TEMPTATION

He looked at her, his pale eyes once again willing her to join him. Pulling her palm to his lips, he softly kissed her hand. "Come on, Julie. I know what you like. . . . Let me—"

She fought the tingle spreading through her body. Heat began a slow course upward. "Listen to me. . . . I don't know you."

The look in his eyes was confident, seductive. "Sure you do. Let me show you."

Bless her soul, she was beginning to believe him. If she listened to much more, she'd be in bed with him before she knew it. She eased her hand away from his mouth. "I'm starving and I need to take a bath."

Light came into his eyes, and the purity of the smile that broke across his features nearly melted her heart. "Sure, okay. I'll wait," he whispered. "I'll wait forever."

The Stranger

Jean DeWitt

HarperPaperbacks
A Division of HarperCollins*Publishers*

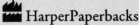 HarperPaperbacks
A Division of HarperCollins*Publishers*
10 East 53rd Street, New York, NY 10022-5299

This is a work of fiction. The characters, incidents, and
dialogues are products of the author's imagination and are not
to be construed as real. Any resemblance to actual events or
persons, living or dead, is entirely coincidental.

ISBN 0-06-101359-5

Cover illustration © 1998 by Robert Hunt

First printing: November 1998

Printed in the United States of America

Visit HarperPaperbacks on the World Wide Web at
http://www.harpercollins.com

❖ 10 9 8 7 6 5 4 3 2 1

This is for the real Julie Ryan,
for Teddy Z, who fell in love with a stranger,
and for Denise, who believes in starting over. . . .
with fond homage to Jim and "Rose" and Leo,
who successfully remade history
with a suspenseful tale of love
and adventure

1

THURSDAY

A full moon on the rise above the forest lit the surrounding, secluded canyon, and a man in his early thirties, undecided about the wisdom of a campfire, stood studying a thin fall of water, luminous under the moonlight.

As he delayed his decision, a sudden fierce wind kicked up from the north, and dense clouds moved in to blacken the night. A heavily canted cedar, long accustomed to the canyon's lee, emitted a series of dull groans amid complaints from nearby timber and the steady rattle of dying leaves along the stream bank. It was several moments before the gale actually toppled the ancient tree in a violent twisting motion that wrenched its century-old root wad from the soil. Tiny orbs of translucent pearl, white and round as the moon, sprang from the ground to dance in the darkness.

The lowermost limb struck the camper, knocking him senseless, and crushed his green canvas tent; the door flap shot open in a whoosh of air to expel a rush and flutter of papers. The dead cedar's tip plunged into the nearby stream, sending a crest of water surging onto the far bank. As the treetop sank deeper into the water, smaller, central limbs driven into the soil began to splinter and give way, unable to support the weight of the mass. Following each snap of wood, the heavy trunk settled lower, descending finally onto the inert man's body.

Loose bark, pine needles, and empty seed cones being carried to the bottom broke away from the wooden corpse to join twigs, dried leaves, and an unlucky field mouse that had been swept into the muddied vortex as the wave receded.

After several minutes the stream regained its regular rhythm, and night proceeded as if nothing were amiss.

2

FRIDAY

Julie Ryan pulled her rental vehicle to the side of the road. With twenty miles of sidewinding two-lane highway remaining, it was time to make a decision. She'd arrived at the turnoff; if she detoured now, it would be dark before she could reach her motel, and her night vision was awful. Still, she was so close . . . and there *were* four hours of daylight. Plus, as much as she disliked change, arranging her rendezvous with the realtor could wait another day. "What do you think, El?"

Typically feline, Elmore ignored her question to groom his forepaw, conveying the attitude of one who does not choose to tackle the situation.

"Find our room and do this tomorrow," Julie persisted, "or take a look now?"

"*Now.*"

"Now it is. Just to check things out, then we'll go on to Nighthawk." She turned the four-wheel onto the gravel road and drove fifteen minutes into the forested countryside. They passed a cleared field buttressed against the roadside. "That's Mrs. Cumberland's place."

Elmore stared past her out the window.

"Well, not yet," she amended. "The house is just ahead."

They'd driven nonstop since breakfast and Elmore had a case of the sulks; she stroked his cheek to soothe his feelings. "Hang in there. This won't take long." She eased the Bronco into the Cumberland drive and stopped behind a mauled and muddied pickup truck that might have been any color. It was parked on an angle in front of a cedar-log house built half in and half out of an earthen embankment.

A screen door opened and a large plaid suitcase flew onto the porch; teetering briefly, it fell over to block the door. A stout gray-haired woman stepped onto the porch in its wake and foot-shoved the suitcase out of her way. A long red scarf escaped from a loose loop around her neck, as she yanked the door firmly shut; she stared in Julie's direction and deliberately turned the key in its lock, then let the screen slam into place.

Julie rolled down her window to stick out her head. "Mrs. Cumberland? It's Julie . . . Pearl Russell's granddaughter."

The woman addressed her immediately, scarf trailing in the breeze. "What are you doin' way out here?"

"I couldn't find a phone listing for you, so I wrote I was coming. Didn't you get my letter?"

"Do I look like I got your letter, young'n? You

couldn't find a listing 'cause hain't got one. Anybody knows me, knows my number." Mrs. Cumberland lurched down the walk with the huge suitcase. "I'm on my way to Spokane."

Disappointed, Julie climbed out of the Bronco on prickling legs. "Right now?"

"*Now.*"

"Yes, ma'am. Hain't got more'n ten minutes if I'm gonna get my connector plane." The woman tossed the cumbersome piece of luggage into the back of the pickup, then advanced to throw her arms around Julie's shoulders. "What you doin', visitin' your grandpa's place after all these years?"

Julie staggered under her grasp. Mary Ellen Cumberland had the embrace of a warm and friendly mother grizzly. "Good grief, young'n, you don't weigh thirty pounds."

"Hundred and thirty," she conceded happily. She'd lost ten since June—there were some compensations, after all—and on her five-foot-five frame, it had been a welcome loss. Struggling to contain Mrs. Cumberland's lumberjack strength and girth in her arms, she succeeded in giving her grandfather's closest neighbor a substantial hug in return; Mary Ellen responded with renewed vigor, and Julie threw in the towel, no match for the woman's might.

"How long you stayin'?" Mrs. Cumberland peered into the Bronco at Elmore, who peered back.

"A couple of days, a week maybe." Depending on how fast things happened. "Sorry we'll miss each other."

Mary Ellen sniffed the air like a deerhound. "Storm's comin' . . . next day or so if this wind's any indication. Pretty good blow through here last night. Don't get snowed in, y'hear?"

Not having thought to check the weather report for the area, Julie eyed the scattering of burgeoning cumulus high overhead. "I was planning to use Gramp's old cabin for a while and look over Joann's property, but you're right, I may have to cut it short."

"Me, I got a plane flyin' all the way to Miami." Mymi. "Then I'm gettin' on a big ol' cruise ship to the Caribbean." Kare-been. "Be gone near two months." Mrs. Cumberland's hand descended into her monstrous purse and emerged with a clutch of keys. "Use the house." She separated out two old-fashioned keys and thrust them into Julie's hands. "Them's the door." Then, plunging into the purse again, she came up with a pad and pen and scribbled a note as she spoke. "Don't count on Pearl's place. Roof's probably caved in by now. Hain't been over there this year." She ripped off the page. "I'll leave this in the mailbox. Wes is my mailman and he knows I'm gone, but I said you're here, and you're gonna put them keys in the box when you leave. He'll pick 'em up."

Julie allowed herself to be swept into Mrs. Cumberland's torrent of goodwill. The older woman jerked open the door to the pickup and swung herself into the driver's seat. "Gotta git."

"Thanks . . . if you're sure I won't be—"

The truck motor roared to life. "What's your sister gonna do with that land? Hain't gonna live on it, is she?"

Julie shook her head. "It was in my letter. She's going to list it for sale. I came up to assess its value. They want me to act as agent."

"Figured. Land next door's for sale, too. They want a coupla million, but that's way too much money. Unless, acourse, you're a drug smuggler. Looks like I'm gonna be real unpopular when I don't let go of mine. I got half the lakefront and, just so you know, hain't gonna sell it." Mary Ellen Cumberland gunned the truck motor.

Julie started for the Bronco. "I'll move my—"

"No need." The pickup shot forward, carved a huge horseshoe in the muddy ground, then stopped short next to the Bronco. "Listen, there's a stranger about. He's on foot with a backpack and hain't seen no car anywhere, so you be careful. Tall, odd-looking duck with white hair. Funny eyes, kinda green and sneaky-like. I caught him crossing onto Joann's property yestiday. Told him to move on. Don't know if he did or he didn't, so you watch out, hear?"

"Thanks, I'll be careful. And thanks for letting me stay in your—"

The pickup was gaining momentum, and Mrs. Cumberland was grinning as the vehicle passed on its way to the gravel road. "Use anythin' you want. You can't find somethin', you just ask Wes," she called back.

She paused the truck at the mailbox long enough to place the note inside and raise the flag, then Mary Ellen Cumberland was down the road and gone. A few seconds later silence descended as the dull roar of the pickup's engine faded into green distance. Julie jammed her hands into her jacket pockets and sagged onto the Bronco's seat to recover her wits. Staying at the Cumberland place would save hours of commuting, and she had enough staples with her to make it the first few days; she and Elmore could drive into Nighthawk for anything else they'd need. She gathered the tabby and made her way up the walk.

Inside the snug cedar home, she freed Elmore to snoop around their new accommodations and called into Nighthawk to cancel her room. He was still snooping when she brought in his litter box and a bottle of champagne for Mrs. Cumberland. "Don't think about it," she warned herself, "just keep busy." She rested the Dom Perignon on the bottom shelf of the all-but-empty refrigerator. Glancing out the window of the tiny kitchen, she counted four metal canoes stacked against the garage and had the answer for the next few hours at least. With the security of Mary Ellen's warm house close by, now was the time to check the condition of her grandfather's cabin and take a small ride on the lake to enjoy the glorious foliage before fall rains bared all but the firs and conifers. Maybe take a few photographs.

The supplies could wait. She returned to the Bronco with Elmore in close attendance. Pushing aside a small hand shovel, her luggage, and the balance of the champagne, she made room for a pair of wooden paddles. "If memory serves," she told her companion, "it's about twenty minutes from here, and we'll have plenty of time before dark." Since she was somewhat rusty in her skill with oars, she chose a wide-bodied, medium-weight canoe that seemed less likely to tip, and, under Elmore's astonished gaze, quickly wrestled it onto the Bronco's roof. "Sometimes it rains up here for weeks," she explained, "so we're gonna go—"

"*Now.*"

"Right." Pleased with his cooperation, she evaluated the bulbous clouds once again and sniffed the wind as Mary Ellen had done, then secured the red canoe to the Bronco's ski rack with a bungee cord. "Sure enough, rain by tomorrow. Maybe an early snow. If I'm going to get decent pictures, it's going to be now."

Elmore gave no further comment. He'd been irritatingly silent for 95 percent of the trip from California, and for someone whose job it was to provide company, he'd been a miserable failure. They'd been companions for years, since the morning she'd selected him, the runt from an abandoned litter, at the local shelter; Elmore's health was still good, but at fourteen years of age he was entirely too set in his ways to be parked in a kennel. She'd spent hours on the phone locating hotels willing to accommodate him—in hindsight, a waste of effort all around.

Three miles farther down the county's gravel road, she turned left to follow a pair of faint tracks and recited the childhood chant that had always directed her family's jaunts to the lake: "Hold on tight, a left and a right; mile and a half, a right and a left." The first three muddy lanes were as she'd remembered, bumpy and ill-tended—but the second left was missing. She backtracked and watched carefully for the old oxen trail that led to the lake. After searching for nearly an hour, she had to admit that she'd become hopelessly lost.

According to her odometer, the "mile and a half" of her memory had become fifteen. When she passed a particularly distinctive tree stump for the third time, she realized that at least two additional "right" roads must have been added since her last visit. By the time she'd investigated identical dead ends that led into turnaround tracks, she was more interested in getting back to the Cumberland place than in finding the cabin. It was early twilight when she stumbled across the lake quite by accident.

She was able to reestablish her bearings at once, and since the weather appeared to be holding, it was a simple matter of rounding the shore to her grandfather's cabin.

The lake was as high as she'd ever seen it, full to the shoreline and beautiful. In the waning daylight, its broad expanse was seductively iridescent, blue-black, and under the light of even a dull moon, promised magic. She was highly tempted to stay the night just to see it. "It's bound to be freezing, but I brought a heavy-duty sleeping bag," she admonished her morose companion. "If the place is reasonably clean, we might just do it."

The cedar cabin hadn't changed other than its walls having weathered to the annealed gray of the stones that lined the shore; surrounded by colorful foliage and brush, the structure blended into the twilight and was all but invisible from thirty feet away. With Elmore in her arms, Julie mounted the steps, passed a small store of ricked wood on the porch, and pushed open the door.

Half a dozen flying things went whizzing out a missing windowpane, while another flipped its way past her forehead before darting through the doorway. "Haint owls," she said, borrowing Mrs. Cumberland's vernacular. Her docile tabby morphed into a crouching, teeth-clacking predator. Leaping to the floor, he hunkered down to examine the ceiling, eager to launch himself into the slaying of unworthy creatures. "Behave yourself," she warned, unworried. Elmore was entirely too old to catch anything flying that high. "Bats are creepy, but they're good for the world. Besides, they taste awful, so don't do anything stupid."

She gave the cabin a quick inspection. It was surprisingly dry, although unless it was shored up, the slanted roof wouldn't survive another winter's weight of snow, that was certain; pinpoints of violet sky were visible in at least three places. However, on balance, it seemed intact enough to spend the night. The metal vent to the potbelly stove was rusted but still in place, thus cooking and heating were possible. Against one wall a deep, old-fashioned cast iron bathtub was perched high on claw feet and provided a base for a picnic-size tabletop; one side of the solid cedar top was fastened to the wall with huge brass hinges, and it had doubled in the past as a bunk for her parents. She and Joann had shared a sleeping bag on the floor. Wooden chairs that had seen better days flanked either side of the tub.

Lifting the "bunk," she found its thick padding had been doubled into a plastic cover inside the tub, along with an old purple goose-down sleeping bag, patched with her grandmother's patient stitching. Between the tub and the wall a set of bath towels were folded with military precision into a large aluminum container; cooking utensils, plastic glasses, cups, and dishes were tucked inside another. Admittedly the compulsive member of the family, the neatness freak,

Julie acknowledged once again that she and her grandfather were definitely related. Safe from hungry mice in a square metal storage tub under the picture window with a view of the water was a collection of romance novels, her grandmother's passion while her grandfather was out on the lake.

Bait buckets were stored upside down over a lantern, bars of soap, tins of matches, and various other items. She smiled. All the comforts of home away from home. There was also a first-aid kit and her grandmother's sewing box, half its compartments given over to fishing lures.

Enjoying the quiet and the deepening twilight, she transferred a few essentials from the Bronco, secured the bunk, and made up her bed with the pad and her heavy sleeping bag underneath, her grandfather's goose-down on top. Elmore's stalking enthusiasm had waned due to a lack of critters willing to make a run for it; Julie watched him take possession of the newly made bed and begin to groom his toes, vigilantly checking the condition of each bat-catching claw while she lit the lantern and took her time arranging their meal.

The moon was rising, round and pale as new ice, when she took up the bottle of Dom Perignon she'd selected for the night. Its cork erupted with a proud, celebratory *popp!* and champagne fizzed into her plastic glass. "Here's to us, O great and mighty hunter," she saluted with false gaiety. "You and me against the bad guys."

Elmore was silent. A night wind whispered its way around the makeshift stuffing of newspaper in the window and breezed readily upward through the holes in the roof. She counted three of them. Every-thing, lately, seemed to be coming in threes.

Sipping champagne, she stood at the window, looked out at the soaring moon and a few silvered clouds that were reflecting themselves in the silent water, and reinvented the steps that had led to this evening. Three weeks ago her sister had called from Switzerland, and three days ago she'd selected this cabin, safe haven from her childhood, as the best place to withstand the next seventy-two hours. If it was written that she would fall apart, she planned to do it privately, and this was the most solitary place she could think of.

She shook herself out of her reverie, determined to defeat emotion. The date would pass. In the meantime she had a view of a beautiful lake, on a beautiful night, with a warm companion.

"Dinner now or later?"

"*Now*."

The combination of a second glass of champagne, a good dinner, plus a forest silence unnatural to a city dweller gave her the soundest night's rest she'd had in weeks. She woke on Saturday morning to an equally quiet dawn edged with the subtle slurps of lake water. Elmore rose from his own personal hol-low of warmth between her knees to extend and contort his body into a luxurious stretch that rip-pled along his spine; morning exercises disposed of, he marched ankle deep up the length of her sleeping bag to rub his whiskers against her face. "*Now?*"

Julie pushed aside her cover only to discover the

morning temperature. "Easy for you with the fur," she mumbled at him.

Elmore, however, was insistent. "*Now.*"

It was a no-win conversation. The tabby was ready for breakfast. Resigned that the day must begin somewhere, Julie struggled to sit forward in the bunk and looked out the window onto a world paled with fog. Sticking warm toes into cold boots and pulling a sweater over the top of the thick Dodger jersey she'd converted into a nightshirt, she ventured outside long enough to scoop up a panful of lake water. Sometime during the night, the chill breeze had gone quiet and the forest had been transformed into a ghostly portrait, but as soon as the sun burned off the blanket of mist, it promised to be a perfect morning to visit the falls—if she could find them without getting lost again.

The stove had preserved sufficient embers from last evening's fire that by adding a handful of dry pine needles and chips of wood, she had an immediate burst of flame in its belly. While the water heated and Elmore crunched his Kitty Krumbles, Julie dressed and braced herself for the day. The milk in her ice chest was still good and she was soon sipping rich, warm, heavily sugared coffee. She submerged a pair of eggs in a pan of water and set them to cook on the top of the stove, treated herself to a second cup of coffee, and, as she'd predicted, by the time she'd finished breakfast a marvelous fall day was emerging from the fog.

A bank of forbidding clouds still crowned the nearby mountains. Rain clouds, no doubt, but she'd made the right decision. The coming weather would reduce the splendid foliage to a carpet of decaying golds and browns. It would be the last photo opportunity this year.

Photographing footage of the long, relatively narrow lake would take only a couple of hours, and finding the falls would give her a secondary diversion. She'd have to keep as busy as possible to prevent herself from dwelling on the might-have-been; with luck, she'd exhaust herself enough to sleep again tonight. After all, there was only so much thought process that champagne could be expected to destroy.

Breakfast dishes washed, Julie dug a raincoat out of her suitcase, stuffed it in her backpack just in case, and, safely clad in waterproof hiking boots, went outside to manhandle Mary Ellen's canoe off the roof of the Bronco. She slid it down the bank and pushed it into the lake under Elmore's nervous gaze.

"Don't worry, you're going, too."

"*Now?*"

"Yes." Sighing, she added the oars. Selling this land wasn't a job she particularly wanted, and if her sister's call hadn't fallen into such close proximity to the leave she'd had planned for months, she might have had the strength to suggest that they use a local realtor. But it had, and she hadn't, so here she was in Washington state launching a canoe onto Osoyoos Lake after a three-day cross-country drive from Malibu.

Their mother had inherited the undeveloped land from Grandfather Russell; Joann had purchased the acreage the following year as an investment. Much as Julie hated the thought of its leaving the family to become time-share condos for sportsmen, or worse, she couldn't afford to buy it on her income as a fledgling real estate agent. She'd resigned herself that the property would have to go on the market.

She stowed the opened bottle of champagne next to the bow, dropped in the hand shovel, added her camera and lunch for herself and Elmore, then stepped into the canoe and prepared to cast off. Elmore watched from the shore, his tail jerking with agitation. "Well, come on," she commanded, and waved his pouch.

"*Now?*"

"I don't have all day." She patted the seat in front of her, and Elmore jumped into the canoe to take up proprietary residence next to her backpack. He lashed his tail with distaste at the proximity of the water.

"*Noooeow!*"

"I know you don't like it, but I can't leave you here." Julie pushed away from the shore with a paddle; floating backward on the water, she stuffed down the realization that recently life had evolved into lots of conversation between herself and an undersize tabby with a decidedly limited vocabulary.

3

SATURDAY

He'd been dreaming . . . lolling about in deep water, splashing and teasing a young girl seated in a rowboat. A pretty, careless young girl, slick with water and sunlight. A vague haze of pain crept through and the dream opened up to a gaping hole, swallowed him whole, and sent him tumbling into a terrifying space. He'd fallen asleep again. Three times so far today, and the same dream each time. He was losing strength in spite of everything he could think to do.

Yesterday, after his initial panic had subsided and he'd been able to reason again, it had occurred to him that he was the unluckiest son of a bitch imaginable unless he could get himself free. That had been roughly thirty-three hours ago. He'd been immobilized for that many hours, plus an unknown length of time before becoming conscious. The back of his head hurt like hell and an area the size of his fist was swollen from contact with the tree or the ground, or both.

Shadow-length told him that it was midafternoon. Lifting his head, he stared at the aching portions of his legs that were visible. Twisted one over the other at the ankle, they were neatly pinned under a limb of the massive, half-rotted cedar.

Left shoulder and upper arm were pressed into the earth, held fast under the trunk of the tree, and frighteningly numb. His wristwatch was visible on the lower part of his arm, but he was deliberately saving the strength it took to push himself high enough to read its face. Instead, he'd watched the sun burn through thick curtains of fog and travel with agonizing slowness across the sky. The crisp blue of forenoon had blanded out to a sickly afternoon gray under a growing blanket of clouds. "In trouble, big time." He struggled to hold down the fear. "Big time . . ."

From the chill in the air and the hued foliage he'd determined that it was fall. But day of the week, month, year—not to mention country, continent, and how he'd gotten here—were missing. Things had names: tent, or what was left of it; boots, watch . . . money. And functions: camping gear, time of day, worth. But nothing had a point of origin. All sense of ownership was absent. In each waking moment for thirty-three hours his mind had engaged in a futile search for answers, and his brain had wearied from the effort. Try as he might, everything that surrounded him had appeared at 7:14 yesterday morning.

Adding to the mystery was the money, thousands of dollars of it, scattered on the ground like so much trash. Two feet to his right a banded packet of money riffled in the breeze and the whispered *flip-flup* of the bills had the sound of eerie, evil laughter. In the day that had passed, he had watched bills escape from under the broken band of a second bundle and into the nearby stream. Several had sunk into the clear water, and he could make out waterlogged presidential visages plastered against stones along the bottom.

It was American currency, ostensibly an indication that he was somewhere in the United States, but there were no guarantees. Foggy, pine-filled forests grew in half the countries in the world. As he speculated on the meaning of the cash, another bill settled onto the water and spun in merry circles before sailing downstream. The money was nothing more than an ironic feature in the whole grisly joke. The only thing in the universe that had importance was freedom—which money could not accomplish.

Under him, the canvas had prevented his efforts to dig himself out. He'd smeared damp soil from its edge on his face to ward off biting insects, but the tent was new and held fast by the base and limb of the tree; he'd bloodied the ends of his fingers but couldn't tear through it.

Failing in that attempt, he'd felt diligently with his right hand for anything to scrape away at its fibers. The soft silt of the stream bank had crumbled through his fingers without so much as a stone. "This isn't happening," he muttered furiously. "Cannot be happening!" His fervent words were a foreign sound in the canyon, and small, hearing creatures went momentarily still before continuing their activities, aware by now that he was not a threat.

He'd become cognizant of his thirst sometime in

the dark. Muscles in his throat were raw and swollen against the dryness, and contracted at the idea of a cooling liquid against his tongue, while his brain resonated with a giant pounding ache, the price of ignoring his head injury to shout himself hoarse most of yesterday and this morning. He knew also that he was feverish and had taken to whispering out loud to keep himself from losing it.

"In trouble . . . big time," he repeated. The tree's incessant weight had all but paralyzed the left side of his body, but he took grim pleasure in enduring pain from cramped leg muscles that had not as yet gone numb; he reminded himself that had his legs been fractured or his ribs crushed, he'd be bleeding to death, or worse. Most of yesterday the toes on both his feet had moved on command, but today the sensations were gone and he was helpless as a mouse in a bear trap.

In the freaky nature of happenstance, his prison space under the tree was large enough that he was without gross injury; the horrifying joke was, there wasn't enough room to escape. Lightheaded, he chuckled at the stupidity of it all: How could a tree fall on you and not kill you? Not even damage you enough that you wanted to die, just pin you down and put you slowly out of your mind. If he passed that point, he hoped to hell that someone *didn't* find him. He'd rather go out like this than wind up with a permanent berth in the land of strange. No tickets home from there.

Unless he figured a way out soon, it was going to be a toss-up between dying of thirst or going out on starvation. All he needed now was a pack of wolves to locate him; providing dinner for something hungry would be the capper of all cappers. The croak of his laughter increased the anguish inside his cranium, and his skull screamed for silence. "Not happening," he panted stubbornly, in spite of the pain it caused, and began a new search for the smallest of pebbles. Anything.

Julie let the canoe drift toward shore and glanced over the top of the canyon at the sky she'd been watching all day. Pale gray clouds were massing rapidly and pushing over the midrange mountains. A few minutes ago the chill breeze had quickened and was flickering insistently across the lake, serving notice that the storm was on the move again. "If this isn't the one, we're calling it a day," she announced to Elmore. "It'll be raining soon." Her watch read quarter to four as she hauled the canoe well up onto the sand and shipped the oars.

Settling Elmore into his leather pouch and fitting him into his space in her backpack, she eased the bundle of cat and camera over her shoulder. With the dramatic pictures she'd taken this afternoon, Joann should have no trouble finding a buyer. Shots of the waterfall—if she could find the blooming thing—would be the clincher. She eyed the sky again and estimated the time it would take to explore the canyon. Too much longer and she'd be hard pressed to make it to Mrs. Cumberland's before the storm arrived. Once she was there, rain could pour, winds could blow—hell, the sky could fall; as long as she was sipping icy champagne in front of a warm fire tonight, she'd be all right.

Stuffing her plastic raincoat into a side pocket of her jacket, she grabbed the spade and began to wade upstream. The waterfall marked the property line. If it had shifted or disappeared, she'd have to get a surveyor out to re-mark the boundary in order to prevent delay in a sale; a new owner would doubtless demand a specific demarcation of the land, and providing an up-to-date survey would move things along.

There were only two canyons left, and if the falls weren't at the base of this one, she'd have to come back after the rainstorm and search again. Raindrops as big as strawberries splashed onto her head and shoulders, and the sky darkened suddenly to a sinister gray. The storm was moving in faster than she'd expected, and underbrush was obscuring her view into the canyon. Elmore was anxious; placing his front feet on her shoulder, he pawed at her ear to make his point. "*Now?*"

"You're right," she soothed, and reached up to scratch his chin. The sky wasn't terribly ominous as yet, not the hard smoke gray that signaled a thunderstorm, and if the waterfall was in this canyon, a picture would take thirty seconds. More rain splashed, and Elmore took a direct hit; he shook his head furiously, sending tiny droplets of water crashing against Julie's ear.

"*Now!*"

"Okay, okay. I got it." The storm was closing in, and they were going to get wet no matter what. She stopped to pull the raincoat out of her jacket; fashioning it into a hood, she draped it over her head to shelter Elmore and her camera under the plastic. She'd get a better picture if she waited for the sparkle of sunlight, and unless she left immediately, they could count on another night in the cabin, but to be this close . . . Elmore pawed at her ear again, and she was caught in indecision. Raindrops began to bash her in the face: the deciding factor she needed. Turning around, she headed downstream toward the canoe.

He forced himself to assess what he knew yet again. Had he missed *anything*? Any possibility? The giant chunk of tree was immobile. Forty men couldn't lift it, and there hadn't been a human sound—not even the jet trail of an airplane overhead—since he'd become aware, thirty-four hours at last calculation.

Rain began, startling him with a hard, giant splotch that shattered against his forehead, another on his cheek. He opened his mouth and waited, glad to savor the water, glad to feel a revival of strength and spirit, and realized suddenly that he'd drifted very close to lethargy. A dangerous state; next would come acceptance. He reintroduced discipline into his thinking.

Beyond the tree was a waterfall. Of the area he could observe, there was no vehicle, so he might have walked some distance to make this camp. If he'd come into this godforsaken place with another person . . . maybe they'd gone for help. He forced his thoughts away from the immobile lump under the flattened tent.

There was nothing in his pockets, no identification of any kind; worse, not a coin or a key to scrape against the canvas. He was dressed for hiking in a tan leather jacket, denim shirt and jeans, heavy boots— but why on earth would he be carrying so damned much money on a camping trip? Assuming it was his tent—and his money. Foreboding rose in his chest, as it did each time he addressed the matter of the cash. A feeling that something, entirely aside from his current predicament, had gone terribly wrong.

Maybe none of it was his . . . maybe he'd found someone else's camp. And someone else's money. If there'd *been* a someone else, unless they were dead in the tent, they'd been gone for two whole days. That much he could attest to as fact. From there, possible scenarios began to thin because he had no memory from which to build explanations.

The raindrops accelerated in pace, hitting him in the face, cooling his tongue and his fever. At some point the welcome rain would soak his clothing and the ground and the tree on top of him. In the chill wind, the wet would drain his body of heat more quickly than before. Perhaps it wouldn't be starvation after all; maybe his life would end in the ancient manner of simply going to sleep. Hypothermia. He raised his free hand and watched the rain wash blood from his fingers; he felt no pain. Not an unpleasant way to die, if it came to that. Maybe he'd have a stroke of luck after all.

Over the noise of the rain, however, came a new sound. He was no longer alone. Something large was splashing through shallow water in his direction. Small, muffled animal sounds reached his hearing, then went silent as the thing moved toward him. He waited with the instinctive quiet of the helpless and hoped to hell that whatever it was, it would pass him unnoticed.

4

"I don't believe . . . *here!* Over here, damn it!"

The strident words were muffled in the rain. Startled, Julie stepped sideways and nearly lost her footing. A swamp creature, his hair and face covered with dirt, was lying on the ground ten feet in front of her, frantically motioning her forward with a muddied hand. For a moment the pale eyes glaring at her didn't look quite human. She hesitated, then stepped toward him with caution, unsure if he was drunk or had fallen.

"Where the hell have you been?" His rasping voice was furious, and it was obvious that he needed help.

It wasn't until he'd slumped back onto what had been his tent that she realized he was trapped. Shocked into silence, she thrust her backpack under the massive trunk of the tree and sheltered Elmore with her raincoat. The enormity of the man's situation was overwhelming; incredibly, he'd escaped a terrible death. Less than a foot in her direction and he'd have been crushed outright. But there would be injury, broken bones . . .

Don't panic. Her stomach began to roll. *Don't panic!* She overruled the images, intent on keeping a clear head. The tree was immense; she was the newly appointed one-person rescue team and had to decide what to do. Quickly. "Hang on," she managed. It would be dark in an hour. Maybe she should go for help and not waste time trying to get him out. Clutching the spade, she returned to his side, trying to prepare herself. If she could free him, going for help would be a waste of precious time, especially if he was bleeding. . . .

Reddened eyes continued to glare up at her expectantly, and his attempt to contain severe emotion was apparent. "Good Christ, am I glad to see you!"

She nodded, mind occupied with first-aid basics: Assess his condition. Evaluate the situation. Well, that was simple. The situation was awful. "Just hang on," she assured him again, with a confidence she did not have. Raindrops were crashing into his face, causing him to blink rapidly, and it was evident that he was in pain. Nothing red visible so far; no blood on the ground. Her breathing eased a bit.

"You're going to dig me out with *that?*" Passion shook his voice. "There's no one to *help?* It's been *two days!*"

Two days! If she'd been trapped like this for two *hours,* she'd be crackers! "I'm sorry." She caught hold of his fingers, cold as ice. Out here alone on the wet ground last night while she'd slept warm in the cabin, desperate for help while she'd circled the lake . . . no wonder he was freaking. Going the shorter way around, she'd have found him hours ago. Unnerved, she let go of his hand. "I'm sorry, I could've been here . . . I didn't . . ."

Thousands of dollars were lying nearby, and her alarm at the man's circumstances took on a sharpened edge of caution. His unusual eye color identified him as the stranger Mary Ellen Cumberland had warned her about, and he'd obviously hidden in this canyon after being warned off the property—which constituted willful trespass. The excessive amount of money was beyond suspicious, it was menacing.

She tried to concentrate. What to do next? Keep him calm. Stabilize existing wounds. Prevent further injury. It was a fluke that she was here at all. Halfway to the canoe a hundred-dollar bill had sailed past her foot; in spite of the rain, when bills two and three had come tumbling down in the current, she'd traded off a night at Mrs. Cumberland's to investigate. In a real-life treasure hunt, she'd collected four more by the time she'd located the waterfall. But who could have imagined this!

She'd been thinking about D.B. Cooper. In campfire stories from her childhood, the ill-fated hijacker had tied himself to a bag of money and parachuted out of an airliner. His body was never found, but years later some of the ransom money had washed up on a sandbank here in Washington, weathered and disintegrating.

Unless this guy was D.B. reincarnated, the biggest cash business on earth was the drug business. Maybe she should go for help after all.

He groaned, obviously in pain, and she put her apprehension aside to focus on his injuries. "I don't have an emergen—"

"Just get me out!" he hissed at her, and struggled to push his shoulder off the canvas. "What the *hell* are you waiting for?"

She stiffened her voice against his manner. "Can you tell me what's broken?"

"Maybe the arm, below my shoulder, I don't know. Can't feel much. I think my legs are okay." The effort exhausted him and he sagged onto the canvas, panting for breath. "Everything's . . . pretty numb."

"I'd better take a look." She laid the shovel aside and opened his jacket. Gently pressing the ribs on each side of his chest and around his back, her fingers encountered no overt swelling or injury. Relieved, she trailed her examination across his pelvis and hips through the fabric of his jeans. "None of this hurts?"

"No, I told you! Just numb."

Rain danced along the backs of her hands as she quickly felt her way along the length of each thigh and around his knees. When he didn't wince and she didn't discover blood, she rose, ill at ease at being so familiar with an unknown man. "So far, so good," she mumbled, surprised and somewhat appeased. At least he didn't have a gun anywhere.

Grabbing the spade, she stepped over the money to circle the limb and have a look at his feet. Grateful not to find bloody boots and bone splinters protruding from thick woolen socks, she probed his ankles and found no obvious breaks. This man led a charmed life. "I'm going to start here," she called out. "It's going to take a while, so try to conserve some strength." She leaned against the shovel and began to dig.

"You didn't answer me!" he shouted at her. "What took you so long . . . finding the camp?"

Floating over the limb of the tree, his voice was curt and demanding. Julie paused in the downpour, increasingly annoyed with his behavior. The guy was not only rude, but wrong all the way around. Finding his camp? If he hadn't been trespassing, he wouldn't be in this mess! And she wouldn't be terrified and cold and . . . suddenly responsible. Her irritation built. Obviously he was helpless, obviously he needed her—so why was he barking orders and giving her an attitude? "Look, I can stand here and get yelled at, or I can dig," she called back tersely. "Why don't we make the best of this and let me try to get you out of here?"

When there was no answer, she stepped down on the shovel.

Situations reversed, she'd have been mindlessly grateful—apparently all he wanted to do was fight. She dumped the dirt aside and watched water run into the hole. If it was already going this way, maybe freeing him wasn't the best idea after all. Leaving to locate someone else to rescue him wasn't an option: It would take hours, and in a storm this size, he could very well drown once the water level rose in the stream. It was already muddy from runoff, and both of them could be in trouble if she didn't get a move on. She heaved more muck aside and resumed digging in earnest.

She'd stumbled across this arrogant jackass, and

he was hers to deal with. He didn't seem to be aware that she was saving his life! And he hadn't mentioned the money. She sure didn't plan to open the door to *that* conversation. If he was somebody weird, a crook or a criminal or something, the less she knew about him the better!

Men in general were on her short list of things to avoid today, and if he *was* a drug runner, she didn't want to know so much as his name—especially if intimidation was his idea of gratitude. On the other hand, there was no point in antagonizing a defenseless, angry man. Fortunately, he'd decided to keep his mouth shut, and she bent to her task, determined to ignore him.

Rain drummed onto her head and shoulders and back. The camping spade was short-handled and awkward to use, but its sharp edge bit through the canvas with ease. Rainwater filled up the hole as fast as she tossed the mud aside, and a few minutes later his feet were free. "That should feel better."

She heard him suck in his breath, and a heartfelt groan was audible through the gloom.

"What's wrong? You all right?"

"Circulation . . . hurts like hell."

Emotion had been staggering through his chest, disjointed and jolting as lightning; above all else was the experience of profound, overwhelming, colossal relief. He was found! He'd been braced to face death as best he knew how, expecting it to emerge from the rain in the form of a bear or a beast, and had looked up instead into the face of this woman: an apparition in a clear plastic raincoat, carrying a cat!

But who was she? As tired and lost and desperate as he was, the moment he'd seen her he was *sure* that he knew her. The woman he'd been waiting for! And yet older, more . . . It didn't matter! He stared over the limb at his rescuer, his angel, unwilling to let her leave his sight. Grateful out of his mind, he waited for knowledge of her to come to him from the void.

Translucent blue-green eyes had coolly appraised him; strong brows were knit in concentration. Fair skin with what might be a few freckles. The rain had flattened strands of wet hair across her forehead, and the rest was pulled into a droopy ponytail. Mud had splashed onto her face and was smeared across her cheek and lips. As she labored, the smears slid along her skin and dissolved in the downpour; she licked the rain away from her mouth with the tip of her tongue. How could he not know her? He'd been expecting her. He was sure of it.

A thousand gratitudes crowded his thinking, but outbursts of frustration kept boiling their way to the surface and causing him to rage at her. Under the ache, his brain was screaming at her, too. *Faster, damn it! Stop wasting time and just dig me out!* He knew he was saying things that annoyed her, things that didn't make sense even to him. Who cared where she'd been? He'd have a thousand days to find out the answers to his questions, the rest of his life to wipe the nightmare of the past two days out of his head. She was getting him free; nothing else mattered! He'd keep himself quiet until she did, if it killed him.

Julie hurriedly retraced her steps and positioned herself next to his shoulder, placing the point of the shovel at the bound edge of the canvas and as close to the tree as she could manage. "Watch your head," she warned, and put her foot on the spade, but the double seam held stubbornly against the metal. She shifted her full weight onto the shovel. The canvas parted abruptly and the shovel head slipped into the soft ground; the toe of her muddied boot clipped his ear. He cried out in pain and his face constricted as he jerked his head aside. She was mortified. He might be a twenty-four-karat jerk, but adding to his misery made her feel guilty all the same.

"Sorry," she murmured. "I'll be more careful." Bracing her hip against the tree, she gained enough leverage to rip the canvas, then folded it aside to get at the ground; for the next few minutes she used the spade without talking, intent on his rescue—and on not hurting him further. Her mind worked ahead. Getting him out from under the tree was one thing; transporting him somewhere he could get treatment for his injuries was the next hurdle to consider. She hoped 911 was operational.

Rainwater had long since seeped under the raincoat to soak her clothing; now it was dripping off her chin and nose and forehead, and icy rivulets were running down her chest. D.B. the Ungrateful here was some plenty lucky she wasn't warm and dry in her grandfather's cabin, snug in her double-down sleeping bag with a hot cup of tea to ward off a chill!

She scooped wet earth from under his shoulder, aware that he was gazing directly into her face; he blinked away raindrops to keep up an intense stare with those clear-as-glass eyes as if somehow his life depended on it. Or on her. Which, in point of fact, it pretty much did. Most people would be babbling about what had happened, or what kind of pain they were in, but she had the oddest impression that he was being silent at a great cost.

He reached up and grasped her shoulder, but he lacked the strength to hold on and lowered himself carefully. She saw him wince as the back of his head touched the canvas again. Most of the mud had been washed from his face, and heavy floral bruising was visible around his eyes, a sure sign of trauma. He'd taken a whopper of a blow somewhere, which could explain a lot. She hadn't checked for head injury. Her resistance softened. Crook or not, it was entirely possible that this guy's brains had been knocked out of the ballpark and that he'd sustained a pretty severe concussion. Concussions were dangerous.

"I need to know where you've been." This time his voice was restrained, but as raw and insistent as his gaze.

She was out of her depth here. If she'd been trapped for two days . . . bad head injury—no evidence that he'd had either food or water, and who knew how bad his arm was going to be—she'd be riding a pretty thin line of sanity. Her instinct was to continue keeping him calm. "Listen, D.B." She deliberately shortened her breath, and continued shoveling. "I'll tell you later, okay? Here's what I know at the moment: We're at least fifteen miles from the nearest phone." This was true. And probably thirty miles from the nearest town, which she decided not to mention. "I'm getting tired, and it's going to take everything I have left to get you out of here." True also. She would play him along until she could get him to a hospital and let the people who dealt with these kinds of situations take over. Professionals.

"Right, you're right." He gestured toward his side, grimacing with every move. "Make a hole here. I can dig, too."

She shuddered inwardly at the thought of him scraping the ground with those abraded fingers, but she hadn't exactly lied: She was reaching the point where she could use all the help she could get. Anything he could do toward freeing himself was welcome, and would help keep him occupied. It took a moment to cut through the canvas next to his waist, and he began scooping mud from under his body before she could withdraw the shovel.

His name was Deebie? Dee Bee? What was that, a nickname? He dragged his hand in and out of the hole in the canvas, thankful for something to do at last. She was right. Explanations could wait. As soon as he was free he'd have all the time in the world to figure things out. Time to learn from her all that was missing. Reassemble the confusions. She'd know, he was sure of it. She had fit instantly into his mind; only people you knew well could do that, surely. Somehow it would all come right.

He'd reached up to touch her with the impulse to pull her close, but hadn't the strength to embrace her. Kiss her. Thank her. But he'd do it soon, and often; he was indebted for his life to this woman, and he would welcome their relationship, whatever it turned out to be.

Dee Bee. D.B. His energy deserted him, his arm became a useless, leaden weight, and he was forced to rest; panting for breath, he watched her lick the rain from her lips again, and followed the soft contractions in her throat as she swallowed. Had he made love with this woman? Loss of memory or not, it wasn't likely he'd forget someone so—

Then it struck. Suddenly he was aware of her singular lack of emotion where he was concerned. Since finding him she had neither kissed him nor acted in a familiar manner. Hadn't voiced personal feelings for him. Hadn't gotten upset at the mess he was in. No tears or assurances that he'd be all right. She had operated at a distance; was still doing so. Unemotional. Professional, almost.

And what was with the *cat*? A cat in the forest made no sense whatever!

5

He made himself start over.

He was certain he knew her. She fit in his mind. And he was reasonably certain that she knew him. She had arrived prepared with a shovel. Apologized for being late. More important, she'd made no mention of the money and didn't seem surprised by the ten or fifteen thousand dollars that was lying in the rain. It was almost as if she'd known he was trapped and had returned for him. If she'd come back for the money . . . wouldn't she have taken it in the first place?

She hadn't asked his name. Or told him hers. It had to mean she *knew* him. Maybe their relationship had other ramifications.

The realizations shook him to the core. He was free, but still powerless! He knew nothing. She knew everything, which made him dependent on a woman he could not name! In a place he did not know! Maybe the money was hers. He was certain he'd been waiting for her. Some sort of rendezvous . . .

Hell, it could be anything!

He forced his thoughts under control and began digging again. Okay, she held all the cards, therefore caution said to find out everything he could before revealing the depth of his situation. But it took the physical effort of clenching his jaw to abstain from interrogating her.

When she finally managed to pull him out from under the tree, his shoulder muscles were deadened and his arm flopped uselessly, but, hallelujah, no bones were broken! He shouted with joy. Almost immediately mental and physical exhaustion caught up with him, drained his strength, and he was too weakened to sit upright. Blood jammed itself through his arteries, propelled by the agonizing intensity of his heartbeat. She was massaging circulation into his shoulder, her chest heaving from exertion, and he saw that she was full-breasted. Part of him was appreciative, unsurprised at the beauty of her body. He *must* know her. His arm and hand began to pulse as painfully as the rest of him, and he moaned in celebration.

"Do you want me to stop? Does this hurt?"

"Sweetheart," he said darkly, "it all hurts . . . including breathing." He tentatively tried out his name. "But D.B. here ain't giving that up."

She smiled at him, and it was a genuine smile for the first time since she'd arrived, softening her features and allowing him to connect with her. "I wouldn't, either," she answered, eyes crinkling at the corners.

He was right after all. She *did* know him. His

name was D.B., and she'd responded to him! But her demeanor changed instantly, became remote once again. Confused, he held silent, his caution reasserting itself.

"I'll have to drag you," she announced, and walked away to begin cutting and ripping the balance of the tent until she had a piece of canvas large enough to hold his body. The lump inside was revealed as a backpack and bedroll, apparently his, which she covered with her raincoat against the driving rain.

By the time she guided the piece of canvas to his side, he was still frustratingly weak but able to help roll himself onto it so that she could slide him down the bank toward the stream. She immediately abandoned his side to begin picking up money, and seemed to be talking to the cat. Riddled with uncertainty, he concentrated on flexing his hand and fingers, trying to regain feeling. As circulation seared its way through his body, new spasms churned in his chest. Rage. At her. And his mind searched for the reason.

For being helpless. For not knowing who she was. For her interest in the cash. All of it! *To hell with this!* He was going to demand some answers! Admit he didn't have a clue! The questions were simple: *Who are you? Do you know me?* He'd demand until he received some blessed information! "*Hey*—" Pain raced through his skull, and the shout died in his throat as he caught sight of his left hand. Slightly bent and pressed into the flesh of his finger was a ring. He rinsed his hand in the stream and identified the gold of a wedding band. Surprised, he shifted his gaze to the woman retrieving the bills, studied her hands long enough to confirm that she wore no rings of any kind. He was married . . . apparently not to her.

The stranger was well formed, taller than she'd first suspected, legs so long that his feet had all but hung over the edge of the canvas. Miraculous and improbable as it seemed, he was reasonably uninjured. Deeply grateful that all she had to do was get him to a hospital without creating makeshift splints, Julie moved about quickly retrieving the money, troubled at her interest in him. She'd let down her guard for a moment, and there'd been a definite connection between them.

"*Neow?*"

"In a minute," she crooned automatically. Poor Elmore's voice was agitated, and he'd lost his usual assurance. Clearly the animal was bewildered by her behavior. It had taken more than an hour to free the man, and a rush of darkness was descending into the canyon along with the full force of the storm. Rain slanted down in gray sheets in front of her, making it difficult to see more than a few feet. Water in the stream was muddy and rising. With the coming night, her own poor vision would come into play, and there was every chance she could lose her way on the lake, let alone driving to Mrs. Cumberland's. They had to get out of here as soon as possible.

The amount of money was boggling! She was holding at least two thousand dollars when the stranger shouted for her attention. She glanced up to see that his eyes were angry and watching her hands, alert to her every move.

She deliberately matched his tone. "Yes?" He immediately looked elsewhere. What did he think, that she planned to steal from him? It was only money, for crying out loud, and she'd yet to hear a "Gee, golly, shucks, ma'am, thanks for saving my life." He seemed oblivious to the fact that her being here to rescue him was as unlikely as his accident happening in the first place!

His retreat into silence was eerie, and worrisome. He didn't appear to be badly injured, but she was no doctor and for all she knew he could have internal bleeding or something. He was already hassling her again; the last thing she needed was a hostile man who was able to move around. The next step would be getting him to an emergency room. Aside from dealing with his attitude, of course, was the problem of getting his all-but-immobile body to the canoe before she could row anyone anywhere. Somehow she had to manage it.

Carrying the wad of wet money, she returned to his pack and found one of its pockets unzipped. Inside were more bills, bundles of them. And a lethal-looking handgun with a clip of bullets! If she'd needed anything further to upset her, the weapon certainly accomplished it—not to mention the immense quantity of money. The sooner she rid herself of this character, the better! Did she dare drag him to high ground and send someone back for him? But if she did, and he died, or disappeared like D.B. the First . . . She couldn't justify digging him out and then leaving him in the middle of a rainstorm.

"*Neeeoow!*" Elmore was flattened under the tree's trunk; she'd used the raincoat to keep the stranger's gear dry and light enough to carry, and he'd gotten drenched. The cat was fed up, and she couldn't blame him. Enough was enough. Uttering a curse under her breath, she unzipped another compartment. This one contained a shaving kit, two tins of chipped beef, a change of clothes . . . and more money.

"*Neow . . . neow . . . neeeow!*"

"Yes, now." *And the sooner the better.* She prayed for a second wind and made a couple of decisions. "I can't carry you, so I'm going to drag you downstream in the water," she told the stranger. "You need a bath anyway."

He didn't laugh at her joke, and she was unnerved by the intensity of his gaze. "I'm serious, I don't have a vehicle." She paused, willing him to tell her he had a Land Rover stashed somewhere in the bushes, but he was maddeningly mute. Jamming cold hands into her pockets, she found the bills she'd collected from the stream. "These are yours, too." She stuffed the soggy cash into his shirt pocket. Taking deep breaths to build up her strength, she pressed on. "There's a canoe, assuming it hasn't filled with water, and then it'll take about an hour to get around the lake to my car."

He spoke at last. "Don't try leaving without me."

Unsure if the statement was intended as a threat, she rounded the tree to attend to Elmore. Wiping him down as best she could, she stooped to put him back into his pouch and saw her grandmother's faux pearls dangling in the rain. She poked at the fragile tin that she and Joann had buried nearly twenty years ago, and half a dozen plastic rings and bracelets threatened to spill onto the muddy ground.

"At least I found these." She freed the tin and jammed it into her pack. "Like I need something else to carry." With the tabby's head sticking wetly out of his pouch and his ears flattened against the rain, she added Elmore as well and slipped her arms into the straps. Last, she approached the man on the ground and grabbed the edge of his canvas. Deliberately facing him down, she gestured at his mountaineering pack covered by her raincoat. "I can't drag you and that, too, so—"

"Leave it."

"What about the rest of the money?"

"Leave it."

Genuinely shocked at the stranger's lack of interest in so much cash, she took him at his word and grabbed hold of the canvas. It was all she could do to move his weight on level ground, but once she got him into the water the rising current helped her bump him downstream.

Eventually they arrived at the canoe and she parked Elmore on the sand. D.B., the maybe crook, was able to use his hands and knees to cantilever his weight into the boat, with her lifting his legs over the side after him. It took her a minute or so to untangle his shivering body, get him wrapped in the canvas, and seat him on the bottom, and then she changed her mind. "I'm going back for your things. It'll take about ten minutes." She grabbed a small bait bucket and shoved it into his lap. "Try to bail while I'm gone," she instructed, and removed the oars just in case. Of what, she was no longer sure; just that she didn't want to be stranded like D.B. senior in case the stranger decided to whack her with one of them and try to row away.

She caught him staring at Elmore. "He's going with me," she said firmly.

The old tabby was shivering as badly as D.B.; she removed him from his pouch and guided him inside her jacket next to her rib cage, then started upstream. Shivering was a bad sign. The stranger's bedroll at the campsite would still be dry, and it'd be worth ten more minutes if she could wrap him and Elmore in it before they crossed the lake, maybe keep them both warm until they got to the Bronco. She wasn't entirely sure she was doing the right thing, but there was also the money.

The cash belonged to this guy, crook or not, and she couldn't fathom his willingness to leave all those dollars to the mercy of the elements. Unless he was brain-damaged, which was entirely possible. As far as the gun was concerned, she'd feel a whole lot safer if it was in her possession until she was rid of him and the whole situation. He and his money were on their way out of her life; let the hospital deal with it. Or the police. Whoever.

She'd been tempted a dozen times to ask his name, to find out what on earth he was doing on foot in a forest, carrying very little food and a ton of money—but common sense said he was armed with a gun for a reason. None of it could be good, in which case he'd lie to her anyway, so she'd held her tongue, determined not to get more involved than she was already.

Stomping upstream as fast as she could manage, she did her best to regroup. She'd driven three days to spend this night in a place she'd known and felt safe in as a child. But it would be far into tomorrow morning before she was out of this mess. "Talk about biting off more than you can chew."

"*Now?*"

Elmore's shivering had stopped and the welcome sound of the tabby's gentle voice made her smile, even as rain slammed her in the face. She gave him his standard answer. "Yes, now, old son. Definitely, unquestionably now."

She'd wanted diversion and exhaustion to get her through the next couple of days, but, working her way toward the money-heavy pack, she came to the conclusion that not only was this more than she'd had in mind, this was quite possibly dangerous.

6

MY NAME IS ELMORE. IF YOU FIND ME, PLEASE CALL JULIE RYAN. Wet fur had covered enough of the small silver medallion that he hadn't been able to read the phone number, but he didn't care. It was information at last, and his mind caressed the knowledge with inordinate pleasure. So elated that he no longer gave a damn if he was cold and shivering and beginning to recognize the need for food, he settled in to wait. He didn't care if it took hours for her to return. He was free, he knew his name, and Julie Ryan was his rescuer!

He pulled the canvas tighter around his shoulders to shut out the wind and considered the woman who'd dragged him down a stream on it, had pushed his legs into the canoe and yanked them around the bottom of the boat so that he could sit upright after two days flat on his back. Subtle, she wasn't. After heaving him into the canoe, she'd sheltered Elmore inside her jacket, hadn't asked his opinion, simply announced she was going back for his pack, then tried to be casual about removing the oars before disappearing into the rain. Evidently she distrusted him.

Well, he had big news for Julie Ryan. Her concern wasn't warranted. *I ain't leaving you, sweetheart. Not a chance in hell.* However, the basis for her apprehension was something else he'd have to discover about their relationship, and it didn't bode well.

He put the thought aside and freed the wedding ring from the wad of money she'd stuffed in the pocket of his shirt. Still shivering, he examined the expensive band in a dimming twilight, read the inscription again: *All my love, G. R.* Unless Julie was a nickname for Geraldine or something, G. R. did not equate to Julie Ryan. Therefore, it wasn't likely that he was D.B. Ryan. And since finding out her name hadn't as yet opened any magic doors to his own identity, there was little to gain by wearing the ring, but she might notice and comment if it was missing, giving him something to go on. He slid the band into the pocket of his jeans and picked up the bait bucket. Until he knew their relationship, caution worked both ways.

Bailing water from the bottom of the canoe, he worked until his teeth stopped chattering, enjoying freedom of motion and movement after days of being immobile. He was alive. And his strength was returning rapidly. Sooner or later she'd tell him something about herself and everything would fall into place. It had to.

Under his seat he discovered a bottle of Dom Perignon with a cork pushed halfway into its opening. Rocking it gently, he felt the subtle shift of liquid. A good three quarters full. He eased the cork out of the bottle, and a whiff of alcohol confirmed the contents. The champagne belonged to his rescuer, but he could not resist a small celebration—one that just might keep him warm. "To life," he justified. "And to Julie Ryan, whoever she is."

His arm muscles quivered a bit from the weight of the bottle before champagne foamed into his throat, smooth and elusive as vapor. Excellent—even tepid and somewhat flat from having been opened for a while. Amazing how a near-death experience altered a man's perspective on what's to be celebrated. Every breath of air. Every sound. Every taste. He closed his eyes and took another appreciative swig; champagne was something he'd obviously known somewhere in his life. Maybe she'd brought it along for a purpose. He'd have to wait and see.

He bailed for the next few minutes, taking an occasional drink from the bottle, glad she'd decided to retrieve his pack. Distracted by gaining his freedom and leaving the hellish place behind, it hadn't occurred to him until they were well out of the canyon that, in addition to the money she'd salvaged, there might have been identification. Her decision to go back for it also made sure that whatever was in the pack didn't disappear before he could retrieve it on his own.

They hadn't talked much on the trip down the stream, mostly back-and-forth "Are you okays?" She'd reserved her strength for pulling him through the water and had been approaching exhaustion when they arrived; he found it interesting that she'd been willing to continue carrying the cat rather than leave Elmore in his care. Not that he knew anything about cats, or whether he even liked them. Just that she'd been concerned enough for the animal's well-being to keep it with her.

Definitely didn't trust him.

He took another drink from the bottle and noticed that his watch had stopped. No matter. He was here, bailing water and waiting for Julie, swilling her champagne with an ascending feeling of calm. The aches and pains in his body were beginning to give him some peace, probably dulled by the wine swirling in his stomach; his hunger had diminished as well. Maybe, if he got drunk enough, his memory would show up. . . . Woozy, he dismissed this as wishful thinking. Maybes weren't going to restore the world for him.

In her absence, the rain had increased and was pouring now in opaque sheets that obscured his vision, isolated him from the rest of the world. He looked out in the direction she'd taken, hoping to see her, wanting her presence. Echoing the hollow sound of the downpour into the metal canoe was an empty feeling in his chest. She'd been gone entirely too long, he was sure of it. Maybe she'd gotten lost. Fallen, was injured. His anxiety built. And here he was helpless in this damned canoe.

A new thought leaped at him. Maybe she wasn't coming back. What if she'd taken the cat because she planned to abandon him after all? People did strange things for money.

The slashing rain covered the sound of her return until she was almost upon him; his brain and heart were jolted at the sight of her. Relief and comfort intermingled as he called her by name. When her eyes traveled to the bottle in his hand, he put it aside. "Damn near killed it," he admitted. "Buy you a case when we get out of here."

"I already have a case. Take this off." Her voice was abrupt as she pushed aside the canvas and helped him out of his sodden jacket. "Finish it if you like. There's plenty more." Shaking out his bedroll, she wrapped it around his back and across his shoulders before topping it with the raincoat, then buttoned the plastic coat loosely under his chin. Satisfied, she transferred Elmore from inside her jacket to a space under his armpit. "Keep him dry, too." Then she tipped both their backpacks into the canoe without ceremony and pushed them under the canvas, out of his reach.

Dry, welcome warmth from the bedroll spread through his body, escalating the effect of the champagne. He switched Elmore to the space under his other arm, rechecking the animal's collar in the process, and watched her leverage her body against the bow. *Julie Ryan.* Hardworking, no-nonsense Julie Ryan. Cat owner. Pretty, tired Julie Ryan was shoving the canoe away from the shore.

He and Julie Ryan and a cat in a rainstorm that seemed bent on drowning the world. He picked up the bait pail. "Hey, Elmore. Welcome to the ark."

Julie retrieved the oars. Somewhere in the last half hour she'd gained a second wind, which was a very good thing, because with D.B.'s added weight, it had taken a healthy push to launch the canoe into the water. With the gun and its clip of bullets a searing, secret presence in her jacket pocket, she climbed inside and took her first pull on the oars. It was apparent from the burn in her shoulders that it was going to be a long trip around the choppy lake.

As he finished her champagne D.B. had taken to staring again, but he was also bailing water, so she couldn't complain. Curious, she studied what she could see of the drinking man. Other than being mud-stained, his clothing seemed to be new, with no wear on his boots—few of the scrapes and scratches normally associated with use in rough terrain. His jeans were heavily blued, indicating that they hadn't been worn to any great degree. The fingers on his left hand were swollen slightly, but the pads and palms of both were uncallused. Outdoor activity could not have been a normal activity for him. Not recently, at any rate.

A few minutes later he'd emptied the bottle and appeared sleepy; it was apparent that after two days without food the alcohol had gone to his head. Preoccupied with the weather and busy taking photographs most of the day, she'd forgotten it was in the canoe, but after what he'd endured at the falls, champagne couldn't do too much additional damage, she reasoned. And it would keep him quiet until she could figure out what to do with him.

Eerily enough, the initials D.B. were correct. His name was Derek Boyd Rocklin, a fellow Californian, according to his driver's license: thirty-two, a resident of Santa Barbara. She'd found a high-school photograph of his wife as well. TO MY DARLING HUSBAND, LOVE FOREVER, GINA was scrawled on the back.

Not more than eighteen, the young girl was a blue-eyed strawberry blond, prettier than average in a powder blue sweater and a strand of pearls. His driver's license picture, with longish blond hair that screamed surfer and wire-rimmed glasses, had been taken five years ago, and the license was due to expire on his birthday next month. She glanced at the barren finger on his left hand. If he was married to Gina, he sure wasn't wearing a ring. It figured.

He was a sneak. A trespasser carrying a gun, and a sneak who knew who she was. He'd read Elmore's ID tag. She'd seen him do it, and it had become another of the reasons she'd gone back for his things: to see if there was anything else in the tent she should know about before she called the Nighthawk police to come and take him to the hospital.

Other than yet another bundle of money, there'd been nothing incriminating. No map or note to hint at his purpose. Touching the gun had given her cold chills, but once she'd removed the thing and its bullets, it had seemed silly not to discover his identity; when she'd moved his shaving kit to make room for the last packet of money, his wallet had practically fallen open. Now she was honor bound to call Gina Rocklin as soon as she got to Mrs. Cumberland's, let her know her husband was injured; then she'd call the police on the trespasser and the sneak who didn't wear a wedding ring.

D.B. swayed with the motion of the boat and fought sleep. He needed to stay awake. Couldn't have her find him sleeping. She should have been here by now. "How much longer, Julie?" Her name rolled off his lips with ease.

She looked away from him and through the gloom toward the shore before she answered. "Another twenty minutes, I think."

It came to him then in a flash. Her face was barely visible in the downpour, and he wished he could see her more clearly. She was licking rain from that full bottom lip again. A champagne thickness was skimming airily along in his brain. "When are you going to kiss me?"

She blinked at him, eyes huge and astonished. He could see she was flustered. "Because I would very much like to kiss you." He was absolutely sincere. He had a wild desire for this woman, and tantalized himself with the thought of her body under him. He wanted the warm feel of her skin against his. To make love to her again, for he knew at last who she was.

7

"Death do us part, remember?"

Julie stared at the man in the canoe with growing unease. He was utterly serious and scaring the daylights out of her. She'd been wrong to go after his belongings. She should never have stopped until she'd gotten him to a doctor. And the champagne had been a huge mistake as well. Derek Rocklin was not only roaring drunk, but possibly delirious. Or somehow his head injury was causing him to say crazy things. Whatever it was, it was frightening.

"Why'd we take the cat?"

"I never go anywhere without him," she said firmly.

"Oh." He went still for a few moments and she thought he'd gone to sleep, but he began to thrash about again, greatly disturbed and mumbling things about their being married. He looked at her lovingly. "Till death do us part," he repeated solemnly, his eyes intense. "Remember? I took you as my wife.

Richer or poorer, and nothing he can do about it."
Then he was quiet.

She pulled the oars with all her strength, desperate to get to the cabin. If she could just reach the Bronco, she'd be reasonably assured of getting him proper medical care before things got worse. The cabin came into view at last, renewing her strength. She rammed the canoe onto the shore and jumped out to pull it far enough into the mud to prevent it from drifting away, then scrambled under the canvas for her backpack and the Bronco's keys. Before either of them could protest, she grabbed Elmore from under Rocklin's arm and ran through the rain for the car.

Easing the vehicle down the slope to the lakefront, she positioned it as close to the canoe as she dared and left the engine running. When she reached his side, Rocklin had resumed his urgent mumbling. "You know I loved you." He produced a gold wedding band from somewhere, waved it at her, then stubbornly worked it onto his finger. "I never loved anyone but you. No one else ever mattered."

"I know," she said to placate him, too exhausted to think of anything else. "I loved you, too. Now come here—we have to get you into the car." She tossed his jacket and sleeping bag into the backseat, threw in both backpacks, then pulled him forward bodily and positioned his shoulders above the side of the canoe; reaching under his arms, she locked her hands across his chest. "As soon as I lift, you push with your feet. This is probably going to hurt." With that warning, she heaved him backward. He came over, but his knees caught on the side of the boat; she lost her footing and they both went down in the ooze. The gun in her pocket jabbed her in the ribs.

Panting, she wriggled out from under his body and forced herself to her feet. Freeing his legs, she opened the door to the Bronco's passenger seat and, with his help, managed to stand him close enough that he was able to sink backward inside. Closing the door, not daring to think or to feel relief for fear her energy would disappear, she sagged against the vehicle long enough to catch her breath. There was still the matter of driving them out before the roads became quagmires, and she racked her brain for the location of her glasses.

He was staring at her through the rain-streaked window, and the look on the man's ruined face was unmistakable. He loved her. Openly, totally, nothing in reserve. And his eyes were full of tears, or she was crazy. She fought sudden, foolish tears of her own, then ran around to the driver's side and succeeded in charging the Bronco up the bank on the first try.

She braked to a stop next to the cabin and turned on the heater. "I'll be right back. Don't move." Refusing to hear an argument, she shut him inside the car and ran into the cabin. Its roof was leaking like a sieve.

Dreading the next leg of her journey, she pushed bait buckets under streams of dripping water as she circled the room, trying to think. They were both filthy with muck and had muddied the car's upholstery; Hertz would not be pleased. So be it. Accidents happened. He had clothing in his pack, could change at the hospital; she would find something at Mrs. Cumberland's. Finally, there was no avoiding it any longer. Resigned, she grabbed a tin of tuna to appease Elmore and, most important, spotted her glasses next to the cup she'd used for her morning coffee. It couldn't possibly have been this morning. She scooped up the glasses, then hurried out into the rain.

Popping the pull-lid on the can of tuna, she bribed Elmore long enough to keep him in the Bronco while she slid onto the driver's seat. Her tabby'd had more than enough of rain and adventure with a stranger, and she couldn't blame the poor animal for being skitsy, but he was along for the ride, like it or not. Hungry, he plunged his nose into the can and, completely out of character, growled a warning at her passenger not to get any ideas.

Next to her, Rocklin sat silent. He had regained his composure, but Julie could see in his eyes that he could not understand her behavior. It was obvious that his soul was naked and in torment, and she felt terrible that she had no idea how to deal with him. "I do love you," she said tentatively, and saw in his face that they were the magic words. Something changed in his eyes, softened toward her. Forgave her, almost. "But right now we need to get to a hospital."

His eyes went dull and helpless, but he nodded and seemed to understand as she strapped him into the seat belt. "Are you okay sitting up, do you think? Would you rather lie down?"

He shook his head. Not knowing what else to do, she turned on the radio, found a station, and donned her glasses. ". . . on these mid-Pacific systems, which are known as the Pineapple Express," reported the announcer. "We haven't had storms of this magnitude since the last major El Niño event, a decade ago. If it's not an emergency, by all means stay home."

"No kidding, Sherlock," she mumbled absently. Unfortunately, this qualified as an emergency. Mentally crossing her fingers, she put the Bronco in gear. Rain was gushing onto the windshield so heavily that the wipers were all but useless, and the headlights gave her only a few feet of notice as to what was ahead of them. The radio announcer repeated the warnings as they crept down the track. "Residents in low-lying areas are encouraged to seek higher ground." Water was running across the road in several places. Not a good sign.

Another few seconds passed before Rocklin began shouting at her to stop. She slammed on the brakes. Instead of a trail, the Bronco's headlights were shining into wavering sheets of rain. The ground in front of them had disappeared. Then a tree branch swept by, illuminated in their headlights, and she vaguely made out the surface of a muddy river.

"The road's gone!" Rocklin was yelling at her, and the extent of their danger sank into her brain. A flash flood was washing sideways across the trail, taking everything in its path. It could dissolve the very ground from under their wheels at any moment! She threw the Bronco into reverse and backed wildly along the road until she could turn around, then drove toward the cabin as fast as she could manage.

"The only safe place is next to the lake," she babbled. Rocklin was nodding in agreement, eyes on her face. "It'll have to rise six feet before the cabin's in danger," she assured him frantically.

He looked at her, his muddied face and green eyes haunting in the dash lights. "Julie, if it rains that hard, we *will* need an ark," he said gravely.

It was suddenly too funny for words, and laughter burst from her throat. He joined her for a few moments, but his face soon squeezed up with pain. Her hysteria built all the way to the cabin. By all that was rational, normal, and recognizable in the world, both of them should be dead. He should have died under the tree, and had they gone an hour or so earlier down the road, she and Elmore might well have disappeared into the floodwater that had torn a channel across the road. Rescuing this man had very probably saved her life.

Finally her laughter ceased.

"Are you okay?" His eyes were liquid in their adoration, disconcerting, taking her breath away.

"I'm fine, honest. Just a little hyper, that's all," she joked uneasily, but it took her a long time to leave the safety of the Bronco, and her legs were wobbling. Rocklin, who'd been mercifully quiet until she'd pulled herself together, agreed to wait in the vehicle with Elmore.

Reassessing the cabin under lantern light, she concluded that even with the leaks, it was better than sleeping in the car. With a strong fire in the stove, the damp would be tolerable; she threw generous heaps of pine needles and wood chips into its belly, tossed in a match, and opened the draft, then busied herself getting kindling. Within minutes the blaze was big enough to add a dry log from the supply on the porch. The sooner she got him inside and shut off the Bronco's engine, the better. She'd intended to fill her tank in Nighthawk, and with only a few gallons of fuel remaining, they'd need every bit of it to get them past storm damage between here and Mrs. Cumberland's.

She could manage with a can of tuna, but Rocklin would need a warm meal. Snatching up an unoccupied pail, she took it outside and caught a couple of inches of rainwater from the downspout, then plopped the bucket onto the hood of the stove to heat for tea. Next she opened a can of condensed soup and put it alongside the pail, then grabbed up a half-full box of wafers and took them outside to Rocklin. "I'll be ready for you in a few minutes. Snack on these until I can get something warmed up, okay? I have a fire going. It'll be a few more minutes."

"I can make it." He grabbed his jacket and made a move for the door.

"Please wait." She shut off the motor and pocketed the keys. "In case you need help." While he attacked the wafers, she brought Elmore and both backpacks inside. The bunk was already made up and best of all, dry, but she and Rocklin were still covered in muck. Somehow they would have to take turns getting into clean, dry clothing. Heating enough water to fill the tub would take hours; for now they could make do with a bucket of soapy water. She routed out soap and towels and the first-aid kit from behind the tub. Then she had a better idea.

Powered by her solution, she retrieved Rocklin's change of clothes and added his toothbrush. It was going to be the proverbial dirty job at the end of a long, dirty day, but she was still the someone on the hook to do it. She took off her boots and socks and removed her jacket; once again the weight of the gun she'd taken from his pack jarred her senses. She quickly slipped it under the bunk mat and put the clip in her purse. Then, seeing no alternative, she rolled up her sleeves.

He watched her disappear into the cabin and loved her, loved her courage and her stubborn resilience. He'd loved her for years, no one *but* her, from the day he'd first heard her laughter ringing from her father's office. And they were married now. They'd celebrated with champagne. It was all perfectly legal.

Knowledge of her had come welling out of the blackness in his head, rushing forth in such a flood that he'd been swamped with emotion. He *had* been waiting for her. He'd lost her at the lake, and now he had her back.

He finished the last of the wafers, grateful for their taste and the comfort they generated in his stomach. Half an hour ago he'd have sworn that he didn't have enough strength to talk, let alone shout, but when the road had disappeared in front of them he'd found certain death to be one hell of an incentive. She'd reacted instantly, saving both their lives this time, not just his, and he loved her. Adrenaline was still coursing its way through his veins when she ran down the cabin's steps toward him and approached the car.

"Before we go in, I'm going to give you a shower."

She opened the door, lifted out his feet, and removed his boots. "Gonna prop you under the rain spout and soap you down, okay?"

Now she was unbuttoning his shirt, bullying his arms out of its sleeves, and he was too happy at her attention to be concerned. If she wanted to soap him up, down, or sideways, he didn't care. That she was near was all that was important. She loved him. She'd said so and he believed her. He watched her toss his jacket onto the porch, then rinse his boots and socks under the spout and set them aside. He was able to walk the ten or so steps to the cabin, and took hold of the roof with both hands to keep himself upright while she helped him step out of his jeans, but he was baffled when she tied his shirt around his waist for modesty before pulling down his underwear.

They were married now; it seemed odd that she was so shy. And other things were upside-down as well. She was the one they'd been taking to the hospital, not him. He forgot his confusion as she produced a toothbrush and he let go of the roof with one hand to scrub his teeth, then gratefully rinsed his mouth. Meanwhile, she had lathered a washcloth with soap and began to smooth the foamy cloth onto his face, beard, and neck; she slid it carefully across his bruised shoulder, under his arms, and down his chest. She gentled the soap onto each of his hands, soothed the lather softly against the tips of his damaged fingers. Her touch was incredible, deft and sure, sending peace and lightning through his body.

Standing on tiptoe, she worked the soap into his

hairline, her fingers gentle as air on the back of his head where it ached like a son of a bitch. Using her body to brace him upright, she washed his back, and he felt her breasts through her sodden sweater, hard-nippled against his forearm and his chest; the feeling was unbelievably arousing. She felt his hardness and stepped back, breaking their contact and refusing to look at him. Maybe she was angry. Sometimes she got upset if he came on too fast. All this was pretty new to her, after all. She was new to him, too, but he couldn't help it. They'd never get out of the bed-room if it was up to him.

But her busy hands slid down his back, scrubbed gently around his ribcage, over the hollow of his belly. White heat stabbed though his body when she deliberately skipped his erection and stooped to lather his legs and feet instead. His weakened hand gave way and he lost his hold on the roof; he slumped against her as she handed him the cloth. "You do the rest." She shifted her hands to hold him upright against the side of the cabin.

Even under the shirt it was obvious that he was standing out at a hard angle, rigid as a flagpole. Feeling proud but foolish, with one hand on her shoulder for balance, he complied with her edict and lathered himself, unsure why she wasn't washing him. She had in the past. Lots of times. And with her hands, not a washcloth. It was a whole lot better with her hands.

She still wouldn't look at him and seemed to be trying her best to be elsewhere—and he couldn't for the life of him think why. Couldn't think of anything except his hard-on and, oh, God, how good it was going to feel when she let him put it in. The hot slickness of her body was what he wanted, not this cold, soapy bath, and no amount of pretending would alter that fact. God, he needed her!

"I love you." He said it as gently as possible and bent his head to kiss her exactly the way she liked.

She met his lips and sent his hopes soaring. It had become a very sweet kiss, half a step toward passion, when she pulled away, and the next moment she maneuvered him under the downspout. Cold water gushed in torrents onto his head and spilled over his face, sluiced down his body, and he felt himself soften. She bumped against him, holding him in place, and he could still feel her nipples. The sensation mixed need for her with his enjoyment of the warmth of her hands and the shape of her body as she kept him under the downspout. It was a game, and he let her play with him.

Eventually she helped him into the cabin, discreetly untied the wet shirt from around his waist, and exchanged it for a towel. He couldn't help it— her attentions restored his erection. He made no resistance when she sat him on their bed; he'd wait forever if that's what she wanted. After a cursory scrub of his hair, she dried his arms and legs, avoiding his arousal all the while. She wiped an oily gel with the sharp odor of medicine onto the back of his head, then over the bruises on his ankles and shoulder, and finally worked it around his fingertips. But she turned aside while he rolled onto his back, harder than ever. "Come here, sweetheart," he coaxed reverently.

She was embarrassed and adjusted the sleeping

bag, making sure to cover his flag. But she'd looked at him; she'd taken a good look, had seen how hard he was for her, knew how much he wanted her in bed with him, and her cheeks were flushing rosily as she spoke. "In a little while. I have to get some food in you first. Keep your strength up."

Aware his strength *was* up, he smiled, convinced in his heart that she would join him.

Face still burning, Julie circled the cabin, unnecessarily emptying pails of rainwater from under the leaks, checking the temperature of the heating soup, and busying herself in general. Derek Rocklin's gorgeous body had nearly undone her discipline. She had a weakness for wiry men, and his long, narrow torso, lean-muscled as a long distance runner's, was looking pretty damned good—even for a married crook with too much money in his possession. Trying to ignore Rocklin's uncircumcised penis bobbing high and pink in the air above those thighs was like pretending there was no gorilla in the corner. Her judgment was close to disintegrating, and her hormones were hopping like popcorn on a griddle.

After the day they'd both had, that either of them could consider sex an option was ridiculous. In some instances, apparently, nature's reproductive rites managed to override common sense. But for her, Rocklin might not have survived this night, and half an hour ago they'd both nearly died. Maybe it was some sort of bizarre affirmation of that survival. Who knew?

What she did know was that, tired as she was, she was excited by his nakedness, by the pale baby-smooth skin easing onto her sleeping bag, sliding into dark places where she'd slept last night. She closed her eyes, saw again the sight of him protruding from thick golden hair, and realized she was more turned on than she'd been in years.

She considered herself enlightened, accepted the enjoyment of sex as a pleasant occupation for normal, healthy adults, of which she was one, and a moderately essential part of her life on occasion. Being engaged to Ned hadn't given her these kinds of racy, breathless responses, but whether she was engaged or not, sex with strangers—with or without zillions of dollars—was out of the question. Particularly someone who wore his wedding ring only on occasion. She peeked at his hand on top of his chest amid the bedding. The ring was still on his finger. That much was good, at least.

This was absurd! She was getting weak in the knees over a stranger when she should be figuring out how to get out of soap-streaked, clammy clothing without him watching. But those bizarre glass-green eyes refused to close. With a shave, he'd be handsome—as soon as the black and blue swelling left his face. His hair and beard were drying to an even paler shade than the intimate body hair she'd witnessed. All but snow white, actually, now that they were washed clean. Classic features completed the picture: a strong, aquiline nose and full, sensual, perfectly shaped lips. Soft, when he'd given her that slow, dizzying kiss. And how on earth had she permitted that to happen?

Curiosity? Well, it was satisfied.

She spooned condensed soup into the coffee cup,

added warmed water from the stove, and took it to his side. He raised himself onto an elbow and cleared a space so she could sit next to him without muddying the bedding, but eased back to touch her once she'd tipped the cup to his lips. Her awareness of him increased, if that was possible, and she could feel the heat of him, and the hardness. She was beginning to react in spite of herself. Tempted to look at him again.

His eyes were endless, incandescent, enticing her into his fantasy. "I love you," he said fervently. "I'd do anything for you."

She tried to avoid his eyes but couldn't pull herself free. "What about your wife?"

He looked at her strangely; something flickered and then disappeared in the clear, liquid green before he answered, eyes now blank with confusion. "She's gone." He was clearly confounded at the question.

Julie watched him closely. "I thought I was your wife."

He blinked at her, then sank onto his back, pale eyes once again willing her to join him. It was as if he were two people at the same time. "You are." Pulling her palm to his lips, he softly kissed her hand, skimming the tip of his tongue lightly along the surface of her skin before speaking. "Come on, Julie. I know what you like. . . . Let me—"

"Listen to me." She fought the tingle spreading through her body. Heat began a slow course upward. "I don't know you."

Eyes above her palm smiled at her, confident, seductive. "Sure you do. Let me show you."

Bless her soul, she was beginning to believe him.

If she listened to much more, she'd be in bed with him before she knew it, mud and all. She eased her hand away from his mouth. "I'm starving and I need to take a bath."

Light came into his eyes, and the purity of the smile that broke across his features nearly melted her heart. "Sure, okay. I'll wait," he whispered. "I'll wait forever."

Elmore wound his way through the brigade of buckets and jumped onto the bunk; he made himself at home next to Rocklin's chest and began to purr. Julie knew she was in trouble. Elmore hated Ned with a passion. For him to accept this stranger, this person who thought they were married, who'd nearly convinced her that black was white, that straight was no longer narrow, was the last straw.

She eased herself off the bunk and concentrated on fixing a cup of soup for herself, doing her best to bring her emotions under control. Nothing this man had said since they'd met had made the remotest amount of sense, and she'd been well on her way to denying reality and getting into bed with him!

Fortunately, her sanity was growing stronger with each nourishing spoonful of soup. Across the room, a long sigh issued from Rocklin's body and he closed his eyes. The soft rasp of his breathing permeated the room as she gathered the soap and a fresh towel, then collected undies and her Dodger blue sleeping jersey from her pack. She let herself onto the porch, skinned out of her clothing, and pushed herself down the steps into the driving rain for a quick shower of her own.

She'd gotten used to the warmth of the cabin,

and the cold rain grabbed her breath; nevertheless, it felt good to scrub away the mud and sweat from rowing and digging and dragging this man halfway around the lake. Adapting to the cold, she freed her hair from its ponytail to give her scalp a brisk soaping and was conscious of her breath steaming into the night. Tipping back her head, she let rain crash into her face and restore logic, remove interest in the seductive stranger's words, take away his nakedness. Cleanse her own tired body in the process.

She rinsed her hair under the downspout, then, still wet, retrieved Rocklin's sleeping bag from the Bronco and brought it onto the porch. It had a few soggy spots from its journey from the falls but was dry enough to sleep in. She stood on the porch and dried herself with a scratchy towel before stepping into her underwear. Her skin was still damp as she lifted the nightshirt over her head and let it float around her body. Moving into lethargy at last, her senses demanding sleep, she wrung out D.B.'s socks and took them in with his boots to dry by the stove, then hung his jacket on one of the chairs. The fire was low, so she carried several pieces of wood inside and placed two of them in the stove.

Most of the cabin floor was wet from the leaks, and none of the dry spaces was big enough to sleep on. In the short time she'd taken to shower, the buckets had collected an inch of water; they'd be overflowing by daybreak, so she emptied them out the door again. She was beginning to chill. If she wanted to stay dry, she'd have to sleep in the Bronco after all, which wasn't fair. Tired, resentful, she gathered Rocklin's sleeping bag and was crossing the room to douse the lantern when she saw that he was awake and had been watching her.

His arms spread open his covers, exposing his torso, straw-golden in the light from the lantern. The pink of his sex had retracted and lay soft between his thighs. "Come to bed," he said sleepily. "Let me take care of you."

Crook or not, it was the best offer she'd had in months. She blew out the lantern, wrapped the sleeping bag around her body, and crawled in next to him.

8

SUNDAY

The face held no visible emotion; pupils of the small brown eyes behind wire spectacles, however, were contracted to pinpoints and held hatred for him beyond measure. He felt himself shrinking before the accusation. *You murdered her. You did it for money, and nothing you can do or say is going to convince me otherwise.* The face came closer, the voice dead calm, the accuser's breath strong in his nostrils. *I have made it my business to see that you rot in hell before you profit.*

Fear jerked him into a cold sweat of panic. Rain thrumming onto the roof was a foreign sound that kept pace with his heartbeat. *What the hell was that about?* He fought to hold on to the words he'd heard in his head: *murdered.* That she was dead he knew beyond doubt, and a cold chill worked its way through his chest. The nightmare skipped away to nothingness as he struggled to understand, then desperately sought the source of the threat, the knowledge, but came awake instead.

He felt himself surrounded by heat and darkness, and things gradually took shape; still, it was several moments before he confirmed to himself that he was actually free, warm, and safe in a cabin. Inch by inch, he placed himself: in a bed, next to a woman. Julie. It was close to morning.

He studied her sleeping face. She'd given him a bath, soaped him down in the rain with caring hands. Or had he hallucinated that as well? Her hair was feathered across her cheek and throat, a rich color between nutmeg and coffee. Last night he'd watched her dry it with a towel. The window had been coated with condensation, but he'd seen the ivory of her body outlined by lantern light as she moved about on the porch; she'd been naked and he'd watched her pull on her nightshirt, a gentle wash of blue.

She was really pretty, he decided, with her mouth open slightly, sending light puffs of air against his shoulder as she slept. They'd both been exhausted, and his memory of the evening had more than a few vague spots, so waking up next to her was a mild, and pleasant, surprise. Her lips had a soft appearance, flushed and innocent, with moist insides. Yesterday they'd been slick with rain. . . .

Yesterday he'd come near to death on two occasions! The where and how of her rescue of him returned in waves as his eyes adjusted to the gloomy, predawn light in the cabin's interior. Less than three feet away from him were the alert eyes of her cat. Unwinking in its observation, Elmore had taken up residence on the purple comforter, and was snuggled into the bend of her knees. Satisfied that he wasn't losing ground in his ability to recall, he avoided delving into the vacuum that comprised the balance of his life and assessed his own physical condition. Body: stiff but functional. The back of his head was still sore, but most of the ache had disappeared. It seemed there was a name for his situation, but it wouldn't come to mind.

His bladder was full and he had a morning hard-on so fierce that its pulsing put to rest any suspicion of damage to that most vital of areas. He eased himself cautiously onto his side, allowing a draught of cold air to sneak past his chest and make him aware that he was completely nude under the sleeping gear. Had they . . . ? He was about to question his ability to remember after all, then recalled the champagne. He'd had a lot of alcohol in a short space of time. Which settled *that* question. The spirit might have been willing—as it damn sure was at the moment— but he was sensible enough to know that even now his body was entirely too depleted to follow through.

His stomach growled in empty protest. Food was a top priority on his list today, but nothing, *nothing* was more important than finding out who the hell he was. Surely there would be something in the pack, and he wanted to be regrouped and as prepared as possible before she woke up. The only thing that wouldn't wait was his bladder.

He and the cat had a staring contest as he eased himself past their sleeping partner and out of the bunk. Sore muscles everywhere on his body cramped and ached in complaint at having to move into cold air. Circumventing buckets of rainwater that were threatening to overflow, he navigated the wooden floor, slick and cold under his bare feet, and quietly eased himself out the door. The hard sky promised a dull, gray day of rain with no letup in sight. He checked through the window to make sure she was still sleeping, then relieved himself over the railing.

The cold forgotten, he returned inside and tried to hold down an excitement of anticipation as he located his backpack. It was surprisingly heavy, and he strained already sore muscles in his arms and shoulders lifting it onto a chair next to the window. How the hell had she managed to carry it from the campsite? Sliding open a compartment zipper, he caught an astonished breath, taken aback at the massive quantity of cash it contained. Wet cash, with half an inch of water in the bottom of the pack. No wonder it weighed a ton.

Something major strange was going on, that was for sure. Here he was, boggled to find a fortune in his backpack, but his rescuer hadn't turned a hair. Small wonder she'd insisted on going back for it. Who the hell *was* Julie Ryan?

More to the point, who was he?

He found more cash in another compartment, equally soaked, and finally an expensive leather wallet; water dripped onto the floor as he fumbled through it to locate a driver's license. *Derek Boyd Rocklin* seared its way through his brain. Empty of meaning, the name might as well have been Santa Claus.

Fighting a sinkhole of disappointment, he tried again, mouthing the syllables, willing recognition. *Rocklin*. It seemed for a moment that the surname generated a sense of approval, but he couldn't be sure. It was entirely possible that his mind was registering the name as familiar simply because he needed an anchor for his sanity. He tried again. *Derek. Boyd?* Still nothing.

He peered at the picture on the license, praying for self-recognition. A vaguely comforting feeling responded somewhere in his cortex, but no Disney ride rescuing him from oblivion. If anything, he detected an enigmatic sense of acceptance. The photograph seemed no more familiar than the name, and without a mirror to compare himself, he couldn't even be sure it was him.

One thing, however, emerged from the enigma. D.B. suddenly made sense . . . his initials. She *did* know him. No one gives accurate nicknames to strangers. Encouraged, he read Rocklin's statistics: Six-foot-one, 152 pounds, green eyes. The body hair on his forearms was nearly white, as pale as the hair and eyebrows of the man in the picture. He was unable to compute his age from the birthdate, since he didn't know what year it was, but the guy on the license looked to be in his mid- to late twenties. Issued in California, an address in Santa Barbara.

He flipped through the card section of the wallet, unable to accept this version of himself until something clicked. The dividers gave up wet plastic information, page by page: an auto club membership, a home shopping club, half a dozen charge cards. *Apparently this guy has pretty good credit,* he thought, dimly amused. *I wonder what else he has.* He looked at Elmore. *Cat, maybe?*

In the slot for paper money, he found a few twenties and a couple of ones, stuck together. No point in separating them. It wasn't like he was short on funds. He glanced at the banded money in the backpack. *He has a whole bunch of cash, that's for sure. Wonder if it's his.* The wedding band on his finger caught his eye, and he reread the license. There was no indication of his marital status. He heard a sound of indrawn breath and turned to look behind him; the woman he'd just slept with was staring at him with no humor whatsoever.

"I'd really appreciate your getting dressed."

Engrossed, he'd forgotten he was naked; with her stiff admonition, awareness of the cabin's chill air descended and he looked around for something to cover himself. "My clothes are wet," he said defensively under a gaze as unyielding as the cat's had been. Unwilling to let go of the wallet, he used it to shield himself and awkwardly sidled to the bunk to sit next to her.

She allowed him to make use of an edge of one of the sleeping bags, but immediately inched away. Deeply discouraged that discovering his name hadn't solved any part of his dilemma, he was caught off guard by her attitude and anger barreled to the surface. "I'm a little confused here." He set his jaw, irritated. "I've been naked all night, and suddenly you want me to get dressed. As I remember, you took my clothes off and gave me a bath . . . hell, you were walking around without anything on. What's the problem?"

She continued inching away from him until she was stopped by the cabin wall. "When *I* was naked, Mr. Rocklin, let me assure you I thought you were sleeping."

"Well, I wasn't. I was waiting for you." He returned

her stare, daring her to deal with him. "What happened to D.B., darling?"

Her bravado increased. "Your name's not Rocklin?"

"You know it is." Furious that the information he needed was still in her court, he ran out of ideas. Taking a breath, he lowered his defenses. "I give up. You're going to have to tell me what's going on with us."

"Us?" She recoiled visibly, her eyes defensive. "There is no us."

"Me naked and you naked," he challenged testily. "You don't count that as *us*? I suppose we didn't sleep together."

"I'm not naked . . . and I was exhausted. It was either here inside with you or outside in the Bronco. Inside was warmer." She blinked at him. "Nothing happened!"

A snarky response slipped out before he could stop himself. "Honey, I don't claim to be Hercules."

She arched her body away from him like a wary cat, obviously upset. "What do you want from me? I wake up to find a—a strange man walking around without a stitch!"

For a moment he lost it. "Just tell me what's going on! I don't have a—" He subdued the impulse to put everything on the table and started again. "Okay, have it your way. Since I think I'm relatively normal, how exactly am I strange?"

He watched her fuss with the sleeping bag that covered her legs, one hand grasping the fabric tightly in her fist, the other creeping under the bunk's padding, searching for something. Finally she answered. "Last night you tried to tell me . . . no, you *insisted* that we were married. I qualify that as strange. Now you're acting like you have some sort of right to embarrass me. One of us is crazy and I thought it was you, but I'm beginning to wonder. . . ."

He had no idea what she was talking about. Why would he tell her they were married? Unless they were, and some part of him knew it. Something pushed at the back of his mind, trying to surface. A meeting . . . with a woman. This woman? This woman knew him. She'd called him by name. "Are you saying you weren't trying to locate me?"

"Mr. Rocklin, I do not know you," she said emphatically. The sleeping bag slid to one side as she gestured with her hands to make her point, exposing shapely legs; in spite of his need for information, small bits of his attention splintered off to assess them, then crept upward to follow the motion of her breasts under the soft shirt. No wonder his spirit had been willing.

"We are not, never have been, anything except strangers." She bristled at him. "We simply passed the night."

As the content of her words penetrated, he refocused to stare at her, refusing to give over without one last shot. "Then explain how you knew my name. Deny you've been calling me D.B."

She stopped adjusting the bedding and froze, eyes blinking guiltily under his gaze. "You told me."

"Unh-uh, sweetheart." Julie Ryan of the gorgeous body, his rescuer and bed companion, was lying to him. What else was she lying about? Everything? "I happen to know that I have never mentioned my name to you." He zeroed in icily and watched fear enter her eyes. "I've been very careful about that."

"Look, all I did was find you under a tree." She began to stammer. "I don't want to . . . I don't know anything about what the money . . . I-I don't care where it came from, or where it's going, anything. All I—"

"Found me? You were carrying a shovel," he reminded her sharply.

"Yes, *found* you." Moving off the bunk, dragging his sleeping bag in her wake, she dumped an indignant Elmore onto the floor in the process. Pausing at the stove, she bent to toss in a handful of kindling with short, jerky motions. "I sure didn't put you there, and I have yet to hear a thank-you!"

He was thrown. This wasn't going the route of his fantasy. She was supposed to give him answers and resolve the mysteries, but nothing she'd said so far was making sense. Maybe she *didn't* know him. Hell, he didn't know himself and he was holding enough information in his hand to identify three people! He folded another edge of the sleeping bag over his crotch, feeling the rage and vulnerability of a naked, displaced man.

She shoved a length of wood inside the stove, then picked up another one, unquestionably for self-defense, and he understood then that he was frightening her.

"Thank you." It took him a moment to choke down a small mountain of emotion. "For saving my life."

"Well, that's a start," she said sourly, and poked at

the fire. Small flames had begun to lick at the kindling.

"I'm sorry," he said edgily. "I hadn't realized. . . . I've had a little trouble adjusting." His headache returned with a bang and he was suddenly terribly tired. "I need food, I think." It was all he could do not to sag backward onto the bunk and seek the oblivion of warmth and sleep. "Food, rest, and—unless I'm the guy in this wallet—a pretty good lawyer."

She was regarding him suspiciously, still holding the stick of wood, and ready to jump out of her skin. "What are you talking about?"

He couldn't blame her for the challenging tone. It was a pretty weird situation, after all. It took conscious effort to make himself trust her. He was going to have to trust someone. "I really thought you knew me. I thought that's why you were here. That we were here, together. Apparently that's not what's going on."

"'Apparently,' nothing. It's not the situation, period." She was studying him carefully. "All I know about you is what I saw in your wallet—yes, I snooped—and this is getting very strange." She placed the wood back on the floor. "I want you to turn around while I get dressed, and then you're going to get dressed, and when nobody's naked, maybe we can concentrate on getting you to a doctor."

He laid back on the bunk, studying the foreign male face in the wallet and listening to the subtle sounds of fabric on fabric as Julie rummaged through her backpack. He fought the void that was closing in by flipping once more through the wallet's dividers. He found a picture of a beautiful young girl and carefully eased it out of the plastic. A high-school graduation photo, from the look of it, and something fundamental moved inside his chest. *To my darling husband, love forever, Gina. 1989.* Gina Rocklin would explain the *G.R.* engraved in his wedding band. Turmoil began deep inside, dragging him into its wake. He was supposed to meet a woman . . . sometime soon.

"How'd you get into the canyon?" Across the room, Julie's voice was curt, bringing him back to the present. "Maybe there's another way out."

He eased the wet photo back into the sleeve as the black space in his head expanded. "I don't know. I don't remember." The feeling in his chest was numbing, beyond pain. He shook his head, willing it away.

"Well, did you come in from the county road?" She was impatient. "Mrs. Cumberland said you were walking."

He forgot not to look at her. She had one leg into a pair of Wranglers up to a soft, feminine thigh; the other was long, bare, and led to a glimpse of scarlet before she yanked down her shirt. Given his recent discovery of Gina, legs and scarlet panties were areas of her anatomy he oughtn't to be looking at.

"Turn around!" Her eyes flashed with dangerous indignation, and he obediently looked away.

Closing the picture of the young girl into the wallet, he forcibly dismissed all but the business at hand. "Who's Mrs. Cumberland?"

"She lives a few miles from here." Her voice grew increasingly testy. "She saw you three days ago. How many women did you meet up here?"

"Two, I guess." Here he was, swimming in the sea of strange after all. He laughed and decided to stop doubting everything she said. "Three days ago was . . . ?"

"Thursday."

"Which makes this Sunday." Grasping the welcome knowledge, he sat up to face her as she worked on her zipper. The upper half of her body was hidden under the Dodger shirt, but her breasts were bouncing with a saucy energy from her efforts. She turned her back. The heart shape of her rear end was pleasing as well. Being married didn't have to stop him from appreciating the view. "What month is it?"

She stopped short, her features quizzical as she turned to face him again. The blue shirt slowly ceased its motion. "Last I heard, it was September."

"And the year is . . . nineteen . . . ?"

She gave him a measured look before answering. "Ninety-eight. What're you, going to tell me you're a hermit?"

He scratched his beard, then held out his hands; turning up his palms, he scrutinized the pads of his fingers before holding them out for her inspection. There were no calluses, only the abrasions from the tent canvas. "If I am, I haven't been one very long. What do you think?"

"Oh, please." She stood for a moment, open-mouthed, then squinted at him, disgusted. "Amnesia? Give me a break."

The term provided closure to a question that had been dangling in his head. "Thank you, *that's* what it's called. I couldn't think of it."

"I don't believe you. Nobody gets amnesia."

"I assure you, Julie, I wouldn't lie to someone who saved my life." He saw that she was leaning toward belief but not entirely convinced. "When you showed up with the shovel . . . I thought you'd come back to help me." He searched for an adequate way to convey his feelings. "*Gone,* I guess, is the best word to describe the sensation. There's this giant . . . nothing where I used to be. It's mostly blank and it just doesn't quit." For a moment the blackness won, and inadvertent tears blurred his vision. But a weight had lifted off his back in the telling.

Julie stared at Rocklin, incredulous, but a part of her was disarmed by his sudden emotion. "I was after treasure," she said slowly.

His face expressed genuine bafflement at her explanation. "Treasure?"

"I'll show you." She crossed to her backpack, buying time to think. Of all the things she'd considered—concussion, mental illness, drugs, con artist, even a basic nut case—amnesia hadn't occurred to her. What she knew about loss of memory could rattle in a thimble. Would amnesia explain the crazy "I love you" talk last night, and his thinking she was his wife? The lump on his head would point in that direction, but losing your past was one of those things that didn't actually happen to people.

Except, of course, it did, otherwise there wouldn't be a name for it. If this guy had no memory . . . he could have mentioned it a whole lot earlier than this morning. Now what? Even if it was true, it sure didn't explain away the money and the trespassing. Or the gun she'd have dragged out from under the padding a few minutes ago if she'd been able to find it—and was going to put back in her pocket the minute he left the cabin. He could be Derek Rocklin the Backwoods Killer for all she knew. Cautious once again, she carefully extracted the crumbling food tin from her backpack and showed him the pearl beads and plastic jewelry. "My sister and I buried these years ago." She grinned nervously. "Under the cedar that beaned you. What can I say?"

He extended the soggy wallet and exposed the driver's license. "Am I this guy?"

Still skeptical, she took it from him. "You don't think you're him?" It had been too dark last night to make a comparison; she'd simply assumed he was Derek Rocklin.

"I have no idea what I look like." He gave her a thin smile. "Or what I'm *supposed* to look like."

She ventured close enough to the bunk to compare the photo to her stranger. "Hair and eyes sure match. Can't be sure about the face. This is about to expire, so it's an old picture, and you're pretty bent up." She squinted at him in appraisal, calculating. "Birthdate says you'll be thirty-three next month. I'd say it was you—without the glasses." She returned the wallet, cautiously curious. "Must feel odd not to recognize yourself."

"*Odd* isn't the word. . . . Mrs., uh, Cumberland didn't know me?"

Julie shook her head, still wary. "She called you a stranger with sneaky eyes."

He looked at her, hurt. "Sneaky?"

"Well, they are an odd color green. Very Nordic." She found her purse and showed him his face in a compact mirror. "You look like you lost a bout with Mike Tyson."

He gave her a blank look, which changed for a moment to something more before he glanced away. It was a small cabin, and she'd just seen that expression that men get when they have sex on their brain. He returned his gaze to the mirrored glass, and she was suddenly aware that she was very much alone with him in a deserted area; battered or not, he was a whole lot bigger than she was. And until she had his gun back in her pocket . . . "Never mind. Makes a fortune boxing. Speaking of fortunes . . ." She plucked a bundle of money out of his backpack and was surprised to find it soaked. "This was dry when I brought it in."

A steady drip of water was falling from a rafter onto the floor where the pack had been. "I suppose you don't know anything about the money, either," she added, determined to gauge his response.

"Not a clue." He seemed fixated on something inside his head. "Saw some of it on the ground when I came to, but I had no idea there was more in the pack until just a few minutes ago."

His answer seemed genuine enough, but it was hard to stay concentrated. When he shifted his full attention to her, it was like stepping into a white-hot spotlight that caused her to blink like a guilty kid facing the principal. "Well . . ." The blue jeans and shirt she'd laid out on the bunk last night were wadded against the cabin wall. She rescued the clothing and placed it next to him, trying to ignore a growing interest in this attracted, married man. Not a good situation, and escalating by the minute. "You get dressed and we'll decide where to go from there."

Not a good situation, indeed. While he struggled into the shirt she located a bra, quickly stuffed it under her jersey, and grabbed a cable-knit sweater. He was watching her closely, waiting for her to leave so he could put on his jeans; she shrugged into her jacket, gathered her purse, then paused at the door. She saw his look of appraisal and tried to keep her cool. "I'll wait out here."

His gaze didn't waver. "I'll let you know when I'm dressed."

"Do that." She stepped outside and ran through the rain toward the Bronco.

9

Ron Hathaway damned himself as a fool for smoking again and blew cigarette smoke toward the ceiling. He looked out his motel window at the pouring rain and listened to his boss, who was worried, irritated, and unhappy. Deke's tired voice rasped through the phone. "Walk me through it again."

"Three days ago," he replied wearily, "he checked in at five, said the contact had come from a woman and she wanted the drop made sometime Saturday morning . . . early. She'd call and let him know what time and where. He'd just been—"

Deke interrupted, exasperated. "Yeah, yeah, run off the property by some old lady and had to look for a new location. Then what?"

"He said it was going to take a while to find another campsite in the dark. Haven't heard from him since."

"How'd he sound? Do you think he was in trouble?"

Hathaway inhaled deeply, going over the conversation again in his mind. He'd sounded fine, he was sure of it. "No indication," he said firmly.

"Anything odd or unusual?"

"Not a word. I'd stake my life on it, Deke."

"Maybe the old woman was bogus. Maybe they're jerking us around."

"Could be, but I doubt it. He said she was a local and he'd passed her place when he was setting up."

"When did the phones go down?"

"Yesterday late afternoon, until an hour ago," Ron justified. "I've been using the cell phone to try to reach him. Either he's turned his off or it isn't functioning. The contact insisted she hadn't reached him, either. Real skitsy, says we're trying to set her up. She wants a new meeting and the money."

"Yeah, and hell's short on ice water! She can wait. How many guys you got out searching?"

Hathaway inhaled deeply; he'd known this was coming, and he wasn't looking forward to the conversation. His words came out in a thin stream of smoke. "None. Here's the thing—"

"Why the hell not?"

He adjusted the phone cord and sat heavily on the bed. "I don't think you understand. It's a mess up here."

"I know it's a mess. I watch the same TV you do."

"Then you know they got a bridge out," he explained patiently. "Flash floods, mud slides . . . there's no manpower to go looking for some guy who may not be lost."

Through the receiver, Deke's voice iced over. "Just what the hell does that mean?"

"I mean local authorities here aren't too sure he's in trouble." Ron closed his eyes. "They're saying it's possible he crossed into Canada. The border isn't that far and—"

"You mention the money?"

"No, of course not, but they can add two and two."

"Well, he didn't cross the border with it! He knows that area. That's why we used him."

Ron took another drag, determined to keep calm. "Yeah, well, all they're willing to do so far is put out a missing persons."

There was a slight pause. "I'm coming up. You get a team out looking for him."

"Looking where? No offense, Deke, but he's had forty-eight hours in at least a dozen directions. He was on foot, but it's possible we're looking for a vehicle now. I drove by the drop-off when I knew the storm was coming in, saw fresh tire tracks. Looked like a four-wheel-drive of some kind going in, but nothing coming out. Figured it might be the contact, and I didn't want to mess anything up."

"You said the drop didn't go down!"

"*That* call came in a few minutes ago. I didn't know it yesterday. I'm flyin' blind here, you know?" He pulled his irritation under control. His boss had a right to be moody. "Anyway, while I was out at the old woman's place, I ran across a note she'd left for the mailman." He unfolded the slight piece of paper to read from it. "Apparently she went on vacation, but get this. Someone named Julie shows up at the last minute—no last name—supposed to leave the house keys in the mailbox."

"Maybe his contact?"

"Could be." Ron tried to relax. "While I was there the mailman came along, so I asked him about the meet property. Didn't tell him about the note, just if he'd seen anyone out there. He says it's owned by people in Switzerland and there was a cabin on the place, but it's been vacant for years. Her showing up is a little too coincidental, I'd say." Hathaway got to his feet, uncomfortable.

"Yeah . . . I don't like it."

"So what are we going to do about the drop? The woman's pretty antsy, says she's going to call with a new meeting place in the next twenty-four hours and if someone doesn't show up with cash, the deal is history."

"I don't give a damn about the deal! We can always fix the deal. Tell her I said to keep her skirt on." There was a frustrated pause. "We have to find him. Get a search team out there! I'm on my way."

Hathaway nodded, unsurprised. "Spokane airport's closed and the bridge on the highway south of here is the one that's out, so you can't drive in. Like I say, it's a mess. Not going to let up until sometime tomorrow night, then there's another storm coming in right behind. In the meantime—"

"I'll be in Nighthawk in ten hours by helicopter."

"Yeah, well, good luck finding a place to put it down. We got ten-foot visibility here. I can't see the street."

"You get the men, I'll be there!"

The line disconnected. Hathaway hung up the telephone and stubbed out the butt of his cigarette. "Well, if he didn't drown, he's in Canada with that money, sure as garbage stinks." He shook the last cigarette out of its pack, vowing for the thousandth time to quit, and reached for his lighter. "Either way, you can kiss his ass a long goodbye. And all that cash with it."

10

Rocklin adjusted himself and zipped the front of stiff, unfamiliar jeans, every nerve ending in his body celebrating the simple act of walking around— still creaking a bit, but a freed man. Apparently the clothing was his, as the fit was adequate. Which, by implication, meant the money probably belonged to him as well. Not that it mattered at the moment. It damn sure wasn't fixing the memory problem.

He rolled his sleeves and strolled onto the cabin's porch to let her know he was dressed and waiting. The plaid flannel shirt she'd laid out for him was warm against the chill mountain air. Impatient, he took a sip of coffee as he peered at the maroon Bronco, barely visible in the rain and mist. Now that he'd confessed his situation to her, he was avid for conversation. Information. Anything she could tell him.

Plus he was hungry, and if she didn't come in soon, he'd start breakfast without her. She'd taken off ten minutes ago and he'd panicked at first that she was doing something stupid, like trying to leave without him. It was dangerous as hell out there, and he'd been anxious until Elmore had wrapped himself around his ankles, meowing for breakfast. He'd decided she must be checking the radio for a weather report, because there was no way she'd abandon the cat. Him, maybe, but not Elmore. Waiting for her, he'd emptied the pails, boiled coffee, prepared a makeshift breakfast of peanut butter toast for the two of them, and opened a can of food for the insistent cat.

Her leaving the cabin had shaken him. For the first few minutes her presence had taken on the importance of air, and him a drowning man. Having so little in his life that made sense, the thought of losing anything known twisted in his stomach like a snake. Shocked by his dependence on this woman, he was still uneasy with the knowledge of it, and more than a little unnerved. According to her, they were strangers; as soon as the weather gave them a break, she'd very likely disappear from his life with an amusing tale to tell her friends about finding some yokel in the woods.

Until his memory came back, he was going to be dependent on strangers, so getting information from her was vital.

He was losing patience and tempted to go get her when the car door opened and she climbed out with a grim look on her face. The sight of her eased a band of tension that had locked itself between his shoulder blades—but called to mind the fact that at the moment he knew as much about her as he did about himself.

"Weather report says this will let up tomorrow," she called out to him. "Then it's going to get worse." He watched her hurry toward the cabin, sailing the plastic coat high above her head and shoulders, running up the wooden steps in a rush. "Another storm coming in. Maybe snow." Her face was slightly flushed, and she'd changed into a thick cotton sweater; it rode lightly on her hips but didn't hide too much of her figure. Raindrops were balanced on the sweater's weave. He had the urge to brush them off. "They mentioned a flash flood near the lake," she continued. "That's us. Apparently it's following an old stream bed. If that's the case, it should be lined with a pretty solid layer of stones and gravel. We may be able to get out that way after all, if the water gets low enough."

"That's two very big ifs," he said slowly. Suddenly, getting out meant an end to his access to her. A fine mist was glistening in her hair; she ruffled the sides with her fingers, shaking out the rain. The drops on her sleeves flew away as well. He frowned at his inordinate interest in the process as he caught sight of the wedding band on his hand. "Next time you decide to disappear, I'd appreciate a little warning," he said flatly.

She regarded him with a cool look. "I didn't disappear."

"You know what I mean. You've been out there for twenty minutes." She hadn't, but it felt like twenty minutes. It *felt* like hours.

Her chin took an obstinate set. "I was a capable person before I met you, Mr. Rocklin. I'm still a capable person, and I can find my way in and out of a car."

"I'm perfectly aware of your abilities, Miss Ryan." He bowed slightly to make his point. "As a matter of fact, I stand before you as testament. However, I'm also aware that you took the car keys."

Her face became subtly defiant. "Okay, so I was thinking about going out to check on the road . . . but I've decided there's no point until visibility's better. I'll walk down later and see how bad it is before we take the car. There's less than a quarter tank of gas."

"If we get mired, we're screwed," he said soberly, and watched higher color climb into her cheeks at his inelegant choice of terms. Not only was she pretty, she was sharp and level-headed into the bargain. It wasn't usual to find all those qualities in the same woman. It occurred to him that in order to know this, he must have had experience with several women. Otherwise, his opinion of her would be as blank as the rest of his life. Which didn't square with nine years of marriage, unless Derek Boyd Rocklin messed around. He carefully filed the thought away for future consideration and turned to something he could handle. "Breakfast's ready." He stood aside to allow her to enter the cabin.

Julie watched him pour her a cup of coffee and took it from his hand, comparing the breadth of his knuckles to her smaller fist; she was aware of his scrutiny. "There should be milk if it hasn't—"

"Soured. Choices are black, or black and sweet."

While she'd been in the Bronco, he'd obviously been through the food supplies. A quick glance at the bunk assured her that its pad hadn't been disturbed. He hadn't found his gun. So far he didn't seem to be aware the weapon was missing. Maybe he really did have amnesia and didn't remember that he had one. Of course, if he started looking for it, she'd have to do some pretty fast talking.

She'd deal with that when the time came.

He was waiting for her response. "Black," she said stubbornly, craving sugar. Unless they could cross the creek, she'd be sharing the cabin with this man again tonight—indefinitely, if they were caught in the impending storm. Maybe they could use the canoe. Row across the lake? To where? She'd circled the shoreline yesterday, and her grandfather's was still the only cabin in the area. And Rocklin was right: Until they'd determined how badly the road had washed out, it wasn't a good idea to use up gas exploring avenues of escape unless there was a reasonable expectation of making it to safety.

"Anything else on the news?"

"Not much. No missing hikers on the broadcast I heard," she said, guessing his intent. "Not a big tourist area. The locals discourage it."

For the next few minutes she endured a quizzing about being at the cabin and what she knew of the immediate terrain. Information that she'd found him a quarter mile from the Canadian border seemed to surprise him but did little else except bolster her opinion that he and the money were part of something illegal. At one point she drew a rough finger-map on the floor, locating the border, the lake, the approximate distance to Mrs. Cumberland's, and the route to Nighthawk for him. "What else can I tell you? Clinton's still president, but—"

"What about you?"

She was rattled for a moment, unprepared for his interest. "I told you, I came up to look over my sister's property."

"No, I meant who are you?" He smiled at her with his eyes, pupils vaguely iridescent in the early light. "Besides capable."

It was a reasonable question. Julie stared back while she summoned a suitable response. Who was she indeed? Exactly how much of your past defined you? Oldest child? College dropout? Control freak? Former secretary, now fledgling real estate agent? And most recently . . .

"Married?" He scanned her ringless fingers. "Divorced, engaged?" he pressed.

"Yes." His look grew deeper, eyes shifting to the sky color between silver and white, intense in their interest. "Engaged," she clarified, trying to concentrate.

"Mmmmm." He gave a slow nod and his gaze left her face to come to rest again on her fingers. "You're about . . . twenty-five?"

"Twenty-eight." She struggled to anticipate him. If he asked about an obviously missing engagement ring, she'd tell him was at the jeweler's, being sized. No, it was none of his business. These were personal questions—too personal under the circumstances, particularly from a married man, and painful. Then there was the fact that despite his bruise-mottled features, he was awfully good-looking. The shape of his mouth was as close to being perfect as she'd ever seen, and acknowledging that she'd noticed, was still noticing, made her edgy.

Maybe she should tell him she wasn't wearing a ring because thieves tended to take such things away from you in isolated cabins. Then she realized that aside from his penchant for walking around without clothing, he'd done nothing to give her a reason to assume he'd steal from her or do her harm. "Twenty-eight," she repeated. "I had a birthday last month." Defensive, off balance, she clamped her mouth shut.

"Mmmmm," again, and another nod, which could mean anything. Inquisitive eyes, heavily fringed with blond lashes, returned to her face, but he lapsed into silence.

"We have a wood situation," she said, determined to change the subject. "Everything dry is on the porch and it won't last the night, particularly if it gets colder. It could snow, and if for any reason we don't get out of here . . ."

He came to attention and smiled at her. "We'll bring some inside so it can dry out."

She saw that he'd fed Elmore and thanked him, but avoided meeting his glance any more often than necessary. She satisfied her craving for sugar by topping the melted peanut butter with spoonfuls of fruit from a jar of boysenberry compote, and as they sipped second cups of coffee, he gestured toward the buckets lined up under the holes in the roof. "The tent canvas is still in the canoe. We can tack it to the rafters and funnel the leaks out that window. Make room for wood."

"Now who's capable?" Grateful for something concrete and possible to do, she leaped up to wrestle her grandfather's tackle box from behind the bath-tub. "We can tie it up with fishing line."

An unwritten truce of sorts fell into place. She topped her jacket with the plastic raincoat and made the run to the canoe for the canvas. When she returned, Rocklin was seated next to the tackle box and had lined up half a dozen fishhooks on the wooden floor; under Elmore's fascinated gaze, he was using a rusty pair of scissors to cut lengths of fishing line. He began attaching the hooks every few feet along the edge of the canvas while she raided the supply of firewood stacked behind the cabin.

When there was a creditable pile on the porch, she reentered the cabin to find him struggling to tie the lengths of slippery filament to the hooks. One of his fingers was bleeding, making it difficult. She hung the raincoat in the corner to dry and slid her jacket onto the back of one of the rickety chairs; the smell of heated wool joined them in the room as she sat cross-legged on the floor to help.

Within the hour they were ready to put the canvas in place. He helped her onto the stronger chair, but when he handed up the canvas, the chair wobbled under her weight. She clutched his shoulder to keep her balance and felt him wince. "Sorry." It seemed as if she was destined to cause this man pain.

Rocklin flinched under her fingers; the chair's ancient frame creaked but held together, and she released him to reach for the ceiling. If it gave way, he realized, she'd fall toward the metal stove. He grabbed her waist with both hands and eased his shoulder against the back of her thigh.

When he was certain she was steadied, he repositioned his far hand onto the chair, not because holding her by the waist was straining sore muscles throughout his torso—which it was—but mostly because embracing those decidedly feminine hips was purely messing with his head. His arm around her body had transformed itself into a gesture far more intimate than cautionary. "Careful," he warned, unsure if the comment was meant for her or himself.

Intent on her mission, she didn't seem to hear. She'd been like that at the waterfall as well, focused and goal-oriented as she'd dug him out with the shovel and dragged him down the creek bed to her canoe. Those memories were indelible; after he'd had the champagne, however, his recall was a little shakier. She'd propelled them around the choppy lake, then things sort of reappeared in patches . . . mostly of him naked and her naked. And what had she accused him of this morning—pretending they were married? There was a vague something of that nature in his memory, but it was hard to be sure.

She reached up again to tease the line around a rafter, and her sweater took a subtle hike upward as well, emitting silky, feminine whisperings that complicated his thinking and invaded his senses with force. Slightly above his head were the globes of her breasts, firm and unswaying, and if he were to tilt his chin the least bit, his mouth would be scant inches from the scrap of red satin he'd witnessed earlier. Less than inches.

Pouting satin firmly nestled between pale, soft thighs . . . warm against his shoulder and bringing on the beginnings of an unmistakable fullness. Married or not, rubbing up against this woman's body was beginning to work on him. D.B. Rocklin was having thoughts . . . of removing ruby satin panties and getting laid. Guilty, he eased the pressure of his shoulder away from her.

She felt the shift. "Don't let me fall." Her voice was distracted, her concentration elsewhere.

"Me either," he muttered fervently.

She looked down at him, sudden concern in her voice. "Are you dizzy? You want me to—"

"No." Her blue-green eyes were pale as water, and her hair, freed from its ponytail, had tiny glints of golden highlights from the window light and held the tantalizing scents of clean and woman. All sorts of male-oriented knowledge was rising to the fore, intimate and enticing, and having nothing whatever to do with memory. He pulled himself under control. "I'm fine."

They were sharing a very small space. For the next twenty-four hours or however long it took to get to safety in her vehicle, they'd be sharing an even smaller space. It might be okay to enjoy the view, and God knows he was planning to, but anything else would be off-limits. Something in her voice, some lack of passion, perhaps, had made him question whether or not she'd been honest about being engaged, but *he* was married—and already entertaining impure thoughts.

And if he continued to entertain such thoughts, one thing was guaranteed to happen: the room— and the Bronco—would get a hell of a lot smaller. He might not know himself as Derek Rocklin, but whoever he was, he knew females—and, engaged or not, Julie Ryan wasn't the kind of woman who would overlook a wife. Not that he would, either, but it would make life a great deal easier at the moment if he *felt* married around her. "I'm fine. Really," he assured her.

He was fine, all right. If she hadn't found him last evening—a time ago that he could count in hours—he could very well be dead by now. And there were still no guarantees they'd make it out of this storm alive. At the moment every instant of life was unbearably sweet, and restriction, moral or otherwise, seemed frivolous. Besides, he justified, looking was different from engaging in action. "Take your time," he heard himself insist. He moved closer once again and took up his former position against her body, deliberately reaching his arm around her hips for the express purpose of enjoying the sensations that touching her set in motion. *Take all day.*

Julie felt the burn of Derek Rocklin's shoulder through the seat of her jeans, and pressure from his chest, warm and powerful, ran the length of her thigh. Heat from his arm surrounding her hips and the push of his fingers at her waist was sinking into her marrow from her knees to her rib cage and had started a curling, narrow path of heat below her stomach; he'd released his hold for a moment, but the curl had lingered. Not good. The man with the blunt ivory beard was much too close. Much too attractive, and much too everything. Tall, interesting, married . . .

Those mystical eyes ten inches from her own were jolting her nervous system and disconnecting her conscience. Glancing down to check on him, she'd seen the look in his face. A sexual look again. In the shadow of her body, his eyes were a much richer green, and it was evident that he was as aware of her as she was of him. If anyone was getting dizzy, she was.

She wrenched her thoughts elsewhere and stepped down.

He repositioned the chair and braced her as she climbed up again, but this time he held himself away from her when he let go of her hand. Immediately she missed the reassuring pressure of his shoulder. Working another line into place, she was aware that he'd stationed himself less than an inch from her body, but the heat and curl he'd generated were there just the same. His crown of hair and the stubble of his beard were white-gold and bordered his features like a halo. Sun-bleached brows shaded his eyes, green as celery when they looked up at her. If they were indeed a window to his soul, they told her very little. And too much.

Maybe she was being foolish by taking his explanation at face value. It was unlikely that amnesia victims couldn't recognize their own picture. He was a pretty smart cookie, and not having a memory very neatly eliminated any explanation of trespass with a ridiculous amount of cash in his possession, not to mention a gun. His intelligence shone through every time he looked at her—when he'd scolded her for going out to the Bronco, for instance. And now this new complication: their interest in each other. So real it was becoming a presence in the room, gathering between them, hanging like a swollen, translucent curtain of smoke, there and not there; and, if she wasn't entirely crazy, growing. On her part as well as his.

Tying the last two lines was less difficult. She quickly pushed the soggy newspapers out the empty pane, and he helped her thrust the tail of the canvas through the window. Determined to regain her equilibrium, she jumped to the floor, causing Elmore to crouch at the sudden thump.

"*Now?*"

"Yes, now, my man," she said, exuberant that they'd solved the leak problem, and determined that the next thing on her agenda would be bringing her libido under control. Avoiding Rocklin's glance, needing space, she opened the door to the porch. "All we need now is this wood inside."

Rocklin managed to keep pace with her, but by the time they had gathered the wet firewood and ricked it into a crisscross pattern to dry, his strength was gone. He sat on the bunk, breathing hard from the exertion as the pain in the back of his head clamored forward into his temples.

"Why don't you take twenty minutes?" Her look conveyed concern, and he was torn between anger at being weak in front of her and gratitude that she was watching out for him. "You haven't stopped since daylight."

"Neither have you," he countered.

"I didn't lose round one to a tree." She laughed lightly, making it okay. "And like you say, you're not Hercules."

"Not this week," he admitted. But he wanted to be. Working at her side, he'd wanted the strength of two men: a married one who could keep his distance and his hands off, and a buck-horny single guy who'd pounce on her in an instant, fiancé be damned. He'd have that gorgeous body in bed in seconds, throw those legs in the air and bury himself in her. Make Hercules look like a wuss.

One thing he knew: D.B. Rocklin, whoever he was, was definitely entertaining thoughts. He studied Julie's hands as she stroked the cat. Another thing he knew: Women in love didn't take off engagement rings, except maybe to wear them on a chain around their neck. They didn't leave home without them, either. Something was wrong with this picture.

"Take twenty minutes," she repeated.

The *last* thing he wanted to do was sleep, but the only thing his body was listening to at the moment was her voice. Twenty minutes took on the aura of heaven, but with his luck she'd check on the exit road the minute he closed his eyes. He tried to eliminate suspicion from his voice as he sounded her out. "What are you planning to do?"

"I'll find something quiet, I promise. And no, I won't go anywhere."

He laughed. He must be pretty transparent, because she kept seeing right through him. "Okay." Relieved for the moment, he scanned her honest face. Something she'd said earlier had nagged at him all morning. "Last night . . ." He watched her glance away and try not to look back at him. "Did I really tell you we were married?"

She nodded, her gaze still drifting in and out.

"Was I, uh, trying to . . ." He was unsure how to

phrase the question without being crude. ". . . hustle you?"

She seemed embarrassed and crossed the room to plant Elmore on the seat of the wooden chair. Finally she looked full at him, blinking nervously. "Tell you the truth? I'm not sure. You sounded pretty convinced at the time. 'Course, you were whacked on champagne."

"Of which you have a case."

Her discomfiture dissolved into surprise, and she tried to laugh it off under his observation. "You have a pretty good memory for someone with amnesia."

"Three days aren't all that hard to keep track of." He rolled onto his side and closed his eyes.

This time he woke to the smell of something good. Beef stew, or he was crazy. She'd covered him with his sleeping bag and Elmore had taken up residence between his legs. The little tabby roused himself, stretched as only a cat can, and jumped off the bunk. Rocklin stretched as well, luxuriating in the ability to do so. "What time is it?"

Her answer came in from the area of the porch. "Little after five . . . you hungry?"

"Famished." Five joyous hours of uninterrupted sleep! He rolled over to find the cabin transformed. Drunken clothing was dancing around the walls and just under the ceiling, lengths of laundry line with a wavering fringe of U.S. currency were crisscrossed throughout the room; the money alone must have taken her hours. Heavily wrinkled towels and shirts, jeans, and sweaters had been washed and were strung on fishing line at crazy angles. Water from their lower edges dripped softly into repositioned buckets. His underwear, which he'd have bet money had been standard-issue white, now appeared to be a medium shade of blue. He decided not to mention it.

"You've been capable again." He pushed his sleep-stiffened body to sit up.

She came through the door; her hair, twisted into a loose knot on top of her head, gave her a charming, hoydenish appearance. "If we can dry wood, we can dry clothes. And money. It'll be lighter to carry."

He was hungry, and she looked delicious. He felt his interest in her react again, this time with immediacy, and quickly covered himself. "You are a downright genius." She was crossing the room toward him, the front of her sweater laundry-damp and clinging to her breasts. She detoured to stir something on the stove top, and her fanny, gently in motion from her efforts, added to his awareness of her. He'd best take a walk. Soon. Like now. He swung his feet to the floor. "Do I need the ignition key to use the radio?"

"No." She didn't turn around. "Just remember the battery."

There was a long pause as he moved through the room behind her, forcing leg and back muscles into use, distracting himself with the aches brought on by stretching his arms from side to side. "Five minutes of news," he assured her, "that's all."

Outside, the rain was discernibly lighter, the air strengthening and clean as it braced his lungs. He firmly rescinded any permission to entertain lascivious thoughts, stepped off the porch into the wet, and walked to the far side of the Bronco to commune with nature.

When he opened the door, the interior of the car held the scent of her. He breathed it in: feminine, fragrant, a mixture of expensive perfume and body lotion, profoundly pleasant. The radio announcer confirmed what he already knew from the lack of horizon: rain all night. A local state of emergency was still in effect, and a drop in temperature was expected. The second storm was forecast to hit the state within the next ten to twenty-four hours. It might give them time to get out after all, so they'd best make plans. Being snowed in was a very real possibility, and dangerous, with their current low level of supplies.

As he listened to the radio he poked through the dash compartment, found the Bronco's rental papers, and noticed her Malibu address. A fellow Californian. When the broadcast information began to repeat he snapped on the ceiling light and craned to inspect the contents of a box on the deck where the backseat had been turned down. If it contained food, he might as well take it inside. Classic dull green bottles were visible in the case. Four slots were empty, but the balance was filled with fine French champagne.

So. The savvy lady from Malibu, who claimed a fiancé but didn't appear to possess an engagement ring, did in fact have a case of champagne with her. The big question was why. And why did he have the impression that she hadn't come up here to celebrate?

11

Not having the faintest idea how to use the weapon other than point and squeeze the trigger, and hoping she'd never have to find out, Julie settled the slick, blue-black handgun safely into the bottom of her purse side by side with its clip of bullets, and winced at the telltale clunk as she set the purse on the floor. Out the window, she noticed that he'd turned on the dome light in the car. What was he looking for? Nervous, she picked up one of the bottles of Dom Perignon and dangled it in front of Elmore. "What do you think, El?" The tabby stared at her, unblinking, and his lack of comment added fuel to her indecision. Was it really wise to reintroduce champagne into the situation?

All the time he'd been sleeping, she'd been thinking about her cabin guest. Rocklin's lack of memory seemed to be somewhat selective; however, champagne had provided some very interesting information during their boat trip, some of which was currently being denied. She wasn't setting a trap exactly, but it would be enlightening to see where a few drinks would take his memory this time. How could he claim, for instance, to clearly recall her mention of a case of champagne, but not what he'd had in mind when he'd made a pass at her? What else did he "not remember"? Kissing her?

Small threads of heat warmed her cheeks. It would be a while before she forgot about it. A kiss that great was rare, in her experience. The last time her heart had done a double-dip of that magnitude had been at her high-school reunion, when she'd soul-kissed Warren Bentner. He'd been handsome-but-married, too. Selective memory indeed.

Waiting for Rocklin to wake up, she'd begun preparations for tomorrow's departure. Threading the money onto fishing lines had been an admittedly crude method of getting it dry, but it seemed to be working; as soon as these bills came down, another batch could go up. Her cabin companion might deny knowledge of all that cash, but she very much doubted he'd leave without it. She wondered idly if drying it constituted "laundering." Whatever—water-logged, it was too heavy to carry, and much too valu-able to leave behind.

Her mind turned itself over to other details: the clothing strung around the walls would probably still be damp tomorrow, but wearable; the Bronco would have to be lightened as much as possible if they were to obtain maximum distance from the remaining gasoline. Leaving Mrs. Cumberland's canoe wasn't a problem; tethered, it would ride the lake indefinitely, and someone could retrieve it at a later date.

And they'd need energy. With that in mind, she'd

been lavish with the food supply before bringing in a couple of bottles of champagne from the car.

The dome light went out. Setting the champagne aside, she checked on the food. Footsteps sounded on the porch, and Rocklin came inside. "Nothing new," he reported. "Rain's easing up somewhat. Looks like we'll have a couple of hours between storms to get out of here."

They pushed back the bedding and, with the addition of the lantern, the cedar bunk became a low but serviceable dinner table. Rocklin arranged the two chairs while she spooned hearty portions of stew, green beans, and applesauce onto her grandmother's vintage Melmac dinner plates.

"Smells delicious." His smile was disarming.

"I handle a mean can opener. I've heated rainwater for tea." She gestured toward the champagne. "Or there's this."

"This," he said immediately, and took one of the bottles into a firm grasp. "By all means this. I say a celebration is called for."

She watched him unwrap the foil and wire, then use his thumbs to leverage the cork. Elmore raised his eyelids to half-mast at the resultant *popp* and fizz, then returned to dozing next to the stove. Rocklin poured two glasses.

"To a special lady." The green eyes were forthright. "Here's to a good life. Yours and mine." He clicked his plastic glass lightly against her own.

Julie sipped her wine, unable for a moment to think of anything appropriate to say in return. "Success . . . in all our endeavors," she managed thinly. What kind of stiff-necked toast was that? Both of them had looked death in the eye within the past twenty-four hours. "To . . . getting the hell out of here in one piece," she amended, and was pleased when he grinned and tapped her glass again.

The champagne went down smoothly during their meal, second glasses as well, and he filled her in on specifics of the weather report. No longer hungry, Julie spooned generous second helpings onto his plate while she explained her decision to abandon the canoe. He continued eating, openly enjoying the food and nodding agreement as she spoke. Finally he closed his eyes and smiled in contentment. He shifted to one side and made room for his legs to sweep past her chair, then leaned back comfortably and raised his glass again. "You've been going nonstop while I've been sleeping," he said to her earnestly. "I promise to make it up to you."

She felt the impact of his interest and the undercurrent of curiosity. "I'm a type A personality," she explained warily. "Have to stay busy. Nothing makes me crazier than downtime." She deliberately refilled his glass.

He seemed not to notice as he surveyed the strands of drying money. "Innovative. I'll bet the manufacturer of that fishing line never thought about this particular use." He leaned forward to examine the near-empty bottle. "Pretty good stuff to take to a cabin in the woods. How long have you been up here?"

"Three days." Three again. The number that wouldn't go away.

He glanced at the waiting bottle, obviously tallying. "One a day?"

So he'd counted the missing slots in the carton in the Bronco. "I like champagne."

He took a sip, studying her over the rim of the glass. "You were planning to drink all nine?"

She shook her head, then nodded, her mind pumping furiously, annoyed that she hadn't been prepared with a story. She took a long swallow, forgetting to let the wine melt into the back of her throat. It *was* good wine. Fit for a celebration.

As soon as she put down her glass he topped it off, emptying the bottle. "Goes flat unless you drink it all." His voice was lazy. "A case is a lot of wine for one person. So's a bottle, for that matter."

"You should know, you drank most of the last one," she shot at him, and saw the remark hit home.

"I won't forget what I owe you. Count on it." Shifting his legs again, he settled in closer, making her nervous. "Since your case seems to be dwindling . . . I assume more of the same will be acceptable?"

Defensiveness crept under her skin, and she'd had just enough to drink to let him know she resented his presumption. "I'd rather you didn't." The sharp remark stung the air between them.

"Sorry."

"It was a wedding gift," she admitted finally. "From his parents."

He raised his eyebrows and looked over at her, openly inquisitive; she slid her left hand out of sight. "You're getting married?" His voice was appraising and somehow her life had come under a microscope.

Still defensive, she was unable to turn it around. "That's what engaged people usually do."

"Mmmmm, usually." His eyes punctured holes in

her faltering confidence as the air in the room thickened and danced. "Rustic ceremony in the woods?" His gaze didn't leave her face. "Is this the honeymoon cabin?"

Not that he'd stated the question in a manner loaded with innuendo, except they both knew it was. Something was going on—a living thing was being created between them, with an agenda all its own. She sought refuge from dealing with him by lowering the level of champagne in her glass. How had he become the person asking the questions? She tried to counter with questions of her own, but her brain had gone on vacation. Identifying this as a "honeymoon cabin" prickled her skin, made her edgy. Why couldn't he just be single? It would be so great just to let go, close her eyes, and go into his arms. Be safe. Be comforted, at least, and not care where her attraction to him would lead.

"What's his name?" His scrutiny continued, bringing heat to her face. "Was he supposed to meet you here?"

"Of course." The response was flat even to her ears, and the warmth in the room increased. She struggled onward. "He'd have been here already, but . . . obviously we didn't expect the weather." His pale eyes were mirrors. She tried to look away from him and failed. "There's more stew if you're—"

"Hey." He shook his head and smiled at her knowingly. "If you don't want to talk about him, I don't mind. We can discuss the weather. That's always safe."

He was teasing her now, and she knew she hadn't fooled him for a second. "I wanted to do some thinking," she conceded. Concealing the state of her emo-

tional life receded in importance and she was lost in
the bantering smile, and the eyes, the bruised face
with its perfect mouth, source of the most wondrous
kiss she'd shared in ages. Even, white teeth gleamed at
her when he grinned. Under the restraint she sensed
in him, a core of strength was overwhelming. He was
charming away her caution again, enchanting her
good sense. She realized suddenly that she was on the
brink of losing control of the situation, and reined
herself in. "Marriage and children are the biggest
commitments you make in life. You're married," she
said pointedly. "So you already know that."

The smile didn't falter, but the look in his eyes
drifted slightly. "Right now the only thing I know for
sure is . . . I'm here with you, drinking champagne."
He swirled the wine in the bottom of his glass and
pierced her with a probing look. "Cold feet?"

She held her breath and met his eyes as long as
she dared, unsure if his meaning was intended as
provocative, while deep inside things began to slip
and sway. Finally, determined to head off the tears
that the question had aroused, she responded, aware
that he would not understand. And that it didn't matter. "I'm not certain, actually."

His expression changed as he registered the
remark. Tilting back his head, he drained his glass,
openly interested and watching her closely. His Adam's
apple worked strongly, propelling the skin of his
throat as he swallowed. God, he was gorgeous! Disturbed by his silence, she pursued the opening into
his personal life in an effort to regain control. "You
don't remember being married?"

"No." He dropped his gaze at last. "I don't think

so, anyway," he added after a pause. "I was having hallucinations when you found me—dreams, maybe, I don't know. A woman that looked something like you. One of the reasons I'm confused, I think."

She'd succeeded. The sonorous spell between them was broken now, dissipating the emotion that had been brooding in the air, and she tried not to regret it. "You told me your wife was gone," she said hesitantly.

His expression turned to surprise. "I did?"

She nodded, watching him carefully. A small scowl of concentration furrowed his brow line. "We were in the canoe," she reminded him. "You showed me your wedding ring and said you'd always loved me—obviously you meant her, but you were very sincere. You also said . . . no one else had ever mattered." She stopped. He'd been more than sincere about his wife, he'd been passionate, and the memory was no longer comfortable. Maybe they'd had a fight. "If she was up here with you, is it possible that your wife left early and that's what you meant by 'gone'?"

"I don't know what's possible." He worried the damaged gold band around his finger as he spoke. "Anything, I guess."

Julie pursued the point almost against her will, poking at the wound she'd created, needing it larger, more permanent. "There was only one bedroll in the tent, and I didn't see anything in your pack that normally belongs to a woman."

He nodded, reflective. "If anyone else was here, they left before the tree came down. That was a full day before the storm, so it's reasonable to assume they're safe, at least."

She noted his unemotional tone and the impersonal use of *anyone* and *they,* and wondered if he was aware of the shift. Almost as if he knew he hadn't been with his wife and wasn't telling her. "Maybe she's on her way home," she said tentatively.

He seemed disinterested in her theory. "Did I say anything else?"

"You said there was nothing anyone could do about it."

He pursed his lips, preoccupied for several moments, his eyes far away. "Let's not assume someone will come looking for me. How about you? Besides your fiancé, who knows you're here?"

She dodged the fiancé part, her defenses on the alert once again. "Mrs. Cumberland," she responded, knowing full well her neighbor was somewhere in the Caribbean. "And my sister." There'd be no help from Joann, either; a giant rainstorm in Washington wouldn't be news in Switzerland. Maybe this guy was perfectly harmless, but he'd been carrying a gun, and she'd be an idiot to admit that no one would realize she was missing. "They'll be worried," she improvised. "Probably have rescue teams out searching for me."

He seemed relieved to hear this, and Julie quickly seized the opportunity to gather their plates and utensils. Stepping outdoors, she rinsed them under the rain spout. Her trap, such as it was, had yielded a married man concerned, albeit mildly, for his wife, but he seemed to have no mysterious or clandestine purpose, merely an inordinate interest in her perverse method of disposing of wedding champagne. Maybe her imagination was working overtime. And maybe there would be a perfectly logical explanation for all that money after all.

Only vaguely comforted, she acknowledged that it had been much more fun allowing herself to be slightly attracted—baloney, *very* attracted to him! Now that his matrimonial status was further established, if she had any brains whatever, she'd get herself under control and *stay* that way.

When she returned, he was taking the soggy bundles of cash out of his pack and piling them onto the seats of both chairs. The gun! Apprehension shallowed her breathing. If he was going to miss the thing, it would happen now. When he'd emptied both compartments and made no mention of the missing weapon, she was able to relax and help him count forty-seven banded packets in all. "Four hundred and seventy thousand," he said, surprise in his voice. "How many did you put on the lines?"

"Two hundred, plus all the loose ones. I lost track and was going to count it when I took it down."

"Looks like there was an even half million." He shrugged and glanced at the long strands of money waving above their heads. "How'd you string it?"

"Squeezed it first." She demonstrated by placing a dripping packet of cash on the floor and stepping down on it with all her might. Water oozed from the paper bills onto the wooden floor. "Peeled them off a few at a time and poked that big fishhook through the corner. Then ran the line through the hole."

While he followed her example, Julie tossed more wood into the stove before taking down the lines of dried money. They removed 293 bills from the filament, and she helped him string three more packets of money in their place. A light rain continued its dance on the roof. As the heat in the cabin increased, the money began to dry even faster, but perspiration dampened the hair at the base of her neck. "It's hot in here." She fanned herself limply and opened the door a few inches to breathe in fresh air.

Rocklin was overheated, too, she noticed; he'd unbuttoned his shirt another two buttons, and his hair was moist at the neckline as well. She watched him run his hand along the length of the second bottle of champagne and shake his head at her. "This is warm. How about one from the car?"

Cold champagne seemed a lovely idea, and she turned to go outside. "Hey." He caught her by the elbow and guided her under the lines of bills to seat her on the bunk. "My turn for a change. You stay here."

He returned in a few minutes, both he and the bottle wet from the rain. Cold champagne flowed into their glasses, and as they worked in tandem on an impromptu assembly line, pressing and stringing hundred-dollar bills above their heads, Julie sipped the icy wine and answered his questions. She told him about Joann and her husband, Gerd, described her grandparents and burying the treasure box when they were kids, explained her decision to change her life and apply for a real-estate license—everything he asked about, except Ned, whom he did not mention.

As they worked, the air space in the cabin filled with cash, and eventually they were spreading layers of money on the bunk. Elmore roused himself long enough to jump onto the bedding and bat several bills to the floor. Soon bored, he curled himself into a ball next to the stove once again and went to sleep.

A little after midnight, Julie swallowed the last of her champagne, stretched out on the floor, and looked up into the musty, swirling green. "Money, money, everywhere," she pronounced sagely, and handed Rocklin her emptied glass. "And not a drop to drink."

He canted his handsome face down at her. "Three more to go."

"Three?" She grinned stupidly, attempted to sit up, and changed her mind. "Threes are the bane of my life. Bad number."

Rocklin smiled. Julie Ryan, would-be bride and cabin companion, was flushed of face and higher than a kite on French wine. He'd made certain that she'd received the lion's share of the second bottle; type A personality or not, there was pain in her, palpable and clear as day in their conversation about marriage, in which she'd managed not to mention the guy's name. Whoever the fiancé was, something was making this savvy, good-looking woman deeply unhappy, and had created grief enough that the still-Miss Ryan was driven to fill every waking moment with the doing of something.

She'd been in motion since she'd appeared out of the mist to rescue him. An hour ago recognition of her frenetic behavior had startled him with its resonance, its strong aura of the familiar—apparently a reminder of something in his own life, or it would be when his memory returned. At any rate, he'd determined that it was past time for her to take a break. If it took champagne to slow her down, so be it.

He, however, would have to take care to make sure

his growing attraction to her didn't get out of control. All the time they'd worked with the money, something in the back of his head kept reminding him that ordinary guys didn't take a walk in the woods with this much cash. Next door to Canada? Between the money and the nightmare that had shaken him awake this morning, something had to be very wrong in his life. Very wrong, and this woman had stepped into the middle of it by saving his life.

It wouldn't take much effort on his part to take advantage of her, and while the line that established acceptable behavior still held sway, the longer he was this close to her, the thinner it was becoming. He picked up the thread of conversation. "Personally, I think it's a damn fine number," he contradicted pleasantly. "In my life, this is day three."

"Rocklin, my friend, let me tell you about threes." He watched her attempt to sit up again, and this time she made it with his help. "Bad number," she repeated restlessly.

He looked into candid eyes that were sea blue in the lantern light, saw dewy cheeks moist with perspiration and an imminently kissable mouth . . . already kissed, that he wanted to kiss again, keep kissing. Own . . . Thoughts were definitely being entertained tonight.

He closed his eyes for a moment, searching for an impetus to keep his distance. This morning's nightmare leaped at him. *You murdered her. You did it for money.* Jolted, he suddenly made the connection to the cash in the room. *This money?* Lacking denial, his mind sped to terrible speculations. *I could be . . . anyone. Someone she doesn't deserve . . . shouldn't be around*. Sobered, he forced himself to return to the conversation. "What's wrong with threes?"

She grinned at him bravely. "Three months ago Ned Tanner, whom you do not know, invited his bride—bride-*to-be*—to dinner." She licked her lips thirstily, glistening them in the lantern light; soft gold refractions bounced off wet pink skin and the small, perfect teeth of her smile. "There's nothing to drink? I know there's more in the car. And it'll be cold, that's for sure."

If he was to remain responsible, a third bottle of champagne was definitely a bad number. "You're blotto," he countered quickly. "Both of us. How about some water?" He grabbed a bucket and, dodging under the strands of money, made his way onto the porch to catch a thin stream of rainwater from the downspout. Rain in his face and cold air blowing against his chest cleared his senses. The temptation to take advantage had been strong in him, and touching her was entering dangerous ground. He confronted himself bluntly. "Until you know who you are, don't even think about it."

Of course he would think about it, but he was disciplined enough now to go back inside, fill her glass with water, and keep his hands to himself.

He waited until she'd taken a deep drink. "You and Ned were having dinner," he prompted.

"*I* had dinner, *he* had three scotches," she specified with great clarity. "Then he said, 'Sorry I have to do this'"—she ticked off fingers as she spoke—"and 'Sorry I waited so long to tell you' and 'Sorry, I can't go through with the wedding thing.'" Three fingers raised, she bumped against the tub and laughed, a wry, sad sound. "What is a 'wedding thing'? Can you tell me that? Getting married isn't a thing, it's a commitment."

What idiot in his right mind would walk away from her? Rocklin shook his head. "Nice guy," he said acidly, more annoyed than he had a right to be with Ned Tanner.

"That's what I thought. Would you believe I took *three* years to decide on him?" She took another drink of water. "My parents hated each other. Our house was nothing but a weekly screaming match for years—drunken arguments, the whole miserable picture of two people who should never have gotten married. When they finally divorced, Joann and I swore we wouldn't marry anyone who didn't take making a family as a life commitment. So I was very careful."

"That's understandable."

"Jo married Gerd two years ago. Moved to Switzerland. I didn't like him, but . . ." She chewed her lip for a moment, then continued, eyes beginning to glaze with tears. "So the wedding was three months away. And we were about to send the invitations."

It began to add together. Alone in a deserted cabin. No ring. A case of champagne. She'd come up here to get through what would have been her wedding night. Chills ran through his chest. No wonder she was in pain.

"I'm better off. I know it's a good thing he changed his mind, because if we'd gotten married, I want to have children, and children need fathers . . . otherwise we'd just be another divorce stastif—stasif—"

It was no good. It didn't matter who he was. He wanted to kiss her, long and sweet like last night in the rain. He'd tried to write off that memory as something he'd dreamed or a drunken fantasy, but it had happened, as sure as she was sitting on the floor next to his feet. "Statistic," he finished for her.

"Whoa!" She grinned up at him, impish and tempting him further. "I'm drunk, aren't I?"

"I think both of us are a little whacked."

"No, *I'm* drunk." She smiled at him. "*You* are gorgeous." She stared at him in surprise, eyes widening as she realized what she'd said.

"So are you." It was said quickly and without reservation. A simple truth. Kissing her took over his mind, the need to do it huge in his chest. Ned Tanner, whoever he was, was a jerk; and D.B. Rocklin, whoever *he* was, was wa-a-y past entertaining thoughts. He went down on his knees, opened his mouth to her, wanting her, needing her to want him. He kissed her, natural as breathing, sweet as joy. A heady, mind-wrecking emotion built between them. Shrieking through his body, it grew with the speed of light, abandoned caution.

Suddenly she pulled away, grave as a judge. "I can't do this."

Fever for her filled up his thinking. "I know."

"I have never dated a married man," she told him solemnly. "Not ever."

He didn't want to date her, he wanted sex with her—right here on the cabin floor, right now, a celebration of their own personal wedding night, and he leaned forward to convince her.

"I kissed one." She stopped his advance with her

hand on his lips. He tasted her fingers. "I've kissed two, actually, but I didn't know the first one was married. I knew about you." She visibly gathered strength. "And I won't. You understand that?"

It was a message to be heeded. "Yes."

She looked away for a long moment, then took a huge breath, obviously tormented. "Three months ago I tore apart a wedding that it took me years to . . . get to. Returned my wedding dress. Canceled reservations . . . for my honeymoon." She sobbed a breath. "I can't do this."

"I know." He sank back on his heels to remain at her eye level, willing an ease to the pressure in his body.

"I got rid of everything. Except the champagne. Then just before my sister called . . . three weeks ago . . . I found out he and a friend of mine had driven to Vegas and gotten married." She held up three fingers in front of his face and shrugged at him, eyes brimming and glassy with pain. "Apparently . . . she was three months pregnant."

His tension found release in anger. *The cheating son of a bitch!*

"So I decided to bring it up here and pour it in the lake." She laughed with tears in her eyes. "But I've been drinking it instead. *We've* been."

Aware of the depth of her grief at the bastard's betrayal, and aware that short of taking her to bed, which would be his solution and not necessarily hers, there was nothing he could do, he made a hard decision. "And we, pretty lady, are plotzed. You better stand up so I can put you to bed." He began to help her to her feet. "We need some sleep."

"You know what hurts most?" She was drowsy now, from the wine and the warmth in the room; her eyelids finally came to rest on flushed cheeks, spilling the tears and shutting him out as she rose on unsteady legs. "I was so careful. I tried so hard to do everything right."

He felt the heartache in her as she opened this very private door into her life, and kept his hands occupied unlacing her boots. Damn Ned Tanner for doing this to her! And hallelujah that the son of a bitch hadn't married her.

"I never played around, never even looked at another guy . . . not even once. I followed the rules." She lurched to one side, and he caught her. "And he walked out. I feel like such a failure."

"You're not a failure, sweetheart," he assured her, and swept aside the money on the bunk, guiding her carefully onto the sleeping bag. He pulled off her boots and tucked the bedding around her body, then sat next to her as she curled onto her side and sank into sleep. He inspected the bent gold ring resting against his knuckle, twisted it in endless circles, seeking strength. "You're smart. And you're funny . . . and a little too honest for your own good." *And if I knew who I was . . . if I knew I was safe for you . . .*

He gently threaded his fingers into the mass of her hair and slid it away from her face, exposing her profile. "Any guy who doesn't see that doesn't deserve you." Cupping her cheek, he traced the fullness of her lips with his thumb, heady sensations on the build again throughout his body. *Oooh, sweetheart . . .*

12

MONDAY

He was kissing her, the sweetest imaginable kiss. Soon his hips grew hard against her own and his mouth became possessive, making her whole and drawing her inside out. . . .

"Julie . . ."

She opened her eyes to blackness and a man's insistent whisper. "Now, honey, come on!" Nothing was visible. Firm hands grasped her shoulders, and something wet splashed into her face. "Now! Come on!"

His body was too close, a chill, dark presence next to her! She blinked in confusion against the sudden flare of a match. The smell of sulfur assaulted her nostrils, and the flame reflected a distorted, mottled face looming over her, hair wet and dripping water. A panicky scream grabbed at her throat.

"It's me, Dav—it's D.B., you have to wake up! Talk to me."

Another frozen moment until she recognized the voice as Rocklin's. He'd shaved his growth of beard, and the change was startling. She shut her eyes against the match's brilliance. "What's wrong?"

"It's raining again." There was unsettling urgency in his voice. "We can't wait for someone to find us. We have to leave now."

The flame crossed the room, cupped in his hand; he lifted the glass shell to the lantern, and light infused the cabin as he adjusted the wick. "It's almost five. Stopped raining right after you went to sleep, but it's started again, so I think we should go," he repeated.

The sulfurous odor disappeared, and she tried to make sense of things while he moved rapidly around the cabin. The strings of bills were gone and he was jamming clothing into her backpack. He'd already changed. Her spare sweater and wool jacket were piled on a chair near the stove. "Wear everything you can. It's cold," he warned.

Thick-headed, still half asleep, she found it hard to keep up. She crawled out of the bunk into the punishing chill and stumbled across the room in her socks. Her boots were lying near the stove and she pulled them on in a fog, welcoming their warmth as she fought a growing sense of panic. Elmore was poised on the edge of the bunk, tail twitching nervously at the predawn activity. "Hey, El," she commiserated. Her voice was shaky from the shudders that came with being abruptly roused from sleep. "I know how you feel." Empty champagne bottles lay in evidence, two of them, providing mute explanation for her inordinate thirst. Suddenly she felt terribly vulnerable.

"There's coffee." Rocklin had rolled both sleeping bags and was efficiently securing their ties. "Made a while ago, but it's still warm enough to drink."

Last night she'd bared her life to this man, confessed in essence that she'd lied about being engaged to Ned. She'd also kissed him again, and enjoyed it enough to dream about it. And somehow all of that was all right. But now she was going out into the night with him, leaving the safety of the cabin. Fear gathered into a tight knot in her stomach.

She reexamined the structure of his face. His jawline was harder, the bruises and angular planes no longer softened by the beard. His expression was distracted, noncommittal, as if nothing had happened between them. Maybe it hadn't. She tried to reconstruct the evening, put it in perspective. He seemed totally oblivious to any change in their relationship. Maybe, for him, it hadn't been anything special. Maybe he kissed every woman like that. Maybe she was crazy after all. She took a stab at normality. "Did you sleep?"

He didn't look up. "Some. I checked the weather report an hour ago and they said the next storm was definitely bringing snow, so I started packing us up." He glanced out the window. "So far it's only rain."

She finished her bootlaces and poured a cup of coffee, stirring in three spoonfuls of sugar against the hangover. The fire in the stove was nearly out and the black brew wasn't exactly hot, but her stomach welcomed the sweetness and warmth, and her nerves began to settle down.

"I've been down to the flood area. From what I could see, it's crossable, but we can't dally much longer."

"I'm not dallying. I have never *dallied* in my life," she threw at him irritably. Past a stolen kiss. Or two.

God, he's better-looking than Brad Pitt in that Irish movie. This isn't fair.

"I'm sorry." He gave her a devastating smile. "It was just conversation."

She was instantly contrite. She'd been sleeping so soundly he could have taken the car, the money, *and* her cat, and she wouldn't have known the difference. "I just need a few minutes to get oriented."

"Take your time." He grinned at her, his eyes twinkling wickedly for the briefest of moments. "Just hurry it up."

This time she was able to grin back at him.

In the light from the lantern, Rocklin assessed his smaller companion with care. Disheveled, hung over, and dazed with sleep, she was still spirited enough to give him a hassle even though she had to be terrified of going out into the darkness. It couldn't be helped. They needed to cross the creek bed as soon as possible and get to a proper shelter. Someplace with more than one bed! Even without makeup she was gorgeous, and kissing her last night had broken down at least half a dozen walls that honorable men kept as last lines of defense; any more "dallying" without separate mattresses and he'd bring on the champagne and throw out the rules.

Especially if what he'd discovered early this morning was true. He lost his concentration as she shimmied into the thick white sweater and pulled her hair out of the neck. Elmore hopped into her lap and she stroked the nervous animal as she slugged down the coffee.

It would have been pointless to lie in the bunk

next to her; as turned on as he'd been, there was no way he could have slept. He might not be Hercules, but he wasn't a saint, either, so he'd resigned himself to a wakeful night rebanding the bills into ten-thousand-dollar packets as they dried.

Somewhere around three in the morning he'd had a brainstorm and what he was certain was the return of normal memory—a portion of it, anyway. He'd written his name with water on the dry floor, several times, and two things had happened. Each time, the *Derek Boyd* portion was awkward, requiring his concentration to spell; *Rocklin* had flowed much more easily, but none of the signatures had matched the driver's license. On a hunch, he'd closed his eyes and distracted himself with the idea of crawling in next to that tempting body anyway, fantasizing long enough to let his subconscious take over. Then he'd signed his name again.

He'd written *David*. When he'd rousted her awake this morning, he'd almost identified himself as David; it had come out so naturally that she hadn't noticed, but he'd known instantly. No last name as yet, but deep in his heart he knew he was not Derek Rocklin. And if he wasn't, he was carrying false identification. Added to half a million dollars and a location close to the Canadian border, things were stacking up pretty ominously.

He'd used her hand mirror to shave and to compare himself again to the face in the wallet, without conclusion. Even with his bruises, allowing for five years' age difference, he and the man in the photo were practically identical; still, it was impossible to know anything for sure. The only absolute was the oncoming storm and his need to get her to a safe place before he moved on. If he was in half the trouble he suspected, it was best that they separate, and the sooner the better.

Weather reports had been grim, promising several inches of rain followed by snow and bruising cold. The area they had to cross was dangerous at best. The flood level had dropped, but it had started raining and the low-water opportunity would not present itself again for several days, if then. As it was, it was going to take a lot of luck to get to the other side and safety.

Julie finished her coffee while he took the backpack of money and their two sleeping bags out to the car. Ten minutes later she took stock: embers in the stove quenched with coffee, supplies in the cabin returned to a state her grandfather would have approved of, trash stowed in a plastic bag in the back of the Bronco. The balance of the champagne had been stashed in the ice chest and shoved underneath the porch.

Further procrastination could be disastrous. They had to do this, and it had to be now. She gathered the half dozen remaining tins of cat food into a pile and hurriedly pushed them into her backpack.

When she extinguished the lantern, the interior of the cabin plunged into blackness. She pushed the lantern under a bucket. Stepping onto the porch with Elmore under one arm, she realized that her stomach was calm with purpose. "I'm ready," she said firmly, and latched the cabin door.

Rocklin emerged from the rain and mist to meet her at the bottom of the steps, the masculine strength of him a welcome assurance. They were in this together. It would be all right. His breath streamed toward her in the cold as he took her pack. It was still raining lightly, mostly mist.

"Don't take this personally, but I'll drive." He walked with her to the open tailgate of the Bronco and tossed the pack inside. "It could get dangerous in a rocky creek bed, and I've had more experience with this kind of thing."

She looked at him obliquely, part of her relieved. Another part took note that it was odd that he had sworn no knowledge of himself but knew something like that. Plus, the man she'd kissed last night was still missing; this new, clean-shaven version was intense and determined to get them away from the cabin.

The mist abruptly gave way to a steady rain, and his hand was out, waiting for the ignition keys. Obviously a man's strength could make the difference in a bad situation, so she put her confusion on hold and gave up the keys without argument. He escorted her to the passenger side and helped her into the car, then took a moment to adjust her seat belt, filling the small space with his presence.

"What about the cat? Will it panic?"

The thought hadn't occurred to her. "I don't think so," she said tightly. "He trusts me."

He tightened the strap against her shoulder, his hand briefly tangling her hair in the process. "If things get dangerous, we might have to abandon him."

"No, we won't!" Her stomach rolled over at the thought. "Elmore goes where I go."

"Get a good grip on him, then." His face was sober. "It's going to get rougher'n a cob before we get out of here."

"I know." He shut the door. She coaxed the pliant tabby into his leather riding pouch and tied the opening close around his neck, something she rarely did. Elmore was wide-eyed with suspicion and shocked into silence by her actions. "Just for a few minutes," she crooned soothingly, and crossed her fingers she'd be right.

Rocklin eased the Bronco down the muddy trail. A series of local radio announcements warned them that various roads had been closed due to unsafe conditions. "Do you know the area?"

"Not well enough to know which ones they're talking about," she admitted. The trail appeared ahead of them through the wave of windshield wipers. "I haven't been up here for years. If the roads are out, there should be barricades or something. Wouldn't you think?"

"I sure as hell hope so." His voice was distracted as he concentrated on driving. Another announcement that phone and electric service had not been entirely restored to the region was followed by confirmation that an extensive snowstorm was moving across British Columbia and expected to hit Colville soon.

"Colville's two hours east," she told him, and wondered if the broadcast was live or a repeat of earlier information. Impossible to tell. Either way, they were going to get snowed on. More danger. Her chest constricted at the thought.

"Here it is." Rocklin's voice was tight.

The muddy path ceased and they looked out onto a swath of rain-rippling water that began at the bottom of a two-foot drop and appeared to be a foot or so deep. Trees and brush had been swept away upstream and down; at least three feet of graded soil had been scoured from the roadbed and carried away. Boulders the size of beach balls were visible in the middle of what had been the road, and a slow, relentless current was sluicing against their sides. "Damn." She heard a rugged sigh. "Looks like pockets of deep water. I'd better walk it first."

She scanned the forty-foot width before his statement registered. It was black and dangerous and he was going to walk across? "That's crazy. What if you step in a hole?"

"You'll see me go under," he said carelessly. She had a sudden urge to slap him for the glib response. The water was perilous, and they both knew it. He shifted the Bronco into neutral and stepped out of the car. "If I do, do not attempt to cross." His breath steamed away in the wind as he issued this order and peeled off his jacket. "You understand? I'll get back to this side, but you may have to follow me down the bank a ways."

Horrified, she climbed out of the car and ran around the Bronco, determined to talk him out of it. "You can't do this. You'll die!"

An odd expression crossed his face. "Don't worry, I can swim."

"So can I," she said frantically. "You'll drown, I know it! You're not strong enough. Let's just go back."

"If we get snowed in . . ." He held up three fingers and smiled down at her. "We'd be out of firewood in three days, and Elmore'll be out of food. I don't want to wind up being cat chow. Do you?"

She shook her head, not believing he was actually going into the water. "We'll find another way."

"It's too big a gamble." He was removing his sweater and the flannel shirt underneath. "Look at it this way: If I drown, you inherit a whole bunch of somebody's money." He grinned at her in the ambient light from the headlights. Rain glistened on his face and chest, beginning to form rivulets. "That tree didn't get me, so theoretically I still have an extra life. If things . . . Promise you'll come back and drink every last bottle of that champagne. Say it."

He was crazy. "I promise."

"Every drop, don't forget."

"Every drop," she parroted mindlessly. "This is nuts. Don't do this."

He tossed his boots and socks onto the front seat, took her face in his hands, and kissed her thoroughly. Too dazed to return the kiss and too numbed by his actions to think beyond the moment, she felt his hands drop from her face and watched him walk toward the water; he stopped at the edge. "I may have to zigzag a bit, so pay attention. Look for smooth riffles, and avoid any of the rolling, turbulent stuff. Those'll be rocks big enough to tip us."

He was really going to do it. Nothing she could say would stop him. He had kissed her goodbye and was warning her that in case anything happened to him out there, she'd be left on her own. She crossed her fingers like a petitioning child as his feet disappeared into the water. He staggered forward under the headlights. Three feet out, he was in to his knees.

"Current's stronger than it looks," he called over his shoulder.

Nearly halfway across, he stumbled and went down; she screamed, terrified that she was witnessing his death, but he recovered and forced his way upstream a few feet, then tried again. This time he almost reached the far bank before he went under.

She held her breath, willing him to come up whole. After a moment he did, a few feet from where he'd disappeared. Long minutes later he was able to pull himself into shallow water, still short of the bank. She ran to the edge of the water. "I'm coming to get you!"

He was coughing, barely able to speak. "Don't!" She hesitated while he retched into the stream. Finally he was able to call back to her. "It's too deep there. I need to find a crossing for you. This isn't safe." He plunged back into the deeper water, retracing his path to the center of the creek. "Turn here," he called. "I'll guide you." He coughed again. "Take it slow!"

"I will." She ran to the Bronco, jumped in, and gunned the engine. Her heart was banging against her ribs as she double-checked that the four-wheel drive was engaged. "Cross your fingers, El." She put on her glasses, praying they wouldn't steam up in the cold, and the world came into frightening focus between the wiper blades. She positioned Elmore, secured in his pouch, on the seat next to her thigh.

He was looking up at her with owl eyes, pupils huge and plaintive. "*Neooow?*"

"Absolutely, most definitely now," she murmured, and eased the Bronco down the crumbling bank and into the stream. Water cut into the headlights, and she kept sight of Rocklin's body, steaming in the frigid air as he waited for her. Soon she reached what she gauged to be the middle of the creek. The stream was deeper than she'd thought, or else the heavy vehicle was sinking into the bottom. The current was pushing fiercely against the Bronco's frame, and she had to fight the steering wheel to keep on course.

He motioned to her to come left, and she allowed the car to drift in his direction. When she reached his position, he began to work his way forward in front of the vehicle; his shadow, long and distorted across the turgid water, danced ahead of him in the beams of the headlights. She followed as close as she dared until he abruptly stopped. He fought his way to the side of the car and she rolled down the window. "It's deeper from here to the bank, about two feet, but there's a hard bottom," he panted, voice and body quivering with each word.

He was freezing. "Get in," she pleaded. "This is crazy."

"I'm too cold, and it'll take too long," he insisted. "Whatever you do, don't drift into deeper water. You lose traction, you'll start rolling, so keep your head." He pounded the side of the car with his fist. "You may get wet, but don't be afraid to gun it. Angle right and give it hell. If you feel yourself in the current, give it more hell, you got it?"

"Yes." Her stomach was jumping now in spasms, battling with her heart. Above the growl of the engine, her head was thumping from the sound of her blood. She could scarcely hear his voice.

"Give me the cat. If you roll, you can't get him out too. Keep both windows down. Let the water in and then go out with it."

She handed an unhappy Elmore into Rocklin's arms and opened the opposite window as instructed, then unfastened her seat belt. "Just don't drop him! He can't swim in that thing."

"Don't worry."

She reached out the window and untied the top of the pouch, just in case. "Don't drop him, anyway! He's too old to swim in this."

"So am I. Now wait till we get out of your way," he ordered.

She nodded, determined not to panic. He waded upstream, pulling himself forward with handholds on the Bronco's hood, then leaned into the current and was swept through her headlights toward the bank, one hand raised above the water with Elmore twisting and writhing in his pouch. Julie held her breath until he had crawled onto the bank.

Fifteen feet. That's all she had to manage. She backed up a foot or so to establish her traction, churned the wheels to the right, as he'd advised, then set her jaw and charged the vehicle forward, one foot pressed against the gas pedal, the other braced against the side of the Bronco. The heavy car sank into deeper water. Instinctively she leveraged her weight with the steering wheel as water surged through the floorboards and over her foot on the gas pedal. The motor roared as she pressed harder on the gas, and the tires found solid purchase.

David watched the Bronco shoot forward, spray flying in all directions, and was proud of her. She brought the car to a halt on the bank and jumped out, jubilant. He made it to her side to hand her the frantic, yowling Elmore, and grasped her bodily to keep his balance. "Th-That was perfect!" He stammered the compliment with cold creeping into his center. "Couldn't have done better." The rain had turned to slush, and the slush was rapidly becoming snow; his clothing was beginning to freeze on his body.

"Next time it's your turn to drive." She laughed up at him, her voice charged with excitement, then helped him walk to the car. Eyes still twinkling, she loosed the tabby inside the Bronco, then turned to lean in close to his face and kissed him. Her lips were warm and seared his mouth. He tried to kiss her back, but she'd already stepped away and was studying him head to toe with a wide smile. "Got to undress you again."

Shivering so hard that he could barely stand, he supported himself with the door as she upended herself across the seat, and a heart-shaped fanny was all he could see as she pulled his sleeping bag from the back. Snow began to pelt him in the face. A moment later she tossed a pair of dry jeans across the door and added the rest of his clothing, then stood next to him and unbuttoned his pants. "Getting to be a habit."

Too cold to argue, too cold to do anything, he held on to the passenger door. She was safe, and whatever happened now, they were even. A life for a life. She was a terrific, gutsy lady coming out of a tough situation, and if it turned out he was someone a woman like her shouldn't look twice at . . . well, at least he'd done something right before they parted company.

Shuddering in the freezing wind, he discovered that his hands were too stiff to make his zipper work, so she managed it for him. With her helping, he pushed the soaked jeans down past soggy blue underwear. "I could get used to this," he joked, and meant it. He sank onto the passenger seat so she could pull the icy denim free of his legs. Her warm breath feathered into his mouth as she labored, and he could taste her. "Skivvies, too," she instructed.

He made a halfhearted objection, then complied. Flurries of snow were dancing past them in the wind, blotting out anything past twenty feet away; they had to get moving. His equipment, such as it was, had shrunken to an all-time low in the freezing water, anyway. She'd seen everything he'd had to offer, more than once, so there was little to be self-conscious about, and this was not the time to negotiate for modesty. Still, he couldn't help being aware that he was being undressed a second time—by the same woman—with no sex to show for it! If there was a next time . . .

He lost his train of thought as she used his sweater to rub circulation into his chest and legs, and by the time she'd carefully zipped him into the dry pair of jeans, mobility was returning to his limbs. He slid his arms into the plaid flannel, relishing the warmth. She helped him into his sweater and slid his feet into dry socks and boots before cocooning him inside his sleeping bag, then she closed him inside the car.

With the heater running full blast, they continued along the track, headlights slicing through swirling clusters of snowflakes. The world grew increasingly white, and as soon as he was warm he became sleepy. His eyelids kept sinking, grit in them, and he was yawning openly. The sky was beginning to pink, warming the snow, tinting her skin. "You okay to drive?"

Totally concentrated, she nodded without taking her eyes off the road, cute as a bug in her horn-rimmed glasses. "I'm fine."

That you are, he agreed fervently. And slept.

13

Despite the trembling in her limbs, Julie kept the Bronco at a slow, even pace on the winding road, determined not to skid off the blacktop. Unaccustomed to driving on slippery snow, her shoulders ached from the fear of winding up in a ditch—and her sense of reason was straining itself to the limit as she worked at reining in emotions. From time to time she glanced at the handsome man sleeping against the door. He'd kissed her because he knew it was possible that he'd drown, she was sure of it. But why had he risked his life?

She knew why she'd kissed him—because she'd wanted to, because she'd accomplished something dangerous and important. Without him, she'd never have crossed that water; she'd have played it safe and gone back to the cabin, gambling that she'd be found.

What she couldn't fathom for the life of her was what had driven him to wade across that flooded road in the first place. If he hadn't, they could have capsized, drowned . . . she could be standing at the side of that wash right now, searching for his body instead of looking for gasoline. Forcing the nightmarish thoughts from her mind, she glanced at him again. He'd been restless for the past half hour, obviously dreaming. She tried to think ahead, aware that she was an emotional mess. Eventually they'd reach a town or an authority of some sort. What would happen then? Would he walk away and not look back? Could she?

Entirely too much intimate information about her personal life had already been shared and, against everything that was rational, she was enjoying this stranger's attention and concern. What was worse, she couldn't deny being attracted to him. More than attracted. If she stayed with him to make sure he was settled and okay, her willpower would only last so long and the likelihood of their having an affair would increase.

An affair! Grandmother Russell would spin in her coffin! Not to mention her parents. Unless he was separated and getting a divorce, there was no possibility that their relationship could become something more.

The back of her neck prickled, interrupting her scenarios. Without a divorce in the picture, it wasn't likely there'd be more. Somewhere, soon, she would have to figure out a way to return his gun. Maybe she could slip it back into the money pack without being caught. And remember to wipe off her fingerprints. Just because he was sexy and handsome and kissed her like nobody's business didn't mean he couldn't be involved in something really rotten or illegal. How had she drifted so far from the balanced, sensible person she knew herself to be?

Discouraged, she forced her musings in another direction. She'd have to call Joann about the property, as listing it for sale in the wake of a local disaster was a waste of time. Which meant she'd be leaving for Malibu and taking up her life again, a life without Ned Tanner. Now that someone had risked his life for her, Ned's infidelity and his sudden marriage to Helena didn't have quite the same importance.

"Gina . . ." Next to her, Rocklin had stirred in his sleep. "Hurry, baby." At his urgent, whispered words, Julie took her attention off the road long enough to see that he was smiling, and a hard dose of reality planted itself in her heart. So much for fantasies about strangers with a marriage on the rocks.

Warm and naked and laughing, he was kissing her belly, the soft undersides of her breasts, chasing the pink of her nipples. Her tongue in his mouth, tracing a path inside, was driving him crazy; the taste of her was a hot wash of feeling melting through his brain. *Oh, God . . . oh, God!* The giddy feeling crashed, and horror moved in. *I'm sorry! I'm sorry!* Blood from the wound was seeping through the front of his shirt, painting itself onto his skin, red and awful, and nothing he could do to stop the flow of it, when the earth suddenly heaved, tossing him sideways against the door of the car. He threw out his hands to catch himself, struck rigid metal. Pain radiated through his elbow.

"Sorry about that."

It was a voice he knew, softly insistent, and David came awake, blinking for a moment at the woman driving as he oriented himself. The feeling of horror in his chest eased. This was Julie. Not the woman he'd been holding. The world outside the Bronco was a paste of white, and the car was creeping along a deserted street. "Hey," he mumbled. "What happened?"

"I hit a hole. Didn't mean to wake you." She gave him a taut glance. "You were dreaming. You called someone 'Gina,' do you remember?"

"No," he lied, trying to rid himself of the nightmare. It couldn't have been Gina. Gina was . . . The car pitched into and out of another hole in what might have been paved roadway. Fuzzy, he watched Julie lick her finger and draw a second line on the inside of the windshield. Gina was . . . The thought wouldn't finish itself.

Confused as hell that the woman in his dream was injured and bleeding, he tried to recall the terrible visions, but they melted out of reach, elusive as the rest of his life. He looked over, trying to read Julie's mood, then out at the whirling blanket of snow; his charged body slowly relaxed. "How long's it been like this?"

"About ten minutes." Again they hit a hole, and the car lurched to one side. He watched her make a third mark on the glass. "Hard to see with everything white," she said to him. "Believe it or not, I've been missing most of them." She turned the steering wheel hard to the right and avoided a fifteen-inch puddle of slurried water. On either side of the car occasional snow-topped cabins made themselves visible for a few moments, then drifted out of sight. "Sign said Lake Stillwater. Looks like one of the summer resort areas. Probably closed for the winter."

"I'd say it was little more than a crossroads." He stared at her again, confused. "Weren't we going to what's-her-name's, Cumberland's?"

"Road was out. Flood washed across it, too, and I wasn't about to drive through that water twice, so I went west."

"Good girl."

"We've come twenty-seven miles since then, according to the odometer. We'll have to get gas somewhere."

The fuel gauge was hovering over EMPTY. His watch was still stopped, but the Bronco's clock read 9:15 and his stomach told him it was well past breakfast. In the dim daylight, driving snow made it impossible to determine much of anything else. The car crawled through a group of darkened structures until they came to Mona's, a combination sundries store and gas station. She stopped in front of the building.

"Pay dirt. Hope someone's home."

He pulled on his jacket, made his way up a small flight of steps, and looked in through the store window. A woman was coming slowly toward the door. She stared at him and then at Julie, who was standing next to the car with one eye on Elmore; the cat was ignoring the falling snow to make immediate use of the pit stop.

"C'mon in," the woman invited. She eased open the door and leaned past him to call, "Cats ain't welcome." Two bigger-than-average hounds were lying near a large metal stove, whose warmth radiated across the room. One of them slowly got to its feet to investigate a stranger. "Haggard, behave yourself," said the woman sternly. David warily eyed the dog with the same degree of inspection that the dog's owner was giving him. "M'name's Willie." The woman offered her hand, and he shook an iron palm while Haggard the hound gave him a more thorough going-over, its nose even with his belt line.

"I'm Da—Derek." Julie, who'd caught sight of the dog, was hustling Elmore back inside the Bronco. "She's uh . . . my friend, Julie," he said, trying to ignore the inquisitive hound. Haggard, with a size somewhere between St. Bernard and wolfhound, sniffed him up and down a final time, then lost interest and rejoined his companion next to the stove. David exhaled gratefully, stepped inside, and kept the door slightly ajar while Willie retreated to a rocking chair alongside the dogs, still studying him. "You and Julie got a death wish, that it?"

"We're lost. Got caught in the storm."

"You certainly did. Hit you in the face, did it?" Seated safely within the guardianship of her hounds, Willie was extending a qualified welcome. Correct answers had best be forthcoming.

"No, that was a tree, actually." Julie stepped through the door as he was glancing around the room, seeking a mirror; there was a small one on the near wall, and he saw his mottled coloring. It occurred to him that while both he and Julie had no memory of his face without bruises, strangers would certainly notice and wonder.

He brushed a dusting of snow off Julie's shoulders and was somewhat relieved when both hounds gave her a peremptory glance of dismissal before flopping their jowls back onto the floor. "This good lady is Willie."

Willie threw her a toothy smile. "Your friend here says you're lost."

Julie laughed. "Well, we are most definitely that. And nearly out of gas. Couldn't get through to Nighthawk, so we came this way. We were caught out at my grandfather's old place. Next to Mrs. Cumberland's?"

"I know Mary Ellen." Willie's rocker stopped abruptly. "You're Pearl Russell's granddaughter? Everybody round here knew Pearl. Good man. We still miss him." She got to her feet, suddenly full of energy. "You two look hungry."

Julie looked at him for confirmation, then nodded at Willie. "Well, actually, a little, yes. We didn't bring much with us."

"Well, I can fix that, then we'll see to gasoline. Can't have Pearl's granddaughter running out of gas in these here mountains. He'd come back and haunt me."

David followed the women into a kitchen fragrant with the aroma of strong coffee. Within moments their hostess had located a bowl of eggs and was tossing a tablespoon of butter into a blackened skillet. "I just put up that coffee, so help yourselves." She nudged a knife and a loaf of homemade bread toward him, then began breaking eggs into the sizzling butter with one hand, using a dinner fork to scramble them with the other. "Go ahead and cut some of that and push it in the toaster."

He did as instructed, fascinated with the change in Willie's demeanor. As the women chatted and bantered about Julie's grandfather, he zeroed in on the kitchen phone. "Any chance I could make a call?"

Willie laughed. "Phone's still out. Sorry."

Julie looked sideways at him. "Is there a local doctor? He has a giant lump on the back of his head."

Willie handed off cooking operations to Julie. "Nearest doctor's in Oroville. Let me take a look." He sat on a kitchen chair while she inspected his scalp with surprisingly gentle fingers. "Tree, huh? Fallin' asleep when you don't want?"

"I was for a while." He shook his head. "Not lately."

"See shooting sparks? Bad headache, won't go away? Blackouts?"

"Sometimes a headache, when I get tired."

She nodded sagely. "When'd it happen?"

"Four days ago."

"Hell, if you was gonna die, you'da been dead by now," she pronounced. "You get to Oroville, see Jim Meadows. Tell him I sent ya."

Within the hour they were fed, had a paper sack filled with fried-egg sandwiches pressed into their hands as well as bottles of water and a handful of candy bars from the store, and were following the tip of Willie's finger as it crawled along a local map; the frayed and yellowed sheet of paper was thumbtacked onto a wall behind the stove and had seen hard use.

"At this here fork, you stay to the right. If you go left, ain't no turnaround and you'll wind up at Hawk's Point," she warned. "That's the lookout station and ain't no one up there this time ayear, so you just ignore it." The finger swept on. "This here's a fire road and goes all the way to Oroville. No rivers to cross, no bridges out. Ev'body up here uses it 'cause it cuts about ten miles off the 'scenic route' the state's real proud of. That's a full hour in this weather. Come over it yestiday and it's clear, otherwise I'd make you go around."

She pulled on a saggy mackinaw, wound a thick blue wool scarf twice around her neck, and jammed her head into a tired black Stetson. "Let's see about gas." She led the way to the gasoline pumps.

As Julie pulled the Bronco into position, Willie took a key from a string around her neck and unlocked one of the pumps. Rocklin kept the fuel spout in the neck of the Bronco's tank until the numbers stopped spinning in their chambers, then carefully topped off the tank with a sense of satisfaction. They were set for at least three hundred miles.

"I ain't got change for this," Willie protested when he gave her payment. "Write me a check or somethin'. Or a credit card? Ain't you got one of them?"

"I'd rather you keep the money," he insisted. "Without gas we could have gotten stranded up here."

Julie agreed with him. "He's right. Please," she persuaded.

Willie allowed herself to be swayed. "All right, on one condition, and I mean it. You call me after you see Jim Meadows and let me know you're okay. Number's on that there receipt. If the phone's still out, drop me a note." She winked broadly at him behind Julie's back. "You're a mighty cute couple. You take care of her, son, you hear?"

"You can count on it," he said, and watched Julie's face crimson as she swung around to face him.

"My Bill took care a'me forty-six years. Woman can't ask for more'n that." Willie studied the snowfall and the ominous sky. "Gonna be two, three feet by nightfall. Don't waste a bunch of time saying goodbye."

He turned to Julie. "She's right, sweetheart. We need all the daylight we can get."

"Keep it around twenty—it ain't one of them there freeways you got in California—and figure two hours to Oroville. If you go longer than that, you're lost and you backtrack like crazy." Willie climbed the steps and opened the door to her store. "Come back anytime," she called. "Me and Bo and Haggard'll be here." She disappeared inside.

Anxious to be under way, he was relieved when Julie conceded the keys without comment. If Oroville's phones were working, the first thing he was going to do was see if Derek Rocklin had a listing in Santa Barbara. And a wife named Gina.

Swinging lightly over the lake, the helicopter gingerly landed on its pontoons a good half dozen yards from shore. The pilot slowed the engine. Moderate snowfall obscured their vision for any distance, but the bright red canoe they'd spotted at the shoreline was bucking in the rotor wash.

Hathaway was nervous; this was an incredibly dumb way for intelligent men to make a living. It had taken a major bribe to get them into the air at

all, and the pilot had just warned them they had little more than half an hour before he would pull
rank and fly out—with or without them. Deke had
been giving the man an argument, but he personally
didn't plan to put the pilot to the test. As much as he
loathed helicopters, he sure as hell didn't want to be
stranded here in a snowstorm.

Out the window on his side was the cabin they
were looking for. He pointed it out to Deke and the
pilot. "Can we set down somewhere up on the bank
so we don't have to get wet?"

The pilot revved the engine, and they lifted off to
circle the area. After a few minutes he landed the
bird in a space in the roadway with enough clear-
ance for the rotors. Hathaway helped his grim companion work his leg cast out of the cockpit and
climb to the ground. The pilot idled the engine
while they examined rain-softened tire tracks, frozen
depressions in the mud, barely visible under a thick
covering of snow. "Reasonably fresh," he assessed.
"I'd say within the last two to three hours."

"I want a look inside that cabin."

Hathaway glanced at his watch. They had fifteen
minutes. Anyone who was able to walk would have
come out by now to investigate the chopper. He
hoped to hell that if David was inside, he was alive.
He held his hand under Deke's arm to steady him
and helped the injured man toward the cabin.

At the end of the tire tracks were dozens of footprints, also covered over with snow. Half of them
obviously belonged to a man of David's size, and the
smaller prints might be a woman's. He studied the
scene. The larger prints were unaccompanied to

what would have been the driver's door. In charge and driving, or possibly (but a whole lot less likely in his opinion) hostage and driving.

The lack of footprints in the layer of snow on the steps confirmed that the two had departed while it was still raining. It had been snowing roughly three hours; therefore the trail was at least three hours cold. He knew Deke was making the same assessments. Inside, Hathaway immediately identified the piece of green tent canvas that was attached to the ceiling beams and funneled out the window. They'd spent enough time here during the rainstorm to be concerned with a leaky roof.

Hathaway held one hand on the stove. The metal was cold, but warmer than the temperature inside the cabin; the ashes were wet from what smelled like coffee and not yet frozen.

His boss was limping around the cabin, examining items nearsightedly as he went, and paused at a pile of wood stacked in the corner to adjust his glasses. On the floor, under one of the logs, was a scrap of money banding. "The cash was here." Next to it, on one of the pieces of wood, a long strand of tawny hair was caught in the bark. "Wasn't he supposed to meet a woman?"

Hathaway watched as both pieces of evidence were carefully removed and placed inside Deke's pristine handkerchief. He thought back to the impatient caller who'd insisted there'd been no contact and had tried to demand a new meeting. If David had lied and had connected with the woman after all, it sure looked like someone was trying to buy some time. A double-cross? The question was, who was doing who?

He showed Deke his watch. They were down to nine minutes. "David's a survivor," he offered edgily. "He knows these woods and he had a gun. He'll be fine."

Deke snorted but prepared to leave. "Can't always use guns against women."

They returned to the chopper and clambered aboard. The pilot's mouth was a tight, hard line, and he lifted off without comment.

"Follow this road. I want to see where it goes." The instruction brooked no argument, and the pilot swung the helicopter into an arc that followed the trail.

When they reached the path of the flood, the copter hovered over the bank. There was barely enough light for the helicopter to cast a shadow. Rotor wash blasted snow in all directions, making it impossible to read the ground, but the trail disappeared into water and Hathaway silently contemplated the roiling flood. If David and his friend had tried to cross, he and Deke were very possibly looking for bodies now. The thought made him queasy.

Apparently Deke was having similar thoughts. "Take us downstream."

"You got two minutes, Mac."

"Then follow the water two minutes, damn it!"

Ghostly, devastated landscape slid underneath them, split by a rift of brown water. Hathaway looked down, his spine tight. Stealing wasn't worth dying for. "You think they could have been caught in the flood?"

Deke answered him tersely. "I want it ruled out."

Half a mile downstream another road had been washed away, but there was no sign of a vehicle foundered in the water. At the end of two minutes the pilot veered the helicopter into the wind without a word, and ten minutes later he landed in the Nighthawk High School parking lot. It was snowing heavily, and as soon as Deke and Hathaway disembarked, the chopper ascended into the gathering gloom and ran south, ahead of the bulk of the storm.

"We're going out there."

Hathaway sighed as they approached the Range Rover. There was no arguing with Deke, and it would happen with or without him. He cleared the windshield of its mantle of fresh snow. At least they were back on the ground.

"If there are tire tracks on this side of that wash, I want to know where they go before the snow's too deep to follow."

Hathaway started the motor and moodily reached for a cigarette. David had been in that cabin, he was convinced of it. And he'd left in the dead of night, with another person. He had to know they'd be looking for him by now. Half a million in cash would tempt any man. Was he foolish enough to think he could disappear with it and not be found?

He cupped his hand and struck a match.

Money leaves trails. Foolish men with money leave even bigger trails. It would be only a matter of time. He looked at the somber, angry man next to him and watched him wipe melted snow off his glasses. The metal rims glinted green in the dash lights as Deke methodically worked on each lens.

Only a matter of time.

14

Snow fell steadily, and on either side of the fire lane it had sculpted perfect panoramas of firs and cedars into softly mounded Christmas tree shapes, thousands of them, in all heights and sizes. Miles and acres of forest slid by bathed in a surreal quiet, disturbed briefly by the sound and passage of their vehicle. Ahead of them, occasional groupings of elk melted into the silent trees, with only a bared branch to show for their departure.

The first hour of the trip had been relatively simple. True to Willie's prediction, the fire road was rough but reasonably well maintained, and their progress averaged a consistent twenty miles per hour. By mutual agreement the radio had been relegated to a low presence in the Bronco, dispelling the silence but quiet enough not to discourage conversation had they wanted to talk.

There seemed little to say, and after sharing the candy bars, Julie let her thoughts drift, not wanting to think about the consequences of breaking an axle. Rocklin seemed deep inside himself; however, he was a careful driver and vigilantly watching the road. Elmore was asleep in her lap, blissfully unaware, so she'd fallen into the swing-and-sway rhythm of the bumpy ride.

An hour from now, in Oroville, she'd be saying goodbye to this man who'd inexplicably risked his life for her; she'd leave him at a police station, or a hotel, or some other public place. An hour from now he and his money and his lack of memory would be out of her life. The thought brought a hollow feeling. She'd take over driving the Bronco, and he'd disappear. Maybe kiss her goodbye. What kind of kiss would that be? She immediately tried to separate herself and not unsettle things with speculation.

From time to time she felt his glance. Mostly he looked at her face, but sometimes his eyes slid quickly along her body. Damn, but the man was disturbing. Maybe it was simply the mystery of him. His claim of not knowing himself. Someone with a blank slate, no awareness of his past, unsure of his future. What happened to people with amnesia? If his memory didn't come back . . .

He was looking at her again. "What is it?" she asked finally.

He blew out his breath before he answered. "This is going to sound strange. Are you sure you want to hear it?"

"How strange?" she asked cautiously.

"I don't think I'm Derek Rocklin. I think my name's David."

He described at length an attempt to verify his signature, but all the time he was speaking, she had one thought that wouldn't go away: If all this had happened early this morning, why hadn't he said something before now? The moment they were approaching a town with a doctor and civil authority, he was suddenly laying this on her? Someone named David wouldn't be dreaming about Rocklin's wife, surely. There was a picture of Gina in his wallet. She'd seen it. The wife who was "gone."

He was waiting for her opinion. She reached for a response. Something logical. "Someone should have reported you missing by now." She began to think aloud. "Wouldn't your name be on record with the local sheriff, or whatever they have here—police, maybe? And if Derek Rocklin *is* missing . . . then you'd know."

He nodded agreement. "Makes sense." A few moments later his eyes swung to her face again. "Would you check it out for me?"

"Me? Why not you?"

"I don't know. My gut says not to."

Because of the money. And the gun? Her mind closed up tight as a clam, and she was unsure how to respond.

He shot her a charming, pensive grin. "I'll understand if you don't want to. I wouldn't, if I were you."

"I'll think about it." She stared out her window, uneasy in her skin. In spite of his loss of memory, lots of things about him were enticing: Aside from his ability to kiss extremely well, albeit on decidedly odd occasions, and being good-looking well beyond the norm, he was smart, logical, sensible—all of which could work for or against him. He'd also walked into danger to make sure she was safe.

Or—because he needed her? Because without her, sooner or later he'd have to expose himself to legal authority?

"I'll think it over," she repeated. "But you're right, I'm not comfortable with it."

"Yeah, okay. I understand."

They rode on in silence, and he grew consistently more withdrawn over the next forty minutes. To counter the uncomfortable hush that had grown between them, she set herself the task of making sure they didn't miss the Oroville road. She'd spotted it and was about to give warning when he uttered an odd sound; his features were contorted and rigid. "What is it?"

"Nothing. Headache," he answered tersely. "You decide yet?"

"No." *Who had he wanted to call at Willie's?* The question struck with the clarity of ice water. And why hadn't she picked up on it until now? "I mean, I haven't decided," she revised. She gestured toward the side road coming up. "This should be the turnoff." He slowed for the turn, and she knew then that she was going to bail out on him. She'd been letting her attraction to him overrule common sense. As soon as they got someplace where she could drop him off, she was through—good looks, risking his neck, the whole nine yards notwithstanding. The gun, the money, too many names, too much mystery—topped by his "gut feeling" to avoid the police—outweighed it all. Even the headache.

"I think I'd better see Dr. Meadows, make sure

nothing's fractured. Then if you could drop me at a hotel or something . . ."

Her concern for him increased, but she couldn't meet his eyes. "Sure." But that would be it. End of the line, everybody out of the pool.

At a snowcapped kiosk in a deserted filling station, *Jim Meadows, M.D.* was listed in the directory. The Oroville telephone service was intact. A quarter invested in the pay phone, plus the use of Willie's name, established that Dr. Meadows was in his office and would see them immediately. They followed simple directions to a number on Maple Street, a large private home with a traditional picket fence.

David helped Julie out of the car. She'd busied herself with Elmore, opened a can of cat food to leave with the tabby while they went inside, but hadn't looked him square in the face since he'd called himself David. She was ready to bolt. He'd pushed her over the line with the name thing. Not that he blamed her. He didn't have a hell of a lot to recommend him at the moment. Not even to himself.

The headache was killing him. Something inside his skull was trying to get out. Plus he was getting visions pretty steadily now, none of them good. The voice of his nightmare had come at him again during the last part of the drive, and he'd been some plenty spooked for the past twenty minutes. It wasn't so much the accusation of murder as the depth of hatred that had permeated the man's voice. Increasingly vivid flashes of holding a bloodied woman were rippling out of his subconscious, beyond his control, and he didn't want to know why. Maybe the doctor could give him some insight as to what to expect where his memory was concerned, because he had the feeling the nightmare was real and about to wind up in his lap whether he wanted it to or not.

They walked abreast up the walk, past a small hand-painted sign in the front yard. In the falling snow, Julie's breath was a frozen cloud that drifted into his path. He was running out of time. Maybe it was best to offer to cut her loose. Give her a sense of control. He'd have to do something, or lose her. "You can leave me here if you'd rather," he said. "I can check with the police later."

She nodded pensively and looked elsewhere. Blots of snow were clinging to her hair, whitest white against muted nutmeg, and settling lightly onto her brows; now and then a stray flake, its crystal geometry visible for an instant, landed on her lashes or melted against her lips. He swept a dusting of lace from her shoulder, fighting the sense of loss that was growing in his chest. "You could be on your way."

"If there's a taxi service, I will. Otherwise . . ." She helped him brush the snow from the sleeves of her jacket. "If he says you're okay, I'll drop you somewhere. Your stuff's already in my car."

As they stepped in the door he took two hundred-dollar bills out of his pocket. "I want you to have this. I've put a big hole in your life. I'd make it more, but I wouldn't figure you'd take it."

She looked as if he'd slapped her. "I don't want that."

"I know it's just money," he said carefully, "but I'll feel better if you have it." She was silent. "Please. Put it down as a chauffeur's fee." He tried to smile at her and failed. "I don't consider it payment for saving my life. It's just saying thanks. Buy yourself something to remember me by."

The doctor's wife interrupted them to introduce herself. "If you'll just come this way, Mr. Rocklin?"

Julie hadn't moved. "Car rental, then." He tucked the money into her jacket pocket before following Mrs. Meadows inside. There had to be a way to stop her.

As Derek, or David, or whatever he wanted to call himself today, disappeared into an examining room, Julie sat in the waiting area berating herself for accepting the money. As soon as they were alone he was getting it back! Why in the world was she sticking around, anyway? He'd given her an out. Practically said goodbye on the walkway. Unless she left immediately, getting into some kind of trouble with this man was inevitable.

Mrs. Meadows's smiling face tilted out of the examining room doorway. "We're going to take a few X rays, Mrs. Rocklin. Would you like coffee?"

Julie flushed briefly at her newly acquired status in life, then shook her head. "No, thanks. I'm fine." She made a quick decision. "But I would like to place a local call."

"Use line three, please. Phone book's in the top drawer." The smiling face disappeared.

Julie settled herself at the desk, located the directory, and called the number listed for the Oroville sheriff's office. A young male voice answered through an intermittent crackle of interference. "Deputy Wilson."

She forced a composed voice. "Deputy, I'm concerned about . . . I've just driven in from Nighthawk, and the phones are down there. Can you tell me if anyone's been reported missing in that area?"

"Several people, ma'am. Nobody local, but we got a whole busload of hikers down there somewhere. Missing since Friday. Is he one of them?"

"I don't know. Maybe."

"What's the name?"

She fought the impulse to hang up. "Derek Roc—"

"No, ma'am, your name."

Rattled, she told him.

"And the name of the person you're reportin'?"

"I'm not reporting him, I'm looking for him. His name is Derek Rocklin."

"I can tell you right now, we ain't got a Derek nobody." There was a pause, and static filled her ear. "How you spelling that?"

"What about David? Do you have a David, about thirty-two?"

"We got two Davids. Last name?"

She hesitated. "What names do you have?"

There was a second pause and a slight change of emphasis. "How long's he been missin', ma'am?"

"About four days. Five maybe."

"And his relationship to you?"

"Friend," she lied quickly.

"And you don't know his last name?"

She'd trapped herself. To her left the door to the examining room opened, and Dr. Meadows's voice drifted into earshot. "I'd have to do an MRI to make sure," he was saying. "Unfortunately, we don't have the equipment here. And like I said, the headaches might get a great deal worse before they get better, so expect that. Where can I reach you?"

"Ma'am?" The deputy's voice emanated from the phone as Rocklin and the doctor stepped into the waiting room. "Hello? Miss Ryan?"

Rocklin's eyes were searching her face with speculation. "We're traveling," he said. "Is there somewhere to stay nearby?"

"Not this time of year. We're a resort town, summer mostly. Fishing. The Renicks usually have a room available, but they're visiting back east."

"Can you give me a description, Miss Ryan?" Julie hung up on the deputy and got to her feet.

"Best bet's to go on to Omak or Brewster." The doctor's genial manner was paternal and concerned. "They generally keep Route 97 clear. My boy works the snowplow. He's just finishing up lunch. Heading out in a few minutes, if you want to follow him. Sure sorry about the delay on these films, but they've been telling me for a week that they'll have that thing fixed. I'll get these right over to Ed's office, and you be sure to call me this evening about the results."

Mrs. Meadows came into the room smiling. "That'll be sixty-two dollars, including X rays. Did you make your call, Mrs. Rocklin?"

Julie nodded weakly under Rocklin's gaze. "I was looking for a motel."

"Nearest motel's in Omak, but I'd go on to Brewster. There's only a couple, three in Omak, and they're bound to be full by the time you get there." Mrs. Meadows made change for a hundred-dollar bill, and Julie readied herself for the drive down

Route 97 behind a snowplow. With a man who hadn't as yet been reported missing.

If the man was Derek Rocklin.

Hathaway replaced the car phone in its cradle and returned his concentration to the snow-covered road. "Wheelbase and tires indicate a recent-model Bronco, according to stats."

Deke nodded, then pulled his newly purchased ski cap down over his ears and straightened his glasses. "Probably a rental. Doubt if they'd steal one." He yanked off a glove to fiddle with the heater knobs. "Christ, it's cold. How far's this town . . . what is it . . . Lake Stillwater?"

"Another couple of miles. They got a gas station, that's about it." The phone rang again, and Ron picked it up. "Hathaway."

"Sheriff Magidsy over here in Oroville, Mr. Hathaway. We had an inquiry about an hour ago that I thought you might be interested in."

"Go ahead."

"A woman named Julie Ryan called about a missing person. Deputy thinks she might have said Rocklin and he misunderstood. Anyway, she said she'd driven up from Nighthawk and also asked about anyone missing named David, age thirty-two or thereabouts. It was close enough to your guy that I thought maybe you ought to know about it. Wilson tried to keep her on the line, but she hung up before he could get more information."

Ron relayed the news to Deke. "You get anything else?"

"Sounded youngish, maybe mid-twenties, not

real sure of herself." After a short pause to confer with Deputy Wilson, the sheriff came back on the line. "He said there was another voice in the background. He couldn't make anything out, but he's certain it was a man talking. The line was real bad. Sorry."

"Thank you, Sheriff. We'll stay in touch." Encouraged, Ron hung up the phone and repeated the details. "Sounds like they're still in the area."

Deke was reticent. "She is, anyway. And wondering if we're looking for him yet."

"'Julie' matches the name in the note from the neighbor. S'pose Ryan's her real name?"

"Not likely, but check it out."

Hathaway coasted the Range Rover through three sparsely built blocks of empty and boarded-up buildings. "I guess this is Stillwater. Wonder where they hid the lake." He spotted the gasoline pumps, pulled next to one of them, and blew the horn. After several minutes' wait and a second blast on the horn, an old woman in a black Stetson came out of the storefront, well bundled up against the cold. Two monstrous hounds were visible behind her in the doorway before she closed the door. He quickly got out to meet her at the island, glad she'd kept the dogs inside.

She looked at him with appraisal. "You lost, too?"

"Why, was someone lost earlier?"

"This time of year, it's pretty common."

"We're trying to find someone lost, actually." He found David's picture and showed it to her. "Have you seen this man?"

She looked at him blandly. "Don't see too well without my glasses. Who might you be?"

"I'm a private investigator." He dug his wallet out of his breast pocket and flipped it open to the identification card.

She studied the license, then glanced at Deke, all but invisible behind the darkly tinted windows of the Range Rover. "He a private investigator, too?"

Ron nodded. "He's working the case with me."

"You want gas?"

"No, ma'am, we just need the information." He tapped the picture. "This man is traveling with a woman with long reddish brown hair who calls herself Julie Ryan." He saw a small reaction in her face at the mention of the woman. "We think they're driving a Bronco. Have they been through here, by any chance?"

"What'd he do?"

"It's sort of a family matter. We just want to talk to them, make sure she's safe, that kind of thing. Were they here?"

"A couple in a Bronco bought gas. Can't say he was one of 'em. Coulda been."

Hathaway felt a rush. "Credit card or cash?"

"Cash, as I recall."

He took a stab in the dark. "Hundred-dollar bill?"

"Could be. You want to take it?"

"That won't be necessary. Can you tell me how long ago they were here and which direction they went?"

"Don't you want to see it? Take the number off it?"

"No, ma'am, we're not after the money. Just the man. You think this might have been him?"

Deke's window edged down an inch so he could

listen to their conversation; the top of his ski cap was all that was visible. She shook her head at the picture and shrugged. "Like I say, coulda been. They's here first thing this morning, and as I recall, they was lost."

Deke spoke out the window without turning around. "What did the woman look like? Can you tell us her age, anything about her?"

"Can't say as I noticed. She stayed in the car, as I recall. Sort of like yourself."

Deke rolled up the window, and Ron stepped in quickly to smooth her feathers. "Thank you, ma'am, you've been a great help. Oh, by the way, what color Bronco?"

"Seems it was black, or brown, maybe. Didn't really notice. Must have headed out the way they come in. This is sort of a dead end, you see. If you don't want gas, I think I'll get in where it's warm. Have a safe trip, y'hear?"

The warmth from the heater was intense, and Julie stared sleepily out the window at the plume of snow pounding into a thick mound on her side of the highway. Ahead of them, the blinking lights on the snowplow cast gold and white flashes onto everything it passed as it slogged along, steadily eating snow by the ton and arcing it aside. She fingered the money in her pocket and decided that returning it could wait until they'd reached a destination of some sort. No point starting a hassle in close quarters.

She had expected Rocklin to ask her about the phone call, but there'd been stillness between them since leaving Oroville. Elmore had long since found a place to bunk on one of the sleeping bags in the back. An hour ago she'd fished out one of Willie's sandwiches and eaten it as a late lunch. He hadn't been hungry.

"I called the sheriff," she said finally. His eyes instantly met her own. "They don't have Derek Rocklin listed as missing, but there were two men named David. I couldn't find out the last names." She shifted uncomfortably under his scrutiny and arched her back to ease the tension across her shoulders. "He said they were with a group of hikers, apparently on a bus trip. Doesn't sound like you."

He turned his attention back toward the highway. "If Derek Rocklin's on the level, someone knows he's out here. If he came up here camping five days ago, someone knows that, too. If he's married, his wife or *someone* should have reported him missing by now . . . unless no one wants him found."

Her thoughts exactly. "Or she doesn't know he's in trouble."

"Anyone carrying half a million in cash *is* trouble," he said darkly. "Doesn't look good, does it?"

She shook her head in agreement. "No."

"May as well face it." He glanced at her again. "As soon as we get somewhere I can start out on my own, we'd better separate."

"I think so, too." A trickle of relief eased between her shoulder blades, only to be replaced by an apprehensive hollow feeling. Looking out for her best interests didn't fall in line with someone who was using her. Still, she'd determined that the man identified in the wallet wasn't missing. Maybe it was the information he needed.

She studied the blinking lights as the plow forged through snow that had drifted across the road, her stomach not quite buying the argument. "If you're not Rocklin, then you're carrying phony identification." In which case there were the missing Davids to consider.

"I've thought of that." His handsome face was sober.

Maybe the wedding ring was false as well. She refused to give credence to what would be a highly convenient solution to her attraction to him. "Or no one's looking for you yet," she added. A much more likely possibility.

"I'm not Derek Rocklin," he said strongly. "I know it! That's the weird part. I *know* it. It's like there's this voice sitting at the edge of my brain, waiting to tell me things, but it's stuck there. Out of reach." He rubbed his forehead. "Would you give me a couple of those painkillers?"

One of his eyes had begun to tear. She opened the bottle of aspirin with codeine, shook two white pills into her hand, then held the wheel in place while he swallowed the medication and washed it down with bottled water. "What did the doctor say?"

"Traumatic short-term memory loss. It disappears as soon as the brain swelling goes down in the area that operates the machinery. Could be anywhere from two hours to a week, maybe longer. In the meantime, headaches."

She unwrapped a sandwich and handed it to him. "Better eat this."

He took a bite, his face reflecting the pain in his head. After a moment he handed it back to her.

"Can't. Hurts to chew." His eye was watering profusely.

"You've taken codeine. I think I'd better drive." When he didn't argue and coasted the car to a stop, she realized he must be in pretty bad shape. "Pull yourself over here," she ordered. "I'll come around." By the time she'd climbed into the driver's seat, nervous occupants of the automobiles behind them were tapping their horns impatiently. She set the car in motion as quickly as possible. He dropped the seat back and made use of the headrest, eyes closed, tearstains on his cheeks; his breath was coming in tight gasps.

"Hurts, huh?" Worried, she saw that the lines in his jaw were white and pinched as knuckles. "Keep your eyes closed. The codeine should kick in any minute."

"Yeah, thanks." Gradually his breathing eased. "I really appreciate your hanging in with me, Julie. Not exactly a fun trip for you."

"Try to get some rest." She glanced at the Bronco's clock. It was nearly three, and they'd traveled only nine miles past Omak. It would be full dark by the time they got to Brewster. The severity of his headache was worrisome. Maybe the jarring ride on the fire road had knocked something loose. All sorts of things could be going wrong, and he was in no condition to fend for himself; unless he improved rapidly, she'd have to find a place for him to stay, make sure he called the doctor. Which meant she'd be spending another night with him after all—but in separate rooms this time. She'd see to that.

He was sleeping soundly when they arrived in

Brewster sometime after seven in the evening, and she decided not wake him until she had to. Motel after motel displayed NO VACANCY signs along the main drag, and she began to get worried. The line of cars behind them disappeared as vehicles pulled into this travel lodge or that motel, and she realized that without reservations it would be hard going to find somewhere to stay. They'd both been up before dawn, and with or without poor night vision, she was too tired to continue driving safely. The snow-plow stopped at a light, and she leaped out of the Bronco to speak with Will Meadows; climbing onto the running board, she tapped at his window. "We don't have a room," she called out. "Is there some-place that you know about?"

The young man cranked his window down about three inches, then looked out at the falling snow. "You can have my room, I guess. Doesn't look like I'll be using it." He gave her the address. "It's a hotel, but it ain't much. Tell the night clerk I told you to take it. He might want a few extra dollars, since the county only pays for one person."

"Whatever he wants," she assured him. "And thank you!"

Five minutes later she wheeled the Bronco into the Triple Tree Hotel parking lot. When she asked the clerk for Will Meadows's room, he cut her off with a smile. "Hell, miss, I gave up that key an hour ago. Figured Will'd be riding that plow all night. Sorry, everything else's spoke for."

She opened her fist to reveal a crumpled hundred-dollar bill and slowly straightened the bill to its full length before smoothing it on the counter between them. "Are you sure you don't have anything else?"

The clerk eyed the money. "Well, we do have the honeymoon suite, but like I say, it's spoke for. However . . ." He squinted out the window at the snowstorm. "It's sort of a standing reservation. Maybe I could make a call. Could be the wedding party'll decide not to show up . . . with the snow and all. But it'll be a hundred dollars tonight."

Julie got the drift. Someone local held the room for private use. She took the second hundred out of her pocket on the chance that there was more than one tryst that could be deferred. "You sure you don't have *two* honeymoon suites?"

He laughed and shook his head with genuine regret. "I'd let you have 'em if I did, sure enough, but one's all I got."

Julie pocketed the second bill and pushed the first one under the glass partition. "Including my cat."

The clerk's face wrinkled with displeasure. "Housebroke?"

"For a hundred dollars, he is."

This time he didn't blink. "Cat included."

15

David surveyed the hotel room. He'd have paid more for a whole lot less. And there were two double beds—so much for the "honeymoon" suite. The ache in his brain had revived to a dull galloping cadence after Julie'd awakened him to explain where they were. It was evident that she wasn't happy they were sharing a room, but he was too distracted by the turbulence in his skull to care all that much. The headache had gained on him as they came up in the elevator and was currently culminating in a roar.

He saw her relax at the sight of the second bed, and Elmore was disappearing into the bathroom, so things weren't a total loss. He tottered toward the nearest mattress, dropping his heavy backpack next to the headboard.

"Are you okay?"

"Depends on your definition," he answered through a thickening haze. "Probably overdid things a bit."

She'd located the bottle of aspirin and was reading the manufacturer's directions. "Let's see when you can take another one of these."

He eased onto the bedspread, his eyes beginning to tear again. Her face dissolved into a blur. "The doctor said 'as needed.' I qualify this as need."

She opened the bottle. "How about food first? Your blood sugar's probably dropped off the chart by now."

Smart girl, and probably right, but food he didn't care about. His head was about to implode. "We have room service?"

"No, but I saw a pizza place a block over. I'll have one delivered."

She brought him a glass of water from the bathroom, and he swallowed two more pills. "Wake me when it gets here." The pain had begun to subside when he heard her order the pizza and request change for a hundred-dollar bill. Moments later a blanket came drifting lightly down around his body. "No onions," he murmured, and eased gratefully into the warmth and sleep.

Sometime later, barely audible in the twilight portion of his brain, he woke to hear her in a low conversation. ". . . I know, that's why I called. . . . I'm fine. . . . Well, it took me a couple of days to get out, and the storm's so severe I think we should consider a change in plan. . . ." He drifted off again.

Julie listened to her sister's worried voice.

"I nearly went crazy. The motel in Nighthawk said you never checked in, and there's no listing for Mrs. Cumberland—"

"I know."

"And Aunt Marge read me the headlines about bridges being out, landslides . . ." Joann paused for breath. "You can't imagine what I thought!"

Aunt Marge was sixty-one and tended to worry. "Make sure she knows I'm okay." Julie decided to omit immediate mention of David-Derek Rocklin-whoever and his backpack stuffed with money; Joann had been worried enough without adding flash floods and a gun-toting stranger into the mix, so she glossed over her recent adventures. "I found the treasure tin," she said, to lighten their conversation. "Its tree had gone over in the storm, and remember Grandmother's old pop-it pearls? Right out in the open. All I had to do was put them in my backpack. And Gerd said I'd never find them. Tell your husband it was a piece of cake."

"You tell him, I don't . . . oh, damn." Without warning, Joann fell apart on her, sobbing with emotion. This was totally unlike her unflappable sister. At first Julie thought it was nerves, but what Joann said next really shocked her. "He has a . . . a . . . mistress."

"A what?" She waited through a wave of her sister's anguish, hoping she'd misunderstood.

"He's denying it, of course, but I know it's true."

Gerd the Nerd had a mistress? "How do you know?"

"She had the nerve to call here. Her name is Ilse and she says they've been together for five years! He keeps her in a . . . I don't know what they call it here, but it's a fancy apartment, nicer than this one. She called because *her* rent isn't being paid, either. I have the name of her landlord, and it's true."

Julie's heart squeezed up with pain for her sister. She'd never liked her brother-in-law, and it had been hard work supporting Joann's decision to marry him. Unfortunately, her instincts about him had been right.

"I'm getting out. That's why I wanted to sell Grampa's land. I'll need the money. Gerd has nothing and he owes everyone. People keep calling here—the bank, the phone company, businesses I've never heard of, and they all want money—including *her* landlord, the creep!" Joann paused to compose herself. "We've spent all my savings, and he's told me a hundred times that it's all being straightened out, but I don't believe him anymore. It's been going on for months. He keeps getting money somehow, but no one gets paid. Nothing he says ever happens. It's all lies." Anger crept into Joann's voice. "Then *she* showed up about the time you found out about Ned and, uh . . ."

"Helena."

"Yes, and I couldn't tell you then, but it's been horrible. I've decided to get a divorce."

Julie was speechless. She'd been so upset three weeks ago that she wouldn't have noticed a typhoon. And for her stubborn, proud sister to give up on her marriage, things had to be pretty bad. "Where is he now?"

"I don't know. I locked him out, but he calls. To make sure I'm still here, I guess, but he won't tell me where he is." Sobs came through the line once again, breaking Julie's heart. "I know he's with her because I hear her sometimes in the background. He's such a liar, I don't even care. It's just that I can't believe he's done this," she wailed.

"Come home. I can be there tomorrow and we'll—"

"No. When he finds out I've left, he could show up at your place looking for me. Aunt Marge sent me a ticket to Chicago. I'll stay with her until I figure out what to do." Her sister's voice strengthened. "I have a lawyer. He says to cut my losses, notify credit card holders that I'm no longer on the accounts. I'll pack up things here that I'll need—do all the stuff I can think about now that I know you're safe. I'll fly out sometime tomorrow night. Selling the land will have to wait."

"What can I do?"

"If Gerd calls, don't tell him where to find me."

"You know I won't." A sharp rap on the hotel door made her jump. "Listen, I think my pizza's here." It had been over an hour since she'd ordered the thing, and she'd all but given up. "Hold on."

"No, I'll let you go. And I'll call when I get to Chicago. Love you."

"Love you, too. Take care."

The rap sounded again, louder, rousing Rocklin; Julie hustled to the door. Ears still red from cold, the delivery boy stood in the hallway, snow melting off his parka. With soft drinks, the pizza was nine dollars even, and he'd brought change for the hundred; she tipped him five dollars, and the boy's face lit up with pleasure. "Anything else you want, you just call!" Closing the door behind him, she envied his exuberance. Being young was easy. An unexpected, generous tip could make your whole day. As you got older, however, it wasn't about money. It was about trust and . . . integrity. Who you were; what you stood for. She thought of her sister. And the man across the room. Telling the truth to people you were married to.

Money didn't solve things. It paid for things and eased burdens, but it wouldn't have made Ned love her, even if he hadn't married Helena. Rocklin's backpack was bulging with cash. She could have taken off with it a dozen times, but it had never occurred to her. Besides, she was smart enough to know that any amount of cash of questionable origin was more trouble than it was worth. Across the room, he was watching her, eyes still drowsy with sleep. If a situation had the potential of being more trouble than she could deal with, sharing a hotel room with this man definitely fit the bill; on the other hand, there was a strong possibility that he could lift her spirits in the process.

She mentally slapped herself. Any more thoughts like those, and trouble would land on her like a ton of bricks. "Dinner," she greeted him, and hefted the still-warm box from Napoli's.

Between the food and the aspirin, David was feeling better by the minute. No dreams had marred his sleep, and no residual headache thumped in his temples; his emotions soared. Life was good! He was sharing hot, stringy-cheesed pizza with the lovely Julie Ryan, four feet away on the opposite bed, one foot tucked up and Elmore draped in her lap. A tiny smudge of tomato sauce was perched at the corner of her mouth like a beauty mark. He wanted to lick it off her face.

Safe in her lap, the cat gazed at him with gold,

implacable eyes and smug feline ownership. A ballsy she's-mine-and-not-yours sort of attitude, the arrogant little twerp. His good feelings veered sharply left. Until he knew for sure who he was, he reminded himself, she might as well be wearing an OFF-LIMITS sign around her neck.

Unable to stand it any longer, he reached for the phone and dialed the operator. "Area code for Santa Barbara, California," he said quietly, and took the wallet out of his jacket. Clearing the connection, he dialed 805 information. "Listing for Derek or Gina Rocklin, please." He spelled the names and specified the address from the driver's license, then handed the receiver to Julie. It was important that she hear the information firsthand. Ruffled at being disturbed by the phone cord, Elmore jumped to the floor.

She listened briefly, shook her head at him, then leaned forward to replace the receiver. "Maybe he's unlisted."

Suddenly he was unreasonable. "And maybe he doesn't exist." Trapped somewhere between the relief of *I knew it* and the frustration of being locked into square one, he lurched to his feet. "Maybe none of them exists!" he exploded. Julie and the cat were both watching him with wary expressions. "Are you sure *you're* real?" He looked helplessly at the bedside clock: half past eight. The silence in the room began to pound at him worse than any headache. Confused by his own behavior, he tried to calm his agitation. "Think we can find some news?"

"Probably not until nine." She tapped a small stack of local papers at the foot of her bed. "Bought these in the lobby." Still cautious, she handed him the top one. "I called Dr. Meadows while I was downstairs. You seemed to be sleeping an awful lot, and I didn't know if it was too much, or good for you, so . . ."

She looked at the floor without waiting for his reaction. His annoyance was pushed aside by a huge surge of pleasure; if she'd cared enough to make sure he was okay, maybe she'd care enough to stay with him. The rage passed as quickly as it had arrived.

"He said the X rays confirmed there's no skull fracture," she finished.

"Thanks." He was genuinely grateful. "And I'm sorry about blowing up at you. This is hard enough on you. . . ."

She moved past him to the corner of the room and began tearing ribbons of newsprint onto a layer of papers on the floor. "I told him your headaches had gotten pretty bad," she continued. "He said it's not unusual, but not to let you take too much medication. See another physician if it doesn't get better within the week."

"Right." He crossed to the television cabinet and found the remote, thickly conscious of her presence and the smallness of the "honeymoon" suite. God, she was beautiful. What was going on with him? Why was he down her throat all of a sudden?

She finished Elmore's potty corner and, studiously avoiding direct eye contact, began rummaging through her backpack. "He warned me about the mood swings. He also said you shouldn't be left alone for the next few days." He could tell she was uncomfortable. "It'll take me that long to drive to Los Angeles anyway, so if you want to come with me . . ."

She wasn't leaving him! Emotion leaped and twisted in his chest, and he took care to keep triumph out of his voice. "I'd appreciate it." Relief began to thunder through his brain. The thought of being alone had been weighing on him more strongly than he'd realized. "Thanks," he repeated, more than grateful this time; he was excited. He studied her graceful movements and envied the cat, who was rubbing its fur against her hip. "I'll follow up on the address in Santa Barbara. Got to start somewhere, I guess."

She seemed embarrassed at his effort to thank her, and busied herself sorting through her backpack for clothing. "I guess," she echoed, and he watched her gather personal items and a small hair dryer. "You can start with letting me tie up the bathroom for a while," she said over her shoulder. "It's been a long day and I'm really grungy."

"No problem." He felt grungy, too, and his stomach executed a pleasant flutter kick; the last time he'd had a shower, she'd washed him. The precise timing in the past couple of days was murky, but the memory was certainly vivid. And life? Life was suddenly very good again. Very good indeed! "Take all the time you want," he said exuberantly. "I'll even scrub your back."

The offer took on weight in the silence that followed; she looked up and he froze, unsure of her reaction. When she didn't blink, an unexpected tension built in the room. He felt it brewing in the air between them. "With my eyes closed," he added, with no truth in his voice.

"That's no fun." She blushed and immediately

looked away, clearly nonplussed. "That's not what I meant." Her explanation was fumbled. "I meant, if you're—*were* going to do it . . . I don't know what I meant. I'm tired."

Her embarrassed disclaimer heightened the sense of what might be possible, which flushed through his system in a wave. "Eyes open would be *my* first choice," he said carefully, "but either way, I'm at your service." The vibes danced between them to a higher level, supercharged with a volatile energy that refused to disappear.

He didn't want it to disappear. He wanted Julie Ryan, and he wanted whatever was going on to escalate.

Silent, scarlet, Julie scuttled into the bathroom with clothing and toiletry items in hand. *Idiot!* Blood continued its rush through her body, unnerving her further. What on earth would he think? She'd started it. She'd responded with a come-on to an obviously mundane offer to scrub her back. The comment had flown from her attraction to him, loosed from her subconscious before she could censor it. *I sounded like a love-struck schoolgirl. Practically invited him to shower with me! What'll I do if he comes in the door?* She pushed the lock quietly into place and prayed he wouldn't act on her foolish words.

Then she unlocked the door. And wished more than anything in the world that he would.

David spent the next few minutes with the cat and his conscience, pretending to read the local paper. Nothing on the pages made sense, except that the lady was attracted to him and the feeling was grand. It wasn't a lonely, one-way street after all. Otherwise she'd have shrugged off his flippant remark as an idle comment—or ignored him and not said anything. He was certain of it. If he'd needed an additional reason to establish his identity, her interest in him was sure as hell it.

He knew better than to try to join her. Too much, too fast, and too many obstacles in the way. He opened his wallet to Gina's picture, then shut his eyes against a new assault of brutal images. Gina Rocklin was the young girl in his memory; that he'd held her bleeding in his arms was a certainty—and suddenly he knew she was dead.

His heart fist-hammered the walls of his chest. Did that make him Derek Rocklin after all?

Dr. Meadows had said that he'd seen cases where portions of past memory got permanently mixed up with the present, and not to rely on anything at first. Shaken, he closed the wallet and tried to force details from the blackness in his mind. Surely to God he hadn't killed this girl. People who killed people had dead places inside, or guilt, or an emotion of some kind that made them *feel* like a killer. The problem was, he didn't feel one way or the other about himself. He just was. Did Gina's death—or the money he was carrying—have anything to do with his instinct to avoid the police?

Being around him might not be safe for Julie. The thought was uncomfortable. He needed her with him, and aside from that need, she was the only person in his life he had feelings for! They were . . . protective. And grateful. She couldn't be safer with

him! He was sure of it. Of course, sex was another
matter. Sexually, he wanted her, no holds barred.

Okay, so his feelings were a hell of a lot stronger
than protective, and the fact that she was attracted to
him was exciting as hell. Permeating the sound of
the shower was the idea of her naked under a slow
stream of water; the image began to work on him,
wiping away his fear. In his mind's eye she was soaping perfect breasts; fingers of foam were slipping
down her stomach and into a patch of hair he'd bet
money was dark copper and as curly as anything
nature provided. Her body was slippery-shiny but
not so soaped that anything important was covered.
Her feet, maybe. A little dab between her . . .

He stopped, angered at himself. She'd offered to
stay and help him when she could have been gone by
now—had saved his life, for Christ's sake—and here
he was, hard as a rock and leering at her inside his
head like a pervert, having no right whatever to take
off her clothing and invade her privacy. Was that the
kind of person he was—would be—when he regained
knowledge of himself? A bozo who wanted to invade
a whole lot more than her shower? Someone dangerous?

Determined to find distraction, he punched the
remote and surfed through TV channels until he
found a station devoted to local news. Their lead story
was the snowstorm, with a recap of recent footage
from the Northwest: various mud slides, snowfall
estimates—and the rescue of a group of stranded hikers. He punched up the sound. ". . . missing for four
days in mountainous terrain near Nighthawk, and
although well supplied with tents and rations, they

couldn't manage to sustain a signal fire large enough to defeat the downpour. Tonight they are all present and accounted for."

No missing Davids. Maybe he *was* Derek Rocklin! Disconcerted, he changed channels until he found an old movie. Cher as a sexy biker chick with Sam Elliot on her mind; motorcycles swept across the screen against a backdrop of roaring engines. Something about their motors resonated inside his head—just out of reach, like everything else. He broke into a sweat, suddenly uncomfortable, disturbed by something he couldn't define.

He strained to interest himself in the film, refusing to think of Julie in the next room under a stream of warm water. On-screen, Cher was kissing Elliot's rival, messing with his head. He changed the channel back to the news. No use. The sounds from the bathroom were deafening, and he was rigid.

Julie stood, her chin lowered to her chest, letting hot water shatter against the back of her head and neck, funnel down her back. She'd shampooed her hair, soaped herself clean, shaved her underarms and legs, and was currently wasting water rerinsing her body. She couldn't stay in here forever, and she couldn't go back into that room with him until she got her act together.

Something had broken loose and was out of control. Something primal. Headstrong and uncooperative. Not like her at all. Something directly related to the beautiful man in the next room, who was interested in her as well. She turned toward the spray and hot water beat into her face, muddling her thinking.

He was entitled to shower, too, and was no doubt waiting for his turn. This time he'd have to wash that gorgeous body all by himself. He'd never said anything about her giving him a bath. Probably didn't remember. Except she knew somehow that he did. He remembered everything that had happened between them since they'd met, she was sure of it. And he knew that he'd kissed her, that she'd let him, and that she'd enjoyed it. He knew that she'd let him sleep naked in her bed. There'd been nothing private from him for the past three days.

Somehow she would have to pull herself together, put things back in order, and get through this evening. She'd offered to drive him to California. In the glass shower cubicle, which was steamed over and felt as though it were shrinking in on her, the trip loomed to an overwhelming size, large as forever. Two more days in close company could have disastrous results. Her feelings about him were already bordering on being out of control. How would she deal with meeting his wife? If he *had* a wife. If he *was* Derek Rocklin. The bottom line: No matter who he was, he was a total stranger—less the past three days.

She abruptly turned off the hot water and caught her breath, unbraced for the shock of cold that streamed onto her body. She forced herself to endure the chill. Her commitment to stay with him would have to be altered. It was as simple as that. She'd tell him she'd changed her mind. Regrouped, invigorated, she turned off the shower and stepped out of the stall. She'd made the decision to stay with him, and she could damn well unmake it. Tonight she'd get some sleep, tomorrow she'd see how she felt, and if she and Elmore decided to move on alone, that's the way it would happen! Besides, he had plenty of money. It wasn't as if he couldn't rent his own car or take a taxi to the nearest airport.

She scrubbed gooseflesh with the hotel towel, rubbing energy into her body. D.B. Rocklin was on his own! As quickly as she could, she dried her hair, dressed, and threw open the bathroom door. He was lying on his bed, Elmore curled at his side. "All yours," she announced snappily.

"Promise?"

The single word, softly spoken, cut a path through her defenses, and one look at his body revealed his obvious intent to pursue the point. "I meant the shower," she added hastily.

Grinning, eyes on her face, he carefully raised himself off the bed and walked in her direction. "I know what you meant."

Rationale, resolve, certitude, decisions . . . everything melted. Damn the man!

16

Julie stared at the ceiling, stiffly awake, feeling as if she hadn't taken a breath since their charged exchange. She'd instantly announced her intention to make it an early evening; he'd said a polite good night before continuing his way into the bathroom.

With one ear tuned to the sound of running water, she had undressed and slipped into her Dodger nightshirt, gotten into bed with the remote, and buried herself under the covers; she'd flipped through television channels for nearly five minutes before finally turning the thing off, unsure what Rocklin would do. Or what she wanted him to do. *All yours.* What a ninny! As the thoughtless quip repeated itself again and again, her mind attempted to alter the content. *The bath's all yours. . . . The room's free now. . . . I'm finished, it's your turn. . . .* She rewrote the meaning, and his rejoinder, into a hundred variations that dismissed the innuendo he'd read into two innocent words.

That maybe she'd placed there for him *to* hear.

The fullness in her body was unmistakable; she was tight with the eternal pressure that lovemaking could ease. After her engagement to Ned last spring, and until three months ago, she'd had a bed partner on a fairly regular basis, so there was no mistaking her mood. But this time her feelings were for the unknown man in the shower. It was illogical and ridiculous. Her mind was aware of these things, but her body had *no* such knowledge and was primed to engage in sex. With him.

When he turned off the shower, she pretended sleep, then nervously watched through lowered lashes as he emerged from the bath, clean-shaven, wearing a T-shirt and underwear. She saw him glance briefly in her direction as he crossed the room, but he climbed into his bed without a word. Elmore, the traitor, joined him. Disappointed that he hadn't at least said something, she felt even more ridiculous keeping up the charade of being asleep. *All yours, indeed.* Wasn't he even going to try to make love to her? So at least she could say no? Restless and miserable, she turned onto her side and faced the wall.

David heard her roll over and wished to hell he could act on the words that were haunting him. When she'd emerged from her bath, dark hair flyaway, shining clean, backlit . . . he hadn't been quite prepared. He'd considered her attractive from the moment they'd met, but now she was . . . *All yours. Honey, you don't know the half of it.* In spite of the hottest water he could tolerate, followed by the proverbial cold shower, his body was charged with the raw, abrasive drive that it took a woman to erase.

He wanted her, with the same blind need that he'd wanted his freedom.

Listening to her breathing, soft in the quiet room, he tried to relax. It would have to be enough that she was still with him. He moved onto his side, displacing Elmore, and tried to sleep. Giant gravestones rose up in his mind, gray and cold in orderly rows along a small hillside. People he knew but could not name walked by him, some extending their hands, giving him flowers. Others ignored him totally.

MORGANER. DAUGHTER OF EARL AND . . . The second name scored into the pale gray marble was indistinct. Then he saw GINA, and the blood that was running from her name sank into dry, crumbling earth, wetting it, soaking it into a thick, viscous mud that coated his hands and shirt. Voices shrieked at him, a chorus of young and old, mourners and priest. Above them all was the old man's, screaming at him with a shrill and hellish venom. "Get out, you murdering son of a bitch!"

I love her! His voice was nothing against them, a whisper. He couldn't make himself heard. Men were dragging him away and he tried to fight them. Helpless. *I have a right.* A woman was pushing at him, too, shouting into his face.

"No!" His voice rang through the room, shocking him awake with its intensity.

Julie was shaking him. "David?" Her voice at his elbow was frightened.

He pulled her into his arms, terrified, and crushed her to his chest, assuring himself that she was safe. And whole. And then he was kissing the slippery softness of her mouth, with the taste of her heating his senses, driving him onward; feeling the warm pressure of her breasts against him under the blue nightshirt, his hands crept inside, caressed her urgently, his need building to a new intensity. Blood throbbed through his veins in a wild rush to his scrotum, to the place between his legs that would make him hard for her.

Against all that was possible, she was kissing him back, her agreement evident, her body curving inward and pressed hard against him. His erection grew, frustratingly confined, superheated, the length of it exquisitely squeezed against ruby satin panties. She made no effort to stop him as he stripped away their clothing and moved her to the center of his bed. Ready to burst, kissing her, breathing into her, blindly sucking at the slickness of her tongue, he opened her knees, found the moist bud of her center already hard and waiting for him; with blood raging in his head, he tumbled into oblivion, unaware of anything except his hunger for her, keeping some part of himself focused just long enough to give her a climax before he lost control.

Julie realized she was lost, and did not care. Somewhere between hearing his cries and the time it had taken to shake him out of sleep, it had happened. He'd kissed her, was still kissing her, and something sweetly chemical was occurring between them—a mixture of controlled madness and a mindless, glowing pleasure, flushing her skin, swelling her body with sensations and needs that crossed out thought and logic and caution.

She was heedless of anything except the growing

pressure of his mouth as he deepened their kiss, of hands that had urgently caressed her breasts, fingers that had grasped and kneaded nipples already sensitive and distended, then confidently traced her torso past the curve of her waist and were at this moment deliberately driving her toward a climax she could no longer avoid. As her shuddering began, he unknowingly deprived of her of a fully realized orgasm by repositioning his body; only partially released, she was rigid as he carefully fit his length inside her, his testicles taut and smooth. As he began to thrust, she was twice as sensitive, and felt the return of her need, more desperate this time, and the sensation of her breasts swelling with blood.

She'd gone headlong into this reckless place with no thought of turning back. She'd fitted herself beneath his body, opened to his touch without reservation, reveling in his embrace. They were perfect together, and she was straining against him, sealing their union. Uncertainty was gone; misgivings no longer ruled her life. There was only this moment, this man, this pleasure.

What had started slowly, fervently, was now a rhythmic, voiceless violence heaving into her core, with mounting impacts as his heavy testicles slapped against her body; soon her flesh was swollen and tight around him, holding him inside, her sex violently sensitive. He ground himself into her, fiercely, with intense purpose, and a shattering climax sent her gloriously over.

She was somewhere dimly sublime, with a moan of profound pleasure issuing from deep in her throat; an immediate rising up, and his shout before collapsing on top of her. He was dragging huge breaths of air into his lungs as delicious ripples began trilling along her insides, causing her torso to quiver under him.

Their return to the present advanced quietly, blissfully, until his exhausted voice sounded against her neck. "You okay?"

Unable to speak, unable to draw enough breath, she nodded; it was enough to drift in euphoria new to her experience. Orgasms had been achieved with Ned, not always, but they'd been nothing like this. She shivered again as another luscious spasm tilted through her body. Definitely not like this.

Still somewhat breathless, he eased his weight off her body and pulled the bedcovers up to their shoulders, then raised himself onto an elbow to kiss her lightly on the lips. "I don't know if that was this guy's best work. . . ." He sighed with intense depth. "But I know *I* sure enjoyed it." He snuggled against her and pulled her close, melding his body with hers, his mouth humming against the shell of her ear. "If you'll stay right here, I promise to do better in the morning."

With her back muscles cozying into the heat of his chest, she chuckled out loud, sleepily content as she tucked her head under his chin. "I don't think that's possible." The earth could stop spinning and the sky could fall, however, before she'd talk him out of trying.

The next morning she woke to the coolness of his skin as he eased back into bed beside her, followed by the tender pull of his mouth against her nipple. After a moment he paused long enough to say good morning, then kissed his way up her throat, across to her mouth, then continued down, attached his lips, and began to suck deeply on the opposite nipple. She lazed onto her side to take full advantage of his attentions. His fingers cupped gently between her thighs, then eased inexorably into a slippery, methodical teasing. Hard-wired, tingling messages twisted and coiled between her nipples and the fingers lightly in friction with the nerves of her sexual center, stealing her breath as he readied her body, augmented her pleasure. Capturing the smooth, fat penis prodding at her thigh as it hardened erect, she began to match him stroke for stroke, adding a few inspired motions of her own with her thumb. "Now," she whispered hoarsely, with an urgency she could not restrain. "Hurry."

His breathing rumbled against her flesh. "Unh-uh, not this morning." And he deftly positioned himself between her legs, slid his face down the length of her body, kissing and caressing her skin as he went, and proceeded to keep his promise.

It was unquestionably the best sex of her life. Of any life. A skilled and intense lover, he probed the hairline of her inner thighs with the tip of his tongue, then gently located the knot of her sex. He teased and then isolated the ultrasensitive flesh with exquisite care before gently taking it captive. Alternating between tender nips and controlled pressure, he stroked repeatedly with the softest part of his tongue until ribbons of orgasms began to flow through her body.

Engulfing her one after another, the sensations peaked and multiplied until she was ringing like a bell. After the first four or five, she began to lose count. Only when she pled for mercy did he let her rest—then began again, until she lost herself, lost awareness of anything except his touch and her ability to feel. Eventually he fulfilled his own pleasure, not once but twice, and it was a full half hour after that before she could gather the strength to leave his bed and take refuge in the bathroom.

Eyes languid, body still weightless, she stared at herself in the mirror as reason tried its best to return. The pleasure of her body overruled her head. *It's not like you planned it.* It had happened, and was done. Could not be undone, and she could not honestly say that she was sorry.

Poor Ned. Poor Helena! If nothing more, David had shown her what was possible when two people made love. If it had been a mistake, then she'd have to deal with the consequences. At the moment she didn't care. And if the next two days bore any resemblance to this morning, it didn't look likely that she'd be changing her mind.

All that having been decided, her mind had its say anyway. *What if you've committed adultery?* she thought hazily. *What are you going to do then? Plead insanity?* Doubt wormed its way into her consciousness, and she stepped into the shower to try to wash it away.

Listening to the dull hiss of running water, David eased into the warmth of her side of his bed, feeling wonderful. If he'd had the strength, he'd have chased her into the shower. He might have been Hercules an hour ago—he'd felt like it, anyway. An hour ago he'd been the supreme and almighty ruler of Julie Ryan's sexy little body, in charge of driving her from climax to climax, her responsiveness to his touch inventing and extending his methods as well as fueling his own delight as he deliberately exhausted her sexually—but at this moment he was just a tired, relaxed, intensely happy guy who could think again. Of course, he was missing the opportunity to scrub her back. . . .

"*Now?*" Elmore stared at him from the opposite bed with the attitude of a displaced lover.

He shook his head as the shower ceased. "Couldn't get it up now if I tried," he confided lazily. "So she's all yours for a couple of hours, but I'll want her back." She'd been like no other woman he'd encountered. Ever. Amazing what great sex could do for your attitude. He wondered what Derek was doing this morning; he'd sure as hell be shocked when he found out about this little turn of events. He'd been on his case forever to—

Adrenaline shot through his body. Derek was someone he knew! Had to be!

Julie came out of the bathroom, wrapped in a cheap hotel towel too small to cover the lower curve of her butt cheeks—which he knew from experience perfectly fit into the palms of his hands. Pale cream breasts he'd ruled all morning were bulging over the top of the terry cloth, and the combination of the two almost made him a liar where Elmore was concerned. Eager to share his discovery about Derek, he pulled his covers aside to make room for her. "Come here," he invited happily. "I have news."

She shook her head at him and crossed the room, the bottom edge of the towel parting flippantly at every step.

"Come here." He was lonely in the bed, wanted her next to him—under him, as soon as he could do something about it. Impatient to share his discovery, he watched her kneel, causing the towel to cover even less territory.

She was poking through her suitcase. "I need something," she mumbled.

"Me too." Hearing the message in his voice, she reached back to tug self-consciously at the towel.

"Listen," he said urgently, "I really do have something to tell you." He saw her turn her head and surreptitiously slip something into her mouth. Was she all right?

He'd been careful with her, he was sure of it. Last night had been fast and furious, trimming little more than a thin edge off his need, as it turned out, because he'd wanted her again this morning, big time.

Rising early, he'd used the bathroom half asleep. Sliding back into the bed next to her, relishing the soft, moist skin of her breasts pliantly molding themselves against him, he'd started without her, enjoyed her nipples for breakfast until she'd been awake enough to join him. He'd taken his time and had gotten off on giving her orgasms for a while, a dozen at least, before he'd taken his turn. But she'd driven him crazy in the meantime, teasing him out of his mind. He was a big guy and she'd been awfully tight; maybe . . . He sat up, concerned.

She saw his reaction and mumbled, "Birth control."

Yikes. The last thing on his mind. In fact, it hadn't occurred to him at all. Past a point, nothing had mattered except staying hard and enjoying her body as long as possible. But his heartbeat was still above normal. "Come here. Please. Let me hold you."

She shook her head, and he was obliged to join her in the middle of the room. "What is it? Are you sure you're okay?" He clasped her to his chest, but under the towel, her body was reluctant. "I'm glad one of us was responsible, because I've wanted to take you to bed for so long, I sure didn't think." He kissed her, and the feel of her body under his hands began to mess with his head again. "Hell, I want you right now."

She gave him a sober, guilty look and handed him his wedding band. "This was in the bathroom." Tears were building along her lashes; he felt like a dolt. She still didn't know.

"I took it off. That's part of what I want to tell you." His excitement returned as he related his discovery about Derek. "I don't know who he is yet, but he feels like a . . . I'm not sure, a best friend or something. Someone I would normally talk to." She blinked doubtfully, and he rushed on. "I'm not him, I swear I'm not!" He kissed her, met unresponsive lips. "I'm not married, *he* is. That's why I was wearing a wedding ring."

"Oh, that's clear. . . ." Tears spilled onto her cheeks, her confusion evident. "Are you saying your memory's back?"

He led her to the bed. "No, but I'm starting to remember things." He described portions of the funeral in the dream. "Her name was Gina . . . Morganer, and her picture's in the wallet."

"You're David Morganer?"

"No. Morganer is her father's name." Information from the black side of his brain seeped forth, astonishing him. "His first name is Earl." *He thinks I killed her . . . and I don't know whether I did or not.*

Unnerved, he pulled Julie's body closer to him and reexamined the wedding band. "I know this is mine, but I can't explain why my identification says Derek Rocklin."

"And you're positive you're not him."

"If I am . . ." He trailed off, unhappy with the direction his mind was taking. *If I am, I'm in total denial. Is it possible? To not want to be someone so badly . . .* His reason rebelled. "I'm not. I'd stake my life on it."

She eased out of his embrace. "Morganer? As in Morganer-Pacific? That Earl Morganer?"

He explored the name. For a moment it held additional significance for him, but the link was unclear. "Maybe. All I could see was his name. . . ."

"Well, if it's that Earl Morganer, he's pretty high up the food chain. More money than . . . any one person ought to have." She rewrapped her loosening towel, granting a distracting glimpse of unfettered cleavage before ruthlessly rebinding her breasts with terry cloth. "Among other things, Morganer-Pacific is an investment empire. Banking, holding companies, and timber interests, not to mention real estate, which is why I know the name."

"Investments. I think so." Little by little, the black was gaining ground and closing in again. "It sounds right." Then, without warning, a headache began, pounding its way forward inside his skull at a low volume. He tried to concentrate on the portion of her breasts that were escaping from the towel, but the ache in his brain was on the move.

"You were married to his daughter?"

He nodded, aggravating the monotonous cadence;

he held his head rigid, trying to stave it off. "She's dead," he repeated. "I went to her funeral." *There was blood.* . . . He turned away from the image, met an unreadable expression in Julie's eyes.

"Can I ask how she died?"

He scoured his mind for the answer. Found the red on his shirt, and on his hands, and knew he could not tell her these things. "I don't know. It's all going away."

Julie saw the pain in his face and desperately wanted to believe that he hadn't made the whole thing up; when he dodged the question about Gina Morganer's death, she knew there was more that he hadn't told her. Whatever the truth, with a megamillionaire family tossed into the mix, things were becoming more and more strange. David's features were going pale. "You want an aspirin?"

"Let me try food first. It's not quite as bad as it was yesterday."

While he ate two leftover slices of pizza, she put on a bit of lipstick and began to get dressed, trying to assimilate what she'd learned in the last few minutes. She managed to disregard her general lethargy in order to process new information about the man who was now her lover. Morganer-Pacific. If it was true that he'd married into that family, the cash in the backpack could be walking-around money.

In addition to food, he needed aspirin for the pain; the medication was in her purse. She handed him the bottle, then retrieved the gasoline receipt from Mona's. "We'll have to check out soon," she reminded him. "We promised to call Willie. If I can manage to reach her, do you want to say hello?"

"No, just give her my best. Ask her how the storm was up there." He took the aspirin into the bathroom and closed the door.

Phone service to Lake Stillwater had been restored, and Willie answered on the second ring. Julie was reporting on their visit to Dr. Meadows when Willie stopped her. "A couple of fellows was looking for you yestiday. About four hours after you left. Said they'as private investigators."

Julie stopped breathing, and cold crept up the back of her neck. "Looking for me?"

"Both of you is what they said. They had a picture of your young man. Said they was trying to find him because they'as worried about you." Willie's urgent voice took on a trace of petulance. "If you ask me, what they was really interested in was finding out what I knew about you—that, and some money they think he's carrying. Honey, they didn't even know what you looked like, exceptin' the color of your hair."

Willie continued with a careful rundown of the conversation, emphasizing that one of the men had been invisible behind the darkened windows of a Range Rover. "I could see he'as white, but that's about all. The other's a black fella, suit-and-tie type, good-lookin', but kinda the grim sort, if you ask my opinion. His identification said he was Ron Hathaway. Talked to me like I was a fool, though. That first one, he just eavesdropped, no manners whatever. And me being a cantankerous soul, I didn't help 'em none." Her voice took on an overtone of caution. "I tell you, something's rotten for sure when a man won't show himself for who he is." Willie paused. "Now, honey, you strike me as being real level-headed, and if you was in trouble or needed help or anything, you'd tell me, right?"

"Certainly." It wasn't possible. No one could make love like that and . . . "Of course I would."

"Good enough. You take care, hear?"

Julie hung up the phone and became aware that her hands were shaking. What on earth had she gotten into? Was she being an idiot after all?

"*Now?*" Elmore was caressing her ankles. She had a fleeting impulse to grab him up and make a dash for the Bronco.

David couldn't be dangerous toward her! He'd been too caring, too generous. This morning, his lean, powerful naked body, abdominal muscles straining, holding himself back . . . The whole idea was ridiculous.

His shower was still running. Feeling the traitor, she furtively made a second call. Los Angeles information had a Morganer-Pacific listing in Beverly Hills; she pressed the star button to be connected "for an additional dollar and ninety cents," before she could change her mind. A receptionist answered.

"Is this your home office?" she demanded. "Does Earl Morganer maintain an office here?"

Apparently so, because screening began immediately. "Who's calling Mr. Morganer?"

Not having the slightest idea what she was about to say, she stared at Elmore for inspiration. "Detective Katt, LAPD."

"Hold on."

Dear God, I'm impersonating a police officer. That's against the law! Moments passed, and she deliberated frantically about what to say next as she listened to the continuing shower, her nerves jumping each time the phone clicked and buzzed.

"Earl Morganer's office," said a voice, smooth and cultured as frozen yogurt. "This is Mary Welles."

"Demetra Katt, Fourteenth Street in Los Angeles," she said quickly, deliberately jamming the words together. "May I speak to Earl Morganer?"

"He's not available just now. Can I be of help? I'm his assistant."

She racked her brain to remember how it was done in TV shows. "We're following up on an earlier investigation. Does Mr. Morganer have a daughter named Gina?"

"Excuse me?" The woman was instantly suspicious. "What's this about? Following up on which investigation? There were several."

Julie went for broke and blew past the inquiry with as much authority as she could muster. "Please answer the question, Miss Welles. It's important."

"Gina Morganer is dead. She was killed several years ago. Now what's this about?"

Julie's heart did a double flip at the unexpected confirmation. She scrambled to follow up. "Can you tell me how and when she died?"

But her had voice had faltered, and Miss Welles seized the upper hand. "Mr. Morganer's unavailable until Friday," she said icily. "Leave your number and—"

"Was her married name Rocklin?"

"That's something you'll have to discuss with—"

Julie's nerves gave out. "If he'll be in his office Friday, I'll call back then."

"Her death was investigated extensively. . . . Detective, was it?" Miss Welles was determined to head her off. "There are official files with this information, and unless you have new evidence in this regard, I suggest you not distress Mr. Morganer with idle questions." Clearly accustomed to being in charge, she became the interrogator. "Which division did you—"

The shower came to a halt. "I'm working privately on this," Julie stated firmly, but her heart was quavering in her throat with the fear of being discovered. Pretending to be a private investigator was probably breaking some kind of law as well. "I'll call back." She hung up the phone two seconds before her knees gave out, and she sank onto the bed. It was true, Gina Morganer was dead. And the death had been investigated. What could that mean? She waited for her heart to calm down, unsure how she felt.

David opened the bathroom door holding a razor, looked her up and down, and uttered a semisalacious whistle. Shaving foam covered his chin and cheeks and trailed down the planes of his throat. "Did you reach her?" She nodded and answered with something that satisfied him, but he didn't close the door, and she watched him begin to shave.

It was too late to run, so she forced herself to begin preparations to check out.

Gina Morganer was killed. Miss Welles's statements could not be misinterpreted, and the knowledge bounced wildly in her brain. Shivering and apprehensive as she prepared to leave the hotel, she took little comfort in the fact that she wasn't an adulteress, but she'd have felt a whole lot better if she hadn't discovered this new can of worms in the process.

17

TUESDAY

Deke's ankle was not only aching, but itching. Down where he couldn't scratch it with a pencil. Worried about David, and frustrated at the continuing storm and an inability to move in any direction, he was about to dial out again when a call-waiting signal beeped insistently. Hoping to hell it was Walde, he punched the lever to switch the line and was disappointed to be speaking with his secretary. "What is it, Melba? I don't need another crisis right now."

"I know, I'm sorry."

Why the hell was she bugging him?

"And I wouldn't have called—"

"For crying out loud, get to the point!"

"Mr. Walde is coming unglued. . . . I wasn't sure I should bother you, but he said if he didn't hear from you within the hour, he'll cancel everyth—"

"What's the number?" He wrote in ink on the back of his hand. "Christ, I've been trying to reach him for two days! If he calls again, tell him that! Anything else?"

Melba was cowed by his manner. "Mr. DePasse called." DePasse was his boss. "He wanted to know if I'd heard from you. I think you'd better check in." She took a deep breath, and he knew what was coming. "I don't suppose there's any news—"

"No! Don't you think I'd have called if there was?" He took a deep breath to calm down. "Forget it, I have a lot on my mind right now. Wait ten minutes to tell DePasse you located me so I can get this jerk off my back." He broke the connection before she could blabber on with something else, then dialed rapidly and got the *pleep-pleep-pleep* that identified a beeper. Not surprising—it was always a beeper with this guy. Jittery with tension, he punched in his location, hung up, and waited. The phone rang three minutes later. When he heard Walde's voice, he lost it. "Where the hell have you been? Why'd you change your goddamn number?"

Walde was equally furious. "Do you think I am stupid? Where is the *money*? If you think you can trick me, you are wrong."

Part of Deke relaxed for a second, the part that was worried about David. The part that was bordering on paranoia, took over. "Screw the money. We need to talk, and we can't do it on the goddamn phone! Where are you?"

"Do you really expect that I would tell you this? One of us is a fool!"

Deke had had all the double-talk he was interested in. "Either we meet, or I blow this out of the water and you and me with it! Where are you?"

There was a brief pause while the asshole thought it over. "You want to talk, you come here. There will be a message. Motel Six in Omak." Walde disconnected.

Deke sighed, ran his hand through his hair, and readjusted his glasses. Things were totally out of control. Totally! Half a dozen men were out in the storm, searching for signs of David. The footprints at that cabin couldn't have been his, or he'd have checked in. Unless something had happened to him.

Or was it conceivable that he'd actually taken the money? He knew Hathaway thought so.

And what the hell was going on with Walde? For the past two days he'd had a recurring nightmare that the son of a bitch had murdered David and disappeared with the money. Unless it was some sort of mind game, Walde was still in the area. Which brought things back to David's being missing. Five days now. Something had to have happened. He would never . . .

Harried, he hobbled down the motel hallway and knocked on the door to Ron's room. Hathaway answered immediately. "Hey, DePasse just called. He wants me to come back for a meeting, and I'm on my way to the airport."

Deke's stomach shrank. "Is it about David? What about me?"

"He said it didn't involve you. I gave him an update on the situation, and he said to tell you he hopes everything is okay."

"I'll give you a lift to the airport."

"He authorized a helicopter."

Deke's stomach lurched again. Helicopter use was

unheard of, except for emergencies, and since when did DePasse speak to Hathaway and not him? "So I don't need to talk to him? You're sure?"

"It's up to you. He knows the storm's preventing all but a cursory ground search; he's current on the footprints and the call from the Ryan woman. He asked me to tell you we'd spoken."

Deke made the supreme effort to appear unworried. "Okay. Roads are closed north, but the highway's open south of here. If they did get out and haven't holed up somewhere, they'd have to go through Omak. Might take a run down there and ask around a bit."

"What about your ankle?"

"Itches like a son of a bitch, but I can drive. No problem."

Hathaway tossed him the keys and picked up his briefcase. "I'll keep the room in case he tries to contact me. If you're going to be gone, maybe we should have calls referred through to DePasse until you get back."

"Don't." Deke did his best to stay cool. "Send them to my room. I'll check in periodically, and I'll be back here this evening. I'm not leaving until we find him."

"I understand. So does DePasse."

Hathaway grabbed his overnight bag. Deke's casual attitude was out of character for a guy who had a problem temper and a fifty-five-gallon screwup on his plate. Something in DePasse's demeanor a few minutes ago had been out of character as well. It wasn't like Deke's boss to avoid talking with him, and while DePasse had been careful not to say so, Hathaway had a strong feeling that the meeting he'd been summoned to in such a rush related to this being David's first assignment, and to a whole bunch of missing money.

They parted at the motel's front office. Ron watched the Range Rover drive away, then, ignoring the directive and Deke's seniority in their partnership, made arrangements for transferring calls anyway. "Anything for either of us goes to my office," he directed, and gave his number in Santa Barbara. He took out David's photograph and showed it to the clerk with a fifty-dollar bill. "If this man comes in any time of the day or night, make sure I know about it."

He watched the clerk study the picture. David was good-looking as hell for a white guy. It would take a blind man to miss him. Tall, with pale blond hair and a California golden-boy tan, he was personable for the most part, with a laid-back, suffering-bastard charm that women got off on.

Ron had worked with Deke for the past several years, and they'd been on a first-name basis for five, but when David had been switched in at the last minute, Ron had taken the precaution of pulling his file. On paper the guy was a flake: no wife, no family, work record suspicious—five nothing jobs in five years. No letters of reference. But Deke had vouched for him, DePasse had okayed the hire, and a week ago the two had agreed to turn him loose in the woods with half a million dollars, so it was their butts on the line, not his.

He sighed, already tired. He hated helicopters

and wasn't looking forward to the long ride to the Wenatchee airport. Dealing with thieves and lowlifes was always for the birds, and in his humble opinion, this setup was particularly rinky-dink. If somebody upstairs hadn't agreed that the payoff should go forward in the first place, he wouldn't be out here freezing his ass trying to clean up after an amateur.

Julie watched him come into the room. In spite of her reserve, her heart leaped at the sight of the man whose inspired lovemaking had given her such pleasure. His lean waist was wrapped in a towel that hid none of his assets as he gathered his clothing, then gave her a kiss. She was unable to hide a guarded response to his embrace, however, and he cornered her instantly. "What's wrong?"

She decided she'd better warn him about the men who were looking for them. "Investigators?" He was genuinely baffled, but she noticed that he seemed to physically withdraw as he proceeded to get dressed. "It has to be the money." His face changed abruptly. "If Willie didn't say anything, how could they know about you?"

"I have no idea. She said they had your picture, never once mentioned your name, and claimed it wasn't about the cash." Instinctively she edited Willie's conversation to omit mention of her safety, and repeated their inquiry about the money instead.

He shook his head, frowning. "Not possible. I don't care what he told her. If he asked about hundred-dollar bills, he knows about the cash," he said tersely. "It's not the first time I've been investigated. Maybe someone saw the license plate or something, and they ran a check on the car to get your name."

Totally rattled at how calmly he'd made the damning admission, Julie knew she wouldn't tell him that she'd called Morganer's office. Frightened by being the subject of a search, one panic at a time was about all she could handle at the moment. "The only person who knew I was at the cabin is Mrs. Cumberland. Well, my sister," she added, "but there's no one for her to tell." She stopped. "Mrs. Cumberland left a note in the mailbox. Maybe the mailman . . ."

"He wouldn't have known about me." Obviously restless, he heaved his backpack onto the bed. "They're looking for the money, they have a picture of me, and they know about you. Whoever they are, it doesn't sound safe." He took her in his arms and gave her a light kiss. "Maybe we'd better get you the hell out of here."

Julie shivered in his embrace, jangled at the upsetting events. This morning's erotic adventures were becoming remote memories, something that had happened between two other people. Unknown men were looking for her. Strangers. It was entirely possible that she was in danger, but from whom— this man she'd decided to trust? Made love with? Was she that witless? Every instinct she had about him told her he was worried and protective where she was concerned. Surely she couldn't be that far off the mark.

18

Hathaway took note of the slender ebony cane next to the chair and reached down to shake the older man's hand. The fact that he hadn't been informed until five minutes ago that the meeting with DePasse would also include Earl Morganer sent his nerves on a high-wire act. The silver-haired white man seated in front of him was in his mid-sixties, wearing a light charcoal gray suit cut from the kind of wool that held its tailoring in a hurricane and had to have cost thousands of dollars in fabric alone; impeccable oyster shirt, perfectly knotted power tie executed in maroons and wines with a touch of pewter—the precise shade as his four-hundred-dollar shoes. The effect was not remotely dapper, and exuded a prescription for power that heads of state would recognize. The clotheshorse in Hathaway groaned with appreciation. Earl Morganer would probably buy and sell three quarters of Rhode Island more easily than he would change his tailor, and with probably less thought.

"Pleasure to meet you, sir," he said formally, hoping against his best instincts that there was something, anything, he could do that would please this man to the extent that a job offer might follow in its wake. Morganer nodded a small acknowledgment; his handshake had been solid, trustworthy, and sufficiently masculine, but his eyes were the unreadable brown of stale coffee, and his demeanor put Hathaway on guard. *He doesn't like something or someone in this room,* he realized. *Hope to God it isn't me.*

DePasse motioned for him to be seated. "I wanted this to be an in-person meeting, Ron, for reasons that will become clear. Mr. Morganer, how would you like to proceed?"

Never in the twelve years that he'd been on board—and certainly not during the three in which DePasse had been his superior—had Ron witnessed power being deferred to an outsider. Whose meeting was this? He held down his fascination at his boss's decision and kept an impassive face with great effort. Morganer's manner was brittle as he waived the privilege. "Please."

DePasse began immediately. "Mr. Morganer has information that bears looking into. It seems that David was a trusted employee of Morganer-Pacific several years ago—"

"Nine years ago," interrupted Morganer.

"—and Mr. Morganer feels that we've made an error in hiring him."

Morganer's iron gaze ignored DePasse as he took the floor. "I control a great deal of power, Mr. Hathaway, as I'm sure you must be aware, but past a point, this man has managed to stay beyond my reach." The seamless voice could have been describing a monument and Ron was fascinated. "I am sorry to say that not only did he break my trust, but he was able to take something from me . . . which I cannot replace."

Not a ripple of emotion had crossed Morganer's features as he spoke; his rage was evidenced only in his assiduous avoidance of speaking David's name.

"I say past a point, because during that time I have used my power to maintain a personal watch on this man. . . ." Morganer's eyes did not waver. Hathaway met his glance, supremely glad that he was not the object of Morganer's vengeance. What the hell had happened nine years ago?

"To attempt to prevent him from damaging others, you understand. Which is why I have taken it upon myself to contact your firm." Morganer swung his glance to DePasse to give what passed for a nod.

DePasse picked up the ball. "I've made Mr. Morganer aware of the fact that David is missing with a great deal of money," he said quietly, "and since Deke not only has personal concerns but was instrumental in positioning him for this matter, I felt he should not be party to any discussion until we decide what to do. I'm afraid we have a . . . situation."

Hathaway's neck prickled uncomfortably, and he rapidly spun through various possibilities. If it was true, and if Deke was involved . . . the pieces could be made to fit, but not entirely. Unless his partner was one hell of an actor, he was genuinely strung out over David's disappearance, and the cash was secondary—unless, of course, Deke had been double-crossed. He held the thought aside and made no response, waiting to see what additional information would be forthcoming.

DePasse was openly angry. He pushed a series of papers across his desk. "Mr. Morganer's provided me with verification of his past investigation of this man, and I have to say, it looks pretty grim. Had I known even half of this information, I never would have taken him on."

Both men paused. Ron knew he was expected to comment. If any of it was true, he was in an awkward position. As far as he knew, he'd been the last person to talk to David. Rock and hard place were colliding, with his sorry ass in the middle. "Well, I agree we have a potential situation," he said diplomatically, having learned long ago not to set fire to a bridge until he was safely on another one. "Unfortunately, bad weather has prevented an all-out search, and there's still the possibility of finding his body. . . ." The possibility, however, was admittedly remote, given the footprint evidence at the cabin. He shifted in his chair, deliberately giving the appearance of being uncomfortable. "I'd hate for any of us to jump to conclusions and be wrong."

"You won't find him." Morganer was implacable. "He used the money to disappear, and the storm was a bonus. Convenient way for him to gain more time before the theft was discovered. You've been set up. Believe me, he's capable."

If I had you on my case, I'd disappear, too. Hathaway shifted again, this time ill at ease. *Wonder who's watching me . . .*

"If the two of them are in this together, logically they'll contact each other at some point." Hathaway tapped the papers on top of DePasse's desk. "Can I take a look at these? Perhaps there's something I can use."

"Of course," said Morganer, rising. "One other thing you should know." He steadied himself with the cane, and Hathaway got to his feet as well. "My office received a call this morning from a young woman asking highly personal questions about my family. She was pretending an investigation, and gave a false name." Morganer was blinking rapidly, the first outward show of emotion Hathaway had detected since the meeting began.

"And you're certain it's connected with this matter?"

"Positive." Morganer's eyes were coldly adversarial. "It was done as a warning. Something to upset me, which it did. He knows that sooner or later I will involve myself in his sad affairs, and that I have always told the truth about him. It was a warning," he repeated strongly. "Take my word on it." He offered his hand first to Hathaway, then to DePasse. "Please keep me informed, if you will."

"Certainly, sir." DePasse ushered him out, and Hathaway stood alone in the room, an unwilling feeling lodged in his spinal cord. He picked up the papers. David had a very dangerous enemy. If he'd been on Morganer's hit list for the past nine years, short of changing his name and moving to another country, David had no future whatever that Morganer couldn't destroy; in fact, his life didn't appear to be worth a dime unless Morganer said so. It sure made a case for skipping out with a bag of untraceable money.

Hathaway left DePasse's corner office and walked down the hall toward his own. He passed Melba coming out of Deke's office, and she voiced the concern of every female on the staff. "Any word on him?"

"Not so far. Hold a good thought."

"I will. How's my boss doing with his broken ankle?"

"He's managing."

"Do you know if he reached Mr. Walde?" She shook her head. "Boy, is he a piece of work. One of our guys is missing out there in a storm, and all Mr. Walde cares about is himself. I don't get it."

"Never underestimate the power of money." Walde had been a pain in the ass for months. Let Deke deal with him. When he arrived at his own office, he called in his secretary and asked her to track down the proper assessor's office in Washington state. "I want to locate the owner of that property. And keep it confidential, please. Nothing on the street."

Twenty minutes later, he had a name: Joann Ryan, Geneva, Switzerland. Purchased three and a half years ago from Irene, who'd inherited from her father. Copies of title documents were being faxed to his office. When they arrived, he found what he was looking for. Until two years ago taxes for the property had been billed to an address in Malibu—in care of Julie Ryan. Bingo. And Julie Ryan had a current phone listing in Malibu. Double bingo! He dialed Melba on the intercom. "When Deke calls in, tell him I had to take care of another situation and I'll get in touch with him later."

Then he set about reviewing Morganer's investigative files.

David looked up from the Washington state map that he'd been studying for the past fifteen minutes. "We'd better eat in Wenatchee."

Julie started at the sudden break in silence and inadvertently jogged the steering wheel. The Bronco wavered slightly as she corrected.

"Then it looks like an hour on to Interstate 90, so we'll have enough daylight for a straight run to Seattle," he continued. "And you haven't said anything for fifteen miles."

He was right. Since they'd left the hotel she'd been chasing her thoughts from one tree to another. In and out of Brewster's supermarket for Elmore's cat food, in and out of a gas station to refill the Bronco's tank, obtain the map, and decide that she wanted to drive—the outside of her was functioning, but inside, anywhere she looked, things were unstable.

He was no longer wearing his wedding band, and the knowledge gnawed at her insides. Why had he taken it off? Why had he worn it in the first place? For the first half hour outside of Brewster, he'd gotten really excited and described memories of working in the timber business, but his were not the hands of someone who topped trees for a living. Then he'd gone silent for the past several miles to study the map.

She'd spent most of that time comparing his comment about having been investigated to Miss Welles's statement that an extensive inquiry had taken place regarding Gina Morganer's death. One inescapable question remained on both counts: why?

"You're upset."

At his accusation, the wheel joggled again. It was a good thing that the road wasn't slippery; the light snow spitting against the windshield was melting as fast as it came out of the sky. "I was thinking about my sister, actually. She's having trouble in her marriage." It was true, but it was also a lie. She had forgotten about Joann's troubles late last night and hadn't thought about them the entire morning.

The crackle of paper scraped against her nerves as he folded the map. "Sorry to hear it."

"Why? You don't know her." The response was sharp and unjust in its criticism, but she was too provoked with him to care.

"You're right, I don't. It's just the reaction I had." He looked at her searchingly; his facial bruising was beginning to fade, and his clear eyes reflected the spotty green of the Wenatchee National Forest on either side of the highway. "This is about us, isn't it?"

Nervous that the subject was on the table at last, she nodded. "I think so. I'm very conflicted about what's happened. I don't know how to feel. One minute things are . . . and the next, I find out someone's looking for me and suddenly everything's weird and . . ." Her voice trailed off, unwilling to finish the thought.

"And it's all my fault."

The town of Wenatchee emerged from the forest. "And it's all your fault," she agreed.

He placed the folded map on the seat between

them, brushing her thigh in the process. She tried not to flinch, but he caught her at it. "Julie, those men have nothing to do with us. Last night and this morning? That was just you and me."

"Whoever *you* are." Her comment was cuttingly glib but accurate. She wanted to believe him, she really did, but there were too many things piling up. Too many names. Too many unknowns.

"My name is David. I made love to you last night because I wanted to, and because I let you." He scanned the passing restaurants, suddenly fidgety. "Let's discuss this in neutral territory. What do you say? MacBurgher's, Babe's, what's your pleasure?"

You, of all people, know what my pleasure is. Furious that it was messed up, that her feelings for him couldn't be trusted, and that more than doubt was crowding into her thinking by the minute, she ignored his question and stubbornly continued through town until she saw the Wenatchee Family Restaurant. She made a hard right into the parking lot and was forced to wait until a young couple in a station wagon had vacated a space near the front entrance. By the time she'd parked, David had pulled his pack out of the backseat. "I'd better keep this with me."

"Whatever." She made certain to crack a window so that Elmore had plenty of air, then entered the restaurant with David at her heels. Not remotely hungry, and definitely not ready to deal with the situation, she felt as if she were being backed into a corner. It *was* his fault. All the turmoil and anxiety she was feeling, his fault. His fault that she wasn't enjoying herself on what had started out as an incredible day. His fault for not having a last name, for crying out loud! She'd made love with David *who?*

But it was her fault for having stayed with him. And for winding up in bed with him. *Her* fault for wanting to do it again—and that was the thing that angered her most. Her error in judgment. People were looking for this man. Private investigators. Probably the police, too. And because of him, people were looking for her.

They were shown to a booth, and they quickly placed food orders with the waitress. Julie played with the car keys to give her hands something to do until he reached across the table and tapped her on the fist. "Let's talk about this."

Miserable that it couldn't be real, she laid the keys aside. "I'm upset about last night," she admitted stiffly. Looking him in the face was dangerous, so she kept her eyes on the place setting in front of her. Its menu was gibberish. "I shouldn't have gone to bed with you."

"Why not?"

Unwilling to enter the minefield of private investigators and the matter of his dead wife, she took the easier route, which held embarrassing pitfalls all its own. "I didn't know . . . you weren't married."

"So it's about guilt? If I was married, maybe you'd have a point."

"You could have been." She glanced up in spite of herself. "I'm disappointed in me." The confession was painful. "I thought I had more character."

"You have plenty of character. You could have ignored me last night. All you had to do was pretend you were asleep, but you didn't." His eyes were convincing her, his voice, his sincerity making it so. "I could be anybody, and you've been taking care of me since you found me. That's an enormous amount of character." His words were spoken with an intensity that revived the passion she'd shared with him, rekindled it in her mind. "You've taken me on faith, let me make love to you, which is what I needed more than anything in the world. I think it's what we both needed. And enjoyed," he reminded her. "How was that wrong?"

She was off balance and defensive, torn between the truth of his statements and a fear she couldn't identify. "It just was. And you know it."

"No, I don't. I swear I'm not married. And you're not engaged. We had no commitments to honor, except what we decided to do for each other, so don't tell me it was wrong, because I know better." His eyes twinkled briefly, infuriating her. "It was never righter, as far as I'm concerned."

Sex wasn't the issue. Sex with this man had been incredible: surrealistic, carefree, two people engaged in mutual exploration, a surfeit of experience she'd never have had with Ned. As if acknowledging this, her heart began betraying her. And her body. "Just because I . . . we . . . that didn't make it right."

He looked at her, candor bright in his eyes, and something else. Something final. "In my opinion, it would be very right to make love with you forever." His smile became the impudent grin of a teasing lover. "Or for an excessively long time, at least."

Their food arrived. Flushed, Julie waited until the waitress had been assured that everything was satisfactory. Her nerve endings were jumping and her senses were so heightened, so tuned to his every movement, that her breasts were aching and she was too scattered to take up the conversation. He didn't pursue it, so they shared the booth in a pregnant, humid silence. Eventually the waitress poured coffee and cleared their service dishes.

Julie dropped three cubes of sugar into her cup and nervously added cream. Within the safety of the restaurant, she got to what was really on her mind. Her confession was perverse and involuntary. "I called Earl Morganer." Her cup trembled violently against her lower lip. "While you were in the shower."

"Oh." For a moment his eyes showed genuine surprise at the monumental shift in topic, then went bleak. "So that's what this is about." He concentrated on stirring his coffee. "What did you find out?"

"That his daughter's death was under investigation. . . . You said you were used to being investigated."

"It sounds right." He toyed with his cup before looking up at her. "So you no longer trust me." His eyes gave her a measured, glacial appraisal. "Did anyone mention that he hates me? That he didn't want me to marry his daughter? I don't suppose you found out my name?"

"No." There was a long, long pause, and he began to rub his forehead with his fingertips. Finally she couldn't bear it. "So that's it? You're not going to tell me anything else?"

"It's all I have right now, Julie." He looked across at her, pinning her with an intense gaze. "Here's everything I haven't said. I know I loved her, I know she's dead, and for some reason I was still wearing my wedding ring." He took a deep breath. "I don't know how she died, but it was bloody and I have the sense that it happened a long time ago," he said in a monotone. "Because I know there have been women since, but I don't think any of them . . . mattered." He looked away suddenly to sweep the room with his gaze, then came back to her stricken face and shook his head in answer to her unspoken question. "No. You're different. I know that, too."

It was too much.

Unable to believe him, she sought escape. Grabbing her purse, she fled the booth and found her way to the ladies' room, stunned by these new admissions. His wife had died a bloody death. He'd been investigated. Was still being investigated, and she was being dragged into the middle of something awful. Somehow she had to get out of this.

More painful than anything was his statement that she hadn't mattered. The honesty of that statement had been unmistakable, and battered at her self-esteem; his belated "you're different" proviso didn't compensate. Fighting tears that threatened to choke her, she stalled for several minutes by putting on lipstick, wiping it off, and putting it on again until she felt ready to face him.

Finally she approached the booth, determined to tell him that she was leaving and that he was no longer welcome to accompany her. He stood as she arrived, a handsome, imposing presence. Women in the room were taking notice. As she opened her mouth to make her pronouncement, he gave her a kiss that nearly weakened her resolve; she enjoyed it as much as she dared, now that it was their kiss goodbye. His eyes scanned her face, and he pushed a strand of hair away from her forehead. "See you." Shouldering his backpack, he disappeared toward the men's room.

How could she be so confused about someone? Part of her knew she wasn't being smart, that she was undoubtedly an idiot on the rebound from her broken engagement to Ned, taken in by a grand, erotic sexual escapade. Unquestionably, sleeping with him had screwed up her thinking. Completely flummoxed, she sank into the booth and saw that he'd paid their luncheon bill. There was a tip of several dollars tucked under his water glass. Seconds passed, then a full minute, and for some reason she was immobilized. *Just leave,* urged her common sense. *Pick up your purse and walk out!* What if he followed her? What if he wouldn't let her leave? It was a public place, so how could he stop her? *Walk outside, get in the car, and drive away!* But the car keys were no longer on the table.

Shocked, she looked again at the Bronco still in its parking space; Elmore was perched on the back of the driver's seat. Why had he taken the keys? To keep her from leaving? Frantic, she felt through her purse but didn't find them—just the cold steel of the gun she'd totally forgotten. Nearly frantic with this new reminder of how much she didn't know about him, she jerked the purse onto her lap for a closer look. There was a restaurant napkin tucked inside.

The keys, along with several of the hundred-dollar bills, were wrapped inside; he had to have managed it a moment ago, when he'd kissed her.

There was a note inked onto the napkin: THANKS AGAIN. TAKE CARE OF YOURSELF. No signature, just *D*. For Derek? She was no longer willing to believe there was a David.

Maybe D.B., after all. He'd taken his money and left by the back door, as gone as the infamous hijacker. She walked outside, furious, knowing full well that she should be feeling relief that he was gone. It was snowing harder, and thin slip-flows of white were scudding across the parking lot, pushed by a chill wind. Waves of sound from departing jet engines sent dull reverberations through the air. He was gone, and she was on her own again. The way she'd planned to be. So why did she feel so abandoned? As if some important part of her had been left inside?

Distracted, she watched a silver outline lift into the afternoon sky, and realization rose faster than the plane. Ten to one he was on his way to Wenatchee's airport! And from there he'd get on a flight and disappear into a snowstorm with his bag full of money.

And she'd helped him do it. The bastard!

19

Arriving at Motel Six by midafternoon, Deke first checked for messages in his name, found nothing, then called the Nighthawk motel from a pay phone in the lobby. More nothing from Walde *or* David. But the clerk had messages for him from Hathaway: A search team had recovered the remains of a tent on the other side of the lake, wrecked by a fallen tree, ripped to hell, and matching the piece of canvas they'd found in the cabin. The good news: no body. Evidence of activity had been destroyed by the rain, but they'd found a matching woman's boot print, size six, at both locations.

It was inescapable—he'd met someone, and the two of them had disappeared with the money. A cold chill of anger crept through his veins. He'd ignored David's past and allowed him to get into this, knowing he shouldn't be anywhere near the area that held his wife's ghost, and Deke knew that if something bad had happened, it was his fault.

The second message from Hathaway: He'd been temporarily assigned elsewhere, would be in touch. Frustrated, his ankle giving him hell, Deke chewed over the information as he moved to a plastic-covered bench and sat down to wait. Across the room, a woman was seated on a matching bench; she was dark-haired, thin to the point of being gaunt, and reading a novel. He'd waited maybe fifteen minutes before she approached to hand him a note. GO WITH HER, it said. SHE WILL DRIVE.

"It's about time," he said irritably. "We could have had this settled by now." He followed her around the building to a dirty green sedan that resembled a dozen other foreign-made imports. "Where the hell is he?" he grumbled. "I don't have all day."

The woman opened his jacket to check for a recording device, and he sighed with impatience as she examined under his arms, around his back, and up and down both pant legs. "You through?"

"No." She probed the ankle cast at length before deliberately placing her bare hands on the fender of the car; he gasped as she rammed icy fingers down his trousers to thoroughly feel him up. Christ, it was a scene from a bad spy novel, and he thought *he* was paranoid! Apparently satisfied that he wasn't part of a trap, the bitch finally unlocked the vehicle and drove them a few minutes away to an outdoor park. Abandoned swings swayed in the wind that whipped across the children's playground.

"Out," she demanded.

He looked around. The place was deserted. "This is ridiculous. I have a broken ankle! You leave me here, I'll freeze to death!"

Her eyes were an implacable dirty gray and reminded him of bad ice: rotten and unsafe for anyone careless. He opened the door and struggled onto his feet. She ran the car forward about ten yards and stopped long enough to close the door, then sped out the way she'd come in. As if he could chase the sadistic moron. Or would. Ten minutes later, thoroughly chilled, he decided to hoof it back to Motel Six and count himself lucky. This was insanity.

He'd walked fifty feet when the cookie-cutter car returned and pulled up next to him. This time Walde was driving; he rolled down the window. "Get in."

"Jesus, get in, get out. What is it with you two?" He managed to jam himself back into the passenger seat.

Walde ignored his outrage. "Where is my money?"

"I don't know!" Deke exploded. "Until you called this morning, I thought you had it!"

Walde's expression was a classic example of astonished suspicion. Eyes narrowed, jaw clenched until the muscle showed white, he glared at Deke, furious. "Why are you saying this? How could I have it? You didn't give it to her!"

Deke matched him glare for glare. "I broke my leg and we had to send another guy, moron. You changed your goddamned phone number, so I couldn't let you know. Anyway, our man's missing. You tell me."

"With my money?" The words were ominous. "You have done this."

"No." Deke tried to ease the pressure on his ankle in the cramped leg space of the car. "We're looking for him. We don't know if he was injured or drowned. . . . He's missing, that's all I know."

"He ran away with it."

The broken bone was throbbing like a son of a bitch, racing with his heartbeat. "No . . . there was an accident. We don't know—"

"This does not matter." Irate, Walde hammered at the steering wheel. "Whatever has happened does not matter! We have an arrangement. I have commitments; you must pay the money!"

"Can't be done." Deke shivered. With the windows down, the car was freezing. "Leave me out of it. I'm through."

Walde was apoplectic. "I cannot!" He was swinging his head from side to side like a caged, demented animal. "It's too late. The sale will be destroyed. I owe money I must pay or go to jail." He was bug-eyed, spittle spraying from his mouth. "I will destroy you. You were paid for information. Give me information!" Walde produced a revolver from inside his coat. "Where is my money?"

It was real. A pistol was aimed at his chest. A bullet was ready to rip its way through his flesh and take away his *life! Bless me, father!* An iron band of terror robbed him of breath, suffocated his thinking.

"Tell me! I have spent two and a half years in this. You will not make a mess of it." The gun wavered for a moment as Walde cocked the trigger, then he pushed the weapon to within an inch of Deke's eye. "Where did he go? You will tell me!"

Deke recoiled helplessly at the man's threat. "I don't know! We're trying to figure it out. He's with a woman named Julie." He poured out everything he could think of. "They stayed in a cabin for a couple of days, that's all we know. We thought she was your contact."

Walde gave him a lethal stare, then jammed the barrel under the soft part of his chin. "Where is my money?"

The man was crazy enough to do it! Deke's bladder threatened to give way. Desperate, he made a bid for time. "He'll call me! Day after tomorrow! That's how we set it up. You'll get your money. I swear it!"

Walde's eyes gleamed alarmingly, but Deke knew he'd bought it when the man demanded to know where.

"He'll call the motel."

"Do not fail." Walde lowered the hammer, then lashed out suddenly and struck him on the cheek with the revolver. Pain shot through his eye while Walde put the gun back inside his jacket. "Get out."

Palms slick with perspiration, he needed two tries to get the door open. The sedan sped away. A few minutes later the woman arrived again and drove him to his car without a word; then she tailgated him to Nighthawk and took up residence in his motel room to wait for David's call. He thought his heart would burst.

20

It was a survivor from the sixties, having escaped Malibu developers, wind-driven wildfires, and mud slides that occurred as regularly each year as spring—a single-story hillside complex consisting of three moderate-size apartments, each with a view of the ocean. An ancient covering of ivory bougainvillea had crawled over the outside of the building and onto the roof; twin vats of Japanese honeysuckle had been carefully trained into a trellis archway. Steps descended to a minuscule, secluded patio, executed in an old-fashioned reverse-V pattern of moist, moss-coated brick. No alarm wiring as far as he could discover. A rustic black mailbox had RYAN hand-painted in block lettering on its side, and was empty of mail.

Hathaway ducked through the greenery. It took thirty seconds to tape the brittle window glass on the side door against breakage, a minute to jimmy the lock. He took a final drag on his cigarette, snuffed it against the heel of his shoe, pocketed the butt before stepping inside. Three minutes to invade her privacy. He exhaled and set to work.

Julie Ryan was a neat freak. Excellent taste, but a neat freak nonetheless. In the late afternoon sunlight seeping through sheer sea-ward curtains, the cream-colored cane print on her living room furniture was warm and inviting. Lemon and celadon silk and rich watermelon velvet throw pillows were perched on either end of the sofa, adding a tropical flavor to the charm. Citrine, moss, and vermilion candles were positioned around the room; needlepoint pillows of sleeping cats had been placed at precise angles on a small wing chair. Paperbacks were aligned on two rows of bookshelves with their spines in an orderly line that a drill sergeant would have admired, with bestsellers separated from mysteries, and magazines in stacks according to title. Real-estate publications.

The second bedroom had been converted into an office, and just inside the door a small table held various pieces of outgoing mail with notes attached indicating mailing dates at the end of the month. No trash of any sort in the wastebaskets; no pens out of their holders, no clutter, no messages on her answering machine. Computer and printer off and covered.

Miss Ryan was organized to the nth degree. Not the kind of place he'd expected. Ivory business cards for a Malibu real-estate firm resided in a gold metal holder. He took one.

Next he made a swift examination of her bedroom. An impeccably feminine, peach-colored bedspread, matching curtains, lace-edged pillowcases and shams. More candles, lemon and aubergine.

Clothing in her closet was relatively sparse for a woman, well-tailored and arranged by color groupings; slacks were separated from skirts, blouses from jackets. The only touch of the color she obviously loved was a small group of summer sundresses that looked to be a recent purchase, with price tags still attached.

Shoes stood at attention in a neat row underneath, red sandals at one end, black two-inch heels at the other—sensible, well polished, and not one pair run down at the heels. All size six. An expensive black cocktail dress and a pair of satin evening pumps were residents of plastic bags.

There was nothing to indicate a man in her life; usually a shirt or a tie in a woman's closet revealed a relationship, but not in this case. If David was her partner, there was no evidence of him. Bricks of moth crystals hung at intervals along the closet's dowel, one slightly to the left of center. Breaking a long-standing practice never to touch anything, he nudged it half an inch to restore order, which in this instance he felt was justified.

He glanced around again. No photographs in this room, either. Odd. People usually had at least one portrait of themselves on display. Pushing the door closed, he abandoned the bedroom for the kitchen and opened the refrigerator. Practically empty: no eggs, milk, open cartons, or fresh vegetables, nothing that would spoil. She'd been planning to be away for several days. Neatly stacked tins of cat food on the food shelves indicated at least one animal; its bowl had been washed and stood empty next to a dry water dish.

Whatever her role in the matter, from the looks of things she had every intention of returning to her apartment. Five minutes had not elapsed before he let himself out. When he reached his car, he called a friend to arrange surveillance, then lit a cigarette. As he waited for the man to arrive, he assessed what he knew and was dissatisfied.

Everything he'd learned about David from Morganer's files didn't fit a profile that Julie Ryan would choose. The man was messy. He'd made a mess of his life and a mess of his future. After pissing off Earl Morganer, the details of which hadn't been mentioned in any of the investigations, there'd been a downward spiral of cheap apartments, sporadic series of short-lived relationships with women interspersed with monastic abstinence, and, in a one-eighty choice from his former career in investments, he'd chosen dangerous occupations in half a dozen states. Bridge maintenance in Oregon and California. High steel work in Nevada, Oregon, and Arizona. Almost as if he had a death wish, and always ending in dismissal. Always moving on.

Finally, labor in the timber industry in Washington and Oregon, topping trees. A hazardous occupation at best, until a year ago, when he'd moved to Santa Barbara and, on Deke's recommendation, had been hired at Ambassador under his direct supervision. Until filling in for Deke and disappearing with half a million dollars, David had been a model employee.

One thing was certain: It had cost Earl Morganer one hell of a lot of money to keep detectives on his tail. There were year-long breaks in which the kid hadn't held a job and had led a quasi-nomadic existence. Unless he was losing his touch, this wasn't the kind of man who'd partner up with a neat freak like Julie Ryan. Or vice versa. Something was out of sync.

When Jack Bailey arrived, Ron briefed him on the layout of her apartment, then headed toward Santa Barbara, still dissatisfied. There'd been two firms keeping track of this guy for nine years. From what he could tell, David hadn't gone to any particular effort to evade Morganer's spies, had always paid his bills and left forwarding addresses. Not the actions of a man with anything to hide, or trying to disappear.

But why two firms? So one could check on the other?

Julie got out of the taxi, weary to her bones but convinced she'd made the right decision. Stubbornly refusing to spend the cash he'd left in her purse, she'd blown out her credit card by dropping the Bronco at Seattle's airport and grabbing a flight home; the need to restore order in her life and return to safety had been paramount.

"If you'd help me with the cat food, I'd really appreciate it," she entreated the driver.

The good-natured cabbie grabbed the carton of tinned Kitty Krumbles that was now part of her luggage and deposited it in front of her door, made a return trip for her backpack and the two sleeping bags, and placed them side by side. Elmore, whirring with annoyance inside his cardboard carrier, was grumpy from being confined during the flight, as well as the ride from the airport, and she was grumpy herself, but desperately glad to be home.

She paid the driver but waited until he'd driven away before letting herself inside. After wrestling everything into the living room, including the sleeping bag she'd inherited, she closed the front door and locked it securely, then freed the cat. Finally, when every light in the living room was on, she paused to draw a deep breath. The apartment contained a vague aroma she couldn't quite identify, and needed a good airing out. Elmore was stalking stiffly toward the kitchen. A creepy feeling settled onto her shoulders as she followed him in, turned on the light, and filled his water dish. The odor was everywhere.

She went into the bathroom, switched on the light there and in the bedroom as well, and dumped her purse and backpack onto the bed. His bedroll was visible through the doorway; she'd tried to abandon the damned thing, but the Hertz employee had found it and caught up to her at the airport shuttle. At the very last minute, she'd decided to drag it home so Elmore could sleep on it.

She returned to the living room. The creepy feeling crawled down her back as she stared at the cat food carton; its flaps had been hastily taped over and her address scrawled on its side. The bedroll wasn't the only thing she'd inherited. Elmore was skulking on stiff legs from the kitchen to the doorway to her office, suspicion in every step, something he did when Ned had stopped by or she'd had a visitor she didn't like. Eyeing her, he returned to the kitchen.

"What? You're making me nervous," she challenged him. "We're home. Isn't that sufficient?"

Three minutes later she had the uneasy feeling that the air was out of place. Hair on the back of her neck stood on end as she identified the odor: a blend of a man's cologne and cigarette smoke. The eerie feeling ballooned when she noticed strange markings on the window of her side door. Three of them, in a crisscross pattern. She was examining the marks when the phone rang, startling her upright; Elmore jumped straight into the air, then came down sideways.

Who on earth would be calling at this hour? She picked up the receiver as if it were contagious. "Yes?"

"I'm sorry to disturb you, dear." It was Mrs. Lieberman, her seventy-three-year-old neighbor. "I saw your lights go on and I wasn't expecting you home until next week, so I just thought I'd call and see if everything was all right."

"I came back early, but I appreciate your keeping an eye out. Thank you."

"That's quite all right, dear. I was up anyway—insomnia, you know. Can't sleep most of the time. Was there a note from your visitor?"

"Excuse me?"

"Well, I assumed he was a friend of yours. He was on your patio earlier this evening. I almost called the police, but then when I saw him go out, I thought maybe he'd left you a note."

Absurdly, her first thought was of David, which she instantly dismissed as foolish and unwelcome. "What did he look like?"

"Tall black fellow, dressed real nice in a tan jacket and navy slacks. Short haircut, very neat, no sideburns or mustache or anything like that. Real nice shoes. Fortyish, I'd say. Attractive—to a much younger woman, of course."

Someone *had* been in her home! "Thanks, Mrs. Lieberman. I appreciate your calling me, but I've been traveling all day and I'm pretty tired."

"Oh, I understand, dear. I wish I could get tired. . . ."

She heard nothing further of Mrs. Lieberman's difficulties. She said a quick goodbye and put down the phone, snatched scissors from a kitchen drawer, and ran into the living room to cut the tape away from the carton of cat food. Yanking open the flap, she grabbed the handgun and its clip of bullets from their hiding place. Luckily, tins of cat food shipped with a cat had raised no eyebrows, because without the gun at this moment, she'd be headed for the door, screaming.

Rattling with nerves, she inserted the clip and used both hands to steady the pistol in front of her. She hadn't been crazy. Someone had been in her home. The door to her clothes closet was slightly ajar, which happened if you didn't close it firmly. She held the gun at the ready and satisfied herself that no one was inside the closet, then combed through the rest of the apartment.

When she was convinced it was empty of threat, she tried to relax enough to think. It was remotely possible that a husband or boyfriend of one of her girlfriends might have stopped by, but not logical. The most obvious person to be spying on her was the investigator who'd asked Willie about her and David. *Tall, good-lookin' fella, suit-and-tie type.* Ron Hathaway had known her name; somehow he'd discovered where she lived. She'd bet money on it. Whoever he was, he hadn't counted on Mrs. Lieberman.

Wired, she went from room to room, unable to discover anything missing; nothing was out of place, not even touched, as far as she could tell. Nothing to tell the police. Unnerved, she went through the apartment again, double-checking the locks on doors and windows; she pushed a kitchen chair up under the doorknob to the side door, piled metal cookware on its seat as an extra precaution, then collected Elmore and laid down on the bed with him. Not likely she'd be able to sleep, but if she did, it would be fully clothed!

The tabby's ears were twitchy, alert to every sound, mirroring her tension. Equally twitchy, and angry on top of it, she tucked the gun out of her sight. None of this would have happened if she hadn't dug David whoever-the-hell-he-was out from under a tree!

She had a thousand dollars of his money in her purse, his bedroll in her living room, and a lethal weapon that belonged to him under her pillow, but she didn't know his name. Try explaining that to a private investigator, or the police.

A little after ten o'clock that night David pulled out of the Avis lot and headed for the San Diego freeway. At the Santa Monica cutoff he nearly gave in to an urge to let the powerful Lincoln take him up the coast, to the address in Malibu she'd listed on the Bronco's rental papers. The knowledge that she couldn't see worth a damn after dark and would have to be holed up somewhere near San Francisco kept him on Route 405 to the Ventura freeway north.

One solace: L.A. freeways were familiar. North of Westwood, he recognized the palatial, hilltop Getty Center. He'd known the airport at Las Vegas, too, enabling him to make an instant walk-on connection to LAX, where the car he'd reserved with Rocklin's credit card was waiting. That the card had been accepted was confusing. False identification shouldn't pan out. Or should it? At any rate, his trip turned out to be smooth as clockwork, leaving his mind free to miss her.

From the instant he'd stepped out the back door of the restaurant, he'd been as vulnerable as an infant. Quite unexpectedly, a raw, painful hole had spread through his chest during the taxi ride to Wenatchee's airport, and waiting for the commuter flight to Vegas had tested his mettle to the breaking point. Only when the plane had left the ground had it been possible to long for her presence.

Thoughts of her hadn't left him for a moment. She was a growing obsession. His statement in the restaurant had been true; he'd been in bed with a number of women over the past several years, drunk and sober, trying to find his wife, replace her, or erase the pain of her from his life, but there'd been no one like the woman he'd made love with this morning. He'd done things to Julie, for Julie, that he'd never even considered with another woman. Somehow she'd filled in the missing piece of him that other women couldn't.

The driving force behind leaving her had been

her safety. The moment he'd heard they were being investigated, he'd decided they had to separate—as soon as he was certain they weren't being followed. Whoever was looking for him wouldn't be able to track her until she arrived at her apartment, which should take at least another day. In the meantime, if he could find some answers at Rocklin's, he'd have a better handle on how to proceed. He'd return to Malibu and make sure no one traced her to California, then figure out his life from there.

The mere thought of seeing her again pleasantly roller-coastered his stomach—though he would prefer having her soft and warm and naked under him. Sweet Marie, he wanted to make love to her again, then keep himself inside that body and never climb out of her bed. He inched up the Lincoln's speed and moved into the fast lane. Missing her was a bigger, blacker hole than the loss of his identity.

But his identity was coming back! And as soon as he knew who he was . . .

The closer he came to Santa Barbara, the more familiar everything seemed. Anticipation built. Maybe there would be an end to this craziness after all. Arriving in the center of town, he automatically took the second off-ramp, traveled north for a dozen blocks, made a right onto Fitch for half a mile or so, and took a second right onto Eldorado. He didn't even have to look for the number; he recognized the gate and pulled into the driveway. The homes in the neighborhood were huge but overwhelmingly familiar. Apparently he lived here. God forbid, he was a cheating husband about to be faced with some hard choices.

Unable to deal with the jumble spinning through his head, he shut everything down and allowed his body to go through the motions of parking the car and shouldering his backpack. He approached the stately, two-story mansion with its elegant landscaping and security lighting, passed a massive swimming pool; a house key was waiting under a small pot of geraniums, and he let himself inside. Terracotta flooring, Southwestern decor, oversize oak furniture—everything falling into place and holding an aura of discovery at the same time.

More and more at ease, he opened the hall closet and sorted through the clothing: a worn brown lightweight wool sweater with a button missing was familiar, as was a ski jacket. Nothing feminine. On the closet shelf was a motorcycle helmet that had seen hard use. He closed the door.

A hallway led to an immaculate kitchen. Down the hall was a bath; opposite, a bedroom. He pushed open the door and recognized the room, then foot-shoved the backpack under the bed and studied the pictures of himself and Derek in frames on a bureau top. He shook his head at the obvious. Julie was going to—

A small sound behind him caused him to spin around. A woman holding a portable phone was peeking through the window at him, her voice barely audible through the glass. "It won't be necessary, Officer. Thank you . . . No, I appreciate it."

He cranked open the window and forced a smile. "Hello, Doris."

"David! Where on earth have you been? Everyone's worried themselves sick about you." She dutifully kissed him on the cheek. "What are you doing here? Why haven't you called? I saw the strange car and nearly had the police over here."

It was close to midnight, and the barrage of questions and accusations was overwhelming; she was punching numbers into the phone as she spoke. He was too exhausted even to attempt to keep up with her. Doris, in her finest hour, reigning over chaos—creating most of it. Images and impressions flooded his brain. He was home.

"Derek's been frantic. I can't imagine what he'll say when he finds out you're here. And what on earth happened to you? Your clothing's a mess. You look like you've been in a bus wreck." She paused for breath, then spoke into the receiver. "It's me. You'll never guess who just waltzed in, bold as you please. . . . No, he seems fine." Half a beat later, she handed the phone through the window. "He wants to talk to you." She disappeared into the shrubbery.

Derek's voice was strained. "Do you have the money?" he demanded.

"Yeah, well, hello to you, too."

"Don't screw around. *Do* you?"

A new headache was taking hold. "Of course. Are you okay? You sound frantic." The bottle of aspirin from Dr. Meadows's office was in the pocket of his jacket. "There's been one hell of a glitch. I assume you've figured that out by now."

"Does anyone know you're there—besides Doris, I mean?" Derek's agitated voice bled into his ear. "Anyone?"

"No, I just got home. We've got a few problems. We're going to need to—"

"Don't talk to anybody until I get there! No one, you got that? And tell *her* not to tell anyone! We can still fix this."

Clearly something was wrong. "Okay, no one. What's goin—"

"Tell me again you have the money! Just say it!"

Derek's voice was wired with tension, and David tried to keep in focus. Strength was draining from his limbs, replaced by a desperate need to sleep. "I have the money," he said dutifully. "Where are yo—"

"I'm leaving now." The line disconnected.

Doris came barreling into the bedroom. "Let me talk to him," she commanded.

"He's on his way here." He handed her the phone, now buzzing with a dial tone, and went into the bathroom for a glass of water to wash down the aspirin. The pain in his head was growing and the world was dimming as he came back into the room; he saw rather than heard her exasperation as the line apparently rang busy for several minutes before she gave up. "He doesn't want anyone to know I'm home, Doris."

Explaining his exhaustion was useless. She understood that he'd been injured and survived a flood, had gotten medical help, had been traveling twelve hours, and would try to make sense of it for her tomorrow, but ten minutes passed under a rain of Doris's disapproval as she tried Derek's number a dozen times. The pounding of her voice was incessant as he did his best to concentrate. Why hadn't he called . . . and why hadn't he let her know what he'd been doing . . . and why wasn't Derek answering his phone? When the codeine kicked in, he politely said good night, lay down on the bed, and went to sleep while she was still talking.

Two miles away, in the San Joaquin Apartments, Hathaway's phone jangled him awake. "She's home—and alone," said Bailey conversationally. "Came in a taxi about an hour ago. Had a cat in a plane carrier."

"A cat," he agreed, and nodded into the darkness.

"Took in a backpack and a couple of bedrolls."

"Two?"

"And a box of cat food."

It was half past twelve. "Thanks, Jack. Let me know if she leaves. Whatever you do, don't lose her."

Two bedrolls. One of them had to be David's. An indication, at least, that she'd be seeing him again. Half the pieces of the puzzle located, Hathaway went back to sleep.

21

WEDNESDAY

In the dark the clock at her bedside marked passing seconds with infuriatingly faithful ticks, faint, lifeless, and more regular than a heart beating.

Every time she sank close to sleep, he eased into bed to press soft, warm skin to her, slide his hands along her body, inside her defenses. He'd make love to her, lips burning through her senses, tasting her, teasing her, dispensing gentle nips and licks and bites in the midst of the deepest, most intimate of kisses. She'd almost lose herself, then come blearily awake unsatisfied, thick with pressure. Alone.

Idiot! She should never have slept with him!

At four A.M. she climbed out of bed, exhausted, to thaw a container of orange juice in the microwave. Splashing warm juice and a healthy amount of vodka into a tumbler, she downed the lot of it without benefit of ice. The last time she saw the clock, it was 5:15, but her eyes opened at seven and would not close again; she hid from the world for another hour, then gave up and dragged her way into the bathroom for a shower—after checking the doors and windows a second time. Drying her hair, she made some decisions.

First she was going to call the locksmith and arrange to have a deadbolt installed on the side door as soon as possible. Then she was going to Santa Barbara. If she could find David, or D.B., or whoever he was this week, he could damn well have his bedroll, his thousand dollars, and his handgun in exchange for some answers! Starting with who was prowling around in her home, and her life.

And why he'd walked out on her . . .

At nine-fifteen Ron Hathaway stepped out of his shower to receive another call from Jackson Bailey. "She's headed north. Got her two cars ahead of me on the Pacific Coast Highway."

"Stay on her." Hathaway hung up, then left word at his office that he'd be out for the morning. Half an hour later Bailey notified him that she'd left 101 and was burning up the interstate. "I pulled up close enough to get a good look at her. She's one pissed-off lady. Cussing and carrying on, giving somebody hell. Nothing in the car except a cat. If she's got anything else, it went in the trunk before she left her garage."

"Let me guess, attractive?"

"Oh, yeah." From the taciturn Bailey's tone, this was a four-star review.

An hour later Jack confirmed that she'd gotten off the freeway, had stopped for directions, and was driving along Fitch Avenue. Hathaway speculated on her actions. Any way it went down, arriving home with camping gear one day and driving to Santa Barbara the next made things a wee bit too cozy between David and Julie Ryan to qualify as coincidence. Somehow they were in this together. No question about it. Hathaway grabbed his keys and headed for David's place on Eldorado.

He debated whether to notify DePasse and decided against it. Nothing blew off cooperation faster than too many suits and credentials. Besides, if David was as smart as Earl Morganer claimed, involving the attractive Miss Ryan in a clubby little conclave with his family wasn't a logical move in this game. More information was required before calling in heavier guns.

Julie turned onto Eldorado Court and stopped in front of the house, conscious of the upscale neighborhood. She'd vented her spleen for the past hundred miles, and now that she was here, she wasn't sure she still had enough steam to go through with it. This was pretty ritzy territory, even for Santa Barbara. She popped the Camaro's trunk and yanked out the bedroll. A gray Honda Civic pulled to the curb half a block behind her, but the driver didn't get out. She realized she'd seen a similar car a few minutes earlier—in the parking lot of a convenience store where she'd asked for directions.

Unquestionably, there'd been someone in her home. If she was being followed as well, she'd led whoever it was directly to Derek Rocklin's address. Jittery, she was undecided whether to drive away or go for it when the front door to the house swung open. A woman wearing absurdly high heels and a genuinely ugly purple housecoat had opened the door to admit a seal-point Siamese. Mrs. Rocklin? Her heart rate shifted to a higher gear. Elmore rubbed his whiskers against the car window, then curled up to wait for her on the driver's seat. The woman stood patiently while the Siamese took its sweet time about crossing the threshold. *Cat lovers can't be all bad,* Julie reasoned, and left the car.

Just inside the entrance to the Rocklin property, she peeked back at the waiting Honda and saw another vehicle approach and stop alongside. The drivers talked to each other for a few seconds, then both cars backed around the corner; when the first one drove away, she decided she'd been mistaken. Having traveled entirely too far this morning to let her imagination run away with things, she lugged the sleeping bag to the front door and rang the bell.

The cat woman reappeared, giving her and the bedroll an acerbic appraisal. "How can I help you?"

The flirty little sundress had been a tactical error, and she was wearing entirely too much makeup. "Are you Mrs. Rocklin?"

"What do you want?"

Julie tried to ignore the woman's abrasive attitude and forged ahead. "Actually, I'm looking for Derek Rocklin. Does he live here?"

"Yes." The woman's curiosity evolved to a stony suspicion. "And who are you?"

"My name's Julie Ryan." She paused for a response that was not forthcoming. "We met during the storm . . . in Washington. I take it he hasn't mentioned me."

"Mentioned . . . ?" Eyebrows rose. "I'm afraid not. What do you want?"

The blond woman was guarding the doorway like a purple centurion, and Julie was tiring of what was rapidly becoming a verbal fencing match. If he'd said anything about being rescued, her name hadn't come into it; obviously there were additional circumstances to their encounter that he'd want to keep hidden. Unfortunately, she'd begun this conversation, and in order to bring it to an end, there was only one safe way to proceed. "I'd like to speak to Derek, if you don't mind."

"I do mind, and I suggest you speak with me first. I assure you it won't happen the other way around."

"Doris . . ." Over the woman's shoulder, she saw him casually enter the foyer, blond hair wetly combed against his skull, still incredibly handsome. A large expanse of familiar chest was visible under a turquoise robe carelessly knotted at his waist. He *was* married. Pain struck, pounding her senseless. He seemed equally shocked, and his pale eyes widened at the sight of her. "Julie! What are you doing here?"

The woman in the doorway retreated a step. "You know this person?"

"She's . . . a friend of mine, Doris."

His eyes were traveling up and down her body as if they were strangers. The hurt was twisting, devastating, taking her breath away, and it took all her willpower to address the man who'd paid her off like a prostitute, then abandoned her in Wenatchee. She'd saved his life! Couldn't he give her that, at least? The indignity of being reduced to "friend" was almost unbearable. Fighting the emotion strangling her throat, she took a death grip on his bedroll to keep her hands from shaking. "I brought his . . ." She tried to focus, to find an exit line so she could retreat down the sidewalk and escape the woman's eyes. "I'm returning this to your husband, Mrs. Rocklin."

"I think you should come inside." His wife's voice was implacable, the purple housecoat in motion. "Maybe one of you will have an explanation."

"As a matter of fact, I do." Stepping forward, he grinned maddeningly and reached for her arm, but Julie evaded his grasp. "I'm just surprised to see her here, that's all."

"I'm sure you are." Julie bit out the words as a warning not to push her. It would take very little to expose his charade; temptation and her temper were both growing. She shook her head. "I'm late. I have to leave."

"I didn't think you'd be home yet, so I was going to—" He looked past her, mild astonishment reflected in his voice. "Hello, Ron."

Julie whirled to find a well-dressed man coming up the walk behind her, silent as a cat, and recognized the driver of the second car. She wasn't crazy—she *had* been followed. The scent of his cologne and a strong presence of smoke and tobacco clinging to his clothing preceded his arrival. "Mr. Hathaway, I presume." Incensed, she found a target for the anger heaving violently in her chest and jabbed her finger against Hathaway's breast pocket. "A free piece of advice: The next place you break into, don't smoke. And skip the cologne. They leave odors. Like a skunk."

She turned on her heel to address the man she'd

been foolish enough to trust ... and sleep with. Under the perceptive gaze of Doris Rocklin, gimlet-eyed and clearly hostile, Julie blushed at the extent of intimacies they'd shared and became even more defensive. "Why is he following me?"

Behind her, Hathaway's voice provided her answer. "Actually, I've been searching for your friend, Miss Ryan. . . . Hello, David."

David? *Not* Derek after all. Somewhere she'd missed a beat, and she tried to catch up. David ... married to Doris. Liar and adulterer after all... brazening it out in front of his wife ... expecting her to go along with the whole thing? Totally confused, she stood aside as David shook hands with Hathaway.

"I've been looking for you, too, Ron," he said. "I think I've straightened most of it out, but there are still a few holes."

"You know him?" Julie was coming out of her skin. "Tell me what's going on, David. Who is he?"

"We'd better go inside," Hathaway responded levelly. "Doris, do you mind? It seems we have quite a few things to discuss."

"Come in, by all means." Doris Rocklin's response was laden with sarcasm. "I love entertaining in my housecoat." Their hostess started up a massive staircase. "Drip on the patio, David, *if* you don't mind."

David had managed to capture Julie by the elbow and was pulling her to his side. "I don't actually live here," he whispered, eyes twinkling at her, "but she lets me use the pool if I'm a good boy. You are gorgeous."

"Fascinating," she said scathingly, and blushed at

the sight of his all but nude body as he opened his robe to flash a wet bathing suit; the covering of hair on his legs was wet as well. She looked away.

"You're jealous," he accused. He gave her one of his enticing grins, then became more serious. "We have a lot to talk about."

Perfectly willing to talk when hell had frozen over, she obstinately clamped her mouth shut. Caught off guard by his accusation of being jealous, still not certain of her ground, she didn't know what to think.

It took a moment to register, but it was impossible not to stare, for the interior of Doris Rocklin's beautiful home was unexpected and jarring: custom grapefruit-colored carpet matched the walls, and burnt metal art pieces and massively intricate paintings in black inks over thick gold and aqua oils burdened a modern decor that had been shoehorned into old-world Spanish architecture. Asymmetrical furniture looked as untouched by humans as it had the day it left the showroom. Self-conscious, Julie dropped David's bedroll inside the door.

He led her down a marbled hallway. "You couldn't have driven. Did you fly from Seattle or San Francisco?"

She refused to answer him. *You figure it out. And you can take that self-satisfied grin elsewhere.* However, she could not deny that his gamboling presence, high-spirited and smiling, plus the pressure of his fingers on her arm, were splitting her focus as sunlit rooms slid by on either side: a massive piano in one, easels and drawing tables in the next; two dining areas, one small and the other gargantuan; a library, the only normal room, with the brief aroma of books and good leather. Her occupation asserted itself in demented sidebar calculations as lesser impressions floated through her consciousness. Metal candelabras, slender floral displays, tortured statuary—in Malibu, bad taste and all, easily $1.2 million, plus the land; on Santa Barbara's hallowed soil, which sold by the inch, bump it up to whatever the traffic would bear.

With a silent Hathaway following close behind them, David was energetically guiding her through the maze of rooms. Knees she'd kissed and thighs she'd scored with her fingernails emerged from his opened robe at every step. Each time she glanced at him, body parts she'd known intimately were defining themselves under the wet bathing suit. Damn the man!

Finally they reentered balmy, coastal sunshine and she was able to inhale deep breaths of salt air, spiked with the heady fragrance of flowers. They'd reached an extensive patio adjacent to a flower garden, bordered on the far edge by a larger-than-average, fully landscaped Jacuzzi. *Another fifty thousand into the pot,* she thought irrationally.

"That dress is, uh . . . pretty terrific. Haven't seen you in one." His attention was total, both teasing and admiring, and she struggled to keep her equilibrium. He seated her at a giant metal and glass patio table, then folded himself into the chair next to her, his blond presence cloaked in turquoise, his interest in her visibly evident. "I've missed you. . . ." The back of his hand brushed her chin, sending her senses into a giddy slide. "You look tired."

"Thanks. Three hours' sleep will do that," she said shortly, determined not to fall under his charm.

When Hathaway sat down, David discreetly covered himself, and she began to fidget between the two men. On one side, a stranger with whom she'd made love, actively attempting to drag her back into his net; on the other, a stranger who had snooped in her closets. At least she could surmise what Hathaway had been looking for: money. Where David was concerned . . .

A maid appeared, shepherding a tea cart across the slate tiling. Carafes of coffee, a fragile Picasso-influenced porcelain service that included cups shaped like sculptures on "painting" saucers, utensils, and finally a platter of cookies were transferred onto the table. The woman left the cart and disappeared as quietly as she'd arrived.

Trappings of wealth didn't necessarily mean that things were civilized, Julie reminded herself, and tried to determine what kind of situation she'd entered. Her tension had multiplied under David's attentions to the point where her chest was aching, but she was determined not to squirm under the scrutiny of either man. Noting the nearest exit just in case, she shook her head to decline a cup of coffee. "I want—"

Hathaway interrupted. "The first thing I need to know is what you're doing here, David."

"I didn't know where else to go." He glanced at his barren wrist. "What time is it?"

"A little after eleven."

"I've only been awake about an hour. I've been trying to reach—"

"Which doesn't answer—"

Julie broke in, determined not to be intimidated, and reached for her purse. "Pardon me, gentlemen, but let me tell you why *I'm* here, okay? I have a busy day, too."

Hathaway stopped the progress of her arm. "Miss Ryan, I'm afraid you'll have to wait."

His peremptory treatment channeled into ferment every emotion that she'd been battling. "Excuse me, but I don't think so!" She shook off his hand and rose from her chair, too wound up to be polite. "You were in my home, without my permission! That's trespassing, so don't tell me I'm going to wait." Incensed, she turned on David. "I want you to tell him, *now,* to stop following me, and to stay out of my apartment! Whatever you two are up to, I'm not involved in any way."

David was staring hard at Hathaway, and she could tell he was disturbed by her accusations. Hathaway looked up evenly. "I went in to see if you had any of the money, but you hadn't come home yet."

David's voice was measured. "Ron, she doesn't."

"I know."

"Really?" Few things were quite so aggravating as being commented upon as if she weren't present. "Well, it so happens I do!" Julie withdrew David's money from her purse and slapped the envelope onto the table, spilling Hathaway's coffee. "Here it is, and now that I don't have it, I'm leaving."

Hathaway looked at her narrowly as he mopped up the liquid with a napkin. "Not quite yet, Miss Ryan. Where's the rest?"

"Ask him. Then you two duke it out, because it doesn't concern me!"

Intent on leaving, she slid David's gun out of her purse. Hathaway drew back and David's calm demeanor vanished. In fact, both men were satisfactorily astonished; having their silent, undivided attention at last, she held the butt of the heavy pistol in one hand while she searched for the bullets with the other and ran down her itemization. "That's the money, your bedroll's in that godawful living room . . . sorry." She found the clip and made room for it in her fist. She shouldered her purse. "And this is me, leaving. I'll keep these until I'm outside, then I'll lay them on the sidewalk. If I see either one of you again, I'm calling the police."

David ignored the gun and caught her by the wrist. "I know you're scared and I don't blame you for being angry, but please sit down." When she refused, he turned to Hathaway. "I gave her the money for saving my life. Sue me." He released her hand and described being rescued.

"Well, it fits with what we know." Hathaway leaned back, less skeptical, but uneasy and keeping one eye on the weapon in her hand as he leafed through the money, counting. "So why is she waving a gun?"

"I am not waving a gun, I'm holding it. It's not loaded."

"Yeah, well, put it away, if you don't mind." He looked at David. "There's a thousand here. Where's the four-ninety-nine that belongs to the insurance company?"

Julie sat down, deflating as the air of anger flowed

out of her chest. Partially reassured, but definitely still at sea, she labored to follow the illogical conversation. "Willie said you were a private investigator."

"I am. For Ambassador Surety." Hathaway read her blank look. "It's an insurance firm."

"If you say so."

"We both work for Ambassador," he said.

She wasn't sure whether to believe them. "I've never heard of it."

"That's possible, Miss Ryan. We're highly specialized." Hathaway produced a business card and handed it to her. Sure enough, AMBASSADOR SURETY was embossed in discreet lettering, and Hathaway's name was on the card. Which proved nothing. He showed her official-looking identification as well, with the company name also listed on the face of his investigator's license. "I take it David hasn't told you that he was acting as courier for me?"

"No." Relief was coming in waves. "David didn't tell me much of anything, actually." She began to laugh, which was what she always did when she was nervous, and placed the gun and bullets on the glass tabletop. The weapon took an awkward quarter turn to the left before coming to rest.

"Whoa, lady! Careful with that thing." Hathaway pushed the barrel into a safer position.

David picked up the gun, verified that it was empty, then put it and the clip of bullets into the pocket of his robe. He shrugged expressively, his eyes seducing her. "I still have a few blank spots."

Hathaway wasn't amused. "What does that mean?"

Julie's laughter died at the sight of an agitated man who came charging through the doorway and onto the patio; eyes frantic, suit rumpled, tie askew, he called out David's name, then stopped short at the sight of Hathaway.

Next to her, David rose to his feet. Her first impression of the strident newcomer was that he was strikingly handsome. And incredibly familiar. She began to wonder if she was losing it as the man came to an abrupt halt a few feet away, then spoke to Hathaway. "Is he okay?"

David answered him. "I'm fine. Doris and I tried to reach you just a few minutes ago. . . . What happened to your face?"

"I fell—a suitcase, on the plane . . . uh, turbulence." He looked around distractedly. "Wow, Ron, this is a surprise, right?"

Hathaway had also risen to his feet. "Deke?"

"Doris called and . . . I drove to Spokane last night, and . . . well, I'm here." He limped to David and pulled him into a rough embrace. "Are you sure you're all right?"

Julie's jaw went soft. "David *Rocklin*," she whispered, dumbfounded.

Hathaway overheard, and while his swift glance was puzzled, she'd found a raft in a sea of confusion: the man who'd gone to her head, who'd made an indelible mark on her sex life, was David Rocklin . . . an insurance courier, not a drug dealer! She stared at the brothers, who were unquestionably peas from the same pod. Not twins, but close enough in appearance to be mistaken for them, down to the bruises on both their faces. Affectionately pummeling his brother on the back, David was obviously younger, twenty pounds thinner, and just slightly taller.

Behind them, a flash of purple appeared in the doorway. Doris's housecoat. The woman was strange, lurking in the hallway of her own home. The whole situation was strange. Hathaway's voice brought her back to the table. "Deke, this is Julie Ryan. Boot size, six."

She looked at Hathaway with renewed irritation. "According to every shoe in my closet." She nodded an acknowledgment to David's brother, but spoke to Hathaway. "Actually, the boots are a seven. They ran small."

They shifted seating to make room at the table for Deke and his ankle cast. Hathaway pocketed the envelope of cash. "We were about to get to the balance of the ransom."

Ransom? This time Julie's jaw dropped.

"You do have it, don't you, David?"

David looked from his brother to Hathaway, apprehension taking hold in his face as he approached the table. "Tell me it's not a person."

Hathaway was staring at him. "What the devil are you talking about?"

"Ron, there are holes! Is someone in danger, yes or no?" David demanded.

"No! What's the matter with you?"

"It's not a person," David repeated, relief in his voice, and sank into his chair. "Then it's a ransom for what? I don't have it all yet."

"Don't have all what? The money?" Hathaway accused impatiently. "Is that what you mean by holes?"

David was inexplicably silent, his eyes locked on his brother's face. Tension was increasing between the three men, and Julie held her breath, waiting for David's response. Cries of gulls drifted in on the ocean breeze, along with the explosive bristle of air being expelled as sprinklers started up in the garden. Uneasy, Julie spoke into the protracted gap in the conversation. "He has amnesia. He didn't know why he had the money."

Hathaway's expression was as boggled as Deke's. David looked uncomfortable. "Technically, traumatic short-term—"

The legs of Hathaway's metal chair scraped against slate, a harsh and hostile sound. He leaped to his feet and began to circle the patio, increasingly agitated. "If you are trying to tell me he doesn't know where it is . . ." His voice grew contentious. "That ain't gonna fly. If you two are in this togeth—"

"You said you had it!" Derek's hand shot across the table to clutch at David's arm. "You *swore* to me that you had it!"

Hathaway's suspicious eyes raked the three people surrounding the table. "Somebody better goddamn talk to me!"

22

Deke withdrew his hand from his brother's arm. It had all seemed so simple at the beginning. A small piece of business, really, in the greater scheme of things. No one the wiser. He'd justified it so often, he'd almost believed it. Now it was chaos, and he was staggering under the weight of the foreign thing in his life that was spinning sideways and negating his ability to maintain a cool head.

Hathaway wasn't supposed to be on the patio of his home, furiously pacing around and demanding explanations. It was supposed to have been just David. And the money. But the money wasn't here. Instead, three pairs of curious eyes turned in his direction. Slowly awareness filtered in: His behavior was causing them to think something was wrong. He did his best to pull himself together.

His ankle was throbbing intensely, and he lifted his foot onto an empty chair for relief. The slow tick of his watch was thunderous. With one ear he listened as David explained to Hathaway the extent of his head injury and why it had taken him so long to find his way to Santa Barbara. From time to time the woman, Julie Ryan, verified his brother's story as truth. Over the sound of his watch, his overriding thought was that he'd nearly gotten David killed. And if he didn't do something quickly to get the ransom to Walde, the next body going into a coffin might very well be his own. He endured the passing seconds with his heartbeat pounding away the remainder of his life.

The rapid sound of heels clicking on the patio caused him to spin in fear. Doris! He'd half expected the hellion working with Walde. In appearance the two women weren't remotely similar, but his nerves were so ragged that for a moment his eyes had nearly convinced him otherwise. His angry wife stalked closer, and he fumbled toward kissing her in an attempt to present a normal facade and give himself an opportunity to calm down. "Hello, honey."

"Don't 'honey' me." She proceeded to exhibit a heavy backpack to the four of them. One of the side compartments had been unzipped, and cash was visible inside the opening. "I think this is what you're looking for," she announced. "I saw him hide it last night, and just so there's no misunderstanding, my husband and I have not been parties to this."

Oblivious to Doris's anger, Deke's spirit went on a dizzying ride. The money was here! Somehow he could fix things!

His wife dropped the canvas bag with a thud and turned on his brother in a controlled fury. "David, I never wanted you here. I've allowed it this past year solely to please my husband, but now I want you out. The sooner the better!"

Her angry stride took her out the patio door without waiting for his response. The sound of her heels died away amid the silence around the table. There was no time to straighten it out now; with the appearance of the money, Deke realized that he had a whole new set of problems. Hathaway and his brother were both moving toward the canvas bag.

"There's something I need to explain," David was saying, "I told you there were some holes."

Hathaway ignored him and opened another of the bag's compartments. Stone silent, Deke watched his partner unzip the opposite side. Suddenly furious, Ron dumped the contents onto the floor of the patio. Handfuls of hundred-dollar bills fluttered onto the tiles, and tumbled among them were scores of paperback novels. "Is this what you wanted to explain, David? I assure you, I'm listening."

It was over. Hathaway had been right all along, and Deke couldn't believe it. "I'm a dead man." Unable to stop himself, he sank to his knees; his ankle screeched in protest as he began to count the bills, part of his mind trying to make the rest of the money appear.

Julie gaped at the scene on the patio. Three men were down on their knees. On one side of her, David's brother and Ron Hathaway were sorting through paperback novels, tossing them aside as they collected loose hundred-dollar bills; David, on the other, was pushing the books away from his feet and trying to hold her attention. His eyes were insistent, appealing to her to listen to him.

"I can explain this." He glanced toward the two men accumulating the cash. "More than that, there are a thousand things I want to say to you. About us. I know who I am, and most of my memory's back, but right now . . ." His eyes darted toward Deke and Hathaway again. "If I don't straighten things out, this could get really complicated. Will you stay until I've talked to them?"

Part of it she understood. Obviously the bulk of the money was missing and he'd be called upon to come up with it. Also missing was the reason that the thief, her lover, the man who'd walked out on her yesterday, wanted her to stay. Her anger was dissipating and she was falling under his spell again. He'd been right; she could deny it all she wanted, but she had been jealous of Doris. Blind with it.

Sticking around to hear the tale had all the earmarks of being emotionally fatal. What she should do was get the hell out. But she was . . . not quite captivated, but definitely intrigued. Somewhere between a restaurant in Wenatchee and the Rocklins' expensive patio, David had replaced a ransom of nearly half a million dollars with a batch of second-hand romance novels. Actually, the last time she'd seen all the money was in the cabin. D.B. Cooper would have been proud.

"Tell me you won't leave. Julie, please!"

Any logic and reason she might have brought to the battle lost out to novelty, and probably showmanship, but she personally gave in to seductive green eyes that had gone mystical on her yesterday morning. "Convince them that I had nothing to do with it," she demanded sourly. Not much of a concession, but better than nothing at all.

"Absolutely. I promise."

"I don't want promises. And I don't want money," she added hastily. "I want explanations."

Next to her, Hathaway got to his feet, a fistful of cash in each hand. "I want explanations *and* money. Gentlemen, we'll discuss this in private," he said abruptly. "Miss Ryan, since you obviously have an involvement in this matter, I'm afraid you will be required to stay."

"Required . . ." She stared at him, unwilling to yield to a man who'd broken into her home and poked among her possessions. "Under what authority?"

He stiffened at her resistance. "Would you prefer bringing the police into this?"

"Or what? You get to break into my apartment and look for money again?" Rage built in her chest. "At the moment, the police sound like a very good idea. Let's call them," she challenged.

"No!" Derek Rocklin's voice was insistent, but Hathaway disregarded the opinion to hold Julie's gaze.

"Okay by me," he said tersely.

David stepped between them. "She doesn't have anything to do with this, Ron."

Hathaway wasn't convinced. "That's fine, David. You come into the library and tell me all about it," he said heatedly, "then we'll see if Miss Ryan's version corroborates. In the meantime, if I were you, I'd strongly advise her not to leave."

Julie gathered her dignity. "I'll stay exactly one hour. Then I don't care what you do, I'm gone."

David kissed her fingers. "Thank you."

The three men disappeared into the house. If she remembered correctly, the library was three doors down the hall corridor, on the left. An uneasy shiver ran up her spine.

Fifteen minutes later, as if summoned by ill fortune, Doris Rocklin appeared on the patio. She'd changed from the hideous housecoat into an elegant periwinkle pantsuit; impeccable makeup and enormous diamond-stud earrings were in place, her hair smoothly fashioned into a French knot at the nape of her neck. She was the personification of chic as she paused to pour a cup of coffee. However, the circlet of diamonds next to a large engagement ring was throwing light unmercifully; Doris's hands were less than steady.

"I see you're still on my property."

"They're in the library. I . . . decided to wait out here."

Seating herself opposite, Mrs. Rocklin folded her arms across her chest, left over right so that her wedding rings were fully displayed. She gave Julie a rude inspection. "At least you're a step up. The last one looked as if she needed a bath."

"I beg your pardon?"

"Just how 'friendly' are you with David? You don't look like his type."

Julie estimated her opponent. At the moment, rage for rage, they were pretty evenly matched.

"Apparently there's some reason we're supposed to be enemies," Julie said tartly. "If so, I have forty-five minutes to kill, so let's get to it."

"Let's do that." Doris set her cup down with a

crash that threatened the porcelain. "You didn't come here to see David. You asked to speak with my husband. And David didn't expect you, that's for sure, which tells me he's covering for Derek." She sat forward aggressively. "If it was an affair, it was over some time ago. And if it's money, you won't get any. I'll see to that."

Mrs. Rocklin's attempt to toss out a peremptory challenge had failed miserably. Julie almost felt sorry for her. Cocooned by wealth and luxury, protected by her zip code and her million-dollar home overstuffed with ugly, expensive art and uglier furniture, Doris Rocklin should have considered herself safe from all comers.

It was an odd feeling to have the power to strike out at the woman. One vicious lie could wreck this marriage for weeks, maybe do permanent damage. But hurting Doris was the equivalent of a karate chop to a child: cruel and pointless. "The only thing I know about your husband is that he's David's brother," she said evenly, and explained the circumstances of their meeting, then improvised enough recent detail to keep it simple. "I took him as far as the airport in Wenatchee," she said wryly. "He left his sleeping bag in my car, so I decided to return it." She described the flood and his having risked his life for her; by the time she'd finished, David's sister-in-law seemed mollified to the extent of voicing concern.

"Do you think he's all right?"

"He seems much better, but he'll probably need familiar surroundings for a while."

"Well, he's going to have to leave. He moved in here a year ago, and my husband's been upset ever since. Now this. Derek's been chasing all over the country—with a broken ankle, mind you—and going out of his mind with worry, and it's solely because of David. You saw him arrive just now, all upset and limping. When David lied about the money, well, it was the last straw."

Julie elected not to pursue the matter. More interested in David than in the money, she framed a question instead. "You *were* talking about David when you implied that I was unusual in his life?"

"Of course I meant David. My husband would never . . ." Defensive, Doris fingered her wedding ring. "Women in David's life come and go like taxis. He's famous for it. I've never seen the same one twice."

Not surprising, given his looks and various other abilities, but disappointing nonetheless. "Odd, that hasn't been my impression at all, and I've spent quite a bit of time with him during the past few days. He's told me about the death of his wife. Did you know her?"

Doris's voice became cautious. "I'm surprised he said anything. He never talks about it."

"He's mentioned her a couple of times, actually. It was a terrible loss for him. I understand she was very young."

"Eighteen . . . *barely*." Doris's emphasis expressed volumes.

"That is young to be married," she agreed. "How old was he?"

"Twenty-two, I think."

Julie tried to tread lightly. "Did she commit suicide?"

"Good heavens, no."

"He said it was investigated. That generally implies—"

"Of course it was investigated. She was Earl Morganer's daughter." The fact was articulated as if it was sufficient reason in and of itself.

"But . . . there was some question about what happened?"

Doris laughed, a small, tight sound. "Earl Morganer was her father, and he wanted an investigation. You wouldn't understand." Her hostess smoothed the velvet of her sleeve with perfectly manicured nails, then spoke to Julie as if she were the high-school dweeb. "Gina was his princess. She was an only child, a classic example of a spoiled little rich girl, and set to inherit the Morganer empire until she ran away to marry someone her father didn't like. Men will give their daughters in marriage, sometimes to a husband they don't approve of, but they *never* let someone take them. And they don't forgive."

Restless, she stared at the horizon. "Wealthy fathers have a great deal of patience. . . ." She collected herself. "Earl Morganer would have gotten her back. I assure you, the only reason he lost the war is because she died."

Doris Rocklin had the conviction of someone with firsthand experience, and Julie was saddened. In the last few seconds an unpleasant subtext of the woman's life had become visible, and it didn't require genius to change the names and fill in the blanks. Nickels to doughnuts, Mrs. Rocklin was an only child.

As if realizing the window she'd opened into her

own life, Doris suddenly changed the subject. "What do you do?"

"I'm a real-estate agent."

"Really . . ." Doris eyed her shrewdly. "So what would you say this property is worth?"

"What's the acreage?"

Doris told her.

She calculated rapidly, determined to pass the test. "Including the furniture but excluding the art, two million three."

Doris raised an eyebrow, indicating a qualified respect.

Julie took her turn. "How long has your husband worked as an insurance investigator?"

"Nearly ten years." Doris's lingering suspicion was overtaken by enormous pride. "He was recruited right out of college. He and David look a great deal alike, but they're very different. David was a business major, had a budding career in investments until he fell in love with Gina, but for my husband, it was always about art. What did you think of our collection?"

"It's interesting," Julie said, resorting to diplomacy. "I noticed it earlier."

"It all belongs to my father. Derek hates most of the paintings, but they came with the house."

Which still belongs to Daddy, Julie concluded, *or they'd have redecorated by now.* "I don't know much about paintings, actually. My sister was part owner of a gallery in Geneva for a while." She was beginning to sympathize with Derek Rocklin. An art lover who had to come home to his father-in-law's garish castle every day? After a few years it could get to be a real bummer. No wonder he looked so unhappy. "Apparently they didn't do too well . . . she had to sell out last year." She toyed with Hathaway's business card, running out of conversation. "So Ambassador insures art?"

"Exclusively. They do a great deal of business with royalty—Middle Eastern and European, mostly. Here in America, it's museum-quality art collections. Anything that's really priceless." She gestured toward the mansion. "My father has several paintings insured with them. Ambassador maintains an internal unit for verification and authentication." Doris's pride softened her face. "My husband is one of their principal investigators; he's been working with Ron for the past seven years. They've had great success in recovering stolen property."

"Mr. Hathaway said David was a courier for him."

"Could be. They're like police officers. Everything at work is confidential and doesn't get discussed with wives. I wouldn't have known David was missing, for instance, if he hadn't been Derek's brother."

The elegant Siamese she'd seen earlier strutted its way onto the patio and cry-whined when it saw its mistress. Julie glanced at her watch. It had been a full hour since she'd left Elmore in the car. He'd be needing a potty break.

"Hello, Eddie, hellooo . . ." Doris became a doting feline owner. "This is Marc Edward Antony the fourth. Say hello to Julie, Eddie. Have you been a good boy today?"

Julie rose to her feet. "Eddie reminds me, I left my cat in the car," she said. "I brought food, but he'll need some water."

"In the car?" Doris was disapproving. "You'll have to bring him inside. I'm sure Eddie has a water dish he can borrow, don't you, Eddie?"

Julie watched in amazement as her hostess granted more interest and compassion to an animal than she'd shown all morning to any of the humans present, including her husband. A truly angry woman.

23

David paced his brother's study, irritated that Hathaway wouldn't let him leave long enough to get dressed. The robe had been flapping around his knees for the past twenty minutes, and the weapon in its pocket was an awkward weight that bumped against his thigh every time he moved.

"You really think I'm an idiot? Just because I didn't know my identity didn't make me dumb enough to run around with half a million dollars in a backpack." The comment was sharper than he'd intended. "I lost my memory, Ron, not my intelligence."

He checked out the window for the fiftieth time. She was still there; halfway to the gazebo, and introducing the diminutive Elmore to his sister-in-law's cat. It was hatred at first sight, and Eddie took to high ground atop the gazebo. Elmore was ignoring him.

Worry that Julie would leave before he could talk

to her had gnawed at his conscience since he'd left her stewing on the patio. It was his fault that she'd been dragged into this mess. Her entry onto the lawn a few minutes ago had calmed his anxiety, but he was having trouble keeping his eyes away from her long enough to concentrate on the business at hand. The past ten minutes of Hathaway's questioning had evolved to another impasse. His brother, seated in the shadows and talkative as a doorstop, had grown increasingly tense.

"I concede you're not an idiot." Hathaway's frustrated voice yanked him back to the conversation. "I'll even concede that we'll find your cell phone buried under the tree—and you wouldn't have known who to call anyway. I've got the whole picture, David, from the tent to the airport to here. What I don't have is a location for the rest of the money!"

"I've *told* you, I'm not sure where it is, but I know it's safe, and that's all I'm going to say until I have a chance to talk privately with my brother!"

"No one's speaking privately with anyone until I know where that money is."

Derek spoke explosively from the corner. "David, I don't have time for this! Just tell him where it is."

"I told you, I'm not sure."

His brother's effort to calm himself was visible. "We need to get the ransom on track as soon as possible. Our client wants his property back, and we've agreed to make that happen. How many times do we have to say it? If we blow this, it'll be disastrous. For me, for Ron . . . for everybody. We all have jobs on the line here."

David had tried to suspend his suspicions, but Derek's dogged concern for a client didn't fit with his frantic arrival half an hour ago with his face busted in. Last night his brother hadn't asked why he'd been missing for the past five days, just verified that David had the money. Derek had driven all night to catch a flight when thirty seconds on the phone could have handled everything, and was scared about something he couldn't, or wouldn't, discuss in front of his partner. It had to be the cash.

Well, boys and girls, the cash can wait until I know what is going on.

Hathaway was losing patience. They'd come around again to the same stalemate in the conversation, and the Rocklin brothers were clammed up tight. Time to move things along, he decided. "Deke, when you spoke to David last evening, you knew he was safe and you knew he was here, right?"

"Yes . . . but I came home because I wanted to make sure he was all right."

Hathaway ignored the beeper sounding at his waist in order to bait his trap. "He'd already told you he had the money?"

"I had some of it," David interjected. "What was in the pack."

"But you thought he had it all."

"That's right," Deke said. "But I didn't want to miss the early flight, and I figured we could talk about it when I got here. I knew we'd need it to set up a new drop."

Same answer, word for word, that he'd volunteered at the top of the discussion. Rehearsed, pat, and full of air. "Why didn't you call me?"

Deke paused, visibly thrown at the unexpected question. "It was late, and I knew you'd be sleeping. I told you, I had to leave immediately or miss the plane. It was a four-hour drive to the airport."

"You drove two hundred miles with a phone in the car." Hathaway repeated the question. "Why didn't you call me? Let me know he'd been found, at least? Give the guys out looking for him a rest?"

Deke's strained voice rasped into the hollow quiet of the library. "I tried . . . but I couldn't get the damned thing to work."

The limp excuse fell on the floor between them. "Were the phones at the airport working? Or didn't you have a quarter?"

Deke went silent, and Hathaway glanced at the readout on his pager. *Office. Urgent-ASAP.* He heaved himself to his feet. "I have to call in. Then I'm going to want a better set of answers—from both of you." He walked to the other end of the study and picked up a phone.

David accosted his brother. "You're lying and he knows it." He had about two minutes to extract an explanation. "I have the money, Derek," he said urgently. "But a few minutes ago you nearly passed out when it wasn't in that bag. Who's going to make you a dead man?"

"Where is it? Just tell me where it is!" His brother's voice was hoarse.

"Answer the question, damn it. Who?"

"Nobody! I was afraid I'd lose my job." Derek was trying to shrink into the furniture. "Do you have it with you?"

David physically crowded his brother, getting in his face. "What you *said* was 'dead man,'" he reminded him vehemently. "Does somebody have a piece of you?"

Derek turned to the wall, refusing to look at him. "All you have to do is give up the money, David. Please."

"Tell me you're not in on this." He did his best to keep his voice down so that Hathaway wouldn't hear. "Either say you're not part of it or tell me who's not supposed to know I'm here!"

His brother's voice was a whisper. "You're going to get me killed."

David's stomach twisted at the admission. "Ron's going to be off the phone any second, and we're running out of time."

Hathaway broke into their conversation, startling them both. "Ron's already off the phone . . . and we've heard from our thieves. It seems they know we found the money and they want to set up another drop. I told them to stuff it."

"No! He has the money! We can give it to them," Derek insisted.

"Sure, we can give it to them." Hathaway was unusually bland. "But how'd they know the money was found?"

Deke's eyes darted away. "I don't know."

"Don't you think it's odd that they know?" pursued Hathaway. "My office got the call half an hour ago, and I'm just now finding out about it myself." He settled himself on the couch. "Is there anything either of you wants to tell me?"

"Someone's threatened his life," David said flatly.

Startled, Hathaway stared from one Rocklin to the other. "Is someone going to put me in the loop?"

"It's not true." Deke's voice was all but strangled.

"That's all I know." David shrugged. "But it's how he got the face, I'd bet on it."

Hathaway pivoted toward his partner and exhaled expansively, clearly troubled. "Deke, we've worked together seven years, and I've learned a hell of a lot working under you. I know you to be a good man, but if you're in trouble, you gotta tell me. *Has* someone threatened you?"

Deke was trapped; slowly his shoulders caved in. "Walde. He thinks David stole the money. I have twenty-four hours to get it back."

Hathaway swiveled to David. "Did you? Is that why you're here?"

David shook his head. "I've already told you what happened."

"Yeah, but you didn't manage to mention where the money wound up." When David remained silent, Hathaway switched to Deke. "Are you two in this together?"

"No!" Deke exploded. "He didn't have anything to do with it! It just got screwed up, that's all. It should have been done with by now."

"You're in collusion with a client?" Hathaway was coldly disappointed. "You'd jeopardize everything you've got here? Your wife, your career? Walk me through this, Deke, because I don't understand."

David read desperation in his brother's face. Derek was scared out of his mind, and they had twenty-four hours to deal with whatever was going down. "He'd never agree to a payoff without a reason, Ron, you know that." He bent toward his brother. "How'd he get to you?"

Hathaway reluctantly set aside his position as the junior man in his partnership with Deke. "If you want my help in saving any part of your ass, run it down for me."

"You won't tell Doris?"

"I'll try to keep her out of it. Best I can do." Hathaway was implacable. "Yank me around one time, and you can tell it to a jury. Let's have it from the beginning. Maybe we can fix it."

Deke sighed and seemed to age before their eyes, but it was apparent that he desperately wanted to get things off his chest. "I met him a year ago, in a Vegas lounge. He was bragging that he'd stumbled onto this rare painting and how it was a real coup that Ambassador had insured it. When he found out I was with the company, we palled around, there were drinks—" He started at a gentle tap on the study door and went pale. "Please . . . Doris can't find out about this!"

David went to the door. "Who is it?"

A faint voice was audible in the hallway. "Martin, sir."

He opened the door to Derek's houseman, who had a stack of neatly folded clothing balanced on one hand, a pair of loafers in the other. "Welcome home, David," Martin said fondly. "We're very glad you're safe."

"Me too. Thanks, Martin. I appreciate your bringing these over." He glanced out the window. "The young lady in the gazebo . . . I need to speak with her before she leaves. It's important."

Martin nodded. "She and Mrs. Rocklin will be having lunch in a few minutes. Are you gentlemen having anything?"

"Later, thanks." Lunch would buy him additional time, but not much. Relieved on that front, David took the clothing and closed the door, but his heart was still sinking. His brother's mention of Las Vegas had telegraphed what was coming. "How much?"

There was a long pause. "Ten thousand."

"You wouldn't blow a career for that."

"You're right, it's worse." His brother's face paled to dead white.

Worse meant something to do with Doris. In a corner of the room, David turned his back to the two men and began to dress. "What . . . he set you up with a hooker? I know it's something rotten."

"Doris'll castrate me if she finds out any of it." Derek squinted into the light from the window. "She didn't know I was up there, and I wasn't gambling, I swear. I wouldn't give her old man the satisfaction!" He reined himself in. "I woke up in a hotel room."

Drugged. It figured. David removed the pistol and ammunition from the robe, then tossed the garment aside, trying to keep a growing rage from running away with him. The pieces came together as he slipped the clip of bullets into his trouser pocket and tucked the empty Walther under the waistband at his back, settling the sweater over the .32. "Owing ten thousand . . ."

"Yeah." Deke swallowed hard. "I don't remember any of it, but my name was on all the chits. Walde said he'd take care of it, but I'd have to return the favor. I knew it was blackmail," he said, defeated, "but there was no way I could come up with ten K without her father finding out. And if Doris got wind of it . . . she'd never go against him."

"You saw Walde pay it?" David asked with less impatience—certainly more understanding. Rich fathers he knew about.

"In cash."

Probably the same money, he thought impotently, *but impossible to prove.*

"He said he'd be in touch in about six months."

"Let me guess." David began to speculate. "He shows up, tells you his painting's been stolen, says the thief contacted him directly and wants a ransom?"

Derek nodded, miserable.

"And the price is reasonable; he just wants his painting back."

"Close enough, except I had half the money I owed him."

"Which he took."

"Yes," Derek admitted with embarrassment.

"Covers expenses." Hathaway lit a cigarette. "What are the details David missed?"

"I was supposed to recommend to DePasse that we agree to the price."

"But you knew he was the thief."

"Not at first. I was suspicious, but I didn't know for sure until he wanted to know what kind of traps we'd be setting up to catch him."

Hathaway wasn't buying. "All this for five grand?"

David snorted. "That's when the photos showed up."

His brother dropped his head. "Yeah. They're

pretty bad and I burned them, but so what? Copies'll be showing up for years."

David sighed. Poor Derek. Somewhere down the road Doris was going to find out anyway. Belham money would be too enticing for Walde not to go for blackmail. He jostled his brain; the photos were a future problem that would have to wait. "Then what?"

"DePasse agreed to the price right off the bat. I didn't even have to hustle him—except he assigns me to do the money end. I called Walde to tell him I was dropping the cash and so I couldn't be somewhere to warn him at the same time. I wanted him to call it off, but he wouldn't. Then he offered me fifty thousand to make sure he didn't get caught. And I decided—"

Hathaway stopped him. "Whoa, whoa . . . up from five? You didn't negotiate that?"

"Fifty. That's what he said, I swear." His brother shook his head emphatically.

David broke into a cold sweat. As much as he loved him, Derek had never been the brightest bulb in the box. Hathaway's guarded look confirmed it. Nobody with blackmail in their pocket gives away fifty thousand. Had things gone down as originally planned, Derek might have taken ransom money into the woods, but he wouldn't have come out alive. No witnesses, no fifty thousand dollars.

Subbing for Derek, more than likely David wouldn't have heard the shot that killed him. Who knew how close he'd been to . . . A chill ran through his body. Maybe Julie, too! Suddenly the threat on his brother's life was terribly real. He ran his hand through his hair. Twenty-four hours might not be enough.

24

David stared hard at his brother. "He was supposed to hand me fifty thousand to give to you? When was I going to find out about it?"

"You weren't. I told him to keep it. The money didn't matter; I just wanted out. All I could see was losing Doris, losing my job . . . I didn't know what else to do."

"What *did* you do?"

"I made sure . . . I couldn't go." Deke inadvertently glanced at his cast. "It wasn't—"

David halted in midstep, astonished. "By breaking your leg? You jumped off that railing?"

Hathaway's jaw dropped with shock. *Sweet Jesus!*

"I would have broken my back. . . . Lucky me, it turned out to be an ankle." Deke audibly exhaled and looked at his brother, shame in his face. "I think it's a dead situation for sure, then DePasse calls me in at the last minute, tells me he's getting pressure from upstairs. Things have been dragging on too long, too many people know about it, and they want it cleaned up before it gets embarrassing. He said you'd already agreed to go in my place and we'd probably save a hundred thousand, but I knew if Walde found out it wasn't me, he'd get crazy and—"

"Wait a second. DePasse decided to use—no offense, David—a novice to save money? What are you talking about?"

"Ron, think back for a minute. We'd been tap-dancing for three months with this guy. Two setups blown, and I had to go in to DePasse for an okay every time Walde raised the ante. First it was three hundred thousand, then it was four . . . now it's half a million. Remember, you kept telling me the guy was an amateur?"

Hathaway realized that he was smoking in Doris's house and stubbed the cigarette out. "Yeah."

"So the longer we waited, the higher the ransom was going to be. DePasse wanted to go while it was still cheaper than paying off the policy."

Hathaway looked up, curious. "Why did I think it was your brother's idea?"

"Probably because I told you I didn't think he was ready." Deke inspected the nearby furniture. "It was the absolute wrong place for him to go." He ducked his head, uncomfortable. "I knew he wouldn't give a damn about safety. Not up there. Time was too tight, things were getting sloppy." He sighed, defeated. "I couldn't go, and I couldn't stop him, so I gave him my wallet."

"You made me put Gina's picture in it," David said slowly.

"Yeah! So you'd remember . . . and be careful, you asshole. A lot of good that did."

Unwilling to defend himself against freak accidents, David nodded reflectively. "You were twitching like a cat."

"It didn't feel right. The timing . . . something was off, and you were sitting on too much cash. The location call always comes in at the last minute. You had no experience at this, things happen . . ."

"Talk to me about Walde," Hathaway said quietly.

"I called him to find out how it would go down from his end," Deke explained. "He was using a woman. She wouldn't know he's not me because the picture was gonna match, so I didn't tell Walde it was David. I said that I'd changed my mind about the money if he'd call things square. He said okay, and I crossed my fingers that nothing would go wrong." He sat down, visibly drained. "Then David disappeared."

David was impatient to get to the crux of the threat against his brother's life. "Okay, so I'm gone. Then what?"

Derek got off the couch and stood with his back to them. "The bastard disappeared, too. When I tried to let him know there'd been a problem, I find out his beeper number's been changed. A day went by, I don't hear from him, and we can't find you. I'm terrified you tried to be a hero and he's killed you or something, so I'm going out of my mind. Then the frigging storm comes in and I'm praying my ass off that you're holed up somewhere, that you didn't drown or something. . . ."

Derek's voice caught and it was a moment before he could go on. "Ron's telling me he can't find you and he's getting calls from the woman claiming you two didn't connect. I don't know if it's real, or this is some new kind of scam Walde's pulling. So I flew up there."

Derek wheeled to face them. "Then I hear from him yesterday, and he's screaming about 'Where's the money?' so at least there's the possibility that you're okay." He described Walde's behavior at their meeting. "Said he spent two and half years on this, and if I screw it up, he's going to kill me. I believe him."

David began to pace again. "You couldn't figure out a year ago that someone this volatile would screw up your life?"

"The guy I met was an ice-cold son of a bitch. Yesterday he was a crazy man." Derek gingerly fingered the welt on his cheek. "Said he was worried about going to jail. I didn't get too much of it. . . . Then he sent that Eva Braun he's working with to sit in the motel room with me. Thank God you called. She heard you say you had the money." He took a deep breath. "They had a long conversation on the phone after I hung up with you, in German or something. I wasn't sure she was going to let me leave."

The room went still, everyone's thoughts in the same arena. Kidnapping was automatically a federal offense and under FBI jurisdiction. Walde had known enough to avoid the feds by not demanding a payoff in exchange for Derek. As the only person who could identify Walde or testify against him, Derek was damned lucky to have walked out of Nighthawk alive.

David joined his brother at the window and they looked out at Doris and Julie, seated in the gazebo.

Martin was clearing dishes and serving coffee. "I'm going to lose my wife," Derek said tonelessly.

Hathaway grimaced. "You'll lose more than that. You'll be lucky if DePasse lets you keep your balls and move to Guatemala."

"DePasse is damned lucky he's not dealing with somebody's corpse!" David faced the two men, furious. "Derek meets this guy out of left field and the *first* thing they talk about is what they have in common—Ambassador! Wham, bam, five hours later, my brother's in his pocket. You're the ex-gambler, Derek— what are the odds?" He shook his head, seething. "Or am I the only one who thinks it's convenient that he just happened to have drugs on hand, a willing hooker, and a photographer in the closet?"

"He's a very organized crook," Hathaway conceded. "A setup, damn straight."

"If he worked two and half years on this, that's a patient man, wouldn't you say?" Controlling his anger, David expanded his theory. "He floats for a year and a half, setting up his insurance policy and finding someone from Ambassador who works in fraud. Then he leisurely takes another six months to put it in place?" David was disbelieving. "No, it went into place when someone put him onto my brother. I'd bet on it. Prior to that, this guy had nothing."

"He had a two-million-dollar painting."

"Okay, why didn't he just sell it? I would have, you would have. Why didn't he?"

"Ransom prior to sale nets him a twenty-five percent cash increase," Hathaway postulated. "Goes in the Swiss account, tax free. I'd think about it if I was him."

David nodded agreement. "Okay, so let's say he's a greedy little crook, not entirely stupid, who knows the system and needs an inside man." He considered the possibilities. "Besides you and me, Ron, who at Ambassador knows Derek gambles?"

"Used to."

"Used to. Who'd know where to find him in Vegas when his wife doesn't even know he's up there? Knows what he looks like, not to mention what his job is?"

Hathaway was following the argument closely. "Someone familiar with his home life . . . his secretary?"

"Melba's a sweetheart, but she's a chatty little Cathy. Who knows who she's talked to? Could be anyone in the firm."

"Or outside," Hathaway concurred. "But I agree, we start with Ambassador. So we have a security problem. Compounded by the fact that our thief is suddenly in enough of a rush to threaten your brother's life."

"He took the time to up the ante twice over the past couple of months. Want to bet something recent has happened in Mr. Walde's life? I say the cash he got from Derek is gone, and he's got a major financial problem that's maybe worth killing over. Something or someone has screwed up more than two years of planning, and it's a wild card he can't control—I'll lay odds that's why he called your office, Ron. The ransom money didn't get handed over, and he's figured out that he's got nothing on me that'll deliver it . . . so maybe he's using company pressure. Maybe letting someone at Ambassador know I have it and he still wants to get paid." David stared out the window. "We stall him, keep the squeeze on, what's he going to do?"

"Self-destruct, if we do it right."

David looked at his brother. "He'd have had you followed from the motel, which means he knows you came home. And he assumes the money is here, or will be." In the gazebo, Julie and Doris were rising to their feet. "She can't leave."

Hathaway turned to David. "*Is* it here?"

He shook his head in the negative, distracted. "I gotta think about this, Ron."

"No, you don't. You have to tell me where it is, or I have to get real ugly."

"Ron, if I'd planned to keep it, all I had to say was I'd already given it over . . . and tell Ambassador to prove otherwise. Which is probably what Walde thinks I'll do." David stood for a moment, allowing his peripheral vision to keep track of her movements. "I *have* the money, but I'm not sure where it is at the moment. Let's start from there. This guy thinks I'm out here somewhere with his ransom, right? But he thinks I stole it from *him*, not the insurance company." He turned to Derek. "Think very carefully, because both our lives could depend on it. Does Walde know I was supposed to be the contact?"

"Not from me. I didn't give him a name. Just told him it was a last-minute switch." Derek blinked. "He didn't even ask, just put a gun under my chin."

David's mind recoiled from the image in order to continue. "Which means he may not know. He wouldn't blow leverage like that. He's off his game plan and making mistakes. Ron, who at Ambassador knows I'm home? Anyone?"

"Not yet."

"That buys us time, but we'll have to stall him as long as possible. Derek has to tell him the money's stashed somewhere and he needs some time to arrange a payoff." He glanced at the empty gazebo. Julie and Doris had crossed the lawn and were entering the house. "It's going to take a rat to catch a rat," David said ominously. He quickly went to the door of the study. "Ron, you still want to talk to her?"

"Not unless she knows where the money is."

"Hasn't a clue. We can discuss this later. Right now I need to catch my lady."

"Your lady?" Genuine pleasure washed over his brother's tired face, and Derek removed his glasses to rub the bridge of his nose. "The girl on the patio? After all these years, are you serious?"

Gleeful, David tapped himself on the chest. "Mine."

Hathaway, however, was disgruntled. "Your lady can wait. We're not finished."

Undeterred, David opened the door. "Ron, Walde's a thorough son of a bitch on a two-year arc. More than likely he knows I live here; maybe he knows everything that goes on. By now he could know about Julie, so I'm making sure she doesn't leave. Give me your word you won't call anyone until I agree to it."

"You're out of favors, David."

"It isn't a favor, it's your word. Yes or no?"

"All right, for the moment."

David closed the door.

25

Hathaway couldn't have said, precisely, why he allowed David to leave the library. Nothing short of getting physical would have stopped the man, and in choosing to follow his instincts perhaps it was no more complicated than having lived a minority's life in America's middle-class society among a majority that prejudged, suspected, and distrusted him on sight without basis in fact.

Rather than fall into the same trap, he'd decided early on that in order to survive in life, liars were liars, assholes were assholes, and decent men were decent men. Hands-on experience would be the only thing that counted when it came to making judgments, and someone's being white, or not, generally didn't have a place in his decision making until well into his appraisal of them. The creed had served him well, and the last hour with David Rocklin had made it apparent that somewhere in his thinking he'd made an error in his opinion of Derek's brother.

Aside from Ambassador's personnel file and the records of Earl Morganer's watchdogs, his knowledge of Rocklin had been limited to the twenty hours prior to dropping him off at the side of a gravel road with a backpack of money, a cell phone, and a tent. The man's conduct hadn't been out of the ordinary, although he had seemed unusually calm given the circumstances. He'd been straightforward in his behavior, his eyes direct if somewhat lacking in vitality, but had barely evidenced interest in his assignment beyond the basics of when and how to make sure Ron would be able to follow the money. In retrospect, Deke was right; concern for his own personal safety had been notably absent.

But, based on the man he'd witnessed in the company of Julie Ryan this morning, it was clear that David had been too silent, too lacking in emotion a week ago. This was a new version: a man obstinately refusing to reveal the location of Ambassador's money because he was passionately consumed with the protection of his brother. David's observations of Walde's schemings had been keenly perceptive and incisive, and his conclusions had been in line with his own—in some instances, a few inches ahead.

He was also aware that David had been watching Julie for the past half hour, unable to conceal the kind of feelings for a woman that a man recognizes in another man and envies. David Rocklin was smitten to the point of obsession and wouldn't leave the premises as long as the woman was here. Earl Morganer's fixation on David meandered through his thoughts. "What happened to your brother nine years ago?"

"David?" Deke shook himself out of his torpor.

"He got married. His wife was killed a short time later." He rose slowly to his feet. "Why?"

"His file didn't indicate a marriage."

Deke slowly processed his words. "It isn't in his file for a reason."

"Which is?"

"She had a high-profile family. There was no way her death would pass the company's notice. If they'd started digging . . . anyway, it isn't relevant."

High-profile equaled Morganer, and the pieces could be made to fit: loss of something that couldn't be replaced. A child. No rage deep enough to cover that one.

Deke got off the couch and touched Ron's sleeve in a silent plea. "God knows, he's been through enough hell because of it. David had four days with Gina . . . please don't ask him about it."

Four days . . . on his honeymoon? Sweet, sweet Jesus! The lifestyle and behavior reflected in Morganer's reports began to make a terrible kind of sense. For the past nine years David Rocklin had been looking for a coffin.

"I'd given up." Deke shrugged, obviously hopeful for his brother. "The only reason he agreed to work for Ambassador is because it was the only thing Dad asked before he died . . . and I promised to watch out for him." He gave a hollow laugh. "Some job I've been doing. But, you know, I haven't seen him this happy in . . . She's the first woman he's given a damn about since his wife."

David met Martin coming down the hallway. "She's in the foyer, sir, saying goodbye to Mrs. Rocklin."

"Thank you." He dodged onto the patio, circled the house at a lope, and caught up to her on the walkway, headed toward the street. He quickly blocked her progress. "You promised not to leave."

"I said an hour. It's been two."

"It was complicated. I need just ten more minutes—that's all, I promise. After that you can tell me to go to hell."

"I can tell you that now." But she didn't stop him from taking Elmore out of her arms.

"Ask me anything," he offered, leading her past the pool and along the path toward the guest cottage. "Everything's back. A hundred percent. Well, almost—I didn't have the ransom thing at first, but I do now." He ushered her inside the cottage and freed Elmore to inspect the rooms. The little cat disappeared into the kitchen.

She circled the small living room, keeping the coffee table between them as she, too, inspected his home. "Insurance is boring. I thought you were a drug runner."

Trying not to spook her, he stood stock still, laughing at her honesty. "So did I, until I woke up this morning. Listen, I want to talk to you until you're satisfied that I'm an okay guy. Then—fair warning—I'm going to do everything I can to seduce you." He took a step in her direction, unable to stop himself. "I don't want you to go home."

She stared at him, innocent and forthright as a kitten—alert and watchful as well. "Okay."

He knew it was too easy, but his body sure didn't. Damn, she looked delicious. Enough of her hair was loose from its topknot to create a nimbus in the late afternoon sunlight cutting through a window. Slender thighs he planned to have over his shoulders as soon as possible were suggestive shadows under the white cotton sundress. He wanted to slide the thing with its saucy pattern of stemmed cherries off her body and grab her up, soft and naked the way he'd had her in their honeymoon suite, let those silly sandals hit the floor and have her again. Crush her cherries until she . . . "What's the catch?"

"No catch. But I have a ton of questions." She blinked rapidly, lashes entrancing him. His body quickened, readying itself.

"Might take a week or so to answer them." From the corner of his eye he saw Elmore saunter out of the kitchen, spring onto the couch, and stretch his belly along one of its cushions. "I'll send out for cat food."

He moved in on her. "Can I please kiss you?"

She stood her ground and he took her mouth, met an answering kiss that melted through him; and again, this time hungrily, selfishly. The world tilted south and they wound up together on his bed, his leg firmly across her body, locking her into his embrace. He kissed her, breathed her in, took possession of her breasts, satisfied himself she was his again. "Christ, I want to boff you. But I can't. Not yet."

"I don't boff," she teased, and kissed him senseless. "But I'll make love . . ."

"Oh, yeah, I want to do that, too. All night long . . ." He took a deep breath to level his head, leaned into the discomfort of the Walther pressing painfully into the small of his back. "But there are things you have to know. Eventually I'll tell you everything." He took another breath, trying to settle himself. With her body halfway under him, it was hard—and he was hard against her. Getting harder. No woman since Gina had affected him this way; not even Gina, on some level.

Dealing with reality was the last thing he wanted to do. He eased himself away from her long enough to take the weapon out of its hiding place. "I meant what I said about you not leaving." He denied his body's drive in order to be coherent for a moment. "I want you to stay here tonight, maybe longer." He dragged the bullet clip out of his pocket and put it and the pistol on the side table.

She stiffened at the sight of the gun, and he felt a sober change run through her body. "I thought all this was about art or something. Are you telling me that I'm in some kind of danger?"

"I'm not sure. I just don't want to be sorry, that's all." He held her tight against him. "I don't ever want to be sorry where you're concerned."

She struggled lightly, and he loosened his hold a bit.

"I should go home. My sister's expecting me there tonight. She'll call from Chicago."

"Call her. Let her know where she can find you."

"You're really serious about this."

He kissed her lightly. "Absolutely. If you leave, I'll have to go with you, and that presents problems."

She thought for a few moments. "I can't tell her to stay away unless I can give her some other kind of reason. She's got enough to worry about right now. And I'm not staying without knowing exactly what's going on." She raised herself on one elbow. "Not some half-baked story to keep me here."

He knew from her manner that it wouldn't be negotiable. While he debated about how much he could safely tell her, she became impatient.

"I guess this is the first test, isn't it?"

"You're right, you should know the situation." He extracted himself from her arms. "But I can't talk to you about it in here. I'm already . . . distracted." He helped her off the bed, keeping one of her hands in his. "The threat isn't against you, it's my brother. He's being blackmailed. If you insist, I'll tell you why, but I'd prefer not to, since it's not pleasant."

"How could blackmail be pleasant?" She darted a perceptive look in his direction. "What you mean is, Doris doesn't know, and you think I might tell her."

"No, I know you wouldn't. It's just that the less you know, the less you'll have to hide."

They sat in his living room, Elmore between them on the couch, and he explained how the foiled ransom had led to the threat on his brother's life. Satisfied that the situation genuinely warranted caution, she left a short message for her sister about car trouble that prevented her from getting home for a couple more days, and the number at the Rocklins'.

Then David buzzed the main house and informed his brother that he'd join them in a few minutes. "I have to get back, help deal with this," he explained. "Will you be all right here for a while?"

She gave him an indignant face. "Oh, I'm coming with you."

"I don't know if that's a good idea."

"My life's being jerked around." Her stubborn came up. "Don't you think I'm entitled?"

"Yeah, but it's not entirely my ball game. All I have is money for leverage."

She hooted. "That's pretty good leverage."

He kissed her impudent mouth. "You're right, it is."

A few minutes later, at the door to the library, Ron Hathaway tried to straight-arm her as well. "This is an Ambassador matter, Miss Ryan."

Obstinate, she faced him down. "Call me Julie, *Ron*. It's also a Ryan matter and, so far, I'm here voluntarily."

"Have it your way ... Julie." Exasperated, Ron stepped aside. "No offense, ladies, but you are observers here, in a highly confidential situation. Since you are both present over my objections, I'd appreciate your remaining aware of that fact during this discussion. We don't need additional security problems at the moment. I'm sure you understand."

Translated, it means "Shut up and listen." Duly admonished, Julie looked past Hathaway to see Doris Rocklin already ensconced next to her husband on the library's couch. She caught the singular look that sprang between David and the investigator, and took the subtle shake of Hathaway's head to mean that Doris hadn't as yet been told about the blackmail. *Fasten your seat belts if that one comes out.*

Platters of sandwiches, soft drinks, and assorted crudités had been provided and, realizing she was ravenous, Julie followed David's lead in helping herself. After seating her in a large wing chair, he perched on the edge of the couch across from her.

Derek Rocklin looked like hell. His bruised cheek had gone a deeper purple, and a pair of darkened circles under his eyes gave him the appearance of a blond raccoon sporting wire-rimmed glasses. "Where do we start?" he asked nervously.

"Our guy's in a hurry, so we stall delivering the cash," began Hathaway.

"And he can't get cash out of the country without declaring it. He was probably going to have me walk it across the Canadian border. Otherwise he'd have to get it into the banking system somewhere. He'll need to make small enough deposits that nobody flags the IRS."

"More time pressure . . . works in our favor." Derek sat forward, clearly exhausted. "I figure another border job."

"Me too. Probably won't go for Canada twice. Mexico's closer. He'd have to have time to scout a location."

"Maybe. Where'd you leave it with him, Ron?"

"Her—he's still using the woman. I said I'd be in touch."

Deke massaged the back of his neck. "Melba called, says he's tearing up the phone lines at the office, threatening to sue us for mishandling this unless we pay the money and recover his painting."

"Sue us? He's got big ones, I'll give him that. Excuse me, ladies."

"He's demanding that I call him. Says he'll go over my head if I don't."

"It's a bluff. I say he's figured out that he's screwed up and is fishing to make sure Ambassador's still on board. Must be getting desperate." David finished his drink. "Let's walk through this again, see if we've missed anything." He disposed of his and Julie's emptied plates as he spoke. "He insures a million-dollar painting a year ago—"

"Two million," corrected Hathaway. "Apparently it appraised out. We wouldn't have insured it otherwise."

"Had it stolen six months ago," David continued, "probably under the assumption that he could drag out negotiations until Ambassador balks at a figure, then settle for top dollar and collect the ransom. Which says he didn't need ready money at the time."

"That tracks."

"Now, suddenly, he does," David mused. "Somebody's got pressure on him. He can't sell this thing legitimately because it's officially 'stolen'—there's a police report on record that has to be cleared. He's faxed money demands from public machines in three different cities, so we can assume that travel expenses are a factor in eating up cash on hand."

"An illegitimate quickie sale wouldn't net him a full price—he'd be out maybe a quarter of the painting's value, maybe more." Ron nodded. "Half a million's a big loss. Plus, he'd have to blow the ransom."

"Another half million out the door. Our boy's not doing too well here. We know he's no dummy. At some point, even idiots cut their losses and disappear. Why doesn't he just 'find' it?"

"Good question." Hathaway turned to Deke. "Tell us exactly what he said to you."

"'It's too late . . . the sale will be destroyed . . . I owe money I must pay or go to jail.' Those are his words."

"So there is a sale. And if it's 'too late,' something with a time factor is going to destroy that sale."

"The ransom was botched. So he didn't get money

he was counting on. Our greedy little guy is trapped pretty good here at the moment. Why *doesn't* he 'find' it?" David repeated, and turned to his brother. "Didn't you say he'd stumbled onto it? Grandma's attic or something? Ambassador checks it out, insures it—so the value's legitimate. If he gives up the ransom, he can sell it. He has a buyer, the value's guaranteed by Ambassador's policy amount, unless . . ."

Suddenly on David's wavelength, Julie broke the rules to speak the question. "What if it *isn't* legitimate?"

"Provenance." Derek, David, and Hathaway all looked at each other. "False. Has to be."

"If the ownership papers are sour, there's no point in 'finding' it, because he *can't* sell legitimately. He'd have to take a bath on the black market. Meanwhile, the ransom's history—so what's he looking at?"

Hathaway grinned, pleased. "I'd say his pants, down around his ankles. Excuse me, ladies. I meant to say: no sale, no insurance payoff—ransom or otherwise. He must have a bigger problem than black-market cash would cover, or he'd have gone there already."

"He owes money. He said that if he didn't pay it, he'd go to jail," recited Derek. "Then he went nuts and hit me."

Hathaway was shaking his head. "You don't go to jail for owing money. You borrow on the street, they break your legs. Borrow it legally, they get a judgment and take your assets—the painting, if he admits he has it—but they don't put you in jail unless you've done something illegal."

"Forgery . . ." David circled the room. "Where do

you get documents that are good enough to fool an insurance firm *within its own specialty?* That can't come cheap. He wouldn't have been able to sell the painting without taking a major loss, so unless he had the cash up front . . ."

"He's had to borrow the money to buy the papers. I met him in Vegas; maybe he was gambling. Maybe he was trying to . . ." Deke's voice failed.

"Vegas?" Doris went deadly silent.

Derek had sealed his doom with his wife, and all eyes turned to Doris's face. "Aw, hell . . . ," he moaned. "Just shoot me."

Her angry voice cut through the room. "How much in Vegas?"

Derek bit the bullet. "Ten thousand, honey, but there's—"

"That's what you owe." It wasn't a question.

"Five. I repaid some of it." He closed his eyes in a shamed grimace. "You may as well know the rest. They have pictures of me. . . ."

"With another woman," she finished leadenly. "You're being blackmailed. Is that why this happened? Is that why we're here—because you went to Las Vegas again?"

"Doris, he was drugged." David's voice was harsh in his brother's defense. "Nothing happened that was his idea."

Julie watched the air leak out of the woman's body; after a moment Doris pushed herself off the couch and left the room. Julie got to her feet to follow her.

Derek, too, withered in front of them. "Nothing like public humiliation," he said softly. "She didn't deserve to find out like that. I should have told her in private."

Julie found Mrs. Rocklin in the lesser dining room, huddled on a chair. "I detest this place!" she burst out painfully. "We should never have moved here. He hates it."

"He must stay because you're here," Julie said quietly, and looked around at the uncomfortable room. "There couldn't be any other reason." Realizing what she'd said, she murmured an apology.

But Doris didn't seem to hear; she sat studying her wedding rings. "Do you know that in ten years my husband has never taken a dime from my father that wasn't spent on me?"

Julie had no idea how to respond, so she remained silent.

"I'm older than he is, you know. Three years. Older than that, really, in a lot of ways." She removed her rings and laid them on the table. "My father spent an absolute fortune on my wedding . . . insisted these were more appropriate than the ones Derek had picked out. Said he didn't want me embarrassed." She reached for the telephone, and Julie watched her dial a number.

"Sherri, would you tell my father I'm on the line?" Doris pushed the rings in circles on the tabletop with the tip of her fingernail. "Thanks, I'm fine. . . . I know you're busy. I'm calling because I need an advance on my trust, fifty thousand. Ask Sherri to have the bank send a cashier's check over by messenger, please." There was a pause. "No, from the trust. It's for me. I thought I might buy a painting. . . . Thank you, Daddy." She hung up the receiver and scooped the rings into her hand. "Or rent an apartment."

26

"Derek, we can take a break if you want."

"No." His marriage was finished; a break would not help. "Let's just get on with this, Ron." It was too much to absorb all at once, and best not to think about it just now. He shook his head to clear the growing fatigue. Too much damage this time—Doris would probably go upstairs, call Martin, and begin to pack his things. It was all but impossible to concentrate. "I'm going to call him. Dangle *him* for a change."

Fighting the urge to go to his wife and beg her forgiveness, knowing it was too much to ask, he held his hands steady enough to dial Walde's new beeper code, then deliberately left the number of a secondary line that would ring into his empty office all night. "That oughta keep him from sleeping."

Hathaway nodded approval. "We're going to stonewall this guy until we check things out. If any of this flies, we have to determine how much we can prove. Deke, you buy us time. Play beeper tag with him until tomorrow noon, then tell him the money's hidden—you don't know where."

David gave Hathaway a meaningful look. "Which'll play, because he doesn't."

"And it's going to take a couple of days to get it," Hathaway continued. "You know him; what do you think he'll do?"

"You mean after he goes crazy?" Deke sighed, too discouraged to genuinely care. "I don't think he'll change much of the original plan. Probably figure out a new place to make the exchange and call us at the last minute. Same as last time."

"I agree. Which brings us to the cash, David. Where is it?"

"Why, are you planning to give it to him?"

"There's no reason you can't tell me where it is. My butt's way out on the line here."

"So's Derek's, so's mine. The minute I remember where it is, I have to give it up. Then I've got no vote in the situation. This is too big a screwup to keep under the rug. Somebody'll have to take the fall. Ambassador's going to say it's Derek, and DePasse will screw him over. My brother could wind up in jail. You know it and I know it."

Hathaway stewed. "Going in without the money, I'm going to look like an idiot."

"So far this is totally outside the office. No one's going to tell DePasse, unless you want to gamble that he's not the leak. Besides, for all you know, I sank the money in half a dozen lakes between here and that cabin. It'll take years to dredge it up if my memory doesn't come back. As far as Ambassador is concerned, you're doing your job—stringing me along, protecting the money."

"So you're holding the ransom . . . for ransom?"

David chose his words with care. "If I knew where it was, it could be interpreted that way. I prefer to think of my lack of memory as . . . leverage."

"Leverage, my ass. I'm going to put a dozen guys around this property, you son of a bitch, and a monitor on the phone. If you even think about stiffing me—"

"Use forty guys. Just give me some privacy this evening. I haven't seen her for twenty-four hours and we have a lot to talk about. For what it's worth, you have my word that I won't leave."

"Privacy is expensive, so don't dick around with me. I need some logistics here if I'm going to keep my job."

"Okay, because I owe you a favor. I have a strong feeling that the cash is in California, within an hour's drive, and it's safe—and as soon as I remember the location, I am the only one who's going to know where it is until I tell you. Under certain conditions, to be negotiated on behalf of my brother, I will deliver it to Ambassador within twenty-four hours. That's all you get."

The sound of light snoring pulled their attention to the exhausted man on the couch. The two of them straightened Deke's body, and David covered his brother with the bathrobe.

"Ron, you're going to have to trust me," he said quietly. "One of us was very likely going to get killed out there . . . and however it *might* have gone down, Derek saved someone's life. He definitely saved this company half a million dollars by coming forward. I don't care if Ambassador fires him—he's got that coming for being careless and a fool. We nail this jerk, it still isn't over for my brother." He looked toward the door, anxious to find Julie.

"I don't want to see Derek in court, or in prison, because he loved his wife," he continued. "Right now this marriage is in serious trouble and doesn't need anything else to break it apart. I've had long, hard lessons in the power of money; therefore I'll be negotiating my brother's future against return of the ransom. That's as straight as I can tell you."

"What about your future?"

"Mine I don't care about. It's been dead for years."

"Really? Then what's this evening's privacy for?" Hathaway looked at his watch. "It's after six, and I'm off the clock. See you tomorrow."

Poleaxed, David watched his boss walk out of the library and damned the man for being right. Clearly there were still a few holes in his head—and through one of them it caught up to him that his life had value for the first time in years. Everything in his world was changed because of Julie Ryan.

Derek's hand slid onto the floor. David crossed the room to push his brother's body deeper onto the couch, then tucked his arm under the robe. Hathaway was right. They didn't have proof, just Derek's word against Walde's. A man that careful would have to be caught red-handed. Unfortunately, by holding out on the ransom money, David knew the die controlling his own future had been cast, and he was committed to playing out his part in it.

* * *

The bottom half of the cherry-splashed sundress was visible behind the opened door to his refrigerator, tempting him to come up close behind her. Elmore, in the corner, had his nose in a bowl with Eddie's name written on it. "We were invited to dinner, but I passed," she said to him, her top half still hidden from sight; the part he could see shifted as she spoke, tantalizing in its motion.

"Thanks." He stifled the urge to grab her hips. "I gave my word to Hathaway that we wouldn't leave. If you're hungry, I can ask the cook to send something over later."

"Cook?" Her head popped up over the door. "They have a cook?"

"Wanda."

She closed the refrigerator. "Actually, I was just checking on what kind of homemaker you are. You can tell a lot from a person's leftovers."

"How'd I come out?"

"You have two kinds of mold on your cottage cheese, half a quart of sour milk, and there's enough stale . . ." She gave him a crooked grin. "What's going to happen?"

"With the ransom? We're going to set a new trap, catch him this time. With my brother? That pretty much depends on Doris. He's going to have to find a new job."

"Are you planning to sleep with me?"

"Hoping," he admitted fervently, adoring her candor. "God knows I want to, but I know you're tired."

"You're right, I am. Come to think of it, I haven't

had enough sleep since I met you." She shrugged expressively, dimpling her cleavage. "But I don't want to be one of your taxis, either."

He looked at her, totally stumped by the reference.

"Never mind. I should change out of this dress. I'll have to wear it again tomorrow."

"I'm sure Doris can find something." The offer to seek out his sister-in-law was halfhearted, at best.

"No, don't disturb her tonight. One of your shirts will do."

"They're in the bedroom."

"Really." She waggled her eyebrows at him. "I haven't looked in there yet. Is it safe?"

"Not if you take your clothes off," he warned.

"Promise?"

He followed the cherry dress down the hallway, impatiently biding his time, feasting his eyes on her as she took command of his closet and sorted through his clothing. Finally she chose a white long-sleeved dress shirt and crossed the hall to the bathroom to change. A few minutes later he heard the shower start up. He kicked off his shoes and rolled onto the bed, aching with anticipation. The bathroom door opened and she tripped barefoot into the room, obviously nude under his shirt, carrying the dress on the shirt hanger, and made room for it in his closet.

"I'll be a few minutes." This time the bathroom door didn't close all the way and he saw her remove his shirt and hang it on the hook on the back of the door; the slender, naked line of her back was mirrored in the glass. She caught him watching and winked at him. "Aren't you the one who offered to scrub my back?" She disappeared into the shower.

Two minutes later he was naked himself and bypassing soggy red undergarments draped over a towel rack to step into the tiled cubicle behind her; he immediately thanked an unknown architect for providing the extravagant, spacious stall. He could see her head to toe under the spray, slick with water, and knew he'd be inside her within seconds.

But he was wrong.

She traded places with him, jollied his body under the water, and as soon as he was thoroughly wet, she turned off the faucet and took up a bar of soap. Lathering his back slowly, tantalizingly, she made him wait for the feel of her hands where he wanted them most as she turned him around and began again at his shoulders, working her way down his skin. He was erect and bumping against her wrist by the time she kneaded foam into his pubic hair, sending static to the base of his testicles. Under, up, and around she moved her fingers—everywhere except his extended, quivering length and the straining, pulsing head at its tip.

Finally she soaped his penis, then handed him the bar and grasped the root and midpoint of his erection with both hands, holding him in a sensuous grip that jolted him from crotch to brain stem. Slick, round breasts were pushed together between her outstretched arms, nipples reaching pertly forward; he lathered his hands and lavished her teats with loving attention, aware that his movements, and hers, were producing the motion of her hands on him, palpating the breadth of his penis, sliding lazily backward and forward in the soapy foam to cause the most delicious of sensations. No way he could last. He'd come in twenty seconds if she kept this up.

To his vast pleasure, he withstood her siege, and was even able to kiss her. She murmured into his mouth, sucked the tip of his tongue. So hard under slippery fingers, so *good!* So near the end of himself. He was forced to plead for respite or give up paradise. But she shook her head, denying permission to pause for relief; sliding one hand higher on his erection, the tips of her fingers came into contact with the thin layer of foreskin, and he shuddered, helpless, as she exposed and explored the sensitive head, circling the center of her palm directly onto the tip. Kneading, massaging, and ruling him with the other, she drove his pleasure. Owned him.

His mouth went dry and he abandoned her breasts to flatten both hands against the tiled walls in a fight for control, tried to hold out against her willful use of him, against the fullness and the wild rush of heat that was bursting into his center, driving and peaking between his legs; his whole body stood rigid from the effort.

But she overrode his resistance and held him prisoner within her rhythm, drew him headlong to the edge and deliberately pushed him over, powerless. His orgasm spurted into her hands as she continued to stroke him, gushed forth to fill the stall with the salty scent of semen, sent his mind and body hurtling into blissful release as a series of spasms emptied his belly, leaving him weak. Somewhere in his coming, a primal sound had issued from his chest, a guttural cry of passion so deep that it strained, hoarse and painful, in his lungs.

When he could, he kissed her again, poured himself into her mouth, loved her for inciting the torrent that had raged over him, and for subduing it. No woman, ever . . .

"Now you know how it feels," she teased triumphantly, and turned the water on again.

Damn near spiritual was how it felt. And exhausting. "I owe you," he said breathlessly. "And I repay debts."

"So do I," she warned happily.

When his strength returned and they'd toweled each other down, he carried her across the hall into his bedroom and lay down next to her, gathered her to him protectively, logy and at peace with the world. After a few minutes she went limp and slipped into sleep; he ran his hand along the bare curve of her hip and the valley of her waist, enjoying the feel of her skin, wanting to pleasure her. Another time. Soon. And often.

Julie opened her eyes, drowsy. It was David, she realized, gently pulling her from a warm, dark place; he was lying next to her with a telephone in his hand. "A woman is calling you. Your sister, maybe?"

She blinked and looked around, disoriented, thick with sleep. In his bed, naked. His bedroom clock read 9:50. Sunlight said it was morning, and her head was full of feathers. On top of their blanket, next to her feet, Elmore was pulling himself into a long, lazy stretch.

"You want to call her back?"

"No, no." She yawned greatly. "I'd better talk to her."

"Switch the call in, Martin, thanks." He handed her the receiver and left the bed. She watched his perfect butt undulate toward the bathroom and felt a surge of energy. It was going to be a *great* morning.

"Julie?"

Recognizing the voice, she guiltily disciplined herself: no peeking at a naked man during the conversation. She rolled onto her side to remove temptation from her line of sight. "Hey, Aunt Marjorie, how are you?"

"Julie, dear, there was a man on the phone."

"I know. This is sort of a guest house, Aunt Marge."

"Oh, I see. Well, we received your message. Is your car all right?"

"It'll be ready any time now," she fibbed. "How's Joann?"

"We went to an early dinner at Publico's last night, and when we got home, Gerd was in the lobby with suitcases. Apparently he'd been waiting for hours and was furious. Geraldo, naturally, hadn't let him go up." Geraldo was the doorman at Aunt Marjorie's apartment building. "Then Joann had an awful row with him. It was terribly distressing, as I'm sure you can imagine. Geraldo actually called the police."

"Oh, brother. Is she okay?"

"She was very upset, of course. Gerd was extremely abusive toward her, shouting and calling her horrible names. Neither of us slept a bit after they made him leave."

"She was afraid of something like this." Concern for Joann drove other thoughts from her head. "Maybe I should talk to her. Is she there?"

"That's why I'm calling. She wanted me to let you know that she's on her way to California. I've just returned from driving her to the airport. I don't think she's safe from him here. He was very angry, and if he should happen to get past Geraldo . . . well, we both thought it was better."

"She's on her way to L.A.?" Julie raced to catch up. "When is she getting in?"

"Somewhere around three o'clock your time. It was all quite sudden, of course, and she couldn't get a direct flight. . . . Anyway, she asked me to call and let you know. Will you be able to be home by then?"

"Of course. Give me the flight information, I'll pick her up."

"She's made arrangements for a car, but if you could be at home . . . She was terribly upset."

"I'll leave right away." She gave her aunt additional assurances before hanging up the phone.

It immediately rang again. "I have a call from Mr. Hathaway for David, Miss Ryan," said Martin.

"I'll tell him." After a lengthy kiss, she traded places with David in the bathroom.

When David picked up the receiver, Hathaway's voice was falsely cheerful in his ear. "Have a pleasant night? No problems with privacy?"

"None of your business. And thank you."

"We have a meeting with DePasse in an hour. Word went through the secretarial pool that you're no longer missing. DePasse is pissed because every female on the floor knew it before he did, so you and Deke get the hell in here. I'm not taking this beating alone."

"We'll be there."

"If I were you, I'd reconsider the money issue."

"Not negotiable." He hung up the phone.

She came out of the bathroom in ruby underwear and pulled her dress out of the closet. "My sister's on her way to my apartment. I have to go."

Disappointed, he watched the cherry dress float down to her knees. "Derek and I have a summit meeting in DePasse's office. Crap's hitting the fan in a big way, and Hathaway stands to catch most of it. It won't take more than an hour, then we can leave."

"It's a two-hour drive, David. If there's traffic, it'll take even longer. I have to stop for gas, shop for groceries . . . If I wait an hour, I'll barely get there ahead of her."

He saw the stubborn look on her face and knew his choices were to frighten her into staying or lock her in the cottage. He tried compromise. "Okay, I'll follow you down as soon as I can. But wait an hour before you start out. Find a market here," he insisted, then spied the gun. "And put the Walther in your purse."

"Oh, come on." The weapon received a grimace generally reserved for cockroaches. "What am I going to do with a gun?"

"You carried it before."

"Yes, when I thought you were dangerous. I wouldn't have *used* it."

"Okay, you're right. Just wait for me to go with you. If you're late, you're late. Your sister's not going to melt. Call a neighbor, have someone put a note on the door."

"I'll call Mrs. Lieberman, but I'm leaving in an hour."

She picked up the telephone, and he was forced to give up any thoughts of having her this morning. He settled for a close embrace and the feel of her body against his lonely groin. *Hathaway, you owe me, you bastard.*

27

THURSDAY

On hold for the past twenty minutes in DePasse's outer office, all three men were impatient. "There's only going to be one voice in there, and unless either of you gets a direct question, it's going to be mine," Hathaway decreed. "Anyone got a problem with that?"

Derek nodded in subdued agreement, but David was moody. "As long as I'm on the freeway in an hour, I don't care who talks."

The secretary answered her buzzer, then ushered them inside DePasse's office. Walter DePasse was furious, his attitude aggressive as he gestured at them to be seated. Six corporate suits were already scattered around the room. Three were introduced as counsel to the firm; the fourth was DePasse's supervisor, Albert Moss; another, Moss's immediate superior, was generally visible only at Christmas parties. The youngest turned out to be a paralegal taking notes, and was introduced as an afterthought.

David, Derek, and Hathaway were each identified in turn. "Walt was right," commented Moss. "If I didn't know better, I could be convinced you two were the same person."

Hathaway took his cue from the expectant silence that descended. "Since I spoke to Mr. DePasse last evening, several things have occurred relative to this matter; however, I haven't had an opportunity to brief him," he said to the room at large. "We've uncovered false provenance on the painting involved, which compounds the insured's fraudulent claim of theft. We now know that the theft was part of a scheme to generate a cash ransom, in which our insured had an accomplice negotiate for its return."

The men in the room were raptly attentive as Hathaway proceeded. "Through an admittedly accidental situation during which our courier, David Rocklin, was injured, the monies were not paid, and Ambassador's funds remain intact. However, the insured, Mr. Walde—who is unaware of our discoveries—has caused injury to our principal investigator and has threatened his life in an attempt to coerce payment. In short, we have two injured agents, each having prevented loss to the firm."

While the three lawyers hurriedly scribbled notes, DePasse expressed open astonishment. "That's a much different story than these gentlemen anticipated, Ron, based on our conversation."

"When you called last night, I hadn't as yet had an opportunity to verify certain of the facts, and I didn't feel comfortable speculating on this," Hathaway said smoothly. "Time delays to various offices in London and New York couldn't be avoided, and I received most of this information a few minutes ago."

DePasse's superiors got to their feet, prompting the lawyers to follow their example. "Well, this seems to be under control at the moment. Walt, I'm sure you'll keep us informed."

"Sorry to have wasted your time. I really didn't—"

"No problem. Good work, Hathaway. Gentlemen, we're certainly glad you're both okay." Murmuring similar remarks, the lawyers shook hands with David and Derek as the men filed out of the room.

Hathaway waited until the door had closed behind them. "Walt, I'd have warned you if I'd known you were going to call division heads into this meeting. I'm sorry."

DePasse was still recovering. "I approved Walde's policy." He ran his hand over a worried forehead. "What's this about false provenance?"

"Documentation on the painting was provided through the Thatchell Gallery in London."

"You're damned right it was. That's why I didn't question it."

"When I asked for a reexamination this morning, Thatchell confirmed that their records had been compromised. On several artists, actually, files have been coming up as altered in their database. One of their employees had been accepting bribes. They are highly embarrassed, as you can imagine. Don't be surprised if we've insured others. Could go as high as fifty, sixty million, and that's just Ambassador's liability. We'll have to wait and see."

DePasse sat silent, clearly in shock at the enormity of the discovery.

"This information is extremely confidential, as several investigations are being launched through Scotland Yard. They're asking us to hold off on doing anything immediate, and I've assured them of our cooperation," Hathaway continued. "I can tell you that the painting we insured is indeed a Chagalier, examined and verified as a legitimate work for the artist. However, we were given a false title. I checked with the Art Loss Register in New York. Under its original title, it is known to have been stolen from the de Luminière Museum in Paris during Nazi occupation in the forties, and was apparently shipped by train to Berlin for some military asshole's private collection. German documentation is a little vague on dates, but otherwise seems accurate.

"When the Allies moved in at the end of World War Two, the painting disappeared, but some of the companion pieces were traced to the Leningrad in Russia. It's been listed as missing for years and could not have been properly purchased by our client. It's subject to seizure as evidence by Scotland Yard, probably British customs, if not the French government—which they'll have to sort out over there. Comparisons to original data indicate Thatchell's records were altered about six months prior to our issuing coverage."

DePasse, red in the face, addressed Deke. "Walde actually had someone threaten your life?"

Hathaway intervened. "When he discovered that David was missing with the money, Walde got paranoid and became convinced that the ransom had been stolen. As you know, Deke flew to the

drop site to look for his brother, and Walde contacted him there. There was a brief meeting with
the female accomplice, Deke received a facial injury,
and his life was threatened unless the money was
paid."

"Can we prove any of this?"

"I haven't had a chance to examine our eviden-
tiary position, but it seems pretty thin on Walde at
the moment. Deke was up there in a personal capac-
ity, concerned about his brother. The meeting wasn't
anticipated, and they were looking for a recording
device, which he hadn't worn, so it's pretty much
Walde's word against ours. Everything we do have
on tape came from the woman."

"That's too bad." DePasse rocked his chair. "Well,
the first thing is to cancel the policy. Then see where
we are legally. If we can't nail him, turn it over to the
FBI, Scotland Yard, whatever."

"I've advised London that we'll cooperate by
avoiding tipping off Walde as long as we can. In
the meantime, we'd like to bring him down. If we
can convince him that he'll be paid, we can get him
on video—"

"No. We already have a financial bloodbath.
Expenses on this thing are running close to seventy
thousand, and according to you, we haven't managed to gather enough evidence to convict anyone
except the woman! I'm not pointing fingers, but
I'm not willing to commit additional resources and
manpower, either. If this man is as dangerous as
you say he is, we don't want further involvement
with our people. Someone will get hurt." He looked
at them, defensive. "We cancel the policy, feed him

to the feds, and that's it." He sat forward in his chair. "At least the money's intact. Where is it?"

"Well . . ." Hathaway felt himself begin to sweat. "That's the tough part, and I'm glad I didn't have to say this in front of the guys upstairs, but the truth is, I don't know. David still has partial amnesia, and he's advised me that he's unable to give us a location at the moment."

"He's *what?*"

"I contacted Dr. Meadows in Oroville, who verified that three days ago he diagnosed David as having memory loss from the blow to his head. The doctor seems certain that David's memory will return. In the meantime, we wait." He pushed ahead. "It could, however, work to our advantage."

DePasse was growing incredulous, shaking his head. "Precisely how?"

Hathaway made certain his glance didn't waver. "It's already out that the money is missing. We circulate a story that David says it was already passed to the woman . . . like we're trying to drive a wedge between her and Walde."

"Accomplishing what, exactly?"

David could keep silent no longer. "With the money gone, Walde will think he caught me stealing from the company—which sets him up to try to coerce the ransom from me," he said urgently, "not Ambassador."

"Not authorized, damn it!" DePasse glowered at him, clearly suspicious.

"You're already in the hole for seventy grand. Why not spend another couple of thousand and catch this bastard?"

"Because it's not my job! My job is to protect the company and the company's money," DePasse said, livid.

David ignored Hathaway's attempts to divert his anger. "And the company's employees! My brother has a death threat staring at him! What about that?"

"I don't believe it . . . and I don't believe you!" DePasse's manner was becoming more and more agitated. "So you don't know where the money is? Well, let me tell you what *I* know. I know a woman *was* involved out there; we have her footprints at the site. I know you left here with half a million dollars. I found out three days ago that you've been hiding a history of instability from this firm, and I know you've been fired from every job you've had in the past ten years!"

"Nine," David corrected rigidly, beginning to understand.

"Amnesia, my balls! What this is, gentlemen, is a very pat, very smooth con, and very hard to swallow. You may be buying it, Ron, but for my money, the whole things smells like week-old fish."

Hathaway handed DePasse a piece of paper. "Sir, this fax from Thatchell verifies that the provenance has fallen apart. The museum was well into their investigation, and it was only a matter of time until it was discovered and they would have given us a call. You can verif—"

"All right! You proved Walde's a thief and you saved this department the embarrassment of paying off a false claim, Ron. Congratulations." DePasse got to his feet, shoved his chair against the wall, and redirected his anger at David. "Trouble is, this man is also a thief! *He's* got it, and I'll bet even money you can't find it. Morganer was right."

David's face flushed with anger, his suspicions confirmed.

"This whole situation stinks! Amnesia . . . What I ought to do is have you arrested for theft."

David rose slowly to his full height, forcing DePasse to look up at him. "If you're going to have me arrested, I'd suggest you do it now."

"Get out!" DePasse barked at him, then at Derek. "Both of you! Hathaway, you stay here!"

David opened the office door and waited for Derek to limp past.

"We'll find it, you son of a bitch!" DePasse hurled at him furiously. "I'll guarantee you that!"

"Whatever you say." He closed the door. Seconds later, Hathaway came flying out of DePasse's office and was chagrined to find the two of them waiting for him. As they headed toward Derek's office the brothers were accosted from all sides by well-wishers, mostly female, with sympathy for their injuries and congratulations on their safe return. It was obvious from various comments that indeed word had already circulated that the ransom money was missing and that they'd been called on the carpet. Male eyes were more direct in their scrutiny of David, and inquiries about his health, and congratulations, were a good deal more circumspect.

"If that ransom doesn't come back, we're all going to be out of a job," groaned Hathaway within Melba's earshot, and closed the door to Derek's office. "I mean it," he said quietly. "You think the three of us aren't going to be under a magnifying glass, you're crazy."

"Good. Let them watch. You'll get the money," David assured him.

Derek seated himself behind his desk, clearly tired, and began setting up tape recording equipment. "Walde's called three times this morning. He's getting so nasty that Melba won't talk to him."

David caught Hathaway's eye. "Maybe you shouldn't be in here."

"You're going to try to set him up without the money," Hathaway accused, and rubbed his jaw in distress. "I ain't in this. I can't be. DePasse'd fire me. I got an ex-wife and two kids."

David smiled. "My brother and I are merely making a phone call. I'll stop by your office in a couple of minutes."

"I hope you know what you're doing." Hathaway hurriedly left the room.

David looked at his brother. "Whenever you're ready."

"Let's do it." Derek dialed Walde's latest beeper number, fed in his own, and they waited until the phone rang, then David picked up an extension as Derek answered.

It was a woman's voice. "Where are you?"

"In my office."

"I won't talk to you there."

"Okay, then listen. The money's out of state and I won't have it for two days. Kill me, destroy my marriage, whatever you do—it's going to take two days. A day to get it, a day to bring it here. So unless you have another plan, call me Saturday and let me know when and where you want it delivered. Anything else, just say so."

The line went dead.

The men looked at each other. "I'd say that constituted a yes."

"How soon do you have to notify Walde?"

Derek shrugged enigmatically. "Someone has to dictate the notice of cancellation, specifying the terms and why there's not going to be a refund on his premium, then Melba has to type it up and send a registered letter . . . that could take a month or so, I think." Derek grinned weakly for the first time that morning. "No additional expenses out of pocket for Ambassador. I'd say Scotland Yard could count on thirty days at least, maybe more if I forget to do it."

"DePasse said he okayed that policy." He tapped his brother's desk with his finger. "He also approved the ransom without your recommending it."

"What are you getting at?"

"And he decided to send me in after you broke your ankle, so this would go down on schedule." He sat back, frustrated. "Except I can't buy DePasse in this thing. Not smart enough."

"You're right. I don't see him staying focused for two and a half years on anything."

"I'm grabbing at straws here." David glanced at the wrist watch he'd borrowed from Derek. "I'm going to drop the rental, then follow Julie down the coast in my car. Probably be gone a couple of days." He smiled at his brother. "If you need to reach me, I have it on good authority that Hathaway knows where she lives."

Derek rose to his feet. "Don't worry, he'll have someone dogging you down there."

"I'd be disappointed if he didn't." David said goodbye to his brother, found Hathaway in his office, and closed the door for privacy.

Hathaway raised both hands in a plea for peace. "Don't tell me what you're doing, I don't want to know."

"I just wanted to thank you," said David, controlling his gratitude with no small effort. "I appreciate your keeping Julie out of it for now and, separate from the money, I owe you for the way you're keeping them off my brother."

"That could all change. Deke's got a lot of problems, and I'm not covering anything, just not naming it yet. Depends on who asks what questions in the meantime. If you do nail this guy, you know he's going to take your brother down with him."

"We know. He's going to do it anyway."

Hathaway sighed, nodding his approval. "We'll be calling on Miss Ryan, taking statements from her. She's material, she has knowledge about the money . . . you know the drill."

"I know, but with any luck, you won't have to do any of that for a while." David waited a moment, then opened the conversation to another painful subject. "When did Morganer show up?"

"Tuesday. They had a meeting about you. . . . I was in it."

He was surprised at Hathaway's frankness—but not that the meeting had taken place. "He leave some files?"

Hathaway nodded.

"Usually does. Generally he waits until I have something to lose, then he comes in and blows it all to hell. This is out of his pattern and about six months early."

"I got the impression that it was a general search-and-destroy mission. Then he stumbled across the ransom situation?"

David smiled indulgently. "So who went through the reports, you?"

Hathaway nodded. "And DePasse."

"Must have enhanced my believability factor immeasurably. No wonder he went ballistic in there. How about you? Do you trust me?"

"Nope."

"I can't fix that at the moment." David went to the door, pensive. "For the record, after Gina . . . I did everything wrong and I didn't care. But there's nothing I can do to fix that, either." He checked the watch again. "I'm late. Is your guy ready to roll?"

"He'd better be." Hathaway paused. "Say . . . why does Morganer use two firms?"

David laughed and then sobered. "Early on, he fired a detective who couldn't pin anything on me. The guy got ticked and tipped me off. Morganer thought I bought him off and always used two after that." He looked at his watch again. "Made it twice as expensive on his end. Didn't change my life any. See you."

A Pacific storm was moving in, cooking the humidity with an unseasonally warm offshore breeze; Julie's clothes were gummy and sticking to her skin. In the few minutes she'd been out of the car's air-conditioned coolness, perspiration had gathered at the hairline of her temple and around the base of her neck.

She took Mrs. Lieberman's note off the door, brought in three sacks of groceries, then opened seaward and living room windows to allow clammy ocean air to sweep through her apartment. Meanwhile she hurriedly transferred produce into the refrigerator and shoved a sack of ice cubes into her freezer.

It had taken forever to get home. After David left for his meeting, she'd taken a quick shower and dutifully waited until ten-thirty, by which time Santa Barbara had been overrun with surfers cutting classes to ride advancing storm waves. Motley vehicles with surfboard racks were butting heads with childless tourists in rental cars who'd waited until after Labor Day and the beginning of fall semester to sample the same beaches. An hour later the Ventura freeway south was practically a parking lot—four lanes of delivery trucks, semis, commuters, shoppers, and soccer moms in sport utility vehicles crawled bumper to bumper past an overturned Safeway rig.

She'd arrived in Malibu a little after two, charged a shopping cart through her local supermarket at a dangerous speed, and had practically thrown food items into it.

Nearly three o'clock, and she was still in her sundress. There'd be barely enough time to get changed before David arrived, and Joann was due within the hour. For an organized person, she was frazzled. Elmore had been skittish since she'd left Santa Barbara, no doubt picking up on her tension; he'd been irritated at being left in the car during her supermarket jaunt, and was stalking from living room to kitchen, unable to settle down.

She gazed around her apartment with a critical eye, trying to see it from a man's point of view, wondering what David's impression would be. Not too frou-frou, she decided, but small and confining for someone his size, and a little prissy with the pillows. They'd have to go. The place was too small to share with her sister for any length of time, too, with the extra bedroom now an office, but she and Joann would have plenty of time to figure that out.

Nervous, she stopped at the loose-fitting side door. The locksmith was coming tomorrow. She filled Elmore's water dish and popped a can of Kitty Krumbles as a treat, with a knot of excitement in her stomach. *He'd* be here soon. She felt like a teenager on prom night, wanting everything to be perfect. All she could see in her mind were his eyes, smiling at her in that ice-cave shade of green that tripped up her heartbeat.

She stepped onto the deck to gauge the position of the storm, trying to unwind, get her feet down, but thinking about him just wound things up tighter. He was interested in more than sex with her. He was attracted to her as a person. Men didn't look at her the way he'd been looking at her if they weren't. And making love with him . . . holy Maria! She'd better hold off thinking about that until later.

As soon as he arrived and Joann arrived, and while her sister was getting settled in, she had hopes of taking a long walk with him, following the steep path down to the coast highway and crossing over to the sand, asking every question she could think of about his life, his future, what he liked, things he hated . . . all the minutiae that make up the whole of a person you're getting to know. The sun was a blur of pale blue behind a thickening band of rain clouds moving down from Oxnard; he'd be here any minute, and she'd been daydreaming instead of changing clothes!

Increasingly nervous, she grabbed up the offending pillows as she quick-walked through the living room and carried them toward the bedroom. Better open a window in there as well, cool the room out before the rain arrived. Inside the doorway, she gasped in shock. The bedroom was a mess, and a man who'd been asleep was suddenly heaving himself off the bed and coming at her. She recognized him immediately, and her breath caught in her throat. "Gerd!"

Her backpack had been emptied; her grandmother's plastic pearls and the rest of the play jewelry from the treasure tin were lying on the floor in the middle of the room. Dresser drawers stood open. Clothing had been strewn from the closet. Rage rushed through her middle. And fear. Joann would be arriving any minute. Obviously he'd been looking for signs of her sister. As if he had a right to break into her home and trash it!

"Hello, Julie. Where is my wife?"

"She's not here." Even angry, her voice was small in her ears, nowhere near loud enough to reach Mrs. Lieberman, on the opposite side of the building.

He stared at the mess, unapologetic. "I can see that. Is she staying somewhere else?" Gerd approached her with menace. He was short but powerfully built, and obviously in a temper.

"I haven't heard from her, and you're going to have to leave."

"She called you from Chicago," he disputed angrily. "You have a message on your answering machine. Where is she?"

She'd spent a total of maybe ten or twelve hours in her brother-in-law's company since he and Joann had been married, and while she didn't know him well, his behavior seemed peculiar, even for Gerd. In the past, she'd considered him somewhat passive, disinterested in general day-to-day events. But today he was consumed by a simmering rage that had a distinctly explosive potential. Apprehension took a larger grip on her psyche, making it difficult to think. "That's an old message. We talked this morning, and she's decided to go to New York instead."

"You lie. No matter." He kicked the pearls aside and picked up the rusted hull of the cracker tin. "What is this?"

"It's the treasure tin from Gramp's old cabin. I found it this week." She clutched the pillows, trying to find reasonable ground. "Gerd . . . Joann told me you two are having trouble, and I know you're upset. But I don't want to be involved."

"There is no trouble. She is my wife."

"Right, and this is something you have to work out with her . . . but she's not here. I don't want to be rude, but I'm expecting a guest any minute. I'm afraid you'll have to leave."

"And I think I will wait."

Anger at his arrogant attitude overrode attempts at conciliation. "I told you, I don't know where—"

"You are a liar!" He brushed past her to march

into the living room. There he began to pace in a circle, raking the room with his eyes. Then he paused next to the front door and put his hand on a glass wall shelf displaying a collection of delicate sea shells. "In one minute I will begin here and tear this room into pieces," he yelled. "I want—"

"Julie?" Hallelujah, it was David!

"Come in," she called quickly.

He opened the front door and came striding to her side, his bedroll in one hand, the other out of sight, then followed her gaze and turned to face the shocked man looking at them from across the room. Weak with relief, Julie clung to his arm. "It's okay. This is my, uh, brother-in-law, Gerd."

Gerd had been startled into silence by David's sudden appearance. Next to her, David's face darkened. "I heard a man's voice all the way across the patio. Shouting. I hope there's not a problem here." He brought the Walther slowly from behind his back, held it loosely at his side. "Is there a problem?"

Gerd charged through the open doorway. "It is not over," he blustered.

Throw pillows slid from her fingers onto the floor, and Julie's legs gave way; she collapsed onto the sofa. David ran out the door, then returned a few moments later. "He drove away." He closed the door and locked it. "What the hell was going on?"

Julie was trembling. "He scared the living daylights out of me." She shuddered. "He must have been sleeping on my bed when I came in. I was late, didn't check the apartment . . . I'm just glad he's gone. He's looking for Joann and she's due here any second. Went through my things. God, what a jerk."

He walked her to the bedroom, and they surveyed the disheveled room. Elmore gave David's ankles an enthusiastic rub as he stooped near the contents of her backpack. Slowly they began to put things in order.

"I tried to convince him she was still in Chicago, but he knows she's coming here. He listened to my messages, the creep."

"Which means he'll probably be back. Hathaway's got some guy watching the house," David told her. "I'll tell him to keep an eye out." He scanned the room and gave her a mischievous grin. "One bed . . . two women. Hmmmm." He gestured toward her bedroll in the corner. "Are we going to need this?"

"If you stay, someone sleeps on the couch," Julie said with a grin. "Won't be you."

David laughed, reminded once again of her strength and mettle; he took a moment to kiss her. "Do we have any time?"

"If her plane landed at three, she should have been here by now." The phone began to ring, and they both hesitated.

"Let it go to the machine," he said firmly, and she nodded.

At the end of two rings Joann's voice came through the speaker. "Julie, it's me. I'm at LAX, but I ran into an old friend of mine on the plane and since you're not home yet, I guess it's okay to go to dinner. I hope you don't mind, but I won't be there until later."

Julie snatched up the receiver. "How much later?"

"Hi! You're there! Should I come on out?"

"That's up to you—I don't want to upset you, but

Gerd just left. He's looking for you, and he's in a real snit."

There was a long pause. "For someone who couldn't pay the rent, he's sure getting around," Joann said bitterly. "He was in Chicago last night, screaming and yelling—I guess he's been home, because he knows I moved out and put my things in storage. I left his stuff in the apartment, and he's nuts because the landlord seized everything. He's damn lucky I didn't burn it."

"Is he dangerous? He seemed really hostile."

"I don't think so. He's always had a temper on him, but he's never gotten violent. Just vocal, but I'll tell you, that wears out after a while. Listen, would you mind if I go to dinner, then let you know? I can't deal with him two nights in a row."

"Sure, call me later. Let me know what you're going to do. If it's late, we can catch up tomorrow." Her heart was jumping through hoops. "Did you have a good flight?"

"Wonderful! Roberta and I haven't seen each other since we were sophomores in college. She's divorced now. Going to give me a few pointers. I'll see you later."

She laughed as David took the receiver from her fingers and replaced it on the cradle.

"The way I count it, 'later' is four or five hours from now." His grin was enticingly. "Gee . . . I wonder how we can fill the evening."

Julie drew herself in. What she wanted to do was go into the bedroom and stay there until further notice. Forget Gerd, forget her sister's troubles, forget the whole world. But for the first time since they'd met, there was also enough time to do something normal with David, like getting to know each other. "How do you feel about a walk along the beach?" she asked tentatively. "We could have an early dinner, maybe. Things have been so . . . rushed, for so long, that I just feel we need to slow down a bit."

"Slow is fine."

She blushed. Slow was terrific. "Good. There are private stairs to the highway."

"A walk with you sounds great, but you know we'll probably have company." He nodded streetward.

"Company's fine, as long as he doesn't eat with us."

"I'll tell him where we're going. Wouldn't want him jumping to conclusions and getting Hathaway all upset. Then we'd be up to our ass in company, and right now I'm counting on at least a couple hours of privacy."

No argument there, she thought happily.

28

The phone rang in Deke's outer office. "I'm out," he said to Melba. "Unless it's my wife, I'm not here to anyone until we finish this. Or my brother. No one else."

His secretary put aside her dictation to pick up the office extension. "Mr. Rocklin's—" Her manner stiffened. "Hello, Mr. Walde."

Deke firmly shook his head. Definitely not talking to Walde.

"He's still not in. . . . I don't have a location for him, but I'll page him again and let him know you're still trying to reach him. . . . No, sir, he hasn't called in all day."

A dial tone was audible as Melba replaced the receiver with a satisfied grin. "What a creep!"

Deke closed his eyes and removed his glasses long enough to rub both sides of his face. "Thank you. He can suck wind until I'm ready to talk to him."

He opened the next file and began dictating

detailed information on the status of the case, determined to leave solid notes for his successor. It was only a matter of time until he was history with the firm—with the industry, for that matter, once word about the Walde fiasco got out—and he wanted everything in order before he turned in his keys.

After completing the balance of his caseload, he changed his mind about dictating his resignation, and wrote it out by hand while Melba was typing. At six he buzzed her intercom. "Would you please call Walde and tell him you've heard from me and I want a phone number, not a beeper, where he can be reached. He won't want to do that, so say I'll be calling back for it in ten minutes."

She made the call, and in a few minutes Walde phoned in demanding to talk to Deke; as predicted, he refused to provide a number, then hung up on her. A few minutes later he called back to leave a phone number with a Los Angeles area code. More hide-and-seek. At least he wasn't in Santa Barbara. Breathing a bit easier, Deke closed the door, then dialed. Walde answered immediately; noise in the background identified the number as a public phone.

"You've been bugging my office for hours," he said with unfeigned animosity. "I told you this would take a couple of days. That means I wait two days and you wait two days, moron. If you're *trying* to screw things up, you're doing a damn fine job so far."

Walde was momentarily taken aback, then tried to jerk him around again. "How do I know to trust you? How do I know you are getting the money?"

"How do *I* know you'll turn over the painting?"

he snapped. "Or give me the negatives? How do I know you're not going to be on my back for the rest of my goddamned life?"

"I will not destroy you unless you mess this up again."

You've already destroyed me, you prick. My wife . . . Something inside him gave way, splintering into jagged, broken pieces, and a black rage broke the surface of his calm. "You know what, asshole? I don't think I give a damn what you do. As a matter of fact, I'm done. Screw you *and* that bitch you pal around with!"

Walde became apoplectic, began to bellow like a wounded bull. "I will kill you! I will kill her, too! You will die for this!"

"Yeah, yeah, right." Right now Walde would threaten anyone if he thought it would deliver the money, and Deke took great satisfaction in having drawn blood. "You think I care? My wife is finished with me. That means I'm poor, and I'm for damn sure not going to give up half a million dollars, so get real. I'm going to need every dime from now on, asshole, so I'm keeping the money! Go for the payoff on theft, because you're not getting anything from me!" His hand was trembling; he put the receiver down on the desk, partly panicked at having lost control, partly savoring the satisfaction of telling the son of a bitch to screw himself. God, it felt good to shove it to the bastard!

Walde was screaming at him again. "I will kill you both."

Deke picked up the phone and spoke over the tirade. "I don't give a damn what you do, as long as you do it in hell!" He took great care in placing the receiver lightly in its cradle. Half the weight lifted from his shoulders, and the ache in his ankle ceased. God, it felt good!

They were halfway down the hillside with a clear view of the ocean in front of them. The Pacific was an oily coal color under the gray sky with whitecaps frothing onto the sand. The concrete steps they followed had been placed in the sharply angular slope long ago to provide community access to the beach and were nearly overgrown with late summer foliage. With rain imminent, the breeze had cooled and was whipping the shrubbery into motion around them, adding to the drama of an incoming Pacific weather front.

"I love the sense of anticipation when it's going to rain," Julie said happily. "The air has this high-strung, edgy quality, and you're not sure what's going to happen. Then nature roars through and cleans house, and everything gets calm again."

"Reminds me of something else," he teased, glancing sideways at her, "but I forget what."

She pretended not to understand. "I'm serious. And after it rains and all the dust's washed away, everything's peaceful and clean and fresh again—a brand-new world."

"I agree. Cuts the tension, all right."

She had to laugh at last. "You're hopeless."

"I have a one-track mind. It's one of the things you'll get to love about me."

It took a few more minutes to wend their way down to the edge of the highway; ten minutes further on, they crossed to the beach side and stopped at a colorful Mexican cocktail bar and restaurant. "I've been here in a couple of times," she said, leading him inside. "It's usually pretty quiet until after dark."

They chose side-by-side seating, with a view of the oncoming storm through thick panes of protective glass. Hathaway's man, who'd followed them down the steps at a discreet distance, came inside and took a seat at the bar; they ordered a pitcher of margaritas and an appetizer of nachos, and cheerfully sent him a beer.

David leered at her comically. "So now that I have a past again, what do you want to know about me, Miss Ryan?"

"Transparent, eh?" She grinned. "Is your memory really back?"

"All the way to childhood."

"In that case, I want to know the usual stuff that women ask about you."

"Let's see." He sat back in the booth. "Lightweight jock, track and field, always in competition with my brother, UCLA business major—"

The waitress arrived and poured margaritas into salt-rimmed glasses for them before she departed.

It was Julie's turn. "College dropout, did secretarial work until the year before last . . . Cheers." She tipped her glass toward his. "Went to real-estate school." She blushed and took a sip of her drink. "Ned, you already know about."

"And Gina, you know about," he said softly. "Both my folks are gone. Yours?"

"My dad's stationed in the Middle East, an air

force instructor, jet engine maintenance. Mom died four years ago. One sister. You'll meet Joann later."

A silence descended. Outside, thin swirls of sand were being picked up by the wind and hurled against the window; in the near distance, the ocean was a menacing presence chewing foamily at the edge of the beach. As rain clouds descended, the twilight grew more dense and ominous.

"Doesn't sound like we have too much in common," she said awkwardly, realizing how little she knew about him and how deeply involved she'd become. There were huge leaps of time to be uncovered between them. "Are you still having headaches?"

He ran his hand to the back of his scalp. "Sore around the edges, but otherwise just fine."

She glanced at their observer, sipping beer at the bar. "Why does Hathaway have someone watching you?"

"Because I haven't given them the money. I intend to, just not right now."

In the dim light from the window, she gazed into eyes that suddenly had no depth, opaque jade with large, flat charcoal centers, closing her out. "And you don't want to tell me why."

"It doesn't affect you. I'm going to give it back when Ambassador and I reach agreement on . . . certain legal conditions regarding my brother." He drank from his glass. "Of course, they can play hardball and have me arrested, take me to court, even, but all I have to do is make bail, and so far Hathaway's still in my corner. I'll remember where it is; it's just a matter of when."

She looked at him, unable to keep a smile off

her face. "Were those my grandmother's romance novels?"

"Yeah. Doris is reading them right now, but I'll make sure they get back to the cabin one of these days, I promise."

"But you didn't leave the money at the cabin?" She took a sip of her drink, pursuing the puzzle.

"It's never left my side . . . well, for a short time, until someone returned it to me."

She choked on her margarita. "*That's* why your sleeping bag was so heavy? I thought it was just wet." Then she began to laugh. "I tried to throw it away, you know. At the airport, when I turned in the Bronco, I left yours in the backseat. I was tempted to dump both of them."

He took a breath, so astonished that she laughed even louder.

"Your bringing it home was the only thing I never worried about! It's a good thing I made the right choice."

She gestured toward the man at the bar. "Tell me I didn't drive it to Santa Barbara!"

"No, it's somewhere else."

"Don't tell me. I don't want to know!"

He held up both hands in acquiescence. "Yeah, well, you're the only one who doesn't."

The waitress appeared with their nachos, and Julie found she was hungry. "Why didn't you get married again?" she asked between bites, unable to mask her curiosity about the one subject that neither he nor Doris had seemed willing to discuss.

This time he didn't smile, and she felt him go away from her, sink down inside himself.

"I thought it was a little more subtle than asking about your wife . . . if you want to tell me."

His face took on a subtly haunted expression. "Talking about Gina," he said unevenly, "generally gives me nightmares, so I don't do it too often. Sometimes I get them anyway." He sat forward to take her hand in his palm. "Are you sure you want to know? It's very unpleasant."

Nervous at the depth of his reluctance, she was momentarily hesitant, then nodded.

He closed his eyes and went further away. "It could change your opinion of me. . . ."

She was silent, uncertain of what she'd begun between them.

"She was sixteen, actually almost seventeen the first time I saw her. I was twenty-one and had a job with her father's firm. Her parents were totally opposed to us, which I could understand, but . . . I gave her father a promise." David gripped her hand. "Which I kept. We were crazy in love for a year, and then her folks served notice that on her birthday they were going to take her out of school and send her to Europe for the summer. They were very open about intending to break us up." He paused and took a deep breath. "I took a week off and rode my bike up to Tahoe. I was trying to decide whether to quit working for her father and meet her there, or wait it out. But she followed me up to the mountains and . . . well, we got married."

A sudden wall of rain splattered against the restaurant window, blurring the outside world.

"That was her graduation photo in the wallet. She'd just gotten them. . . ." His eyes began to tear as he continued. "I won't make it through this without getting upset." He stared out at the storm for a few seconds, composing himself. "She wanted to go camping, so we rented a little cabin, like your grandfather's. Four days into our honeymoon . . . I killed her."

Shocked and stricken by the words, and by the truth she heard in them, Julie grew cold.

"She was . . . so tiny. All crumpled up like a . . . bones broken, through her skin. I remember feeling them move when I picked her up, there's a sound they made . . . still keeps me awake some nights." A shudder rippled through his body. "She was bleeding to death, and we had to get her to a hospital."

Color had washed from his face.

"You weren't alone?"

"Someone stopped to help. He drove us." Tears began to spill down his cheek. "I was holding her when she died. I'm not too clear on things after that, at the hospital and all, I don't . . . Dad and Derek came to get me. I tried to go to her funeral, but her father had me thrown out."

"What on earth happened?"

His eyes veiled over. "She wanted . . . she always drank bottled water, and we ran out." His smile was vacant. "So I took her car and went to get bottled water for my wife. It was such a simple thing. She'd started charcoal. Wanted to stay at the cabin and cook, have food ready for me. She was so . . ."

She saw physical pain take over his body, flattening his voice to a dead monotone as he continued. "I'm driving back, and I have the water. Then the right front tire goes flat. . . . I remember thinking that it was good that it happened when it was me driving, because she wouldn't know how to . . . It was dark by the time I got the damn thing fixed . . . it was dark," he repeated. "And I hit her."

"Oh, my God," Julie gasped, horror-stricken. "She was walking?"

He shook his head. "She was on my bike—a motorcycle, and she wasn't supposed to ride it. It was too heavy for her to handle." He took in a huge breath and let it out slowly. "But she was probably worried. It was a narrow road. She came around a curve and . . . I killed her."

He sat silent in his torment for several minutes, not meeting her eyes, holding back emotions she could only guess at, inside his own private hell. "A few minutes later, a man came along . . . helped me get out of the car, and we found her. She was moving when I picked her up, still alive."

Julie returned his grasp, holding on tightly. "You tried to save her life. Why was it investigated?"

He was blinking, trying to clear his vision. "Her father snapped, I think. She'd lied to him, told him she was spending the weekend with a girlfriend. She hadn't called so she wouldn't have to lie to him again. A state trooper notified him she was dead. She was his whole world, and I think he just came apart." He wiped tears from his eyes. "He tried to prove that she died because I picked her up, and that she'd have been okay if we'd waited for the paramedics. Then he found out we were married, and he decided that I'd killed her on purpose."

Julie blinked, trying to comprehend. "I don't understand."

"I didn't, either. Apparently . . ." He shook his head, voice deadened once again. "Apparently she had some sort of trust from her grandmother that went into effect the day she got married. I had no knowledge of it—God knows I wouldn't have taken the money—but he locked onto the idea that I knew, and that's why I wanted to marry her. He thought I took her up there to kill her. All in one neat little package."

He made a derisive sound. "Damn near proved it, and the next thing I know, my dad is spending his life savings on attorneys' fees. Morganer had a grand jury convened, claimed the impact on the bike was from behind. The bike was so damaged, I don't know whether it was or not, or how they could tell. Anyway, I never think about that part. For me, it doesn't matter where I hit her. I killed her."

Julie sat stunned, unable to think of anything to say. He stared bleakly out at the rain gusting against the window. "Anything else you want to know?"

She looked at him, unable to express the extent of her compassion. "How on earth did you survive?"

He didn't answer for an extended beat. His eyes were focused on the rain, and just as she began to think he might not tell her, he responded. "I'm not sure. Even after the funeral, it was a long time before I could believe she was dead. Her father was insane, determined to make me pay for it. Like I cared what he did to me . . . I bummed around, worked sometimes. Drank a lot. I don't remember a couple of years, here and there. I spent a lot of time trying to . . . replace her, I guess. Then a lot of time trying *not* to. I wasn't a great emotional bargain for anyone."

He gave her a direct look, rejoining her at last, an almost physical broadside under the conviction in his words. "I still may not be. It's permanent damage, I won't lie to you. . . . She's dead and I killed her. That'll never go away." He sighed deeply. "And one of the things that came back with everything else is: until a week ago, I didn't care much whether I lived or died. Not since that night, my brother will tell you that. Anyone I know will tell you that."

He took her hand again. "But for what it's worth, there hasn't been a moment since we met that I've been able to shut you out, or not worry about you. That's new for me. It scares the hell out of me." He shook his head, eyes holding her fast. "And losing you scares me even more."

She felt a warmth in her chest at last, competing against the sadness that had been growing, and a hope that things between them could be nurtured, go forward, grow.

"Sexually . . ." He smiled at her, sad and wearied from the telling. "I don't even know how to tell you how great sex is with you. It's like there's never been anyone, not even Gina, who gets me where you do. I loved her, and I always will—that's part of the deal if anything permanent happens with us. But this thing with you *is* something separate."

A rush of emotion tingled through her body.

"I've thought about her every single day since she died, every time the sun goes down—except this past week. Maybe not knowing about it for a while, not thinking about how she died every time it gets dark . . . maybe it's been long enough to let someone else in my life. I don't know." He kissed her hand, his eyes connected to his soul. "And I need you to understand that I *don't* know. It's all too new, and I'm afraid to trust it. Nine years doesn't change overnight." He stroked a strand of her hair back into place. "Except maybe it has. . . . At any rate, I don't want anything unclear between us. It wouldn't be fair to you."

His sincerity was disquieting but welcome, and she tried to equal it in response. "There's been nothing in my life remotely similar to the tragedy you had," she admitted. "My baggage is not being able to trust. I grew up with it, saw it destroy my parents' marriage. Then Ned . . . And until a week ago, I'd never in my life had an affair—I guess that's what this is." She paused, uncomfortably. "Ned and I were going to get married, and I assumed we were going to have a future. So that part of a relationship with you is new to me, too. It's like I've always been so careful, needed all these guarantees . . . so Polly Perfect, and my sister's never going to believe that I'm sleeping with someone I've only known a week. I'm not sure I believe it."

"Are you?"

She looked at him, confused by the question. "What?"

"Sleeping with me?"

"Oooh boy." The blood of her body rushed into all the right places, and she bit the end of her little finger. Eyes dulled to the sheen of wet jade were taking her measure, faint highlights beginning to flicker in their depth. She glanced out the window at the storm. "Well, right now it's pouring rain, so I don't . . . we're not . . ."

"It's a little after seven o'clock. I met you in the rain, so I don't mind getting wet. We can stay if you want, but if it'll sway your decision, the current score is one to nothing, my favor." Eyes filling with mischief dropped to her chest level, traveled up her throat to her mouth, then met her gaze again, with a more intense expression. "And if I'm going to have time to make it even before your sister arrives, we probably ought to leave now."

"Oooh boy."

She grabbed her purse; he gave a passing waitress thirty dollars and told her to keep the change. On their way out they stopped at the bar and he introduced her to Jackson Bailey. "This my lady, Jack, and we're heading up the hill."

Bailey pointedly studied the storm, clearly uninterested in getting wet. "Looks like it'll let up in about an hour. You're not going to have dinner?"

"Yes, well . . . we're not hungry, but stay and have dinner if you'd like. No rush. I promise we're in for the evening."

Jack grinned tolerantly, shook his head, and avoided Julie's eyes. "Thanks, I'll keep that in mind."

Julie was still blushing when they dashed out into the rain.

The shower stall in her old-fashioned apartment was tiny, built for one person's use—or hedonistic pleasure, depending on the moral outlook of the apartment's inhabitants. After an exhilarating climb up the hill in the downpour, he and Julie had thrown their soppy clothing into her dryer and opted for the latter.

Maneuvering for space was a soapy, slippery business indeed, and exceedingly pleasant. There was a slight roll of thunder as he grasped her shoulder and turned her back to him, gliding himself along as much of her skin as he could manage in the process. He scrubbed her back with a duck-shaped sponge, then abandoned it in favor of working soapy, foamy fingers gently around her breasts, across her ribs, down the hollow of her belly, and lower, taking full advantage of it being his turn to call the shots. However, her proximity and the nature of his activity served to work against him, and he soon gave in to the prospect of greater pleasure.

"Time to rinse," he breathed in her ear, and turned the shower on again. "You're too slippery. And I want to hold on to you . . . from here."

Water rained down on them, melting the slick coating of lather. This woman—what was it about this woman that he could not do without? He turned off the shower and sluiced droplets of water from her skin with his hands in drawn-out delicious moments. Stooping to wipe down her long, sexy legs, he kissed the undercurves of her cheeks, then brought his hands up between her knees, rose to position himself, and entered her from underneath. She was swollen and moist, ready for him. Sliding his fingers over her hips and gripping the base of her thighs with both hands, he rocked himself forward into this most ancient of embraces.

He held his breath to keep control as he listened to her responses, gauged her pleasure, and kept himself on edge in an extended, exquisite experience for both of them. There was a point of internal pressure from this position not possible from any other, and when her inner contractions began, she uttered incoherent cries, inadvertent and unintelligible, confirming each time she came.

God, he loved making love to her! He moved leisurely back and forth, from side to side, protracting and increasing her orgasms. Her breath was coming in shudders and her moans in time with his when he came, emptying himself.

Later he eased her into bed, then retrieved his clothing and returned to her bedroom to get dressed. She scowled up at him, petulant, sleepy-eyed. "Where are you going?"

"Your sister's message said midnight."

She checked her bedroom clock. "It's only eleven-thirty, and I don't care what she said. She probably won't be here until tomorrow."

"I know, but if I don't leave now, I'll get in there with you. The first time I meet her, I'd rather not be the naked guy in your bed, if you don't mind." He kissed her, wanting to slide under her covers anyway, wanting to sleep by her side and wake up warm and toasty next to her—and make love with her again in the morning. By which time her sister would be camped out in the living room. He gave it up. "Besides, she's got obvious problems with her husband, and I think she'd probably prefer some privacy. I'll call you tomorrow."

Jack Bailey phoned Hathaway shortly after midnight. "He's checking into a motel. Mile and a half from her place. I don't know, maybe they had a fight."

"Nah, he said her sister was coming in."

"Well, I can't cover both of them. Do you want me to put Straithern on her?"

Hathaway picked up his watch from the night table and looked at the time. "How long will that take?"

"Half an hour, tops."

"Do it. But you stay with him. Don't even blink."

29

FRIDAY

Three hours ago, sexually blitzed and tired enough to go to asleep on his feet, David had fallen fully dressed across the motel bed in a vague, euphoric haze, full of her; now he was wide awake and his mind was jumping from subject to subject to subject like a leapfrog on speed. His brother . . . Gina . . . his life . . . years of guilt . . . but mostly the impact of this incredible, beautiful stranger who'd filled his world these last few days, whom he'd been sleeping with, had made love to, hadn't wanted to leave this evening.

For the past hour the peace of her had seemed at war with the pain, at war with the past . . . with protecting Derek . . . the money . . . and something else. Something . . . wrong. He could feel it.

His mind continued its free fall, skipping and kiting, his thoughts as out of control as confetti flung from a high place. Events and elements that defined him and were yet to be confronted, dealt with . . .

overcome. The promise to his father . . . promises he wanted to make to Julie.

Could he put his life back together at thirty-two? Start over with a career, build a future? What right did he have to ask her to join him, to live with him and share the sorrow—and the knowledge that he'd kept hidden and could say to no one?

Under the sound of the rain was the hesitant scuff of leather against cement. Someone was outside on the walk. Then came a rattling tap of knuckles on the room's window glass. A burst of nerves rode the length of his spine. "Yeah?"

"Rocklin, it's Jack."

He recognized the voice and opened his door the width of the safety chain to find his boss's watchdog. Bailey was alone, and the man's wary, hangdog expression caused a sensation of alarm to settle in at the base of his brain. "What do you want?"

"Hathaway said to wake you. It's not good."

A creeping numbness closed around his heart. He slipped the chain and allowed the man inside.

Bailey was mercifully brief. "We lost her. She came out with some guy and got in a van about two-fifteen. Straithern got the license plate, but he didn't realize there was a problem until the cops arrived half an hour ago. Husband came in with a gun. Tied up her sister, but she managed to get loose and make some noise. A neighbor called it in."

Three black-and-whites were on the scene in front of Julie's apartment, reflections of their emergency lights slickering red and blue on everything wet. David waded through a pool of fear to see for himself. She couldn't be gone. After all they'd been through, some nut case of a brother-in-law puts her in a van and drives away with her? They'd looked into their future. Made love. It wasn't possible.

In the middle of the living room, a woman identified to him as Julie's sister was keening and staring into space, rigid with hysteria. She was seated on the sofa and a female officer was offering her a glass of water, trying to calm her down. Strips of silver duct tape were lying in a plastic bag on the wing chair. Everything seemed to move in slow motion. David introduced himself, but Joann was too upset to do more than stare through him and nod.

Bailey helped him find an officer who would talk to him as a friend of Julie's. "Domestic situation gone bad, apparently," said the cop. "Angry spouse flies in from Switzerland, hassles the wife in Chicago, follows her to L.A. She comes home late, he's waiting on the patio." The officer worked a kink out of his shoulder. "Anything you can tell us?"

"He was here earlier this evening." David had the sensation of someone else's voice issuing from his mouth. "Broke in. Hostile, threatening."

The officer made a note. "What time was that? You saw him here?"

"Before four, I think. It wasn't dark yet." Floating in and out of a leaden place, he gave the officer a general run-down of his confrontation with the brother-in-law, his dinner with Julie, and the time he'd left her alone.

When Bailey verified the times from his surveillance log, the officer became circumspect. "A better description of the husband will help. All we have from the wife is general: age, eyes, height and weight, black sweats. She's pretty shaken up."

"Julie called him Gerd." Hearing himself use her name, David fought harder to stay present. "No mustache or beard," he said dully. "He needed a shave this afternoon, weak-chinned, dark hair cut regular length, bit of a beer gut, uh . . . seems foreign, an odd cadence to his speech. He was gone within seconds after I arrived. Wasn't wearing sweats earlier, was driving some kind of sedan, navy or black . . . seven-OXD-something plate. Did you run the license on the van?"

"We're working on it."

Information from the officer had come to a halt the moment David had admitted that he was under Bailey's surveillance. A need to talk to Gerd's wife, to find out what she knew, clawed at his concentration. Across the room, the woman officer was gently solicitous. "Mrs. Walde, is there anyone we can call for you?" she asked. "Parents, a friend . . . ?" Joann was shaking her head in denial.

Inside his chest, his heart began a lurching motion. "Walde? This guy's name is *Walde*?"

"Yeah, Gerd Walde. You know him?"

Walde wasn't that common a surname. David shook his head at the officer, blinking, trying to take it in. Julie's *brother-in-law* was Walde? The asshole who'd threatened to kill Derek? His mind rebelled. *How could it be Walde?* And why would he kidnap Julie? What did she have to do with anything? If it was Walde, he hadn't followed her from Santa Barbara—he'd been in her apartment long enough to fall asleep this afternoon before she'd arrived. So what was the connection? What was he missing?

Next to him, the officer began to consult with a detective arriving on the scene. "The suspect's a Swiss citizen. We're working on his passport to find out when he came into the country, make sure he doesn't leave. Some kind of art dealer, married to the victim's sister a little over three years. Recent separation . . . financial problems. She's not too coherent, but it seems he's trying to find some money he thinks the wife took, so maybe he grabbed the sister-in-law to see if he can scare the wife into giving it up."

The money! Of course, the goddamned money! That's what he was after! David's fear built to overwhelming proportions. *Christ, Walde could have it all!*

Still stunned at his discovery, he watched the detective approach Joann. "Mrs. Walde, did your husband give you any indication where he was going when he left with your sister? Anything at all?"

Joann Walde was trembling, her voice thin and ragged. "No, just 'Where is my money?' He kept saying it like he was going to kill her unless he got it." She looked up, obviously bleary with fright and confusion. "There is no money, I swear it! He's spent everything we had. I couldn't get him to understand that there was no money to take! Oh, God, Julie . . . He's crazy, he's gone crazy. It's all my fault. I should never have come here."

On the outside of David's envelope of fear, the detective's voice droned on. "Do you have any reason to think he's capable of violence, Mrs. Walde?"

"I don't know. I don't *know.* He had a gun! I've never seen him with a gun before," she wailed, giving

David's terror a voice, and his mind leaped to the other gun. The Walther. The one he'd left on Julie's bureau.

"I've never seen him like this. Oh, God, Julie . . ." Joann collapsed in tears; the woman officer helped her to her feet and walked her into the bedroom.

With a thin hold on his own sanity, David followed. It was missing! Gone from the bureau. Julie's bathrobe, in a muddle on the floor, distracted him with mute testimony that she wouldn't appear. Why hadn't she used the gun? She'd watched him place it there. Maybe she'd forgotten. Maybe she'd been too frightened. One thing was certain: Walde had it now.

He scanned the room, desperate to find proof of her existence, and relived moments of time that had taken place just hours ago: he'd undressed her to take their shower; he'd tossed rain-wet ruby underwear onto her bureau. Close to midnight, when he'd expected her sister at any moment, he'd retrieved the Walther from her laundry room, laid it on the bureau, and covered it with her panties as a lame erotic joke; she'd given him a mock-disgusted look, then walked with him to the front door. Kissed him good night. Turned the lock behind him.

As far as he could tell, nothing else in the room had been disturbed. He pulled the policewoman out of Joann's hearing. "I left a weapon here." He described the Walther while something that felt like broken glass churned in his stomach.

"Not here when we came in," said the policewoman. "I searched this room myself."

He returned with the officer to the living room to notify the detective in charge that the pistol had been taken; his face impassive, the detective began issuing revised information to his people on the two-way radio he was carrying. "Kidnap suspect has a second weapon, taken from the scene," he stated tersely, and described the gun. "Consider him doubly armed and dangerous."

David grabbed Bailey's arm and charged out the front door. A uniformed officer followed them to Bailey's vehicle and waited within earshot while he put in a frantic call on the car phone to Derek. "Wake up! Walde's got Julie. An hour ago. He's her goddamned brother-in-law, for God's sake. Listen to me! When he calls, you give him anything he wants."

Despite the hour, his brother was alert within seconds. "Oh, damn. I'm sorry, David. Oh, Jesus! When I told him the deal was history," he admitted hesitantly, words laden with guilt, "he threatened to kill her. I told him to screw off. . . . I had no idea he was talking about Julie, I . . . oh, Christ! I'm sorry!"

"Shut up, shut up! I don't want to hear this now!" David held down his panic long enough to speak slowly and succinctly. "Tell him I'll give him whatever he wants, wherever he wants it. Do you understand?"

"Yeah . . . yes! I'll leave for my office immediately."

"Just make sure you reach him, and don't miss his call!"

David gave him Bailey's number and hung up, shaking. Bailey and the officer were staring at him. "You'll have to come with me, Mr. Rocklin," said the officer.

Trapped, he grabbed Bailey's arm. "Keep Hathaway in the loop, let him know what's happening.

Tell him I need his help." Then he followed the officer back inside Julie's apartment.

The next two hours were a blur of questions as he attempted to give the Malibu detectives the history of the ransom that had led to Julie's kidnapping. From time to time dread would rush his thinking and spike through his heart like an alien thing, convincing him that he'd lost her, that he'd find her body broken and bloody, the way he'd found Gina, and be helpless.

Rage at Walde closed his throat and sent him out of his mind. Swaying in his chair, unable to hold down frenzied waves of terror that deafened him to the surrounding men, he blanked out their voices and their concern and their determination to come to her rescue.

Around four in the morning he was driven to the Malibu police station, and FBI agents arrived. He repeated his story, and soon they were questioning him about his eagerness to pay Walde a ransom for Julie's release. Asking more questions about the money. He told them everything—except the location of the cash.

Hathaway came in at some point, confirmed his statements, and clarified his status with Ambassador Surety; after that the questioning subsided. But no word arrived from Derek that Walde had called him. He tried to put himself in Walde's place and determine what the son of a bitch would do, but questions from teams of investigators continued into the morning hours, and he was informed that he'd be detained at the police station until further notice.

Was he certain about leaving the gun on the bureau? If he was worried enough to provide a weapon, why had he stayed at a nearby motel? Why was he under surveillance by his own employer? Why had he called his brother and offered to pay a ransom before a ransom was demanded? Did he want to change his story about the amnesia? Why would he not disclose the location of the money? Was he positive of his description of Walde? The circle of fear tightened into wrath so pervasive that he wanted to scream, to hurt someone. He longed for the freedom to find Walde and kill him.

The rainstorm had passed south. The sky was a dark dove gray above the streetlights, not yet pinking into dawn. In the driver's seat of the van, Julie struggled to stay alert. Carrying David's gun around for a week had not prepared her for reality. She'd witnessed people being held at gunpoint a thousand times, but actors being bad guys and stalwart heroes hadn't generated anything close to the genuine emotional impact.

News footage of a real shoot-out between police and bank robbers and glimpses of paramedics sopping up real blood from gunshot wounds had aroused a sense of being appalled, but in the end the lingering thought had been an intellectual one: recognition that death was permanent and that dying in an attempt to steal money—or because of some adolescent turf war over drugs—was stupid. But *nothing* equaled the fear of a real gun in the hands of a real person who seemed entirely capable of shooting her.

Gerd hadn't been visible immediately, hunched down directly behind her sister as Joann came through the doorway. Sleepy, distracted by the late hour and her disappointment that instead of arriving at midnight, as promised, Joann had obviously closed a bar somewhere before showing up, she'd seen her brother-in-law too late. Her sister's whispered "I'm sorry" and the distress in her face hadn't registered.

"Where is he?" he'd demanded. She'd been too terrified to answer, but Gerd had seen for himself that her bedroom was empty and had gotten furious. After forcing her to bind Joann's arms and legs with tape, he'd manhandled her back into the bedroom and ordered her to get dressed; he'd stood watching through the doorway. She'd forgotten about David's gun until she'd uncovered it, and moments later her brother-in-law had charged into the room to yank clothing from her closet and announce that she would be driving. Holding her at gunpoint, he had thrown a sweater and a pair of jeans at her and waited impatiently until she was clothed enough to discard the robe; defending herself with David's gun had not been possible.

Pleading that she'd need her glasses and driver's license, she'd managed to grab her purse from the top of the bureau before he'd dragged her out into the rain by her hair and pushed her into this hideous van. She'd driven south down the coast for him, then east at Santa Monica, then left and right onto one street after another of darkened houses, with glistening streetlights making it hard to see. With the gun wavering unsteadily as he'd switched it from hand to hand, sometimes he'd sent her doubling back, but always he'd avoided the freeways.

Thoughts of David haunted her. She hadn't had the presence of mind to say anything to Joann, to leave a message for him, even. When he'd left, Jack Bailey would have followed him, so no one would even know she was missing until hours from now. In the meantime, it was up to her to think of something.

Two blocks past a sign that read KOREA TOWN, Gerd had pointed out a phone booth. She'd positioned the van close to the phone and he'd opened the driver's-side door to keep her in full view. Determined to remain calm until she had a clear opportunity to make a move, she'd anticipated his need for coins and offered him her wallet; he'd taken the thirty-three dollars in cash, then fed coins from the change pocket into the telephone. His eyes hadn't left her face, and she'd made no effort to upset him; he was clearly unstable, and doing anything rash could easily give him cause to shoot her. The call had been lengthy, in a foreign language, and he'd used most of her coins before getting back in the van.

After that, he'd made her change directions so many times that she no longer had any idea where they were. She suspected he was lost as well. Urban sprawl along California's coastline stretched all the way from Malibu to the Mexican border and they could be anywhere between. She hadn't been permitted to drive in a straight line, but she calculated that they weren't much farther south than Hawthorne.

She held on to the thought that she'd survived the

past week in Washington by keeping her head, and gradually her terror eased to a nerve-deadened sense of survival. The longer their activity stretched toward dawn, the more she found that she could concentrate on something other than the gun and Gerd's irrational behavior. Pushing her glasses up onto the bridge of her nose, she tried to make sense of his actions. Somehow her brother-in-law was involved with the insurance ransom. He'd seen the treasure tin and knew she'd been at the cabin. He'd known about the money David had been carrying and that the money was missing . . . and he'd seen David at her apartment, with a gun. She raced to add up what else she knew.

Gerd was a small-time art dealer; her sister had bought into his business after they'd gotten married and had sold her interest in the gallery back to him a year or so ago, but to the best of Julie's knowledge, they'd never dealt in million-dollar paintings. Obviously there was another, extremely dangerous side to Gerd, one that neither she nor Joann had known about. Her sister's description of their financial difficulties didn't square with Gerd's owning a two-million-dollar painting. Maybe he'd hidden it from Joann, or maybe it wasn't his.

Gerd barked another direction at her, jarring her into making a too-quick left turn. He was mumbling at her again, words she couldn't comprehend, and was angry when he had to repeat himself in English. "The money. The *money!* What he did with it?"

Admitting knowledge of the cash would not help her. Plus, it could endanger David as well; therefore, honesty was definitely out of the question—at least until she had more information. "Gerd, please . . . I don't know. I've told you, he had a backpack. If there was money, I didn't know about it. We were strangers, and we got caught in a flood together, that's all. All I did was drive him to an airport."

"Don't *lie* to me! He was in your *home!* With the gun."

"He told me that the only reason he stopped by last night was to say hello. I don't know why he had a gun. I don't *know* the man. Why would he trust me with information about money? I never expected to see him again, believe me. But you were angry and threatening me. I was more afraid of you than I was of him."

Sometimes he believed her, sometimes not. His emotional turmoil was apparent as he suddenly gestured toward an open Mobil station and demanded, "Here! Here!" She bumped the back wheels of the van over a center divider as she made the turn. "Be careful, *dummkopf!*"

That word she understood. "I told you I couldn't see at night!" she railed.

The gun disappeared into the pouch of his sweatshirt while an attendant, a young man, filled the van's gas tank. Gerd paid him with some of her cash. "How far is Long Beach?"

The young man scratched the back of his neck. "On the freeway?"

"Yes." The bulge of metal jerked under the fabric pouch.

"Oh, about forty minutes, I guess."

Gerd gestured toward the surrounding neighborhood. "Where is this?"

"Here? This here's Inglewood."

"Thank you . . . Let's go," he ordered. Julie eased the van out into the street and he continued giving her hasty directions. Eventually they passed a run-down motel and he directed her to circle the block, then told her to stop in a small alley. *Too late!* Her mind began screaming at her that she was an idiot.

He walked her to the rear of the van and put her inside at gunpoint. He picked up a roll of tape. "Ankles," he insisted. She complied, each breath increasingly difficult as panic rose in her chest. She'd made a mistake by waiting for opportunity! Now she was helpless. He allowed her to put her glasses into their case, but irritably grabbed them from her hand and threw them into her purse before stuffing it under her arm. Then he climbed in next to her, his breath hot in her face. She did her best to fight as he taped her wrists, but he was too strong; she began to scream as he pressed a square of duct tape across her mouth.

He backed out of the van and quietly shut the door; after a moment she felt forward motion. When the vehicle came to a halt again, he shut off the engine and the interior lights went dark. She felt the van's body shift as he got out. Then he was gone for what could have been minutes or an hour.

Struggling was useless. She fought hysteria as emotion jammed her throat. When he'd instructed her to tie up Joann, she'd managed to wrap most of the tape onto the cuffs of her sister's jacket, but Gerd had wound the sticky, unyielding stuff directly onto her skin. *Please, God, someone . . .*

David.

He'd be frantic. He'd come looking for her. What could Gerd conceivably have hoped to gain by kidnapping her? Unless she was to be exchanged for the ransom. The possibility became hope. David had the money. David would find her.

30

She'd been dozing; she blinked against clear, thin daylight. The kind that signaled a September sunrise, she though hazily. It was shining through a slender portion of windshield visible above the seat backs in front of her. She'd been slumped against the van's ribbed flooring and her cheek was itchy. She rubbed it against the carpeting. Sunlight. David would call soon and wonder why no one answered . . . he'd find Joann . . .

Something brushed against the outside of the van, startling her; she raised her feet to kick against the metal siding. If it was a person . . .

"Over here." Gerd was back, his lowered voice directly outside the rear door, and her determination collapsed. "Ilse! Over here!"

Ilse. Taking a moment to steady herself, Julie tried to remember where she'd first heard the unusual name. Then she remembered: from Joann. Ilse was Gerd's mistress! She'd known when he made the phone call that he wasn't in this alone, but she was offended on behalf of her sister that this particular woman had turned out to be his partner. She held her breath in order to hear more clearly.

"I have four." Ilse's voice was agitated. "I can't believe you have done this!"

There was a burst of unintelligible argument from Gerd, then the passenger door opened and several pieces of metal clanked as they landed inside. The door slammed, and a pounding on the side of the van boomed in Julie's ears, causing her to flinch. ". . . need more time!"

"That we don't have." The woman's tone was deeply angry. "So, we have to be very careful and do this right. If he has gone to the police, it is dangerous. We must call. It's the only way we can decide if . . ." Their discussion went out of her hearing, and Julie's heart began to race. Ilse's involvement changed things. The question was, for better or worse?

It was quarter past seven in the morning, and he'd been answering questions four of the five hours she'd been gone. Leg bouncing at the knee, wild with tension, David sat in a cubbyhole of a windowless office somewhere in a warren of windowless, cubbyhole offices that were used for interrogation. He was certain he was being watched through what appeared to be a large acrylic replica of a nature scene, entirely too large for the room. *Where is she? What's that bastard doing to her?*

He stared past the agent at the blue lake on the wall and scraped his palm over his jaw, vaguely aware that he needed a shave. "If I'm not under arrest, release me," he said heatedly. "You know my brother has a lawyer on the way, and if you arrest me, I'll make bail in twenty minutes. I've answered every question you've asked, seventeen times. Nothing's going to change."

"I can keep you as long as I want, sonny." The agent's name was Bradshaw, and he needed a shave also.

"I know you can. And I also know that my sister-in-law has more money than good sense, and if the Belhams decide that going public will get me out of here, you'll roast in the media if you don't have more on me than you have right now." His voice deepened with frustration. "And I know you don't, because I haven't done anything!"

Bradshaw glared at him. "Wait with us for the call, Mr. Rocklin. Let me do my job or you're going to get her killed."

David ground his teeth. "We're calling a dead number! If Walde was going to call back, he'd have done it by now. He hasn't contacted my brother, so he's already changed beeper numbers. He's sleeping in while we're irritating each other," he said bitterly.

"I don't think so, but if he gets himself a new pager, we'll start over. In the meantime, let's discuss why you won't turn over the money."

David went stubbornly silent while the federal agent tried to hide a yawn, and eventually Bradshaw conceded and left the room. Three minutes later David was ushered into a waiting room of sorts where Hathaway was pacing.

"Don't leave town," advised his escort, and removed himself.

"Have you talked to Derek? These guys won't tell me anything."

"Five minutes ago. Walde hasn't called," Hathaway answered. "What about here?"

"Bastard didn't respond to the page. It's not a number he knows, and he probably figures it's the police."

Bradshaw popped his head through the doorway, gesturing excitedly and snapping his fingers at them. "Get in here."

David shot through the door. In a larger cubbyhole, an agent was muttering into a headphone. "I can't hear you, the connection's cutting out. . . . Call me back." The line disconnected and a dial tone filled the room. The agent indicated a telephone on top of a nearby desk. "It's a woman. When she calls, you answer there. Keep her on as long as you can."

David nodded, a cold rage driving his energy. The two men fussed with equipment attached to the telephone, which rang immediately. David answered. "I have the money. Where do you want it?"

The woman responded. "It's good. We will—"

"You tell that son of a bitch I'm going to want to see her, and she'd better be all right."

"She's fine. We will let you—"

"Don't tell me she's fine. I want to talk to her! If anything's happened to her, *anything*, I'll kill the both of you, I swear it. You hear me?"

"We will let you know."

"When?"

"Tomorrow." The line went dead, and David sat rigid, waves of perspiration coating his body. "You get it?" The agent's answer was affirmative, and he was able to breathe again. "Good job."

"Yeah, well, we're faster than we used to be. Being local helps." The machinery was noiseless as a group of numbers slid onto the video screen. The agent tocked the numbers into an adjacent computer setup and an address appeared within seconds. "Phone booth in Costa Mesa," he said, writing the address on a pad of paper. "She'll be gone, but we might get lucky spotting the van in the area. From now on, every minute counts." Ripping off the sheet, he rushed out of the room to notify the Costa Mesa police.

Bradshaw looked at David. "Told you we could help."

David returned the gaze, no longer angry, just tired. "I owe you one." He picked up the phone and began punching in numbers. "I'm going to get my brother down here, which will take about two hours. As soon as he arrives, I'm leaving. Unless you arrest me."

"What are you going to do?" Bradshaw asked cautiously.

"He's working his way down the coast, probably thinks he can get into Mexico—" He broke off to speak to his brother. "Derek, I just talked to them and I need you down here. . . . Malibu police station. Thanks." He hung up the phone. "I'm going to be following him with the money. I'll be in position to deliver it whenever he wants."

"We can't let you do that. We'll have him before then."

"Bradshaw, this guy is losing control. Everything he's planned for more than two years has fallen apart." David heaved himself to his feet, body stiff and uncooperative. "He owes a lot of money somewhere, is afraid of going to jail, his whole world is coming apart. When Derek told him to take a walk, he thought he was out of options and grabbed Julie. He's desperate, he's not thinking . . . and he's convinced that getting the money is going to save him. It's probably the only thing that's holding him together."

"I agree with everything you've said. Once we're in position, we negotiate and talk him down. We can't just—"

"I'm convinced he was willing to kill to get the money in the first place. He's a cornered rat, and if he decides he's beaten, there's no way he's going to let her walk away!" He held Bradshaw's gaze as he walked to the door. "If he doesn't get that money, nobody knows what he'll do, including you. I'm going to give it to him, and you'll have to shoot me to stop me—and I don't think you can do that."

"He can do just about anything else, David." Hathaway, who'd been listening quietly, was the soul of reason.

"Within the law. And I think the law says that as a private citizen, I can give money to anyone I choose."

"Don't do it. You're gonna get her killed," the agent said coldly. "These guys don't leave witnesses."

"If she gets killed because I wouldn't give him the money, who fixes that one?" David shot back. "It's only money!"

"We'll get him! Just help us do it."

Hathaway cleared his throat. "Rocklin," he said

gently. "The money belongs to Ambassador."

"I'm borrowing it, and I'm buying a real live person instead of a painting. You know the Belhams are good for it; we can sort out the details later, Ron, don't you think?" He glanced at the federal agent. "If Bradshaw here does his job, the money's just going for a ride, that's all. And right now it's going to Costa Mesa."

"We're all going to Costa Mesa, son. Your brother can follow us down there."

Julie felt Gerd climb into the van and saw the top of his head above the seat back. He drove for what seemed like twenty minutes—but she was tired, and time was getting harder and harder to judge.

Finally the van was parked and the back door opened up. For the first time Julie saw the woman who'd spoken. Ilse's forceful voice did not match her face and body, but her appearance was nonetheless striking. Small-boned, delicately featured, and incredibly thin, she had fish eyes. Dead fish eyes: prominent, oddly dull gray in color, thinly rimmed with colorless lashes, and sunken under penciled brows that had been plucked nearly out of existence. Lank black hair had been cut in an attractive manner, but the roots were a mousy, tepid brown.

Ilse used a knife to cut the tape away from her legs, then produced a silk scarf large enough to wind around Julie's head in the style of a monk's cowl; the silk held the stifling smell of oily perfume. The van was situated within a few feet of the back entrance to a motel, and Julie gave up hope of being seen when they quick-walked her between them into a room

and shoved her onto a chair. Ilse removed the suffo-
cating scarf and dropped it onto the nearest bed, and
Julie could breathe again.

Gerd tossed four license plates onto the tabletop.
The sound of their grinding and clattering against
each other scraped another layer off Julie's nerves.
She rested trembling hands on her knees, willing
herself not to lose it. Gerd had taped her wrists so
that her palms faced each other, and the only other
comfortable position was propping her hands against
her chest. So far, they'd left her purse strapped to her
body; mired in a sea of helplessness, she felt its heavy
weight as a comforting presence. She looked around,
trying to get her bearings, and wondered if she dared
ask to use the bathroom.

She'd used her tongue to loosen the tape from
her lips, but where it was stuck to her chin and
cheeks it was beginning to irritate her skin. From the
chipped top of the dining table next to her chair, her
eyes crept along the edges of the frayed bedspreads
covering the two single beds in the room, past an
abused television set bolted to the wall under a
sturdy metal strap, and on to a less-than-appealing
kitchenette with a sink, a hot plate, and a small
refrigerator. In a place this scruffy, even if she were
able to scream, it was unlikely that strangers would
come to the rescue. Shrieking "fire" would probably
be ignored as well.

The door to the bathroom was open. Catching
Ilse's eye, she nodded her head toward the bath a
couple of times, and made a small sound in her
throat. The woman gave Gerd a rankled look and
said something in a foreign language. Gerd flushed

and shook his head, then picked up the gun and uttered a burst of what must have been male justification. Ilse approached her slowly. "I will make it so you can walk and use your hands," she said, "but you will keep the tape on your mouth."

Julie nodded agreement; the woman produced her small, very sharp knife once again and led her to the bathroom before freeing her wrists. "Door stays open," she warned.

Freedom! Under Ilse's unwavering stare, Julie managed to keep the purse in place and sat, no longer caring much about Gerd's sensibilities. Massaging tape gunk from her wrists, she saw only Depression-era flooring tile, uniformly grimy and surrounded by filthy grouting and uneven cement patches where tiles were missing, but her total attention was focused on the couple in the adjoining room.

Gerd and Ilse resumed their battle within moments, going at each other in an escalating argument, using a mish-mosh mixture of languages; it was obvious that they didn't want her to know they were discussing her, and Ilse was gesticulating wildly, muttering in French something about "impossible," "ridiculous," and "why," plus a very clear "imbecile," which Julie took as verification that Ilse hadn't expected a hostage. Gerd was shouting about a *boot*, which might have meant "boat," but nothing else was intelligible.

Julie was afraid to speculate on their intent, except surely they didn't intend to try to get somewhere by boat! She lingered inside the bathroom as long as she dared, trying to understand enough of what they were saying to decide what to do. Ilse returned to the door, knife in hand, while Gerd shoved the license plates around, eyeing her as well. Gerd got to his feet and began pacing frantically as he vented his temper.

Eventually she heard *kaffee* and realized the argument had switched to food, of all things, and who was going to get it. Gerd handed Ilse the pistol and slammed out the door, apparently the loser in the skirmish. The clamor yielded to a silence thick enough to hear the van's engine start up.

Under the woman's assiduous glare, Julie washed her hands before coming obediently out of the bathroom. After her hands had been retaped, Ilse pushed her onto one of the beds, then took a pen and a pad of paper from a gargantuan tapestry purse and moved to the opposite side of the table in order to keep her in full view. She did not speak, and Julie used the blessedly quiet time to think.

She was exhausted and hungry, and sliding in and out of panic. Dealing with Gerd alone might have been possible. Eventually she might have calmed him down, reasoned with him. But Ilse was easily Gerd's equal, and the odds had doubled against being able to help herself out of this mess. It was now two very angry people against one supremely scared one who had no voice in the matter.

She tried to remember how the ransom was supposed to work. From the conversation in Derek's library, David had been delivering money in exchange for a painting, but she had no specific idea of what was to have taken place. How, exactly, did one go about exchanging a ransom for a person? The concept was so foreign, she had no idea where to start.

Ilse's preoccupation with writing material and a phone book began to register. Every aspect of the couple's plans had unexpectedly gone wrong: the wilderness of Washington state had been exchanged for urban Los Angeles, and they had a live hostage instead of an illegal painting. They couldn't have known the money would disappear and that she'd become involved . . . and wouldn't have been prepared with a plan to kidnap her.

They were creating one.

She took a deep breath and began to settle her nerves. Gerd hadn't come to her apartment looking for Joann. He was looking for the money. He'd been convinced that either it was in her apartment or she knew where it was. David had arrived and frightened him off, but he'd come back with a gun. Looking for David? Had to be! It was the only thing that made sense. All the time she'd been taping Joann's arms to the chair, he'd hassled her: "Where's my money? Where's the money!" She'd had no reason to connect it to the insurance money.

David and the money were gone . . . so Gerd had decided to take her with him. Then he'd stopped long enough to call Ilse, to let her know what he'd done; no wonder the woman was furious. Kidnapping was a federal offense. And Ilse the mistress was now Ilse the accessory, through no action of her own. Maybe that's what they'd been fighting about. Kidnapping a person had taken things to a whole new level. And they hadn't had time to figure out what to do with her, or how to receive the cash without being caught.

She wasn't up on state-of-the-art technology, but the police had sure found O. J. Simpson twenty minutes after he'd started using his car phone. Maybe they had ways of finding her, too. But she was a hostage, not a fugitive. She'd be the one with a gun to her head if the police were moving in.

A cold chill ran through her body as she realized another thing that was different from the original plan: identities. The police would have photos by now. Being able to get on an airplane and leave the country was probably already impossible. Neither Gerd nor Ilse had made any effort to disguise themselves to her, which meant they knew it was too late for such measures. Wherever they went, it would only be a matter of time until they were caught, extradited if necessary, and wound up facing a jury.

Unless they changed their names and managed to disappear. Which required money. Following this logic, for Ilse and her brother-in-law, getting the cash had become the only solution possible. And she was the key to their getting it. She could also be the key to making certain no one followed them. Gerd might try to keep her between him and the police. His manner seemed to be deteriorating, approaching desperation, and with weapons involved, things would be dangerous for everyone concerned. Most of all her.

One thing was certain: If a ransom was paid, at some point they'd be faced with a decision about whether or not to let her go. Her best chance was to escape before that happened. The next time her hands were free, she'd have to gamble her life. Until then, she would do everything Gerd and Ilse asked of her. She would be very, very careful, and would try to be prepared.

Gerd returned with a fast-food breakfast for them and a milkshake for her; she sat up and moved to the side of the bed in order to hold the icy drink. Gerd loosened a portion of the tape from a corner of her mouth to make room for a straw. It was a weak, watery concoction tasting of cheap, commercial frozen mix and chocolate syrup, but she was so hungry she didn't really care. Even crummy food provided energy. Three huge gulps into the shake, alarm bells suddenly jangled through her system. An aftertaste, false and metallic, lingered on her palate; she stopped drinking it instantly. David had said something to Doris about her husband having been drugged in Las Vegas. And photographs . . .

Jittery, she set the drink aside, but it was too late. A fluid sense of ease was already wilting her body, and she realized that she'd ingested enough to knock her out in spite of anything she could do. Gerd and Ilse were both watching her, and their conversation resumed in bursts of low, soothing tones that lulled her into a state of jelly. Her eyelids were relentless weights, first sagging into her vision, then impossible to open.

Making a final effort, she clenched her fists and gouged fingernails into the palms of her hands until it really stung; her brain bounced and oozed, but she succeeded in coming to rest in a place of total relaxation, her mind and hearing intact. Her hands softened into mush and she drifted with the rhythm of their speech, fluffier than air, no longer afraid.

"She's out."

"What are we going to do?" It was Gerd's strident, rumbling bass.

"Nothing. He said he would pay the money."

"What if this is trap?"

There was a lengthy, musical rustle of paper. "It is an open parking lot, with a close exit to the freeway. From there . . . to here. And we're gone. Everything must be ready."

"Yes, this should work. Yes. Thank you, I don't know what I would do except for you. . . ." A deep sigh, then an eruption. "Why . . . why?" Gerd's rage was evident. "It is perfect! Everything in place. We would live in Cannes by now!"

"Shhh!" Ilse's anger sounded resigned. "The rest is gone. Accept it. I have three hundred dollars. How much of your cash is left?"

A shuffling and a whispered count. "Less than two thousand." A chair scraping. "Where are you going?"

"It is not enough. She will have some in her purse."

"Thirty dollars. I spent it for petrol . . . and breakfast."

Ilse's voice was above her, speaking quietly. "Are you sure about . . . Have you explained to the owner of the painting that it is best for him if he gives you money to leave? He understands that you can have the provenance traced to his name if you choose?"

"He said he will deny this. No one will question him, and I cannot prove." Agitated sighs. "He is right."

"Fool." Ilse's comments, barely audible in the air above, began to recede. "Only a few thousand is not so much to pay to avoid trouble. Are you sure he—"

"Ilse, I have try!"

"Shhh!"

Gerd immediately lowered his voice. "He will not blackmail. He wants his money back! He knows the provenance is gone bad. He knows I took a deposit for the painting and did not tell him. I cannot repay the buyer, I cannot repay him. What we have on hand is all. It must be enough. We cannot trust anyone."

"Give it to me."

Silence.

A chair squeak.

Silence.

Julie felt her hold on consciousness begin to slip.

"What if they make a trap?"

"How can they? A weekend, everything will be crowded . . . they won't take a chance someone will be injured. They will need time to put police in the area, but we won't give it to them. It will work!"

"We must get rid of the van."

"We can do that while we do a final check. Then we contact them and—"

"What about her?"

"She's not going anywhere. Tape her feet, just to be sure."

Silence.

"God should damn this man!"

"Quiet!"

Julie drifted lower.

"Four hundred thousand from the commission,

Ilse." Gerd's voice was plaintive. "Five from the insurance. Three for making the provenance! After the sale, I am millionaire. I am rich! Now I have nothing."

"Tomorrow you will have five hundred thousand. No more worries. No more planning and hiding like a fugitive. Think about that. Don't think about the other."

"I can never go home."

"We have to get rid of the van," she reminded him.

Chairs squeaking and scraping . . . clothing rustling . . . her ankles being lifted, her legs limp and heavy, while tape went round and round . . .

And she didn't care. David was coming. He'd be here any second . . . and Joann could sleep on the couch.

31

It was half past eleven and Deke stared at the cast on his leg, contemplating the gigantic destructive arc his life had taken since he'd broken his ankle. He'd nearly gotten his brother killed, received a threat against his life, and strained his marriage past the breaking point. In the past thirty-six hours alone he'd lost his career, moved out of his home, and caused the woman his brother loved to be kidnapped.

Seated next to David, he was aware that there was nothing he could do to make amends; he was remorseful beyond anything he'd ever be able to express to his brother for dragging him into this quagmire. David's forbearance toward him throughout the ordeal had been truly amazing. The two of them sat surrounded by three men, drinking coffee and waiting for Walde to call. Or to take a call from his cold-blooded lady friend, now known to be Ilse Weinze, bitch extraordinaire.

The telephone company had rigged the contact number they'd used in Malibu to the FBI's new area of operation, and a haggard David had disappeared with Hathaway, then dragged himself back in three hours ago to continue the wait. Afraid to meet his eyes, Derek looked out onto Long Beach Harbor and saw nothing.

David was too worn down to try to ease his brother's shame. They'd straighten it out between them one of these days, but right now . . . right now, all he wanted in the Western world was to know she was still alive and help bring her home safely.

"They found the van," announced the monitoring officer, holding his hand to an earphone. "Motel parking lot in San Pedro," he relayed to the room at large, then paused to receive more information. "Couple fitting our description drove away about nine o'clock this morning, no third party visible in their vehicle. Van was empty, license plate had been switched. Forensics is looking at hair and fiber to make sure, but they're pretty certain it's the vehicle. No blood, no signs of struggle."

Everyone in the room relaxed somewhat at the last, most welcome piece of information. David set his mind to work on the new scenario to keep from going crazy. So they'd dumped the van. Which they'd been expected to do, and which meant they'd be driving a new, unknown vehicle that would make them that much harder to find. Refusing to sap his strength by being angry, he concentrated all his energy on willing the call to arrive. He and Derek had agreed that when Walde called in, Derek would talk to him to provide a voice he'd recognize; if it was the woman, David would take the call. *Come and get the money, you greedy bastards. Come and get it.* He rocked in his chair and repeated the mantra in his mind until it worked.

The buzz startled them all. The agents sprang to life, and he and Derek both picked up headphones; when they were ready, the agent switched on the sound. As agreed, his brother answered. "Yes?"

"Hello, moron."

It was Walde; David's heartbeat tripled in an instant as impotent rage tore through him. His mike had been turned off to ensure his silence, but he could hear Walde's voice loud and clear, as well as his own unsteady breathing. Powerless, he clenched his fists, hating the man for his contemptuous, brazen attitude, for his supreme cowardice, for victimizing people David loved . . . hating himself even more for not having realized how dangerous he was and allowing this cretin to get the upper hand.

"Which of us is the moron now?" asked the insolent voice.

"I am." Derek was handling it well, speaking coolly and without anger. "You won, I lost. Just don't do anything to the girl."

"I want to hear an apology," Walde retorted haughtily.

His brother responded without a beat. "I'm sorry."

"I didn't hear you."

"I'm sorry!" Derek said loudly. "I'm the sorriest son of a bitch you'll ever meet!"

"No need to shout, *moron*."

Ahead of them, in his brother's sight line, an

agent held up a notepad scrawled with the words SAY MONEY.

Again Derek responded smoothly. "I'm sorry. . . . I have the money. Just tell me where."

There was an immediate dial tone, and David groaned at Walde's failure to stay on the line. It wasn't his brother's fault; Derek hadn't said anything wrong. The agent shook his head, acknowledging that he hadn't been able to trace the line, but seemed unperturbed. "He's mousing with you, having a good time. Probably knows he was cutting it too close. He'll call back. Give him time to find another phone."

Half an hour passed before the line buzzed again. This time it was Derek's secretary, Melba. "We just received a fax," she said breathlessly, "and the police-man here said I should call you. It says: 'Moron. No more phone calls. You and only you will deliver the money. Anyone else in the area I say, and I do not show up. You will know what that means for her. Be ready at three o'clock for the location. You have ten minutes to arrive. When I am safe with the money and not before, I will call with an address.'" Melba took an audible breath. "The police took a copy, too."

David began to quake with rage. The son of a bitch was going to get away with it! Walde was going to get the money without anyone being able to make sure she was still alive. He stood, trying to contain the violence racing through his body. One of them, either himself or Derek, would have to deliver half a million dollars to this bastard and gamble that he hadn't already murdered her! He decided at that instant that it would be him. He wanted another look at the man he would track down and kill if anything had happened to her.

What time had the secretary said? Three o'clock. Less than three hours! Christ, was he cursed with threes as well? "That doesn't leave us much time."

"That's the idea," acknowledged one of the agents. "But he's doing it on the fly and is bound to make mistakes. When he does, we got him."

Bradshaw came in, already aware of the faxed instructions, and part of David's mind broke off to marvel at the speed of modern law enforcement. Maybe there was a chance after all. "We're looking for someone who can double you," the agent announced to Derek. "We'll have to fake the ankle brace."

"No. It's going to be me," David interrupted. "No one looks more like him than me, and if this guy gets spooked, he might kill her."

"Too dangerous." Face grim, Bradshaw was shaking his head. "Rocklin, listen to me. Agents are trained for this. It's a job for them. You're in love with her. You lose your cool, make one wrong move, and he could wind up killing both of you. Then I have a real mess on my hands—for letting you do it *and* getting you killed. Can't—"

"We're wasting time. It has to be someone he knows, and it's going to be me. I'm going to be the coolest guy you ever met." He planted himself in Bradshaw's path. "You guys have half a million dollars put together?"

"We're getting it."

"I already have it," he said calmly.

"We got lucky!" The agent tracking incoming calls interrupted their debate with a smile on his face. "Nailed the little weasel! Long Beach PD had public fax facilities staked out. He walked right into it." He pressed his hand to his earpiece, listening. "He's under surveillance right now, alone in his car."

Across the room Derek met his eyes, smiled hopefully, and raised both hands with crossed fingers.

"Come to Papa . . ." Bradshaw's voice drifted through the quiet in the room.

David's breath died in his body. It was going down, and he was stuck in an office, helpless. *Please, please, please let them be careful! Don't stop him. Don't lose him!*

The listening agent's face changed, closed over. "He just dumped the vehicle and got in a taxi. One passenger . . . a woman, and it looks like . . ."

The silence went on forever.

He nodded. "She's the passenger. He's in the backseat with her. Driver's a woman. Matches the girlfriend." There was a long pause. "Looks like they're heading for the 405. A plainclothes unit has them in sight." The agent listened again for several moments. "Taxi has false tags, phone number on its side is registered to some guy named Moammar something-or-other that I can't pronounce. They think it's a gypsy cab. Poor Moammar's probably tied up somewhere, with his cash missing."

"If he's lucky." David's voice was barely audible. "What happens now?"

Bradshaw's indecision was written on his face. He banged the wall with his knuckles, then turned to David, no longer on the fence. "Okay, we're out of

time, so I'm going to wire you up. But you're going
to wear a vest and do exactly as I say! If I change my
mind, you go *nowhere*, you got that?"

"Exactly what you say," David repeated flatly.
Determined not to show emotion, he was grateful
for Bradshaw's neutral tone. David was certain that
if his feelings were to run any higher, his brain
would explode.

They were in a taxi, in a line of cars on a freeway on-
ramp, and Julie had no idea what to expect next.
Ahead of them, two cars, one in either lane, picked
up speed with every green light and eased their way
into the slow lane. Soon it was their turn, and Ilse
sped the cab onto the freeway.

Julie's feet were free but her hands were still taped
together, with Gerd's fist wrapped firmly around her
forearm. She was still foggy with sleep, blinking into
the clear, bright midafternoon sunlight that generally came the day after a storm. Ilse's scarf was
wrapped around her head again, hiding the patch of
tape covering her mouth. She felt like the prisoner
she was, unable to move or speak, and suffocatingly
defenseless. The green freeway sign looming up
ahead read 405 SOUTH SAN DIEGO, and she took slow,
deep breaths, trying to clear her brain of the drugs.

San Diego meant . . . Mexico? Were they crazy?
You couldn't just drive into Mexico. There were border procedures. INS, Immigration and something . . .
Naturalization Services, patrols looking for anything
suspicious. Gerd and Ilse were Swiss and probably
didn't know. She had no idea how long she'd been
out. Did they already have the money? She looked

around for a suitcase or bag of some sort.

Apparently not, from the look of things. Gerd was agitated and firing off terse comments at Ilse, who was nervously watching the rearview mirror without answering him. Several miles later Ilse abruptly veered across two lanes to take an off-ramp, bouncing the cab across an emergency parking zone and a double row of hazard bumps to manage it. Gerd was thrown bodily into Julie's side, and she deliberately let her head loll against him, trying to appear unresponsive. The car screeched to a stop, throwing her limply forward; Gerd yanked her back in time for her to see the taxi's right front fender come lightly to rest against the overhanging motor of a sleek power boat. The boat moved forward slightly, and Ilse edged their bumper in front of a family camper that had twin Jet-Skis in tow.

The surly boat owner got out of his truck and leisurely inspected his motor, oblivious to honking horns and shouts from drivers behind the camper. Julie did her best to be visible enough to capture his attention, but each time she moved, Gerd gripped her arm until it hurt. The man took a good three minutes to decide there hadn't been damage and to drive on; the driver of the camper was inordinately polite and allowed Ilse to move the taxi into line ahead of him.

They worked their way forward in heavy traffic and entered a public marina, following signs proclaiming THIS WAY TO LAUNCH AREA. Scathing remarks she could only assume related to Gerd's opinion of Ilse's driving ability rang inside the cab, assaulting her ears.

Immediately ahead of them was the calm vista of water taking on a flotilla of pleasure boats. Weekend sailors. Boats! Gerd *had* said something about a boat. How could they get on a boat with this many people around?

The taxi crept forward a few feet at a time until they were able to enter a parking lot. Ilse turned aside and circled the lot to approach a slip area that had rest rooms and a bank of phones for public use. Beyond the phones was a jetty with orderly rows of narrow access docks. Dozens of pleasure craft, sailboats, and catamarans were bobbing in the water, their hulls sparkling in the brilliant sunlight.

Sailboats were arriving with sunburned passengers; outbound fishermen were carrying bait buckets, hampers, and fishing gear; children wrapped in plastic life vests occasionally escaped high-strung, shouting mothers. Ilse stopped the taxi in the middle of the lane and got out. Julie kept her eyes at half-mast and slowed her breathing, trying to prepare herself.

She couldn't believe it when Gerd followed Ilse out of the taxi and the pair walked toward an empty phone booth. She instantly yanked the lock and seized the door handle. It worked up and down uselessly. Swearing but undefeated, she frantically scooted across the backseat and was jerking the handle of the opposite door when Gerd saw her and came lumbering back to the taxi. She'd gotten the door open and was clawing at the scarf, trying to pull the tape away from her mouth to scream, but he was able to prevent her escape. He slapped her for her efforts and held her in place, then slapped her again, concealing his actions with his body. "Stupid, stupid," he said angrily. "You will not do this."

She glared at him, furious, and made as much noise behind the tape as she could manage. He slapped her a third time, so hard her ears were ringing, and shoved her back inside, but she knew now what she was going to do. They'd have to take her out of the car at some point, and the minute they did she'd make all the noise she could muster. She'd lie down, make him carry her. She'd pretend a fit. If he hit her, so what? A man slapping a woman in public wouldn't go unnoticed. People would stare, and if she could get the scarf loose and witnesses could see the tape on her face . . .

Gerd's attention was no longer on her. He was staring out the window toward the phone booth, his face going rigid. She followed his glance. The booth was in use by a large woman with three children hanging on to her arm, but Ilse was nowhere in sight. From the bewildered look on her brother-in-law's face, this was definitely not a part of the plan. But Julie held her hopes in check; maybe Ilse had simply stepped into the ladies' room. Gerd's head swiveled, eyes searching up and down the beach. Then his gaze sought the lavatory door, apparently with the same thought. They sat, motionless, while time crawled by. A minute became two, two became four. Gerd was visibly shaking and had taken the gun out of his jacket pocket.

The brass ends of bullet casings were visible in the revolver's chamber. Terrified, she tried to decide what to do. If she made noise or called attention to them now, he might do anything. People—children—could get killed. *She* could get killed.

"We will go inside," he informed her. He produced a knife and roughly cut the tape from her wrists, then removed the piece from her mouth. "Do not talk."

She nodded, knowing it was imperative that she cooperate. The rest room was full, with women and children outside waiting in line, and Gerd was clearly in no mood to put up with resistance. He hauled her out of the car and pressed the gun to her ribs. "Inside," he repeated, and they walked awkwardly through fifteen feet of sand to the door of the lavatory. They passed the line of people as he pulled her along with him. Then he boldly stepped inside the ladies' room, bent to look at the feet under each of the four stalls, then yanked her back outside, mumbling, "Sorry . . . sorry . . . ," toward the squawking women who were protesting his invasion.

Ilse was gone, she was sure of it, and the look in Gerd's eyes was beyond frightening; it was entirely possible that the least obstacle could tip him over into a shooting spree. "He's European," she said to the women in line, trying to placate them. "Looking for his child. We're sorry."

He hustled her to the taxi, pushed her into the front passenger seat, then drove to a nearby parking space, looking about constantly for a glimpse of the vanished Ilse. Julie was too rattled by the woman's disappearance not to wonder what could have happened. It had been practically instantaneous. Almost as if she'd planned it. And if Ilse could get away from him . . . She hugged the purse still taped to her body and calculated the time it would take to open the door and make a run for it. If she could get him to put down the gun for even a second . . .

"The money." Gerd was mumbling and searching his pockets with one hand, waving the revolver with the other. He found only a handful of bills. "She had the money." He looked at her blankly, his eyes going black, hysteria visibly escalating. "She took my money! The lying whore took *my money!*"

Julie stared at her panting brother-in-law, afraid to move, petrified that he would explode into something hideously violent before she could convince him that it would be okay. If she panicked now, all hell could break loose. "Gerd, I can help," she said soothingly.

He swayed in his seat, not hearing her, and the gun barrel was pointed upward toward her head. She tried again, as calmly as possible. "Gerd . . . we can fix this. I can help you. You were going to make a call. I can do that."

Slowly her words began to register, and his eyes came into focus. "Yes . . . yes. You can make the call." He fumbled in his jacket pocket and produced a piece of paper. "You will call this number. What time is it?"

"I don't know." She carefully pushed his jacket sleeve up far enough to read his watch, desperate to keep him occupied. "It's a little past three o'clock."

"You can make the call," he repeated. "Tell him to bring the money to this address. It is all you will say, this address." He handed her the slip of paper. BAYVIEW BRIDGE, LONG BEACH HARBOR was written on it. "Now."

He walked her to the phone, and she made the

call. As soon as a voice answered, she read the address as slowly as possible; before she could say anything else, Gerd disconnected the line. They returned to the taxi and he popped the trunk, taking out a large Styrofoam beer cooler. "Now we must choose a boat," he said, icily composed and suddenly conversational. "I will decide." Then he stopped her, hissing, "Do you think I am stupid? Do you?"

She shook her head, having no clue what had set him off this time, as he ripped the tape from her waist. She managed to catch her purse as it slid from under her jacket.

"Leave it here," he demanded, and tried to take it from her hands.

She was determined to keep it with her, and shrilly raised her voice. "No, I'll carry it. There are things inside I need."

A couple passing by took notice, and Gerd saw their interest.

"Female items, dear," she improvised, for their benefit.

Gerd was suspicious, unamused. "Do not cause a problem. I do not warn you again."

"I'm sorry." One more error. How many more before . . . She shouldered the purse on remote control, hugging its weight to her side like a lifeline. He handed her the empty cooler to carry and marched her past row after row of sailboats until they reached an area that catered to speedboats with high-powered engines. The dock area was deserted of activity except for a sleek, long-nosed racing craft idling into position at an empty slip. "That one," he said vehemently.

Her heartbeat fluttered out of control as they made their way down the walkway and onto the floating dock before the owner had finished easing the boat into its space. GLADYS'MADNESS was lettered onto its bow. Gerd's arm was linked with hers, his hand and the gun out of sight in his jacket pocket. As they approached the boat Gerd leaned down to grab a mooring line and tossed it on board. "Here you go."

"Thanks." The owner was unappreciative, barely civil.

"Not at all," Gerd said chattily. "It is a beautiful boat. It is new?"

"Brand spankin'. Picked her up today."

Gerd nonchalantly stepped onto the boat and pulled Julie after him; under their sudden weight, it tilted heavily to one side. The owner was apoplectic, glaring at and pointing toward their improper deck wear: grit-laden, leather-soled street shoes that were scratching the shiny new surface of his boat. His dismay was quickly compounded by the supremely bad manners of his uninvited guests.

32

David emerged from the unmarked car feeling clumsy and constricted under the flak jacket strapped around his torso and over the wiring getup that allowed Bradshaw to listen to his every word. "Where are they?" he demanded. He took his place on the hillside next to the agent and his partner, adjusted a baseball cap that hid most of his hair, and pulled off unfamiliar sunglasses to squint against the afternoon sun.

He saw her even as the police officer, José Obregon, pointed out a public phone booth, and his heart jumped. From their distance she was tiny, wearing a scarf that hid her features, but it was Julie! He'd know that body anywhere. She was talking into the phone. The bastard was standing hard against her, but otherwise she seemed all right. Probably scared out of her mind, but not dead! Relief pounded through his body in giant waves. Then nervous energy took over, and the need to get to her. Take care of her.

Bradshaw looked around. "Where's the girl-friend?"

"Took off about ten minutes ago. Henrickson went after her with the dog." Obregon and his part-ner were a K-9 unit. "Suspects approached the booth, left the victim in the car," Obregon explained. "She tried to get out, but he caught her. While he was putting her back, the girlfriend ran around the rest room building, then ducked down and made a run for it into the parking area. I've been waiting for you."

Obregon's voice unit crackled. "Female suspect is now in custody. We also have a site, Bayview Bridge. The brother's ready to decoy if you lose him, and we're rolling out now. We'll be in position in about ten minutes. We'll have a sniper on him from there."

Bradshaw turned to Obregon. "How about here? Can we get a shot?"

Obregon shook his head. "Not high enough. Couldn't get a man in position in time. Everything down there's too level, too many civilians. Our guy's looking for a site."

David had been listening with his eyes fastened on Julie. Gerd was walking her away from the booth and toward a taxi; he lifted what appeared to be an ice chest out of its trunk, handed it to her to carry, then walked with one arm in his jacket pocket, hug-ging her to him as they passed the rest rooms.

"Christ, what do you suppose is in the chest? Why is he making her carry it?"

"Probably brought it for the money, but let's not take any chances," said Bradshaw. "Looks like he's got a boat. We'd better get down there."

Obregon notified his men that Bradshaw had

arrived and was on his way to join them, then took up his field glasses to keep Walde and Julie in sight. David grabbed the backpack of money and slid his arms into the straps, adrenaline pumping full bore as he slid down the grass slope behind Bradshaw and his partner. They headed through the parking lot at a lope, but by the time they'd arrived at the rest room facilities, Gerd and Julie were half a block distant. Joined by two plainclothes officers, the five men quickly began acting like serious fishing buddies hurrying to catch up with a friend; bypassing sailboats by the dozen, they soon cut the distance in half. "These boats are all privately owned," said Bradshaw. "You don't rent these little jewels. He must know someone here."

Ahead of them, Walde stopped abruptly. Winding his arm around Julie's, he walked out onto one of the access docks, pulling her with him. David could see that one hand was still in his coat pocket. At the far end of the dock, a power boat was being guided slowly into its slip by a single driver; Walde and Julie were approaching the boat, then Walde tossed a mooring line.

David and the officers drew closer as Walde stepped onto the boat and yanked Julie and the ice chest aboard after him. Then to David's surprise, the boat owner's angry voice carried across the water: "Hey, get off, you! Get off!" David held his breath, expecting a blast of gunfire at any moment. But the boat owner was suddenly silent. After a moment the speedboat began to drift outward, and would soon clear the slip. He began to panic. They weren't going to reach her in time.

"He's hijacking the damned thing!"

Bradshaw swore and spoke softly into his voice unit. "We got another hostage! Guy driving a blue speedboat. Looks like a random victim. Make sure Harbor Patrol is alerted; find out if they can clear the channel until we see what this fruitcake is going to do." He looked a warning at David. "Okay, we know this guy is armed, so nobody do anything stupid."

"Stay here!" David shifted the backpack and jogged forward before Bradshaw or the others could stop him. He reached the access dock and ran toward the speedboat. Halfway down, he jerked off the baseball cap and began shouting. "Hey, Walde! You want this or what?"

Walde looked up, then frantically checked the wooden walkway behind him, holding a gun at the ready. He seemed completely baffled by David's sudden appearance and unprepared to cope with the situation.

Julie's eyes were staring at him, stricken. David willed her to keep cool, make no sudden moves. "You said ten minutes, I'm here in ten minutes," he called, slowing to a walk. "The moron with the money, right? Bayview Bridge? I was on my way there when I saw you down here. Save us all some time, okay? Let's do this."

Now ten feet away, Walde was blinking at him, nonplussed. David swung the backpack off his shoulders and dropped it with a thud onto the wooden catwalk. "It's all here. Half a million."

Walde's attention immediately went to the pack, and he came to life as the boat was nearly clear of its slip. "Stop!" he screamed at the frightened owner.

"Back, back! Make it back!" The man's head bobbed up and down, signaling frantically that he had every intention of doing so.

"Show me, Rocklin. I want to see the money." Walde was looking around wildly, suspecting a trap, seeing no one.

David thanked his stars that Bradshaw and the others hadn't followed him. "What, I'm gonna show up with an empty bag? Give me the girl. Let's get this over with."

The boat wasn't moving, and Walde aimed the revolver at the frantic owner. The terrified man took a sideways, spread-eagle dive over the side, causing an uncontrollable rocking motion that threatened Walde's stance. He immediately seized Julie and put the gun to her face. "I'll kill her!"

The boat owner swam under the wooden dock, causing more waves and more motion to the boat. He grabbed on to one of the pilings, and David put himself into slow motion. "You, in the water. One sound and I'll shoot you myself," David called down to him, voice calm as ice. "Just hang on and keep your mouth shut." The speedboat was settling down, and he carefully addressed the desperate man in front of him, refusing to see Julie's horrified expression. "Gerd, I'm going to pick up the bag and show you the money, okay? But I'm not going to give it to you until she's on the dock."

"Do it!" Walde snapped at him, eyes in constant motion, still looking for an ambush.

David stooped, unzipped the compartments, and displayed bundles of the cash from each. "I'm here alone," he said calmly, "just like you said. And, as you can see, the money's all here." Walde began to calm down and used the gun to motion him forward.

David picked up the backpack and, holding it by its straps, proceeded slowly toward the end of the slip. The boat's engine was idling, still in neutral, but the powerful vessel had drifted sideways with a slight current, maddeningly out of reach, and was about to bump a neighboring boat. Anything at this point, however minor, could cause Walde to panic.

"You're about to hit the dock," he pointed out quietly. "Julie, honey, can you see if you can put the boat in gear? Don't give it any gas," he warned, speaking confidently, "just put it in any forward gear. That okay with you, Gerd?"

Walde did not object and released his hold on her but stayed close behind as her slight frame slipped behind the steering wheel in the cockpit area. She studied the equipment, obviously nervous, and finally pushed a button. The propeller's gearing immediately engaged, but Walde was expecting the change in direction and kept his feet. The boat began to inch forward. When the bow came within reach, David jumped on board.

Gerd moved toward him to reach for the back-pack, but David held on to the straps and deliberately kept it just out of the shorter man's reach and dangling over the edge of the boat. If he dropped it now, it would land in the water and sink like a rock, and he could see in Gerd's face the knowledge that shooting him would be to lose the money after all.

"Julie, darling, I want you to climb off. Jump if you have to, but I want you off this boat. This is between Gerd and me now. Right, Gerd?"

She was shaking her head, refusing to do it, and he wanted to bash her. Gerd was shaking his head also. The two of them reminded him of irrational, stubborn children; he felt a stab of rage, then brought himself under control. Gerd was waving his gun around, clearly undecided about his next move. Then he did as David hoped—he stepped forward to push the barrel into his ribs.

"I can kill you right now."

Over the coughing idle of the speedboat, he heard her gasp; catching her eye, he mouthed, "Get off." Then he smiled down at Walde. "Of course you can. But what's the point? Everyone within forty blocks hears a gunshot that's going to echo like crazy out here on the water. A couple of good Samaritans call the police, and this whole thing goes up in smoke." Julie wasn't moving, damn her stubborn steak! "Our deal was the money for the girl. I brought you the money, she leaves, and I'm your new pal. I say we should get the hell out of here before somebody comes along that we don't want to talk to." He handed over the backpack. "You know how to drive this thing?"

Gerd looked up at him blankly, the heavy pack weighing down one arm.

"It so happens that I do, so what's it going to be? A chauffeured getaway and half a million dollars; or the police? You're not a stupid man, Gerd. Let's get going." He looked at Julie and hardened his voice. "Get the hell off this boat before someone gets hurt!"

She reacted at last. "Oh, God . . . okay, okay, okay."

But the speedboat refused to cooperate, and with

Gerd holding the gun to his body, David was forced to take over the steering and jockey the boat into a position in the slip that would allow her to climb off. She was moving toward the dock, one hand fumbling inside her bloody purse! Christ, what was it with women and purses?

His heart stopped as Gerd suddenly swung the revolver toward Julie again. "We all go," the man said darkly. "If the money is a lie, make no mistake that I kill her and dump her overboard. Take me out of here, *now*, or I shoot and I don't care!"

"It's not a lie," David said calmly. "Look in the pack."

"There is a tracking device."

"I swear there isn't."

"An explosive, a dye."

"No. Hey, nothing blew up when I opened it a minute ago."

"She stays until I am sure!" Gerd was shaking, clearly unstable. "*Now!*"

Unwilling to gamble, David eased the nose of the powerful boat away from the slip and entered the channel that led to the open harbor, slowly increasing their speed to convince Gerd that he was doing as ordered.

"Faster!"

"Can't," he said reasonably. "We have a speed limit here, or you'll have the Harbor Patrol on your ass."

Gerd brought the empty ice chest forward, pushed Julie's purse aside, and shoved the backpack onto her lap. "Put the money here," he ordered. "So I can see." He braced himself against the side of the boat to watch, and as she transferred bundle after bundle into the bottom of the chest; he began to nod. When she'd finished, he was smiling, his mood shifting rapidly. Finally, exultant, he began to laugh. "That stupid pig! I have done it," he shouted into the wind. "She did not think it would work, but I have the money!"

Julie tried to think what to do. Gerd was acting crazy, and she had no doubt in her mind that David was in danger. When he'd appeared out of nowhere, she'd been shocked into believing that she was actually being rescued, but when no police appeared and it was apparent that he was alone, her relief became horror that she'd be forced to watch him die trying to save her. He'd tried to get her off the boat, but she'd been too scared to leave without him. Men killed men for male reasons—deep-seated instincts and hatreds that defied female rationale. Gerd wouldn't kill her—she was sure of it, because he didn't consider her a threat. But David was a threat; David could get killed.

By some stroke of fate, some fluke, some bit of sheer, blind luck, in the past forty-eight hours neither Gerd nor Ilse had thought to look inside her purse, hadn't found the Walther that she'd grabbed off her dresser mere instants before Gerd could discover it. Her hands were freed now, and the cold knowledge that she would have to defend David and herself against Gerd's madness became a driving force, pushing her forward.

They were approaching the breakwater and open ocean. It had to be now, before Gerd lost control and murdered them both. Now, while he was still raving,

distracted with his fortune and screaming into the
wind. Terrified, but determined that she would
shoot him if she had to, she slid one hand into her
purse, found smooth metal, but—oh, God—the
handle or the barrel?

Approaching on their left was a large catamaran
slowly entering the marina, its crew members furling
sails. Things seemed to happen all at once. David
suddenly grabbed her arm and yanked her toward
him, shielding her with his body; she heard the
sound of the engine change as the boat lost power,
throwing her off balance. Her purse dropped to the
floorboards and he was shouting into her face that
he loved her. Ignoring her frantic attempts to speak,
he abruptly heaved her over the side. She hit with a
giant splash, went under still trying to tell him about
the gun, nose and mouth taking in seawater.

David steered a hard right to keep her away from the
prop in case it was still spinning, and saw her bobbing ten feet behind them within seconds. "Help!"
he shouted at the passing crew. "She can't swim!"

One man had already dived off the near side of
the catamaran and was thrashing toward her, and
another had picked up a docking pole. Behind him,
Gerd was regaining his balance, gun in hand. Satisfied that she was safe, David kicked the boat's big
engine into gear and opened the throttle, this time
steering a hard left, trying to keep her rescuer out of
the wake, then aimed the speedboat dead at the
breakwater. Gerd, mouth agape, was slow to react;
the sudden forward motion of the boat threw him
backward and to the side.

David immediately killed the engine, and the big boat rocked violently as it lost forward momentum. This time Gerd couldn't keep his footing and went down. David threw himself onto the man's body. Gerd managed to get off one shot with the revolver before David took it away from him, but it wasn't much of a contest; the depth of his fury was no match for a man who was merely trying to steal money.

Once he'd wrestled Walde's gun away from him, the man collapsed in tears, making no resistance. David hit him anyway, twice, just to get some of it out of his system; he removed Walde's belt, yanked the man's pants down around his ankles, and secured his wrists with his belt. Threatening Gerd with certain death if he so much as moved, he turned his attention to the pitching boat.

They were drifting dangerously close to the breakwater, but he managed to start the engine and put it into reverse. By the time he was ready to maneuver the stolen boat back into the proper lane to return to the marina, the Harbor Patrol had boats on both sides of him, and an army of pistols and shotguns were staring him in the face. He cut the engine with one hand, as ordered, then carefully held both hands above his head, never so happy to see legal authority in his life.

They'd gotten the two of them and the chest of money on board, and were rigging a tow line for *Gladys'Madness,* when a third patrol boat came alongside and he saw her. Wet clothes plastered to her body, hair a mess, she was scowling at him with blood in her eye. He was going to pay heavy dues for tossing her into the harbor, but she was absolutely gorgeous and he blew her a kiss.

"Hear you been raising hell out here, son," said the officer in charge.

"No, just trying to lift it a little."

The man had absolutely no sense of humor. "That what you call throwing people overboard?"

"Not people, sir! Just the lady I'm planning to marry."

Under his gaze, Julie's scowl turned to owl-eyed disbelief, then she did her best to suppress a smile. Then the scowl returned. Major dues.

"As soon as she's dry," he added merrily.

33

NOVEMBER 10

The wedding was set for December fifth. Invitations had been mailed, her father was flying in from Morocco to give her away, and Doris's dressmaker was putting the finishing stitches into her wedding gown.

She and Joann were lying on her sundeck, enjoying the thin, unseasonably warm Malibu sunlight. Julie flashed her engagement diamond, shamelessly enjoying its sparkle as she reached for the telephone. Elmore watched her movement from his perch on the railing, then, satisfied that she wasn't planning to disappear, resumed grooming his chest fur, but kept one eye on her just the same. He'd been staying particularly close since she'd "abandoned" him and left with Gerd, and the tabby wasn't taking any chances this afternoon.

"I'm calling Aunt Marjorie. Do you want to talk to her?"

"No, we talked last night. Tell her I'm fine and the

divorce is going ahead. I keep explaining that Gerd's not giving me an argument, but she still thinks he's got some new scheme up his sleeve."

"She's probably right. . . . Aunt Marge, it's Julie. Just wondering how soon you were coming out before the wedding. Can't wait to see you." Joann waved goodbye and tiptoed off the deck, and Julie smiled as her aunt voiced concern about her sister's divorce. "She's fine. . . . No, it's going ahead. He's not giving her an argument."

Joann stuck her head out the door and gave her an I-told-you-so look, then disappeared inside.

Aunt Marjorie was insistent. "Dear, is your sister there?"

"Not just now, but I expect her back any minute."

Her aunt's voice became conspiratorial, taut with suppressed excitement. "Are you positive she doesn't need more evidence to get her divorce? Because I found something this morning that I'm certain she could use."

"Uh . . . I don't think so. What is it?"

Her aunt lowered her voice. "He collects pornography! There's an envelope full of terrible photographs hidden in one of the family albums she gave me. It's nothing a decent woman would have in her home, so it must be his."

"Photographs?"

"Yes, my dear. Negatives and everything, so he must have taken them himself. They're all of the same couple, a woman with short, black hair doing things I wouldn't dream of telling you about."

Julie felt her stomach react. "Is the man blond and about thirty-three?"

"How did you know?" Aunt Marjorie was instantly concerned. "Oh, dear. What shall I do with them?"

Julie thought of Doris Rocklin and took a deep breath. "Burn them."

"Isn't that destroying evidence?"

"Not exactly. Gerd was using the photographs for blackmail," she explained unsteadily, then had a sudden thought. "That's probably what he was looking for when he came to Chicago."

"Oh, dear. Are you certain?"

"I happen to know that no one plans to prosecute Gerd for blackmail, so . . . do you think you could have Geraldo put them in one of the furnaces?"

"Oh, I don't think so, dear." Her aunt was quiet for a moment. "It rather makes him an accessory, wouldn't you think? But he might let me do it, if I explained the material was . . . embarrassing."

"That would be perfect." Somehow Julie felt Aunt Marjorie would do just fine "destroying evidence." She also pled silently for mercy that her aunt wouldn't confuse David with the man in the photographs when they met.

With one eye on the clock, she ascertained her aunt's travel plans and confirmed that she would leave Chicago *two* days prior to their wedding next month, and not three. She also wondered if David had arrived in Long Beach for his twelve o'clock meeting with Gerd.

David looked around the cement enclosure that was his half of the visitation room, curious as to why Walde had requested an audience. It was two months since their joyride in the harbor, during which Walde had somehow acquired high-priced legal talent and had managed so far to fend off extradition to England, France, or Switzerland. That was no surprise, as a good lawyer could keep one country pitted against the others indefinitely.

However, according to Bradshaw, Walde's erstwhile girlfriend, companion, and accomplice had already agreed to cut a deal with the federal prosecutor. Ilse was offering testimony in return for dropping the kidnapping charges. The decision would undoubtedly affect the site of Walde's future incarceration.

Ambassador was gathering its own evidence to charge Walde with fraud. Walde's lawyer had already been warned that anything Gerd gave up today, Ambassador would use, if warranted, but had permitted his client to have the meeting anyway.

Walde entered the room on the prisoner side of the glass and was escorted to the assigned booth by a guard. David moved to the corresponding seat and picked up the telephone.

Walde lifted his receiver. "I have information I wish to sell to Mr. Hathaway."

David nearly laughed, but had to hand it to him for brass. The arrogant little man was up on current events: Six weeks ago, Walter DePasse had taken a rather sudden early retirement, Ron Hathaway had been elevated to DePasse's former position, and—after the return of the half million dollars with the unwritten but binding understanding that Ambassador would not prosecute his brother—Derek had quietly resigned in order to move to San Diego with

Doris. The two of them had leased a small condo with an ocean view, and had taken up playing golf as a lifestyle. After a great deal of thought, David had accepted Hathaway's offer of a promotion to private investigator for Ambassador Surety.

Walde was waiting confidently.

"What information?" he asked, disinterested.

"We must discuss the price. Obviously, I must have money for this. I have a great deal of expenses."

"You tell me what's for sale, I'll decide if it has value."

Walde sighed. "Three years ago I have an art gallery in Geneva."

"This I know."

"A man comes in one day to tell me that he has a rare painting he wishes to sell. It is worth two million dollars, but he has some difficulty with the provenance, and I agree to help him. He give me two hundred thousand dollars for this purpose, but the painting must be insure by Ambassador."

"To prove the documentation will hold up."

"Yes. The painting must stay in his possession, but I am to provide papers which establish that my gallery has sold it to him. He sat in the next room while the Ambassador appraiser examines and photographs, then he took it away."

"So it wasn't your painting. Big surprise. None of this is new information, Gerd. No value to me," he said impatiently. "You want to give away a name, give it to your lawyer."

"I have, but this man said it was not his painting, and now he claims that no such painting exists."

"What does any of this have to do with me?"

"He is Ambassador's client. The ransom was his idea."

"Excuse me?"

"His idea. He told me to falsify the thief so there is a police report, and to file a claim—then create the ransom demand. I tell him he is crazy, but he wants to be certain of the provenance. It was his test."

If true, this was an interesting new wrinkle. One he could not afford to ignore. "Who are we talking about?"

Walde stared at him shrewdly. "How much value for this name?"

"I can find him without you."

Walde took a photograph out of his pocket and held it against the glass. "This man is someone in your family."

David stared at the photograph and then at Walde, the tension building at the back of his neck telling him without a doubt that Gerd wasn't bluffing. "I'll let you know." He hung up the receiver and got to his feet, then turned on his heel and left the room.

Two hours later, he was standing in the waiting room at Morganer-Pacific. "Nice to see you again, Mary," he greeted her. "Don't tell me he's not here. I happen to know that he is."

Famous for never losing her cool, today Morganer's assistant was flustered. "He's in a meeting, David. Really. And it's very late in the day. It's not going to be possible."

"I know what time it is, and I don't mean to put

you in an awkward position. Just give him this and tell him I said to see me or wish he had." He handed her a fax.

She returned three minutes later and he was shown into Morganer's office. The furniture, paintings, rare books, and art pieces were exactly as he remembered them, and he had the eerie feeling that time had stopped in this room nine years ago. Not a trace of dust, nor an article out of place. Mary Welles was very good at her job, but she didn't offer refreshments.

Seconds later Earl Morganer entered through a private door, impeccably dressed, clearly agitated. "I've called security," he announced. "You have *exactly* thirty seconds." The older man's hands were steady as rocks.

"I'm here to tell you that I'm getting married again—"

"Is she wealthy? You and your brother seem to find wealthy women your specialty."

David ignored him. "Mr. Morganer, here's what I know. I know you have a Chagalier worth two million dollars. I know it's the one we insured for Gerd Walde because the photograph was faxed down here from his file. It's also the one I saw in your daughter's bedroom a little over nine years ago."

Morganer didn't turn a hair. "Prove it."

"I don't have to. Walde will do it for me."

"So this is blackmail?"

"Yes, sir, I guess it is. I'm getting married December fifth and I plan to take my wife to Paris for our honeymoon. While we're there, we're going to visit the de Lumière Museum to see if they are in possession of a certain painting that was stolen some fifty-odd years ago. If they don't have it, I plan to tell them where they can find it. If, on the other hand, it's arrived, my wife and I will admire it and congratulate them on its safe return." He rose to his feet. "That's what I came to tell you."

He paused in the doorway. "Earl, you didn't cause her death." David took a deep breath. "It's true that it wouldn't have happened if she hadn't followed me to Tahoe. It wouldn't have happened if we hadn't gotten married. It wouldn't have happened if there hadn't been a bad tire on her car. If I'd taken a bus, or flown, or walked instead of going up on my bike. It wouldn't have happened if a thousand things hadn't fallen into place in some sort of hideous order—including your being unwilling to let me and Gina be in love and work it out."

"Don't say her name! You killed her, and you know it."

"And you know that she was on the wrong side of the road!" He forced Earl Morganer to look at him. "You know, because you paid someone to get rid of the skid marks!" He sat heavily on one of the chairs. "I tried not to, but God help me, I hit her. And she died. I live with that every time the sun goes down, just like you do. It's punishment enough, believe me."

The old man began to sob, and David left the office.

34

DECEMBER 10

Julie gazed out the window, fascinated with the sight of Paris powdered with a crystalline layer of snow. Holiday lights scintillating along the curves of the Eiffel Tower turned snowflakes outside the glass into colorful, glistening rain. She scraped a line in the webbing of frost with her fingernail, then flicked the tiny charms on the bracelet her husband had given her as a wedding gift: A tiny fir tree with ALL MY LOVE, D.B. etched on the back shimmered between a stylized cat and a miniature copy of the tower shining in the distance.

"So what do you think?" David's voice was lazy next to her ear, and his arms were warm around her shoulders, keeping her safe from the dark.

"I think life is amazing," she answered. "I think it's strange how things have changed so quickly. How things I wouldn't have dreamed possible a few weeks ago are now a part of our lives."

"What didn't you think was possible?"

She sighed, happy in his arms. "That I could feel this good. That I'd be married to a tall, handsome, gorgeous, sexy stranger I met in the woods." She raised her face for a kiss. "That my father would actually like you instead of being polite, that my aunt thinks you're terrific, and so does my sister—not that she has great taste in men, but she's improving."

"What else?" he said indulgently.

"I didn't think Doris and your brother would stay together, let alone be as dopey as newlyweds at our reception. I never thought you could fit half a million dollars into my sleeping bag."

"Anything else?"

"I never thought Elmore would be happy staying with my sister. I never thought I'd be looking out on Paris at three A.M. Never expected in a million years that I'd be this lucky."

"Anything else?"

She thought for a moment. "No. I think that's about it."

He kissed the back of her neck and began to rub her shoulders in that special way she loved. "Mmmmm . . . so what are we going to do about three A.M.?"

"Well . . . one and two were pretty great." She smiled up at him. "Three is ready when you are."

AUTHOR'S NOTE

On November 24, 1971, a fortyish man carrying an attaché case and identifying himself as Dan Cooper purchased a ticket for cash from Portland, Oregon, to Seattle, Washington, on Northwest Orient Airlines. He wore a business suit, a white shirt, loafers, and a lightweight raincoat. After takeoff he donned sunglasses and gave a written note to a stewardess indicating that he was hijacking the plane; the opened briefcase appeared to have dynamite packed inside. His demand was two hundred thousand dollars and four nonmilitary parachutes.

Two and a half hours later the parachutes and the money (twenty-one pounds of twenty-dollar bills) had been collected and were waiting at the Seattle airport, and Cooper directed the plane to land; the passengers were released.

The Boeing 727 was refueled and took off again at 7:37 P.M.; the pilot was instructed to fly below ten thousand feet with the landing gear extended, wing flaps down fifteen degrees, and the aft airstairs down as well. The hijacker tied the sack of money around his waist with cords cut from one of the parachutes and at 8:12 P.M. leaped out into seven-degree-below-zero weather at 196 mph.

Several years later an eight-year-old boy picnicking with his family found $5,800 in heavily weathered twenty-dollar bills on a Columbia River sandbar. The serial numbers matched money given the hijacker.

The hijacker became known as D.B. Cooper through the error of a United Press International reporter observing FBI agents on a routine investigation of a man named D.B. Cooper, who was immediately cleared. The hijacker's fingerprints were not on file with the FBI, and the case is still open.

Generally, wars are declared and fought for ideological or political reasons. Losing opponents are looted, and anything of value becomes the property of the conqueror. During Germany's occupation of various countries during World War II, priceless paintings, irreplaceable artifacts, and "souvenirs" were taken from public and private sources alike. Entire collections were shipped to Germany's museums.

When Germany collapsed and Hitler committed suicide near the end of the war, Allied forces moved in and the plunder of Germany's museums began. Huge quantities of confiscated artworks had been stored in buildings, caves, and mine tunnels throughout the German countryside, with the knowledge of local citizens and under the guard of ordinary soldiers. There was little or no record keeping. Massive numbers of artworks disappeared.

An estimated one million such items—paintings, drawings, objets d'art, sculptures, books, and archival documents—are hidden throughout Europe (and the rest of the world). Without provenance—legitimate proof of origin—they are illegally acquired artworks, subject to seizure by various public, private, and governmental agencies until legal ownership can be determined.

ABOUT THE AUTHOR

Born in historic Johnstown, Ohio, this multi-published author enjoyed careers in entertainment law, network television, and the motion picture industry prior to writing her first novel. The recipient of several awards in her field, she currently lives in Beverly Hills, California. JEAN DEWITT is a pseudonym, and this is her initial venture into romantic suspense.